CRUEL & BEAUTIFUL WORLD

• BOOK ONE •

BROKEN WINGS

L. STODDARD HANCOCK

To all of my original fans who have been with me on this journey since day one. Your love and encouragement is what made this book possible.

CHAPTER ONE

Deryn Leon awoke suddenly as the van came to a halt, her heart racing as she looked out the barred window to see where they were. She knew the house but not well. It was just on the outskirts of Middle City in Utopia, and the Guardian who resided there liked his slaves fresh.

She hadn't been fresh in a long time.

A girl in the seat across from her whimpered. Deryn looked at her unmarked skin and sighed. She was young. She was beautiful. He would love her.

The door to the back of the van opened.

"There aren't many this time," said the driver as his face appeared in the bright shaft of light. "The president's been disposing of more and more lately. Been in one hell of a mood since they lost track of that damn Leon boy again." He caught Deryn's eye and smiled wickedly.

The Guardian named Wenton Pace poked his head in and thoroughly scanned the goods. He paused on Deryn for a moment. She stared back at him with cold, unafraid eyes that made many of the president's Guardians, the highest form of guard, look right past her since they feasted on fear.

As expected, he quickly moved on to the whimpering girl, not even taking notice of the four other beaten and bruised women or the two men who were also in the van.

"What's this one?" he asked, pointing at her. "Resistance?"

"Don't think so. A group of 'em were caught outside, not

sure how they got out. Thought it'd be fun to breathe the toxic air. After they were quarantined the president had the others executed but Barath requested to keep this one. This is her first run since."

"Yes, I can tell. She's certainly in better condition than the rest," said Wenton, glancing at Deryn. "Bring her out. It's been a long time since I've had such a pretty one in my home." He licked his lips.

The girl struggled and screamed as the driver climbed inside the van and dragged her out by her bound wrists. He slammed and locked the door behind them. The other prisoners listened in silence as she continued to scream all the way to the house.

Deryn looked out through the bars and watched her until she was gone. She'd learned a long time ago that it was a waste of energy to struggle like that. The collar they wore would zap them dead if they traveled more than two-hundred feet from the van. She had seen it happen many times before. There was no means for escape. Of course, some might argue that death was the better option. She certainly thought about it often enough.

"Such a shame."

Deryn turned. The old woman sitting beside her was also staring out the window.

"Only in these dark times could being so young and beautiful ever be such a curse."

Deryn nodded but didn't speak. It was best to keep friendly words and names out of these drives, since there was a fairly decent chance she would never see any of these people again.

But this woman she actually recognized from several drives before. She'd been a slave for years, just like her.

The doors burst back open and the driver shoved a different girl inside. She was bloody and beaten, her left eye so swollen that it was barely visible behind a large, purple mark. She must have been a member of the Resistance, since Wenton always treated them the worst.

The newest arrival settled in a seat and sobbed into her hands. The van started again and pulled back on the slick road.

"Looks like we're headed for Inner City," said the old woman, still staring out the window. "That means you have at least thirty minutes to rest." She smiled at Deryn. "Come here, child and place your head on my lap. Out of all our times traveling together, I've never seen you look so weary before."

Deryn glanced hesitantly at the woman's lap and then into her blue eyes, which still shined bright even after all she'd been through. She tried to smile back but it fell short. How long had it been since she'd genuinely smiled? And then she remembered. It was the last time she'd seen Dakota. When he'd told her he loved her.

"Thank you," she said weakly, lying down and resting her head on the woman's lap.

The old woman stroked Deryn's hair, the gentle touch soothing her enough to drift into a shallow sleep. She didn't know how to sleep deeply anymore.

Deryn wasn't sure how long it had been since she was first enslaved. Definitely several years, but she'd stopped keeping track after the first. Mundane things like time only made her life more miserable.

They had these slave trades every three months or so. A gift to the Guardians for their loyal service and to keep those still fighting in the Resistance from ever finding their loved ones. Two birds, one stone. It was Elvira, the president's demon spawn's idea to use the slave trade like this. Deryn was there when she'd came up with it. In fact, she'd been the inspiration. It was her penalty for being the daughter of the Resistance's leader.

Sometimes Deryn would hear stories about the Resistance breaking into Utopia and bombarding places she had once stayed, supposedly looking for her, but they were always too late.

It had been a long time since she'd heard about any of these rescue missions. The rumor was that her father had forgotten about her. Her last owner told her that President Saevus was considering disposing of her, preferably through a very public execution. She had meant to scare Deryn, but she'd only found relief in her words.

It was hard to believe that not too long ago the world had been such a different place. While many Utopians did believe the outside air was toxic, they would never have fought those who wanted to live there. Not until the day President Saevus took over, voted into power through a rigged election following his father, the former president's death.

At first, the change was subtle. Outsiders only being allowed in certain parts of the city, then they were only let in at all if they agreed to be quarantined first. It was troublesome but nothing they couldn't handle.

And then the kidnapping began.

That was when everything had truly changed, and Deryn had been taken from her home to train and become a guard of Utopia. Of course, in retrospect, that hadn't been so terrible. Not like now, where she was forced every day to do things unmentionable. And all because her father had come for her, but failed to set her free.

CHAPTER TWO

Several Years Earlier

"**D**ad!"
Deryn ran into the large room at Eagle Training Center and searched frantically for her father. It was overrun by battling Guardians and Outsiders, their guns roaring and blood spilling at every turn.

She found her father Godfrey in a heated battle with President Collin Saevus. The two were cousins, though they never knew each other, kept apart by siblings with different views of the world.

Deryn beelined for Godfrey, but was knocked onto her back when a guard's weapons set off a blast that exploded against the wall. It was Saevus's loyalist follower, his daughter Elvira, and she had been aiming for Kara Triggs. Kara was like a mother to Deryn, always taking care of her after she'd lost her real mother at a young age. And she was here fighting. For her.

They were going at it roughly and Kara only had a primitive gun while Elvira had an Element. It was a special weapon designed solely for guards and had everything from powerful explosions to protective shields. Some attacks were fatal, others simply incapacitated their enemies.

Still, Kara knew how to fight and she was ready to finish this woman once and for all.

Deryn waited for her head to stop spinning and got back on her feet. She couldn't believe this was real. This whole battle was happening because of her. To save her from becoming a guard the next day, on her eighteenth birthday.

It had been three years since she'd last seen her father. Not since the night she and several other Outsider children were taken from their homes by Saevus's guards to become one of them. And here she was, one day away from her sealed fate and the Outsiders had come for her, invading Eagle Center and armed to fight with their ancestors' rusty weapons to set their children free. To stop this cruel recruiting process once and for all.

Deryn couldn't let this happen. She couldn't let people die for her.

She scanned the room for Kara, making sure she was safe before aiming her Element at Elvira. But she never got the chance to fire before Elvira noticed her. She switched the setting on her Element and sent a large gust of wind in Deryn's direction, knocking her back off her feet.

Kara was livid. She tried to retaliate by shooting several bullets at Elvira, but they bounced right off of her protective dark-blue Guardian trench coat. It was better than any body armor. The only way to kill a Guardian with the Outsiders' old guns was to shoot them in the head, straight on. Even in the back would never work since they wore hoods.

Having had enough of this, Kara pulled a dagger out of her boot and lunged at Elvira, knocking the other woman off her feet. The two of them wrestled on the floor for a while, Kara trying to find a weak spot in Elvira's coat while Elvira tried to regain control.

Deryn ran for them again, attempting to aim her Element but afraid she might hit Kara by mistake. Elvira's Element was still set to let out a powerful gust of wind. She pulled the trigger, holding it long enough to knock anyone within a five foot radius on their backs.

Kara flew off of her, her knife falling from her hand as she hit the floor hard. Without hesitation, Elvira grabbed the knife, lifted it high and jammed it into Kara's heart.

Deryn watched in horror as blood poured from Kara's chest, her body convulsing and eyes bulging as she had a small moment of clarity before turning her head to look at Deryn. Then all movement ceased, and Kara was no more. Her eyes wide open and lifeless, and aimed right at Deryn.

Loud laughter echoed from across the room. Deryn looked and saw President Saevus glancing around joyously as so many Outsiders fought for their children and their lives. Elvira hurried to be by his side. Godfrey was no longer near him.

"Deryn!"

Kara's son Dakota ran towards her, wearing his steel-blue guard trench coat but having torn off Saevus's crest from the sleeves.

"Dax! Your mom! I'm so sor -"

"I saw," he said, cutting her off as he held back tears. He grabbed her hand and pulled her to her feet. "Where's your dad?"

"I don't know."

She scanned the room frantically. It was large and crowded, and it took her a while before she finally found her father, who was near Saevus once more. He was circling him, hatred pouring from his very soul as he stared at the man who had taken his children from him.

Collin Saevus was not a man. He was the enemy.

He and Godfrey had their weapons aimed, her father now holding an Element.

"It didn't have to be this way," said Godfrey, pressing a button on the top of his Element.

The president laughed. "I believe it did."

"Our request is simple. Give us back our children and we'll leave Utopia forever."

"You know, I don't think I will," said Saevus, his smile unnerving.

A large gust of wind shot through the room and they both wobbled on their feet. Elvira's husband Soren had knocked three Outsiders into a group of guards, who were ready to attack. Then he turned and shot another Outsider in the face, his finger so quick that no one knew the blast would be powerful enough to make the man's head explode. Deryn and

Dakota were close enough that his blood splattered on them.

All around them the chaos was growing, and the Outsiders were losing more fighters. While a few moments ago the outcome of the battle could have gone either way, they had just lost four fighters in a matter of seconds, as well as Kara. More guards were arriving every minute and they were showing no mercy.

Outsiders began to flee as the battle took this turn for the worse. But Deryn and Dakota held their ground, fighting with everything they had. This was what they'd been trained for, even if it was for the other side.

Throughout all of this, Deryn lost track of her father again. At one point, she saw her brother Talon run in wearing his guard uniform, tearing off Saevus's crest like the others who were still loyal to their roots. He saw Deryn and fought his way towards her.

But Deryn was still searching for her father, following the eyes of several guards to find their leader. Saevus and Godfrey had not struck yet, a clear glimmer of panic in her father's eyes as he realized how quickly they were losing control.

"Set our children free!" he shouted.

And then both men got in position, their weapons pointed at each other's chests as they pulled the trigger at the same time.

The blasts from both Elements collided. Godfrey had been more than willing to sacrifice himself, truly believing the powerful explosions that came from the guards' weapons could not be stopped. But he was wrong. A shield burst out of Saevus's Element, blocking the explosion and sending it shooting back at Godfrey.

Right versus wrong.

Good versus evil.

Love versus hate.

There was no question who should have won that day. The man with the strong heart and love for his family should have prevailed. But that was not what happened.

The explosion had been weakened by the shield, but it was still strong enough to hit Godfrey in the chest, sending him flying backwards until he crashed against the wall behind him. He knocked his head and landed unconscious on the floor.

"Dad!" screamed Deryn as Dakota held her back.

Saevus came for him again, his weapon at the ready, but several Outsiders stepped in his path, sacrificing their lives to give Dakota's father Piz enough time to throw Godfrey over his shoulder and flee through one of the doors. Godfrey had given the Outsiders hope when they thought there was none. He was their leader and saving his life meant everything.

Deryn grabbed Dakota's hand. She tried to pull him with her to follow their fathers, but he pulled back.

"Dax, let's go!"

"Deryn, I have to stay," he said, his voice cracking. "Our people are still fighting here. I can't just leave."

Deryn stared off in the direction her father had gone. She gulped and nodded. "Alright. We'll stay and -"

"Deryn, no!" shouted Talon, finally reaching them through the chaos. "Dad came here today for you, and if he dies it will not be in vain! Go! Follow them and find out where Piz is taking him!"

There was another loud blast and someone's torso flew between them. Deryn covered her mouth to hold back vomit. Talon was quick to move into a protective stance in front of them.

"We'll meet at our place," said Dakota, tugging on her hand and catching her eye. "As soon as this is over, I'll wait for you there."

Deryn nodded. "I love you, Dax."

He smiled. "I love you, too." She smiled back and he leaned in to kiss her, holding her for a brief moment before forcing himself to let her go. "I'll be waiting for you."

Gripping her Element tightly, Deryn turned away from him and ran out of the room, only looking back once when she reached the doorway. She sighed heavily and went off in search of her father.

It wasn't hard to trail them. Several Outsiders had followed Piz and left many bodies in their wake. Just a little ways up, the straight path ended and a small amount of blood on the wall let her know they had turned right. She had barely turned the corner when she ran into someone with such force that they both fell backwards.

When Deryn sat up she raised her weapon, but was unsure of what to do when she saw the person she had bumped into was Xander Ruby. His father was one of the highest ranking Guardians and had signed Xander up for guard training the moment he became of age. He had turned eighteen just last month, and at the current moment looked frightened out of his wits.

Deryn lowered her weapon, knowing very well that she could never shoot Xander. While she didn't know him well, she still knew him, and he didn't appear to be armed, even though the entire training center was currently amidst a battle.

Xander put a hand on his aching head, his eyes widening as he looked at something over her shoulder.

Deryn turned just in time to see a guard with a gasmask aiming his Element at them. She and Xander rolled out of its path as the person fired. When she looked again, Xander was crawling on his elbows and knees towards a body lying on the floor, searching it frantically for what she assumed was some sort of weapon. The body obviously held no Element, but possibly a dagger.

"Traitor!" the guard shouted, shooting another blast at Xander.

Xander held up the body and used it as a shield. Luckily, the guard had only used a stunner and Xander escaped unscathed.

Deryn jumped back to her feet and aimed her weapon. Before the guard had a chance to react, she stunned him. Her aim was a bit off and she accidentally hit his Element, causing it to shatter into a million pieces. The guard still fell flat on the floor.

"What are you doing?" shouted Xander, throwing down the body he was holding. "This is a fucking war, Leon! Aim to kill!"

That word rang loudly in Deryn's head. *War.* She shook it off. "No!" she shouted back at him. "He was not aiming to kill so why should I?"

"Whatever." He climbed to his feet and glared at her. "Your fucking funeral."

"What did he mean traitor?" she demanded, following him with her Element while he went to the next body and searched it.

"I'm not a traitor!" He turned his cold eyes on her. "*You* and your people are. But this battle today is pointless. This is not how I die!"

"Coward," she spat.

"Toxic bitch," he spat back.

She rolled her eyes. "Next time just say thank you."

"Never gonna happen, sweetheart," he said with a quick glance up and a wink.

Deryn grunted as he finally pulled a dagger out of the dead man's boot. She was about to continue following her father's trail when someone else ran out of the hallway Piz had gone down, knocking her shoulder and slamming her back a few steps.

"Xander!"

Deryn was whipped in the face by a streak of long hair.

"Mom!" shouted Xander, standing up straight and running into Penelope Ruby's open arms.

With the two of them distracted, Deryn took a step towards the hallway again. She was about to plan her course of action when a third Ruby appeared. Xander's father Atticus. Deryn's heart stopped as she quickly raised her Element, but Atticus paid her little mind as he ran to his wife and son.

"What are you still doing here?" Penelope asked Xander. "I told you to run."

"I was going to but my Element wasn't in my locker," he explained. "I couldn't just walk out the front door without one. I'd look like a deserter."

Penelope blinked. "But who would take -"

"I did."

Every last heart in that hallway stopped. They all turned to see Elvira standing with her Element aimed, motioning to the extra one she had fastened to her hip.

"If your son was a real guard then he would've come to the battle weaponless and ready to fight!" shouted Elvira. "He's a traitor!"

Deryn tried to take a step out of the hallway, but the moment she moved Elvira's Element was on her.

"No!" Penelope pushed her son protectively behind her. "Elvira, you must understand! Xander is not a traitor! He's -"

"You're right." Elvira looked at her and smiled wickedly. "You are." She moved her Element off of Deryn and fired at Penelope's heart. She was hit with a powerful shock that made her body thrash wildly before falling backwards.

"Mom!" shouted Xander as Penelope collapsed in his arms.

"Penny, no!" cried Atticus, falling to his knees and cradling his wife's lifeless face in his hands. "What have you done?"

"What I had to," said Elvira, her smile not faltering.

Deryn took this moment to fire at her, but her damn Element was still on stun and Elvira easily dodged the attack.

The woman laughed. "You think you're a match for me?" She changed the setting on her Element to stun and aimed for the one Deryn held.

When it hit, Deryn tossed her weapon far away before it could shatter and catch her with the remains of the stunner.

Now without a weapon, she darted for the other hallway. Elvira shot another stunner at her but missed.

"Grab her!" Elvira ordered Atticus. "Grab her if you want your son to live!"

Something gripped Deryn's ankle. She fell forward and landed hard, looking over her shoulder to see Atticus's vacant eyes staring at her while he held on tight.

"What do you mean by that?" he asked, looking back at Elvira, his expression lost somewhere between anger and grief. Deryn kicked him, so he grabbed her other ankle, easily overpowering her.

"The man who led the attack today is her father," said Elvira, stepping forward. "He has already fled and our president is not happy about it. If you want to keep your son alive after the cowardice he has shown today then I suggest you give him something to lure the enemy back."

Deryn shook her head frantically. She tried to look at Xander first, so she could plead with him to make his father let her go, but his eyes were still blank and focused on his mother. So she looked at Atticus. He stared back at her, torn for a moment before glancing at where he had her pinned. He reached for something hanging from his belt, which became glowing blue shackles at the press of a button.

"No!" Deryn sat up and swung her fists at him, punching and clawing until his grip loosened. She tugged her feet away and tried to stand, but Atticus pulled her right back down. "Ow!" she cried out as she landed hard on her arm.

Xander's eyes finally focused as he turned his head to look at her. She stared at him desperately, pleading for him to do something, anything more than just sit there. But Xander did nothing. He opened his mouth like he was going to say something but, before he could, Atticus had his shackles around Deryn's ankles. He grabbed her by the hair and yanked her to her feet.

"Xander, head home," he ordered. "Take your mother and stay hidden until I come for you. I want to get this all straightened out with the president before you show your face again. Understood?"

Xander nodded, his mouth slightly open as he stared at Deryn. "What are you going to do with her?"

"That's for our president to decide," said Elvira, walking over and wrestling with Deryn to get another set of shackles on her wrists.

"No!" screamed Deryn as Atticus threw her over his shoulder and carried her through the halls. "Dax! Talon! Please!" She looked back at Xander with one last plea while he sat on the floor, holding his dead mother in his arms. "Help!"

Xander closed his eyes and did not look up again. And then Deryn was around the corner, her last glimmer of hope out of sight as Atticus and Elvira carried her towards their leader. Cheers echoed down the hallway as President Saevus and his guards celebrated their victory, the last of the Outsiders having finally fled.

The world was theirs to control, and Deryn Leon had just received a front row seat to the hell they were going to create.

CHAPTER THREE

Deryn jerked awake as something cold brushed against her cheek.

"We're close," whispered the old woman, her fingers trailing to Deryn's forehead.

She sat up and blinked. She'd been dreaming again, if you could call it that. It never seemed fair to call a nightmare a dream, especially when her nightmares were also her reality.

She looked out the window, staring at the bright lights of Inner City. After President Saevus's defeat over the Outsiders he had locked up the city from the inside out. Those most frightened of the outside world and the wealthiest lived in Inner City. Middle City circled around it, not quite as protected, and those worried about their health wore gasmasks when venturing outside of their homes. Outer City completed the circle and was inhabited by those living in poverty.

The people in Outer City would occasionally drop dead, President Saevus claiming it was from the toxic air leaking in through the doorways the Outsiders had opened when they chose to leave Utopia in the first place. The doors were now locked up and only ever opened when his guards had business outside.

But the toxic air leaking in was a lie. Deryn knew for a fact that he had random people, sometimes entire families, poisoned to keep the fear alive. This was the kind of information you learned as a slave. It was just a shame she couldn't do anything with it.

Most of the Outsiders had fled the city for good after they lost the battle against Saevus. If captured they were executed on the spot, unless they were desirable or valuable in some way.

There were plenty of citizens in Utopia who weren't Outsiders but had still ventured outside at one time or another. After the battle in Eagle Center, Saevus had gathered up as many of these people as he could, killing most but putting the ones he let live through a brutal quarantine. Definitely not standard. Anyone who went through it never came out the same. Deryn had been through it three times.

Those who had evaded capture fled underground. Before Utopia was built, their ancestors had lived in a string of protective tunnels. People hid there, small groups known as Tunnelers moving daily to evade S.U.R.G.E.'s - Saevus's Utopian Robotic Guardians for the Elite. Robots that scanned the tunnels for human life. They were black and the size of two fists with fluttering wings. Virtually indestructible, at least with the Tunnelers' weapons, and designed to kill if necessary.

Something tickled her ear. She winced and pushed whatever it was away. It was the old woman moving some loose hairs out of her face.

"You don't look well," she said with a frown.

Deryn glanced down at her bruised arms hanging out of her tattered coat and sighed. Over the years she had always been tortured, that was a given, but this last place had really done a number on her.

Apparently, the only reason the Guardian had chosen Deryn was because her brother had recently been killed when the Outsiders broke into Utopia and raided his home. Since she couldn't get revenge on who she wanted, she got it on Deryn instead.

"Nothing I can't handle," said Deryn, even though she knew she needed medical attention. There was definitely some internal bleeding after everything she'd gone through. Her ribs hurt the most. Sometimes the pain pressed so tightly against them that she couldn't even breathe.

Trying hard to focus her attention elsewhere, Deryn didn't

notice the old woman take something out of her pocket until it was shoved into her hands. It was covered by a green handkerchief but she didn't need to unwrap it to know what it was. She turned to the old woman with wide eyes.

"W-what -"

"You need this more than I do. Get out of here. Find your family and help them set us free."

"I can't take this," said Deryn, handing the gift back to her.

"But you must," said the woman. "Many of us believe the reason the Resistance hasn't started an official war is because your father fears for your life. If you escape then he will have no reason not to fight."

Deryn was still staring at the handkerchief. "That's easier said than done."

"And I have complete faith that you will succeed."

The left corner of her mouth twitched upwards. "Where did you get this?"

"Slaves like me are not watched as closely as slaves like you."

The van came to a halt. Deryn slipped the item into her coat pocket and looked up. Everyone in the van was watching her. Hopefully, none of them would speak of this. That would be the end of them both.

As always, Deryn stared out the window to see where they were. It was a large house on one of the wealthiest streets in Inner City. She had been here many times before and knew instantly that this would be her last stop of the night. She was, after all, his favorite.

"I have an extra special treat for you, sir," said the driver, opening the door to the back of the van and letting the Guardian have a look.

Soren Tash poked his head inside. He didn't look around for long before his eyes fell upon Deryn. They lit up with his smile. "If it isn't my precious Outsider. You've returned to me at last. How long has it been since you were here? I'd say at least a year."

Deryn had no idea how long it had been. It didn't seem like an entire year had gone by since she last resided at his house -

mainly because he always found her no matter who she belonged to - but she trusted his concept of time much more than hers.

Before he could say another word, Deryn stood up and walked out of the van, not even bothering to wait for the driver to come and get her.

"Eager one you got 'ere," said the driver.

"Yes, she always is," Soren said proudly.

Deryn tried to step down, but he grabbed her by the waist and put her on the ground. Her body winced at the touch, unable to handle such pressure.

He frowned and stroked a bruise on her cheek. "Someone has not taken proper care of you."

Deryn moved away. She looked back at the old woman one last time before the door was shut and locked. Following Soren, with the driver right behind her, Deryn took a good look at the old van. It had belonged to their ancestors long ago and was refurbished for the sole reason of the slave trade. All hover-cars and bikes these days were designed with built-in trackers. Several years earlier, the Outsiders had hacked into Utopia's computer system and tracked one of the hover-van's carrying slaves in an attempt to find Deryn. Unfortunately, they had tracked the wrong one and old, wheeled vehicles, which could not be tracked, had been used from then on.

"Fontaine!" Soren called as soon as the front door was closed.

A young, well-dressed man with sallow skin, a shaved head and dead eyes instantly appeared in the foyer. "Yes, Master?"

"Go and fetch the other slave," ordered Soren. "I want to get this trade over with quickly so the night may proceed."

The young man nodded and hurried off.

Soren looked at Deryn and scanned her from head to foot. "Switch her collar to me and remove her binds," he said, motioning down to her chained wrists and ankles. "I would like to get this coat off of her so I can see the damage."

The driver undid her shackles first, then lifted her hair and pressed his thumb on her collar. When it recognized his fingerprint, the collar's light blinked red. Soren pressed his thumb against it next until it blinked blue.

"*New ownership approved*," said a robotic voice. Deryn hated those words. Even after all this time, the voice still made her sick.

Once that was done, the driver went as far as removing Deryn's coat and hanging it in the closet by the door. She stared after it longingly, wishing she had kept the item on her instead of in her coat's pocket.

Soren walked around so he was facing Deryn, rubbing his hands up and down her arms and making her shudder. He found his way to her hips and lifted her shirt slightly, taking a peek at the bruises underneath.

"Clearly, your last owner did not know what they had. This cannot be fixed overnight."

Footsteps sounded in the hallway. Fontaine walked back in the room with a haughty-looking girl behind him.

"I thought you said I could stay?" she said, crossing her arms and sneering at Deryn.

"That was before I knew what was waiting for me in the van."

"*Her?* This beaten whore?"

Soren's brow furrowed.

"Master, please, I'm the better choice. No one can make you feel the way I -"

He swung the back of his hand, smacking her so hard in the face that she fell to the floor. As she attempted to stand, he smacked her again, causing a loud cracking sound. Her nose began to bleed. All Deryn could do was watch as this girl screamed, trying to grab Soren's feet before he could strike again.

"Master, why?" she cried once she successfully had her face buried in his leg.

"You will *not* speak to her in that manner again," he snarled through gritted teeth. "Do you hear me?"

"Yes," she answered, crying harder. "I'm so sorry, Master. Please, I love you. Let me stay with you!"

"No," he spat. "You will never stay in this house again."

"No! Master!"

She reached for his arms, but Soren stepped back and prepared his free foot to kick her in the face. The girl closed her eyes and waited for the hit but, before he could, Deryn reached her hand out and put it on his chest.

"That's enough," she said, keeping his gaze as he slowly lowered his foot. "I take no offense."

Even though Deryn didn't want to see this girl struck again, she felt little pity for slaves who fell in love with their owners. Of course, she doubted it was really about that. Out of all the Guardians who participated in the slave trade, Soren was, if nothing else, a safe bet. He didn't torture the slaves he took in, though he did do many other things to them. Things that some might consider worse than torture. But as long as his wife wasn't there - and she so rarely was - his house was one of the better ones to be in.

"Fine," said Soren, shaking her off of his foot. He reached down and touched his thumb to the back of her collar while she cried. It beeped and blinked red. "Take her away. I never want to see her face again."

She continued to cry as the driver put Deryn's old binds on her wrists and ankles, pressing his thumb on the back of her collar until it blinked blue.

"New ownership approved."

He pulled her roughly to her feet. Soren took Deryn's hand and led her to the living room as the driver and the slave exited.

"Fontaine, fetch our guest some medicine for her wounds, and call the physician. I would like him to come by tomorrow and treat her properly. We must nurse her back to health immediately."

"Yes, Master Tash," said Fontaine before walking off.

"Let me get a good look at you," said Soren, settling Deryn in front of him and trying to remove her shirt.

She grabbed the ends and pulled it back down. "Don't."

"But I need to see the extent of the damage, my precious Outsider."

Deryn cringed as he spoke the name he always called her. "No. I don't want you to see."

Soren frowned. "Difficult, as always." He grabbed her arm, making her wince. His frown deepened. "Wait here," he said before exiting the room.

The moment he was gone, Deryn ran over to the closet with a limp she only then became aware of and found her coat. She dug through the pockets and pulled out the item the old woman had given her. After removing it from the handkerchief, she stuck it in the front of her pants and pulled her shirt down to cover it. Then she shut the closet door and hurried back to the living room as best she could.

Soren returned a minute later with a bottle of blue liquid. Deryn turned her back on him. She heard him open the bottle and pour its contents on his hands. Then he came up behind her and began stroking her arms.

"What are you doing?" she asked, getting goosebumps on every spot he touched with the cold liquid.

"Numbing you," he answered. "There is no way you'll be completely healed by tonight and I still plan on reuniting properly." He moved her hair aside and ran his tongue along her neck.

"Stop it, Tash."

"Oh, my precious Outsider, won't you call me Master just this once?"

Deryn tensed. "Never."

Soren chuckled. "All these years and you're still so impossible to break." He moved his hands into her shirt and ran them along her bare stomach, just missing the tip of the item poking out of her pants.

Deryn sharply grabbed his wrist and pushed it away. "Remove your hands from me."

"And if I don't?" he asked, seizing her other arm and twisting her around so she was facing him. "You forget that for the next three months you belong to me." He lifted his hand and used a single finger to stroke her cheek. "I have also spoken to my father-in-law about possibly keeping you permanently. If he decides not to execute you then he says he'll consider it."

Deryn recoiled and moved away from his touch. He just smiled and ran his fingers through her hair.

She loathed him.

Perhaps the only thing more pathetic than a slave who fell for her abusive owner was a Guardian who fell for his Outsider slave. Soren would never admit it aloud but he was in love with her. He'd been intrigued by her when he was one of her trainers at Eagle Center, but he hadn't felt something deeper until she was captured and he'd had the pleasure of having her for the first time. Nothing revolted Deryn more than seeing that yearning look in his eyes whenever she was near.

"I said remove your hands from me," she repeated, her words slow and harsh. "This is your last warning."

Soren smirked. "Make me." He pulled her head inward and forced his lips on hers.

In one swift movement, Deryn bit down hard on his bottom lip and pulled out the hidden item.

"Ow! Fuck!"

Soren stepped back, readying his hand to slap her when he felt something plunge into his stomach. He gasped and looked down, finally removing his hands from her to hold them over the bleeding hole in his center. His eyes moved to Deryn's hand, watching as the blood, *his* blood dripped from the knife she held. Then they moved up to her face, her eyes fierce as she stared back at him. He had never seen such fire in her before, or he had chosen not to. Either way, until this moment part of him truly believed that she cared for him as much as he cared for her. But he'd been wrong. So, so wrong.

"W-why?" he asked in a choked voice as blood continued to pour from his gut.

"I told you to remove your hands from me and you didn't listen," she spat. "I don't want you to touch me. I've never wanted you to touch me. And now you will *never* touch me again."

With those final words, Deryn lifted her blade and slashed it across Soren's throat. He grabbed at the new wound and fell to the floor, struggling to stay conscious as he bled out.

Deryn watched him until he stopped moving, only then looking down at the bloody knife she held. She didn't think she could do it, take someone's life in such a cruel fashion, but she had and she hardly felt sorry about it. Soren was a Guardian. A murderer. She had probably saved dozens of lives by ridding the world of him, including her own.

Someone screamed.

Deryn turned to see Fontaine standing in a doorway. He ran away, dropping the medicine he held.

"No!" shouted Deryn, darting to catch it. But she was too late and the glass shattered. "Dammit!"

There was no time to stress over it. She hurried back to Soren's body, grabbed his right thumb, and pressed it to the back of her collar until it beeped and blinked red. She tore the thing off, for the first time in years feeling like she could breathe again.

Then she searched him. The only thing of any use to her was the guard wristband he wore on his left wrist. With it she could get out of Inner City without being questioned like a citizen. Granted, she would never get past Middle City before a trace was activated on the wristband to find her, but it was better than nothing at all.

She lifted her knife and cut the wristband off of him, cringing at the pink, wounded flesh just below it since guard wristbands were designed to burrow into their skin and bones. It was a good thing he was already dead, because when a guard's wristband was removed it signaled desertion. A horrible infection would take over their bodies, killing them within minutes. Black veins were already moving up his arms.

With the wristband in hand, Deryn ran over to the closet. She was just about to grab her coat when she noticed how tattered it was. She would definitely stand out in a crowd wearing that. So instead she grabbed a simple black one and put it on. She reacted a bit when she realized it smelled like *her*. Soren's wife and the person she hated most in this world.

Elvira.

Once the coat was on, she stuck her knife and the confiscated wristband in her pocket. She opened the door and sprinted outside, forgetting all about her wounded ankle and not stopping until she was off of the property.

Pulling the coat's hood over her head, Deryn looked in every direction before walking into the night. She headed for the gate to Middle City, where she would find someplace to get lost in.

The streetlamps lit the way for her like a golden path, giving her hope for the first time in years. It was like they were leading her, guiding her towards what she desired most. To be reunited with her family and friends.

With her father. The man who'd risked everything for her.

With Talon. The brother who'd always looked out for her.

And with Dakota. Her sweet Dakota who'd probably blamed himself for her disappearance. Hopefully, they were all together and still fighting. For her. For everyone. For their future. And, above all else, for their freedom.

CHAPTER FOUR

Several nights later, Deryn lingered outside of a bar in one of the grimier parts of Middle City, trying to stay with a crowd. She had initially hid under bridges that were built over their filtered water source or in dark alleys when it became late, but then the guards started searching those kinds of places for her, almost catching her nearly half a dozen times.

As Deryn stood there, an intoxicated woman stumbled into her without any sort of apology. She pretended to help her catch her balance, while slyly slipping off her citizen wristband. These ones were not burrowed into people's skin like the guard wristbands, so it was easy to take.

Once she had it hidden in her sleeve, she walked to the small market on the corner and put it on her wrist. Citizen wristbands were connected to their owners' bank accounts, so she was able to use it to buy a little food and some medicine to soothe her insides. The one praise she gave Utopia over the outside world was their medicine, which was much more advanced. No physicians had been in the first wave of people to become Outsiders, and those who considered leaving later were the first to die by the 'toxic air' leaking in from the outside. Her people had to teach themselves and they still hadn't gotten it quite right. Of course, the best medicines in Utopia were not available for purchase in stores.

Deryn swallowed the medicine before eating the small amount of food. She didn't want to use too much of someone else's money. President Saevus had really cracked down on the rules over the years, starting with the wristbands. They tracked everything their owners did and were checked by the guards daily. A large purchase at a market late at night would not go unnoticed, but a small one would most likely be ignored. There was no freedom anymore. For anyone.

She had found two gates to Outer City over the course of the last few of days, but security had been heightened since her escape and she was unable to get through before they were thoroughly checking everyone's information with twice as many guards as usual. No one was told why this was being done, which Deryn could only assume was because the president didn't want her father or the other Resistance members to catch wind of her escape.

So it seemed, for now, Deryn was trapped in Middle City, unsure of what to do next.

With the food down, she waited a few more minutes for the medicine to take effect. As soon as that mild relief set in, she stood back up and walked into the crowd, trying hard not to limp. She made sure to drop the wristband somewhat near its owner's foot. Then she continued to the curb, where she stared blankly at the road. She needed to come up with a plan but her mind was not as sharp anymore. Years of torture could do that to a person.

"My band. Where the hell is my band? Someone's stolen it! Someone stole -"

"Isn't that it right there?"

Deryn looked over her shoulder and saw someone pointing at the ground. The woman she had taken the wristband from looked at it, blinked, and laughed before picking it up. "Oh, thank Saevus! The Guardians would've had my head for sure!"

"We need another round to celebrate!" said a man, walking over and putting his arms around her and her friend who had spotted the wristband. "On me!"

The women both laughed and followed him inside. Deryn turned back to face the road and began to think.

"Did you hear the rumor that some Guardian got his throat slashed open?" a man asked his two acquaintances as they walked up beside her. He took out a pipe that smelled like strawberries, a poor tobacco substitute, and lit it.

"Yeah, I heard some Outsider slave did it. Wouldn't be surprised if we're all watching their execution this weekend," said a man with a large cleft in his chin.

"No, I don't think so," said the man with the pipe, taking a large puff. "Word is they escaped, which is why the whole Middle and Inner Cities are essentially on lockdown."

"How annoying," said a ginger man, rolling his eyes. "I hope they catch the damn slave soon. I hate not being able to just walk over here from Inner without all the damn questioning."

"Speaking of which, where is that damn tram?" asked the man with the cleft chin. "We need to get to the gates before they close 'em for the night."

"Don't think it's supposed to be here for another few minutes." The pipe man took another puff, only now noticing Deryn standing there. He turned to look at her, catching a slight glimpse of her profile. Luckily, this was the less bruised side of her face, so she probably looked fairly normal, albeit a little tired. "Where're you headed?"

"Nowhere." Deryn turned her head so he couldn't get a better look at her.

As she did this, a man walked up on her other side, wearing a black coat with the hood covering his face, much like hers. She moved her head so it was facing forward, reached into her pocket and clutched her knife. Just in case. The new stranger rubbed his eyes, appearing very weary.

"I can fix that," said the man with the pipe, grabbing her wrist.

His hand landed directly on a large bruise. It sent a horrible sting through Deryn's arm. "Ow!" she cried out automatically. She didn't mean to, since he hadn't even grabbed her that hard, but the pain was too strong.

The hooded stranger stopped rubbing his eyes. He stood frozen for a moment before glancing sideways at her.

"Shut your trap! I barely touched you!" shouted the pipe man, releasing her with a push so she flew backwards.

Deryn collided with the stranger in the hood. He caught her before she could hit the ground. The sleeve of his coat rode up and Deryn got a clear view of the wristband burrowing into his left wrist. It had President Saevus's crest on it - a dragon shaped like an 'S' with the words 'In Saevus We Trust' in a half-circle around the top, representing the protective shield around the city. Reserved only for his top Guardians. She tried not to gasp and pulled herself off of him. She needed to get out of there. Now.

Deryn turned to walk away, her hand still on the knife in her pocket, but the man with the pipe grabbed her again. "Where you going, princess?"

He pulled Deryn into him. Before she even had a chance to try and get away, the hooded Guardian grabbed the man's arm and shoved him off of her.

"You dare lay a hand on a lady?"

Deryn's heart stopped. Dear god, she knew that voice. She turned her head slightly and tried to get a better look at the man, but he was still well hidden under his hood.

"What's it to you?" asked the man with the pipe, pulling back his coat and showing the blade he had fastened to his hip.

"You have a permit for that?" The hooded man was quick to pull back his sleeve and show all of them his guard wristband, and Saevus's crest only made it more powerful. The men went white.

"S-sorry, sir," said the pipe man, looking nervous. "I didn't know you were -"

"Who I am shouldn't affect your treatment of others. I believe you owe this woman an apology."

"So sorry, madam."

Deryn said nothing. She turned to walk away again but stopped when she saw two Guardians in their dark-blue trench coats standing outside the bar. Wenton Pace and Gordon Mackey. Both had owned her at one time or another. They seemed to be asking everyone a lot of questions, probably looking for her. *Shit.*

The hooded Guardian followed her eyes. He waved at his

comrades and shouted, "I'm off duty! Check their information for me, will you?" He pointed at the trio of men standing frozen beside Deryn.

"Send 'em over!" shouted Wenton.

The hooded Guardian looked back at the men in front of him. "You heard him. Go." He grabbed the blade out of the pipe man's holster. "I'll hold onto this. We both know you don't have a permit. You're lucky it was me and not one of those two who caught you tonight. And you better hope nothing else is wrong with your information. Gordon is an expert at catching counterfeits."

"I-it's all good and clear, sir," said the man with the pipe he had long forgotten about. He and his friends nervously headed over to where the two Guardians were waiting.

Not even ten seconds after they were gone, a large red tram turned onto the road, hovering above the ground and ringing its bell before stopping right in front of Deryn. She was just about to bolt when she noticed Wenton and Gordon were not just scanning the wristbands of those three men, they were scanning the wristbands of everyone.

When she turned back to the tram, the hooded Guardian motioned and waited for her to go first. Her heart was racing. If she ran now then she would surely look suspicious, but what other option did she have? Only one.

Taking a deep breath, Deryn stepped forward and onto the tram, the hooded Guardian following closely behind her.

Upon entrance, the attendant sitting behind a counter stared up at her, waiting impatiently and darting his eyes between Deryn and the scanner she needed to touch her wristband to for payment. Her nonexistent wristband.

"Get moving, lady. I ain't got all night."

Deryn froze. Clearly, this plan was not very well thought out.

"I've got the lady," said the Guardian behind her, reaching his arm past her and scanning his twice. "And give her a chocolate, as well. She's had a rough night."

"You got it, sir," said the attendant, pressing a button so the tram was back in motion and driving itself. He reached under the counter and pulled out a chocolate bar. The Guardian scanned his wristband once more and the chocolate was shoved into Deryn's hand.

She pocketed it and moved into the tram, making sure to grab a map of the area out of brochure holder before heading towards the back. She kept walking from car to car, very aware of the footsteps trailing behind her.

She reached the last car. There weren't very many people but the few she saw were either passed out drunk or possibly fornicating. At least they had the decency to cover themselves with a blanket so she wasn't quite sure. But really she was.

Deryn didn't stop walking until she got to the very back corner of the tram. She sat beside the window and rested her head against it, trying to ignore the sound of the seat across from her creaking as someone put their weight on it.

Keeping her head turned away from him, Deryn opened the map. A small hologram of the tram moved around, so she could see exactly where they were and where they were going.

She debated when and where she should get off. Part of her felt like she should exit as soon as possible, but another part of her wanted to wait until she was closer to a gate to Outer City.

Of course, right now she was also thinking about the best way to get away from this Guardian, whose eyes she could feel burrowing into her. She pulled her hood more forward. There was no way she could get off before him. What if he followed her? She shuddered at the thought.

Having settled on a plan to wait for the Guardian to exit before choosing a stop for herself, Deryn refolded the map and put it in her pocket.

Even though the seats in the tram were not the most comfortable, it still beat sleeping outside in the cold against a metal wall.

Deryn grabbed a pillow from beside her and put it against the window. She rested her head and closed her eyes. It felt good. She hadn't had an owner who gave her a pillow in a very long time. Probably not since the last time Soren had a hold of her, and that was only when Elvira wasn't around to scold him for it.

The tram came to another halt, causing Deryn to jerk forward in her seat and her hood to fall back a little. She quickly adjusted it and glanced sideways at the Guardian. He had finally stopped watching her and was looking out his window curiously.

While the tram normally started up again after a minute or so, this time it didn't. Deryn held out her ear and listened. The bustling activity going on in the other cars had stopped as abruptly as the tram.

"Shit," said the Guardian under his breath.

"What's going on?" asked a woman. Deryn didn't remember seeing any women when she came through the car, so she assumed she must have been one of the people under the squirming blanket.

"I hear -" *Hiccup!* "- Garjens been checkin' da -" *Hiccup!* "- tram a' night."

Deryn went white.

"Ter make sure we all gots our ... ugh ... bands. I needa bucket."

"That'll be three coin," said the tram worker who was patrolling this car. He took a piece of paper out of his pocket, flicked it once and it popped into a bucket. His wristband scanner was at the ready.

"I ain't gots -" *Hiccup!* "- no mer money ter spen'."

There was a strange gurgling sound that Deryn did not find pleasant at all. She put her head back on the pillow and closed her eyes.

"For the president's sake, just give him the bucket!" shouted the woman.

"Three coin," repeated the tram worker.

"Please ... ugh ... no ... Bleh!"

Even without looking, Deryn was quite sure she knew what had just happened.

"My coat!" shouted a new voice. "Are you fucking kidding me?"

"S-so s-s-sorry," sputtered the drunk man. "I-I din' mean to _"

The familiar sound of whip-like beam of light shooting out of an Element made Deryn wince, and that was before the man screamed. She put her hand back in her pocket and gripped her knife tightly.

"Check his information before I lose it, Luka."

There was the clear sound of a scanner as a set of footsteps walked slowly down the aisle. Deryn could hear as the two new Guardians grabbed everyone's wrists, making a few comments along the way.

"You sure are pretty," said the same Guardian to a whimpering woman. "Your body already reeks of sex. Did you do it right here in this seat?"

"No," she cried.

"You toxic little liar."

"I'm not toxic. My aunt and her family went out, but -"

"Same thing," he spat. "Hey, Luka, your shift's done after this, isn't it?"

"Yeah," said the voice of Luka Voclain. Deryn hadn't seen him in years, despite the fact that he lived with his father Barath, who often favored her during the slave trade.

"Maybe you'd like to take this lovely piece home with you?"

"I'd rather not. The last time I brought a girl related to an Outsider home, my father whipped her to near death. Needless to say, she hasn't been over since."

"You're ... you're kidding, right?" she asked.

"I wish I was," said Luka. "She's all yours."

"Excellent," said the other Guardian. "Clean yourself up. I don't want any traces of some other man on you while you're in my bed tonight."

"You're not even going to fight for her?" asked Luka, assumingly talking to the man she was with.

"I ... we ... I mean ... I only met her an hour ago."

The Guardian laughed. "Looks like I got myself a real class act tonight."

Footsteps continued down the aisle. Deryn clenched her

eyes shut and moved her face farther into her hood. Her palm was sweating as she fought to keep her grip on the knife in her pocket.

"Evening, Veli."

Deryn trembled as the hooded Guardian said the name. She knew it well. Veli Tash, older brother to Soren and an adamant hater of Deryn. He couldn't stand the way his brother acted when she was around, so he tortured her every chance he got. He said she made Soren weak. It seemed he was right. If Soren wasn't weak then he might still be alive.

"What are you doing here?" Veli asked the hooded Guardian.

"Just trying to get home. A process you're currently delaying. Could you move this along, already?"

There was silence, followed by another footstep. Closer to her. A presence leaned in. Deryn gripped the knife even harder to stop her shaking. Should she strike? If she did, would there be any chance for her to -

"I would prefer it if you didn't wake her," said the hooded Guardian.

"Why? She with you?"

"Yes she is, and she's a little drunker than I prefer, so I was hoping to sober her up a bit. I don't want to end up with something sloppy tonight."

Deryn knew she had stopped breathing but she couldn't bring herself to start again. He had just lied for her.

"You scan her band?"

"Yes, because I always ask to see a woman's information before buying her a drink."

"Don't get smart with me, you little -"

"Watch your tone! You forget that I am your superior now."

Veli shut his mouth.

"She's not who you're looking for, so get the hell out of here and let me get on with it!"

There were several more creaks on the floor as Veli stepped backwards, away from Deryn.

"By the way, I was so sorry to hear about your brother."

Veli stopped moving.

"Of course, Elvira's another story. She says her lousy husband deserved it, considering his obsession with that slave. Didn't keep a good enough eye on her."

"Fuck you -"

"Ah! Language!"

Deryn's hand gripped the knife even harder. She hated that he was prolonging this. Just let them leave, already.

"I oughtta -"

"You *ought to* what?"

Veli said nothing.

"That's what I thought. Get out of here, Veli. I'm tired and I would like to get home."

"Bastard," said Veli under his breath as he walked back down the aisle. "Just like his father."

"And, Veli!" the hooded Guardian called once his subordinate had gone a fair distance. "Leave the girl sitting up there, will you? I suddenly have a craving for a three-way tonight."

Veli grunted. He left the car and headed for the front of the tram.

Luka laughed.

"Drinks later this week, Luka?" asked the hooded Guardian.

"Definitely," answered Luka before following Veli out of the car.

As soon as they were gone, the Guardian looked at the whimpering woman near the front of the car and said, "I suggest you get home quickly. And don't go out again at night anytime soon. If he sees you then he'll undoubtedly try again."

"Yes, thank you," she cried.

A few seconds later, a bell rang and the tram started again. As it continued to move, Deryn sat there baffled. She had been saved. By *him*.

After taking a deep breath, she released her knife, sat up straight and turned her head to face the Guardian. She kept her eyes down for a long moment before lifting them slowly, first taking in his feet, which were aimed in her direction, then his knees, his chest, his shoulders, his neck, and finally his face, no longer hidden beneath the safety of a hood. It was a face she hadn't seen in years but would never forget. A face she had never wanted to see again. The face of Xander Ruby.

Xander stared back at her with his golden-brown eyes, which were hidden behind two dark circles that made his creamy complexion appear even paler. By the looks of it, there was a good chance his exhaustion rivaled her own.

Xander only held Deryn's gaze for a moment before he lifted his hand and motioned for her to turn around. The old her would have fought him on such an order, but the present her knew he was right. She was not in the clear yet. Someone could still recognize her. She turned back around and closed her eyes, silently wondering what could possibly happen next.

CHAPTER FIVE

Deryn must have drifted off to sleep, because she shot up in panic and nearly attacked when someone grabbed her shoulder.

"Our stop is next," said Xander, fixing her hood, which had fallen halfway off.

She blinked.

He leaned in and whispered, "Everyone here heard me say you were getting off with me, so I suggest you do just that before you risk both our lives."

Deryn looked around the car and saw that everyone was watching them, including the other woman who was trying to get a good look at whomever it was she wouldn't be having a three-way with that night.

Deryn stood. She flinched as Xander grabbed her hand, but he kept a firm grip and pulled her towards the front of the tram.

While taking a good look down at their clasped hands, Deryn felt absolutely sick. Filthy and starved, holding hands with Xander Ruby, *forced* to rely on the help of a Guardian. It really didn't get any lower than this. And that was saying a lot, coming from her. She had been pretty close to the bottom before but at least she always somewhat had her dignity.

Deryn kept her head low as they walked, not making eye contact with anyone.

Xander led her through the tram's cars, each more crowded than the last. When they reached the front, he stopped by the exit and gripped a pole, pulling her into him and holding her tightly as the tram came to a halt.

The doors opened. Xander took hold of her hand again and hurried them outside. They were the only ones who exited. The doors closed behind them and the tram zoomed off, creating a loud whistling sound as it sped through the night.

As soon as it was out of sight, Xander dropped Deryn's hand and the two of them were left standing outside in the cold, damp air.

Unsure where they were, Deryn looked around. They appeared to be in an older neighborhood, with houses and apartments built with brick, as opposed to the steel and glass structures that were favored throughout the majority of Middle and Inner City.

It was pretty dead. Not only were there no people walking around, but every building was pitch black. Many people ran and even more were killed when Saevus came down harder on his citizens after defeating her father. Their population had already been dwindling for years and a lot of buildings were left deserted. Sometimes entire streets were devoid of human life. This looked like one of them.

Without a word, Xander turned and started walking to what Deryn recognized as the east, thanks to the stars they could see in the artificial sky, which Saevus claimed mirrored the outside world. She knew that was another one of his lies. It rained far more in here than it ever did out there.

While growing up on the outside, Godfrey had taught Deryn how to read the stars. The real stars.

After Xander had taken a few steps, he stopped and turned. "Coming?"

Deryn's eyes widened. It was a ridiculous question. Of course she wasn't coming, and she made that very clear by rapidly shaking her head.

"It's not safe for you to stay out here."

She crossed her arms and remained silent.

"If I wanted to turn you in, don't you think I would've done it already?"

That was a very curious question. If he had been any other person - Guardians and guards aside - then she might have said yes, but this was Xander Ruby. Someone history had taught her never to trust, and for good reason. Why should now be any different?

"Look, I understand why you don't trust me."

At least they were on the same page.

"I never gave you much reason to before and the band on my wrist doesn't exactly help. But if you stay out here you *will* be caught and you *will* be executed. They have a plan to capture you and, without someone's help, they will succeed."

Even though Deryn was starting to feel less confident, she still stood up straight and held her ground. This was Xander Ruby. The boy she had pleaded with to save her moments before she was forced into the life she was now trying to escape. She could never forget that.

"Fine. Do what you want. Your fucking funeral."

And with those final, familiar and heartfelt words, Xander turned and left. Deryn watched him walk farther and farther down the road, his figure growing hazy in the fog. Fog she never understood, considering they were in a damn bubble. Her eyes did not leave him until he rounded the corner.

Deryn turned to walk in the opposite direction, but quickly looked back at the corner he had just gone around.

She had never been much of a gambler but, given the current circumstances, every move she made was just that. A gamble. Right now she had no plan. She knew no one in Middle City, other than her former slave owners, and had nowhere to go. Sleeping on the streets was a great risk and she could hang around the crowds all she wanted, that didn't change the fact that, eventually, someone was bound to recognize her. Xander had.

Past prejudices aside, at that moment Xander had given her no reason not to trust him. He protected her from those men outside of the bar, paid for her to get on the tram, lied for her so she wouldn't get caught by the other Guardians, *and* bought her chocolate.

Deryn reached into her pocket and touched the chocolate bar. She closed her eyes and breathed deeply. It had been a great gamble when she used that knife, and now she was going to take another one.

Before Deryn had a chance to talk herself out of it, she opened her eyes and ran in the direction Xander had gone. Her body ached as she moved and a pain she had almost forgotten about shot through her ankle. But she didn't care. She had to catch up to him. Whether he betrayed her or not, he was still her best option. So, for the first time since she had known him, Deryn Leon was taking a chance on Xander Ruby.

She whirled around the corner and stopped to look for him. He wasn't there. She had already lost him. What was she supposed to -

"About time you got here."

Deryn's heart jumped. Xander was leaning against the wall just beside her.

He smirked. "You didn't actually think I was going to leave you alone out here, did you?"

She didn't answer.

"Do you never talk anymore?" he asked, standing up straight. "Back in training, the trick was getting you to shut up. Always so damn opinionated. Where are your snide remarks? Your derogatory comments? Where's your fucking fire?"

Deryn stared at him coldly. She huffed and said, "It's back at Eagle, probably in that hallway we were in before your father dragged me off to a life of slavery."

Xander stared back at her, mouth slightly fallen. But it was not long before his look of surprise melted away and became a grin instead. "Ah! Now there's the girl I know and loathe. Looks like I just have to rattle you a bit. Well, come along."

Xander took the lead and guided Deryn through the dead streets of what was formerly a vibrant city. Back when Outsiders were allowed in as long as they went through quarantine or wore gasmasks, and Saevus hadn't killed off half of his citizens for disagreeing with him. The world had practically ended but two centuries ago, the majority of people had died and yet he still took so many lives from the few who remained. It was their job as the survivors to rebuild the world, not destroy it further.

Judging from the street they were on, Middle City might as well have been a ghost town. Deryn glanced around the eerie sight, unsure of how she was supposed to feel. Even though she had spent a good deal of time in Middle City, as a slave she had always been isolated in a house. Other than her glimpses from the window during the slave trades, she had never really seen how sad it had truly become.

Xander walked rather quickly and Deryn had a hard time keeping up with him. Her ankle was really starting to hurt and she found herself wishing she would have thought to buy something for it.

After several twists and turns through the streets, they eventually stopped in front of a tall but narrow apartment complex. Xander scanned his wristband, then used a key to let them inside. As they walked up the stairs, loud music and voices could be heard coming from one of the higher floors. She pulled her hood on farther.

"Oi! Ruby!" shouted a man as they continued past the third floor.

Xander put his hand on Deryn's waist and guided her up a few steps higher than him. He ignored the way she flinched and turned towards the man who called him.

"Picked these up for you."

Deryn watched him toss something to Xander out of the corner of her eye.

"Thanks." Xander pocketed whatever it was.

"Come on, Ruby. You gotta tell us," said another man, walking over and taking a large swig from a bottle of whiskey. "How much longer we gotta put up with this damn lockdown?"

"Yeah. You Guardian bastards catch whoever it is you're looking for yet?"

"You know I can't share that information," answered Xander.

"Ah, come on! What's the point of having a Guardian as a

neighbor if you can't tell us anything?"

"Favors." Xander winked. "All I can say is that the lockdown won't be ending anytime soon. Actually, starting tomorrow, it's going to be worse. You will receive a formal notice in the morning."

Both men whined in great disappointment.

The first one took a puff of what appeared to be a cigarette, which was strange considering they had been banned several decades ago, along with all other tobacco products. He glanced at Deryn and she quickly turned away. "Who's your lovely friend?"

"None of your fucking business."

"Shier than the ones you normally bring around. What's your name, sweetheart?"

Xander grabbed the bottle out of the second man's hands and said, "I'll be taking this. And I suggest you keep it loud down here tonight, 'less you want to hear something your small and feeble minds won't understand."

Both men gaped at him and then at Deryn. They grinned.

"It's always the quiet ones who are the screamers." The man with the cigarette laughed.

Deryn whipped in their direction. "I beg your pardon!"

"We should be going now." Xander grabbed her arm and yanked her farther up the stairs. "Hold your fucking tongue, will you?" he whispered harshly, once they were a fair enough distance away.

Xander didn't stop pulling her until they reached the very top, which she had counted as the fifth floor. There was only one door here. His wristband was scanned and he unlocked several locks quickly with his key. He stepped inside and turned on the lights. Then he waited for Deryn to come in, but she made no signs of leaving the hallway.

"You already came this far. Seems a bit foolish to stop now," he said, wiggling the door like he was going to shut it.

Deryn looked skeptically at him. But then she took a deep, meditative breath and stepped inside. After all, it was part of the gamble.

She jumped when Xander shut the door. Without a word, he took off his coat and tossed it over the back of a chair, leaving her standing there as he headed for the kitchen.

Deryn stood frozen as he shuffled around in there, her eyes studying every last inch of the apartment Xander called home. It was much smaller than she expected. Not that it was small by any means, but he had grown up in one of the largest homes in Inner City. The Saevuses and the Rubys had been close for generations, often living next door to one another.

The living space was well-sized with a black couch, two matching armchairs, a coffee table, a desk and chair, a fireplace, and a nook with a built-in bookcase that had more knickknacks on it than books. Considering the majority of books in Utopia were electronic, it seemed irrelevant.

There was a small dining area with a hardwood table and four chairs just beside the kitchen. A tacky chandelier hung above it, which she was sure Xander did not choose. Just beside the dining area was the open kitchen, which she only glanced at briefly since Xander was moving around in there.

There were three wooden doors in this apartment, and one large sliding glass door that led out to a balcony. The curtains were currently drawn. Deryn moved to close them.

"Shoes," called Xander from the kitchen.

She stopped and looked back to see he had taken his off by the door. She did the same, frowning as she looked down at the rundown boots she had been forced to wear for years next to his shiny black boots.

Letting out another sigh, she walked over to the curtains and took one last look at the city before shutting it away.

"You can take off your coat, Leon. I'm fully aware of who you are."

Deryn tensed at the sound of her name. It had been a long time since anyone had called her any name at all, unless they were calling her something derogatory. It was interesting to hear it again, even from his sharp lips.

Deryn decided it would be all right to pull off her hood but she didn't want him to see the beaten remains of her body just yet. Or maybe she didn't want to see them herself. It was hard to know.

Once her hood was off, Deryn turned and walked across the plushy white carpet towards Xander. A mouthwatering aroma was currently lingering in the air, and she really hoped that whatever he was making was meant for her and not just a midnight snack.

Xander looked up as she approached, sucking in his breath when he saw the bruises on her face. Deryn halted and instinctually reached back for her hood, her arms aching as she did so.

"Don't," he said, holding up a hand to stop her. "I didn't mean to do that."

She stopped and lowered her arms to her sides, uncomfortably playing with the pockets on her coat as she moved her eyes to the floor.

"When was the last time you ate?" asked Xander as he stirred a pot on the stove.

"I don't know," she said with a weak shrug. "How long has it been since I ..." Since she what? Murdered someone. Slashed his throat open. "Escaped?"

"Three days," he said as he opened a cabinet and pulled out a bowl.

"Then it's been four days. Maybe longer. I've had a few little things but not much," she answered, remembering that her last owner had starved her for at least twenty-four hours before stuffing her in the van.

Xander let out a deep sigh that made her cringe. She hated pity, especially from him.

"Sit down, Leon."

Every bit of Deryn still left inside of her wanted to protest. She didn't like being ordered around by him, but the sharp pang in her ankle outweighed her stubbornness and she took a seat at the table.

Not even a minute later, Xander put a bowl of chicken soup and a glass of water in front of her. He took a seat on the other side of the table and drank from the bottle of whiskey he had confiscated.

"You should eat slowly," he instructed. "Your stomach needs time to adjust. If this is too heavy for you I have fruit or - "

"This is fine," she said, taking several sips of water before picking up the spoon he'd given her and digging in. It tasted damn good. Maybe it was the starvation talking but never in her life had she ever tasted something so delicious, so intoxicating, so ... damn good!

When she was about halfway through, Xander stood up and disappeared through one of the closed doors. He returned several minutes later holding a bundle of clothes and waited for her to finish the last few bites.

"I'm not going to lie. You reek of something putrid."

Deryn wished she could be offended but she knew he was right.

"Shower's through there." He pointed at one of the doors. "You can put these on after."

Xander put the bundle of clothes on the table. Deryn stared blankly for a moment before shuffling through them. An oversized shirt, some black silk pajama pants and -

"Ew!" she screamed, dropping the lacy, red underwear she had accidentally touched.

"What?" he asked, shrugging his shoulders.

Deryn looked at him and raised her eyebrows.

"Sometimes women leave things behind when they come here."

She raised them higher.

"It's not like they're dirty. I've washed them since."

And higher still.

"They're all I have so it's either them or nothing."

Deryn looked down at the red lace and huffed. While she was absolutely disgusted with the idea of wearing some random woman's underwear, she also didn't want to go commando while wearing Xander's pajama's, so she caved. She picked up the underwear and clothes, walked to the bathroom and shut the door behind her.

After turning on the shower, Deryn carefully undressed.

She draped the coat over the closed toilet seat and stripped her body of her tattered shirt and pants, discarding them in the trashcan and hoping to never see them again. It was the same clothes she'd been wearing when her father stormed into Eagle Center and attempted to rescue her. So much had happened to her in those clothes and she loathed them for being present during the darkest years of her life. She would have destroyed them right then and there if she had the means to do so.

Before stepping into the shower, Deryn stared at the mirror for a long moment. She didn't want to look in it but she knew she had to. To finally see the damage that had been done to her.

She took several deep breaths before walking in front of it and slowly turning to face her reflection. She gasped as she caught sight of herself, *all* of herself, for the first time in years. There was no meat left on her. She never had much but now she was nothing but a pale, withered mass of skin and bones. Her entire body was covered in bruises that would fade and scars that would not. She looked at her reflection and traced each one of them, trying to remember how they came to be. Her eyes began to tear. She sucked them back and focused on her face.

While Deryn had never been a great beauty, she knew during her training days by the way the men ogled her that she was at least attractive, but the woman looking back at her now was hardly recognizable. Her mahogany-brown hair, no longer streaked with sun-kissed red, was dead and tangled in a filthy heap on the top of her head, and her face was dirty and bruised. Slight traces of dried blood still marked the spot she had been struck moments before being shuffled inside the van. Her green eyes, which had once been bright and optimistic, were now dull and lifeless, hardly visible under two dark circles that might as well have been more bruises. Even her expression was weary and aged.

Deryn shut her eyes and turned away from the mirror. She tore at the rubber band in her hair, struggling with it so aggressively that she pulled some strands out by the roots before tossing it next to her clothes in the trashcan.

She opened the shower door and let the warm water run down her frozen body. Slavery was in her past now. She was free and she couldn't let the memory of it defeat her. But it was hard not to be defeated when there were still so many reminders of that life all over her, etched into her skin forever.

Taking the bar of soap in her hands, Deryn lathered every inch of herself, determined to get any remnants of those memories that were removable off of her. Every muscle in her body ached as she did this, but she worked through it. She had to wash all of those horrible memories away. She had to be clean again.

Once Deryn was satisfied enough with her body, she moved on to her horrible mass of hair. She put some shampoo in her hands, rubbed them together, lifted her arms and -

Stopped.

She couldn't do it. She couldn't lift her arms high enough to wash the top of her hair.

"No," she cried, finally feeling defeated as she lowered her hands and let the water wash the shampoo off of them.

She tried lifting her arms again, without a reason this time, but was met with the same excruciating pain as before. Turning her head, she attempted to look at how bruised they were but it was impossible to see at this angle.

Deryn continued to cry as her body actually resisted her attempt to forget. She didn't know how long she was in there, but it must have been a great deal of time since Xander started banging on the door.

"Dammit, Leon, what the hell is taking so long?" he shouted before throwing the door open.

"Go away!" she yelled from inside the shower.

"You forget that this is my fucking apartment," he said, walking over to the steamy shower door and opening it.

"What are you doing?" she screamed, not even noticing that his eyes were closed as she moved to strike him.

"Ow!" he shouted, covering his face.

"How dare you!" Deryn hit him again before grabbing the towel he had in his hands and throwing it over her body.

"I wasn't looking, Leon!" Xander grabbed her wrist to stop her from attacking.

"Let go! Let me go!" she screamed, going absolutely ballistic. Her body hurt terribly but she refused to stop struggling.

"Calm down!" he shouted, releasing her wrist and letting her step backwards.

Deryn did not stop until she hit the shower wall, and then she used it to sink down to the tiled floor, not even caring that the towel she still held desperately was getting soaked. She cried into her knees as Xander gaped at her, unsure of what had just happened.

"Why aren't you clean yet?" he asked after several uncomfortable moments.

"I ..." Deryn sobbed. "I can't do it," she finally said.

"Can't do what?"

"I can't raise my arms to wash my hair. I don't know if they're bruised or ... or more. What if I can never raise them again?"

"Well, you certainly had no problem raising them to attack me." Xander looked down at her battered body and sighed. "Let me see."

Deryn hesitated before slightly lifting one arm, the other still holding the towel. Xander took a cautious step into the shower and looked.

"It's bruised pretty badly. Like someone gripped you there."

"They probably did," she said with a sniffle. "I don't remember."

Without another word, Xander walked away from the shower and over to the bathtub. He started running the water, then rolled up the sleeves on his sweater, followed by the legs on his pants.

Deryn stood up and watched him from the shower's doorway. "What are you doing?"

"Helping you," he said. "Get in the tub."

She eyed him curiously.

"Fine. I'll go first." Xander sat on the edge of the tub and dipped his feet. "Eyes are closed, Leon. Now grab the shampoo and conditioner, take off the towel and get in here."

She didn't move.

"I promise I won't look. Now get the hell over here."

With another horrible shot to Deryn's pride, she walked back to the shower and turned off the water. She grabbed the shampoo and conditioner, put them beside the tub, dropped her towel and carefully stepped inside. After sinking down in the water, she settled herself against his legs.

"Okay," she said.

Xander opened his eyes and reached for the shampoo. He squirted some into his hands and lathered it into her dirty tangles.

Deryn tried to keep herself together as he washed her, but everything that had happened that night was just too much to handle. Xander Ruby had saved her. And, what more, he was actually helping her bathe. And decently. Not once did a hand or an eye drift. She made sure by watching him in the mirror.

As Xander used the detachable nozzle to rinse out Deryn's hair, she brought her knees up to her chest and put her face in them, trying hard to hide her tears. But Xander was no fool.

"Leon," he said softly, putting a careful hand on her shoulder. "You're safe here. I promise. There's no reason to cry."

"How long?" The words came out muffled as she spoke into her knees.

"What?"

Deryn moved her head so it was facing sideways and repeated, "How long? How long has it been since that day?" Never before had she cared so much about the answer to that question.

"Five years yesterday," said Xander as he squirted some conditioner into his hands.

"It's September 3rd?" she asked.

"Yes."

"My ... my birthday."

Xander froze. "Oh. I ... That's right. Your father came the day before -"

"Five years. Gone," she said quietly. "And I hardly even felt them."

When Xander was finished washing Deryn's hair, he got out of the tub and grabbed a clean towel, using it to cover her naked body while helping her get back to her feet. He left the bathroom while she dried herself off, returning a minute later with a new shirt for her. One that buttoned up so she wouldn't have to maneuver it over her head.

After she changed, Xander keeping his eyes closed the entire time, he pulled out a spare toothbrush and let her have a moment of peace.

Deryn took a long and much needed breather in there by herself. She felt rather embarrassed and her stomach was twisted in horrible knots. A combination of nerves and eating too fast. She didn't understand why she was here, or why Xander, a Guardian, was helping her. If President Saevus ever found out about this he would kill him on the spot.

As soon as she felt somewhat composed, she left the bathroom. Xander was nowhere to be seen, but she followed a shaft of light coming from the door closest to the balcony. Inside, he was pulling back the sheets on a simple but comfortable looking bed.

"This is my guestroom," he said without looking up. "You can sleep here. I don't know for how long, but the president is setting a curfew starting tomorrow. From now on, anyone who's not in a registered residence between the hours of midnight and four a.m. will be revealed. I don't know how yet, but they will and it's best if you're not outside for that. I'm sure I don't have to explain why."

"How ... how long do you think he'll be looking for me?" she asked, eager to get out of this city and find her way back to her family and Dakota.

"It's hard to say. After a couple of nights of this curfew, he might just assume you escaped Utopia somehow. But he also might not."

"And I can stay here? Throughout this ... curfew?"

Xander nodded. "And longer. If you need to." He looked up and locked eyes with her. "Get in. You look exhausted."

As much as Deryn hated the way he kept ordering her around, she simply didn't have it in her to fight with him. So she obediently walked over to the bed and lay down. Even though she didn't need him to, he pulled the covers over her and somewhat tucked her in. He looked as confused by the gesture as she did.

"Why are you doing this?" she asked weakly.

"I don't know. But when I knew it was you on that curb, I couldn't just leave you there."

"So you saw me?"

"No. I recognized your voice when you cried out as that man grabbed you. The last time I saw you, my father made you fall. Your voice sounded the same then."

"Any normal member of the guard would have turned me in."

"I know," he said. "But I stopped being a normal member of the guard five years -"

"And one day ago?" she finished.

Xander nodded. "That's right. The day I watched that bitch kill my mom for trying to protect me. I do what I must to stay alive, Leon. That's all."

"Some might call that cowardice," she said before turning her back on him. "You can go now. I'm tired."

Xander looked down at the soft traces of her figure in the blankets and sighed. He wanted to defend himself, but he simply didn't have it in him to fight with her. So he left, turning off the lights and closing the door, silently wondering what he was going to do with his new houseguest.

When he arrived in his own bedroom, he leaned against the closed door and whispered, "I'm fucked."

CHAPTER SIX

Deryn awoke the next morning to complete and total silence. She hadn't slept very well, considering she still had to do the one eye open thing, and both her head and body ached horribly.

Glancing around the room, she found no clock and since she had absolutely no concept of time anymore, she didn't know how early or late it was. She supposed it really made no difference. Whether she'd been in bed for eight minutes or eight hours, her sleep was still as restless and unfulfilling as ever.

Through a small crack in the green curtains, Deryn could at least see that it was light out.

She struggled to lift her aching body to a seated position and carefully placed both feet on the floor. With the covers torn off of her, she took a good look at the silky pajama's she was wearing and stroked the material. She didn't like it. It was very cold that morning and silk wasn't exactly forgiving when it came to weather. Something flannel really would have been more appropriate. Of course, she was in no position to complain.

Deryn stood up, needing a minute before she was capable of straightening her body entirely. All of the thrashing she had done to Xander in the shower had really been a bad idea. She hurt even more now than before.

She went over to the window and pulled the curtains aside. It was a bit gloomy outside but, overall, seemed like a fairly nice day. The president claimed the weather in the city reflected how it was in the outside world, but she had lived in that world and it was far less gray than the one currently in front of her.

Hopefully, she would be able to see the outside world soon to prove her theory that Saevus showered the entire city with dread intentionally, but she had a pretty good feeling that at least a few weeks in this apartment was not so farfetched. If she was going to get out of the city, it should have been done within an hour of her escape, and she simply didn't have the strength for that. So, for now, she would have to wait.

Getting on her knees, Deryn crossed her arms on the windowsill and continued to gaze outside. It was still her birthday, and she supposed being alive after a Guardian discovered her was a gift in itself. It was most certainly all she was going to get.

With a heavy sigh, she stood back up. Shivering from the cold, she looked around for her coat. Then she remembered she had left it in the bathroom.

With as quiet a stride as she could manage on her hurt ankle, she went to the door and carefully opened it. She poked her head into the dark living room and searched for a light switch, eventually spotting it near the front door.

Glancing around, she noticed that Xander's shoes were no longer by the door and his coat was no longer draped over the chair. But hers was. She picked it up and put it on, hugging herself in an attempt to keep warm. The pocket felt heavy and it was then that she remembered the items she carried. Her hand traveled inside of it and came out with a knife, a map of Utopia, and a chocolate bar. For the first time since she got it, Deryn had a chance to look at the knife in the light. It was silver with a spear point, and the handle was wooden with two lines spiraling around it that crossed each other. There was still some dried blood on its tip. She picked at it with her fingernail.

The lock on the door clicked and Deryn looked around in panic. As a last resort, she darted behind the couch and ducked the moment the door opened.

"Too slow," said the deep and distinct voice of Xander.

Releasing a sigh of relief, she stood up straight.

Xander noticed her coat and cocked an eyebrow. "Going somewhere?"

"I was cold," she said, fidgeting with the items in her hand.

"Did it ever cross your mind that, instead of trying to hide, maybe you should've raised that knife you're holding?"

"No," she said honestly.

"Is that the knife that did the damage?" asked Xander, walking over and putting the rucksack he was carrying on the closest armchair. He took the knife from her reluctant hands and inspected it closely. "I must admit, Leon, I was a bit shocked when I heard about what you did to Soren. I really didn't think you had it in you." He smirked somewhat proudly before slipping the knife back in her pocket. "You should make sure to keep that close." Xander picked up his rucksack. "Follow me."

Deryn's nostrils flared as he ordered her around again. It was getting annoying. But she wasn't sure if she really had the right to protest, so she followed him to the kitchen.

Xander put the rucksack down on the counter and pulled out two bottles of a green liquid. "This medicine will help with any internal injuries you might have," he explained as he went into one of the drawers and pulled out a spoon. "You take exactly one spoonful every twelve hours. No more, no less. Got it?"

Deryn nodded and watched closely as he poured the liquid into the spoon for her. He handed it off and she drank it down quickly. Minty.

Xander reached into his rucksack again and, this time, came out with a small clock.

"This is for your room. I know I don't have one in there and there will be certain days when I'm going to require that you don't wander around out here. Take a good look at the time now so you remember when to take your medicine."

She did just that. "Is the time right?" she asked, noticing it was only six-thirty.

"Yes."

"You've already been up and about at this hour?"

"I don't sleep much," he said before reaching into his rucksack once more and pulling out a small container holding a blue paste. "Rub this on your bruises. It will help them heal faster."

Deryn took the container and frowned. "Ruby, I know as a slave I'm probably not the most informed person in Utopia, but aren't items like this and the medicine forbidden unless prescribed by a doctor?"

"They are."

"Then how did you get them? Are Guardians above the rules or something?"

"They are when they know where the Black Market is."

Deryn's eyes bulged. "The Black Market?" she repeated. "I thought that was just a myth."

"No, it very much exists. It's always existed but, after the war, supporters of the Resistance took it over. Some Guardians have been searching for it for years, trying to shut it down, but others of us, the majority, simply use it to our advantage."

"Where is it?"

Xander chortled. "You must be an idiot if you really believe I'd tell you something like that."

"Why wouldn't you?"

"Because, Leon, I know how you are. In danger or not, if you knew where the Black Market was, you would undoubtedly try to go there. It's too dangerous. Especially for a wanted person."

"What's safe for you is safe for me."

"In this city, the band on my wrist says otherwise."

"If you're such a great Guardian then why the hell do you live in this building, so far from the rest of civilization?"

"The president wanted one of us inhabiting every corner of the three cities." Xander stuck his hand back into the rucksack and felt around for something. "Besides, I like this building. Other than the noisy bastards downstairs, it's completely empty." He came out holding a small, blue box and put it in front of her.

Deryn eyed the box curiously. "What's that?"

"This may be a bit of a shock but, if you open it, you just might find out."

She rolled her eyes. After all these years, he was still such an aggravating smartass. She reached out and opened the box, her eyes widening as they settled on what was inside. It was a cupcake. A delicious looking, chocolate frosted cupcake with rainbow sprinkles.

"I wasn't sure about Outsider traditions, but around here it's customary to have cake on your birthday."

Without waiting for a reaction, Xander picked up his rucksack and carried it into his bedroom. When he came out a few minutes later, Deryn was still standing there, staring blankly at the cupcake he had given her.

He smirked and walked over to her, putting a hand on her shoulder to get her attention. "Here," he said, handing her a black sweater. "So you don't have to wear that heavy coat all day."

She took it absentmindedly.

"And these are for your feet," he said, putting a pair of slippers on the floor.

Deryn watched closely as he specifically placed them so they would be easy for her to step into. She stared at them for a moment, and then at the sweater, and then back at that damn cupcake. After darting her eyes several times between the three objects, she finally stopped on Xander, giving him her first good look since the tram.

He was the same. Dusty-blond hair, golden-brown eyes, creamy white skin that had never touched sunlight, defined cheekbones and a strong jawline. Slightly older, slightly darkened by the effects of war, but the same. If he was the same on the outside then how the hell could anything else about him be different? No. This was just too weird and she felt like she was going to burst. Her mind couldn't take it anymore.

"No, no, no!" she shouted, throwing the sweater back at him. "Stop it! Stop doing that!"

"Doing what?" asked Xander, furrowing his brow.

"Being like this!" She motioned at him dramatically with her hands. "Like ... like you're nice or something! It's creeping me out!"

"Me being nice is creeping you out?"

"Yes! Because you're not nice, Ruby! You're mean and spiteful! And you're a Guardian! Your father is a big part of the reason why I've been held prisoner and tortured for *five* years! Five fucking years!"

"Yes, I realize that," he said calmly.

"If you wanted to help me then you should have done it then! You should have lifted a hand and stopped them!"

"I was young. And my mom had just been killed in front of me. I didn't know -"

"I don't care!" she screamed, crying freely. "Do you know what they did to me? What Soren did to me every day I was imprisoned in his home?"

"Yes," answered Xander without even a flinch. "I'm aware of what happens to slaves, and Soren was hardly quiet about his delusional conquest over you."

This only made Deryn cry harder. "He never had me! Despite what he thought, he never, *ever* had me!"

"I know. That's why I said delusional."

"I can't stay here," she said. "I haven't even been here twelve hours yet and I can already feel the walls closing in on me. I can't be trapped again. Not by you. Not by another Guardian."

Until that moment, Xander had been holding it together, but hearing her say those words set something off inside of him. A fire he had not felt in years. "Is that what you think I'm doing?" he asked, his cold eyes narrowing. "Trapping you? Like *they* trapped you?"

Deryn said nothing but continued to look firmly at him.

"Believe me, Leon, I don't want you here anymore than you want to be here!"

"Yet here we are," she said, using her hands to wipe her damp cheeks.

"Yes, and that's the way it has to stay. You and me. Here.

You understand?"

Deryn studied him carefully as he finally let that coolness he had been trying to maintain go. "Why am I here, Ruby?"

"Not to be my fucking slave! I'm actually quite certain that I'm the one who's been doing things for *you*!"

Deryn opened her mouth to say something but he beat her to it.

"I fucking bathed you! An Outsider! In *my* bathtub! Where's the gratitude? I mean, honestly. Next time just say thank you!"

Deryn straightened herself up and mirrored him by crossing her arms in front of her chest. She looked him square in the eye, her mouth lowering in a deep scowl, and repeated the words he had said to her in the hallway five years earlier. "Never gonna happen, sweetheart."

With a final mocking wink, Deryn pushed past him and marched with a slight limp towards the guestroom.

"And there is nothing wrong with being an Outsider!" she shouted before slamming the door behind her.

"Fuck you!" Xander tossed the sweater at her door with a frustrated growl, then kicked the slippers across the room.

After feeling to make sure his keys were in his pocket, he shouted, "I'm going out!" at the closed door. He stormed out of the apartment, slamming the front door twice as hard as she had.

CHAPTER SEVEN

Several hours later, Deryn awoke to her stomach growling. She wasn't sure when she'd fallen asleep, but it couldn't have been long ago since her head still throbbed terribly.

She rubbed her swollen eyes and sat up in bed. From the crack in the curtains she could tell that the sun was already setting. Xander had not come back yet.

With a deep sigh, she stood up and walked into the living room. Her feet tangled in something and she looked down to see the black sweater. She picked it up and ran the fabric through her fingers. It really was nice. Much better feeling than the silk pajamas. With a quick removal of her coat, Deryn lifted the sweater and put it on over her head. Her arms were already starting to feel better from that medicine, but she still needed to rub that paste on them.

Once the sweater was on, she hung up the coat in the guestroom closet, but not before emptying its pockets. She put everything in a row on the dresser. The knife. The map. The chocolate bar. This was all she owned. All she had to her name. Two gifts and a free map.

Heading to the kitchen, Deryn stopped near the bookshelf and noticed a frame on it with a photo of Xander and his parents. He couldn't have been older than ten, judging by how small he was. It was funny to think that when this photo was taken she'd been living freely in a village called Redwood with her father and brother. It would still be another five years before the guards came to their small village in their gasmasks, taking her, Dakota and several others in the dead of night, moving too quickly to even give their parents a chance to fight. Still, her father tried. Her brother Talon, who'd been taken two years earlier, was the one ordered to lead the invasion, and even through his mask she could still see the pain in his eyes.

For six months they were kept in quarantine, left with nothing to entertain themselves but each other. At the time she'd thought there could be nothing worse than living in that small space with a dozen others, all as bored and frightened as she was.

How wrong she had been.

Deryn was just about to put the photo facedown when she took a good look at Xander's mother standing there with her husband and son, looking so genuinely happy. She died because she wanted to protect Xander from the dangers of an ensuing war. Deryn couldn't be angry with her.

But she still loathed Atticus, and there was no way she could have his cold eyes staring at her every day. After finding some blank paper in the desk, she tore off a small piece and put it over Atticus's figure. Now only Xander and his mother were visible.

Once that was done, Deryn finally made it to the kitchen, stopping only briefly to put the slippers on her frozen feet. She looked through the cabinets, trying to find something decent to eat. Xander didn't have a lot, but he at least had everything she needed to make a sandwich.

As soon as her sandwich was finished, Deryn stared longingly at the open blue box on the counter. That cupcake looked delicious and she really wanted it. But she had already put on the sweater and slippers. How much more of her integrity could she compromise?

After an innocent lick of frosting, Deryn huffed and closed the box. She went over to the couch and sat down.

"Oh!" she exclaimed pleasantly as she sank into it.

Xander had always seemed like one of those people who owned furniture for style, not comfort, but this was actually quite nice. Plushy but slightly firm.

She sat there for a while, eating her sandwich and staring at the door. When it didn't open she grew frustrated and started pacing around the apartment. Eventually, she grabbed a blanket she found in a closet and wrapped it around her shoulders, slid open the glass door and crawled onto the balcony.

She stayed hunched down where no one could see her, sitting against the wall of the building while snuggled in the blanket. She could hear the two men who lived downstairs chatting animatedly and quickly learned their names were Bronson and Quigley. They were actually quite funny and seemed like two people whose company she would enjoy. But then they were joined by a third.

"Oi! Ruby! What's with this notice we got about a fucking curfew? What am I, a child?" asked Bronson in his deep and pleasant voice.

"I don't make the rules," said Xander sounding slightly on edge. "Give me the bottle."

Several moments passed with nothing but a slight gulping sound.

"Whoa! Easy on the whiskey!"

"I hate your cheap shit, but I fucking needed that," said Xander, slamming the bottle down. "You got a cigarette, Bronson? I left the ones you gave me upstairs."

"Sure thing, mate."

There were a few more quiet moments as, she assumed, they lit up cigarettes.

"So you gonna tell us what's bothering you?" asked Quigley in his softer voice, compared to the other two, at least.

"No."

Deryn chuckled. That sounded about right.

"Then how the hell are we supposed to help you?" Quigley again.

"You're not."

"Come on, Ruby. We always tell you our problems. We're friends, remember?"

"Never having enough whiskey and begging me to buy you more is hardly a problem."

"But you have unlimited resources," said Bronson. She envisioned a smirk.

"I don't want to talk about it."

"Suit yourself then."

There was a long silence.

"Am I *always* an ass?" asked Xander.

"Yes," Deryn whispered to herself.

"Yeah," said Bronson.

"Pretty much," said Quigley.

"So when I try to do something nice, that comes off as creepy?"

Deryn smiled. For some reason she found the fact that she made Xander question himself gratifying.

"How nice was it?" asked Bronson.

"Pretty fucking nice."

A pause.

"Are you gonna tell us?"

"No," said Xander coolly.

"Why not?" asked Quigley.

"Because it's none of your fucking business."

"Aw, come on!" Bronson again.

"No."

"Please!" Quigley.

"No!"

"Pretty, pretty, please -"

"Dammit, Quigley! I'm trying to be serious here!"

"So are we -"

"All I want to know is why when I help someone they always, *always* think I have fucking ulterior motives! I can be nice!"

"Sure you can," said Bronson. Deryn envisioned his smirk again.

"So when I buy someone a cupcake, why the hell would they interpret that as something different? Something bad."

Another pause.

"You bought someone a cupcake?" asked Bronson. Now she envisioned his face all twisted with curiosity, much like hers had been. Even hearing Xander just say the word 'cupcake' was creepy to her.

"Aw, who was it? Was it a girl?" inquired Quigley. "Was it that girl from last night?"

"No."

"It was, wasn't it?" said Bronson. "I didn't get a good look at her but, from what I saw, she looked pretty cute."

"She's not."

Deryn chuckled again. Now *that* was the Xander she knew.

"So it wasn't her then?" asked Quigley. She didn't get as good a look at him yesterday as she did at Bronson, but she was pretty sure she was picturing him correctly as her mind made him cock his head in curiosity.

"It doesn't matter."

"Then why'd you buy her a cupcake?"

"I never said I did."

"Then why'd you buy *anyone* a cupcake."

Xander let out a deep sigh. "Birthday," he said so quietly that she barely heard him.

"A birthday!" said Bronson brightly. An image of him beaming entered her head. "That's not creepy! That's adorable!"

"You both are fucking annoying, you know that?"

Another pause.

"I would be honored if you bought *me* a cupcake," said Quigley with a teasing sincerity.

"And on that note, I'm getting the fuck out of here," said Xander. "Thanks for nothing, assholes."

"You kiss your mother with that mouth?" asked Bronson.

"My mother is dead."

This pause was a bit heavier.

"Sorry," said Bronson, his deep voice cracking. "I forgot."

"Doesn't matter. If you go out, remember to watch the clocks."

"When do we ever go out?"

"Good point."

Deryn listened as their sliding door opened and then closed again. Crap. Now she felt bad.

In a rush, she crawled back inside, shut the door and got to her feet. She limped to the kitchen as quickly as she could, opened the blue box and took one good look at the cupcake before stuffing it in her mouth.

The lock clicked on the door so she chewed faster. When Xander walked inside she had just taken the last oversized bite but there was no time to swallow.

He relocked the door, turned and looked a bit surprised to see her standing there with chipmunk cheeks. "What are you doing?"

Deryn shrugged, thankful that he didn't pay her large cheeks any mind.

"You're fucking weird, you know that?"

Xander walked past her to his room, his eyes slightly shifting to look at the blue box on the counter. She could swear she saw a faint smile when he noticed it was empty.

As soon as he was gone, she tried to finish chewing, but he was back not even ten seconds later with a pack of cigarettes in hand. He headed for the balcony and, when his back was turned, she tried to chew again.

When Xander reached the door he paused, noticing it was open a crack. "Were you out here, Leon?" he asked, turning back around.

Deryn shook her head.

"Are you sure?"

She nodded.

Xander stared at her curiously. "Say something."

She said nothing.

"Did you hear me talking to Bronson and Quigley downstairs?"

She shook her head again.

"Are you lying?"

Another shake.

Xander took several steps towards her. "What's that you have in your mouth?"

Her eyes widened.

"Is it the cupcake?"

Giving in, Deryn gulped, almost choking on her bite.

Xander grunted. "Just swallow the fucking thing, will you?"

She did. "Sorry, I -"

"Not necessary," he said, walking back to the balcony. "But, if you're going to go outside, you better be damn careful." He shut the door behind him.

Deryn remained in the kitchen for a few moments before clutching her blanket tighter around her shoulders and following him outside. She crawled again, making sure to stay low as she settled herself in the same spot, giving her the perfect view of Xander smoking a cigarette in an old chair.

They sat there in silence, both of them gazing out at the street, Deryn through a crack in the stone barrier. While watching what looked like a cat running across the deserted street, she accidentally let the blanket slip off of her shoulder.

"How's that sweater working out for you?" asked Xander, eyeing it with a smile.

Deryn fixed the blanket. "Yeah, it's ... it's really quite comfortable," she answered honestly. Then she sighed. "Look, Ruby, I don't want you to think I'm not grateful, because I am. This is the most at ease I've felt in -"

"Five years?" Xander cocked an eyebrow.

"And one day," said Deryn with a dim smile. "But you have to understand why I'm hesitant about you. Since the day I was taken prisoner, I haven't been around one person I can trust. And you ... well, I know you're already aware of this, but we have a history."

"Yes, we do," he said, taking a drag of his cigarette. "And I'm sure my profession doesn't help."

"It really doesn't," she said. "And, it's just ... I find it odd that, in all this time, I never saw you. Not once. I saw every other Guardian there is but never you. Why?"

Xander sighed and glanced sideways at her. "I almost always knew where you were, Leon. And I made a point to never be there."

"You kept track of me?"

Xander nodded.

"So you could avoid me?"

He nodded again. "I've heard stories about you over the years, and I had no interest in seeing you like that. The way you looked just yesterday, I never wanted to witness that."

"Why?"

"Guilt," he said slowly. "For some reason I have it when it comes to you."

"Gee, I wonder why?"

Xander glanced at her from the corner of his eye. "Before you go jumping to conclusions, I'm not sorry I didn't try and attack Elvira once she and my father had you in their clutches. If I had then I would be dead, and you would be one step closer to execution."

"That's not -"

"You're lucky I was there last night. You were mere moments away from getting caught and you know it."

Deryn took a deep and agitated breath. Her damn pride was really getting a beating. "Fine. I admit it. You saved me last night."

"About time," he said, looking amused.

"Well, if that's not the reason you have guilt when it comes to me, then what is?"

Xander took a long drag of his cigarette and moved his gaze back to the abandoned street. His brown eyes sparkled almost gold in the simulated moonlight, and Deryn realized they were not the most unpleasant things to look at.

"We bumped into each other that day. Knocked each other over. Remember?"

"I do," she said, pulling her knees up to her chest and resting her chin on them. She gripped her nails deep into the blanket as flashes of memories filled her head. Memories of her father, brother and Dakota. Of Godfrey's still figure as he was carried away from her. Of Dakota's loving gaze as he gave her one final kiss. Of his hand letting go of hers ...

"I'd been hiding."

Deryn blinked back to reality.

"Per my mom's request, but the moment I heard all of the

commotion I knew I had to get out. I should've just stayed where I was. If I had then maybe Elvira would've never found out about my mom, and maybe you would've gotten wherever it was you were trying to go."

"I probably would have."

They both went silent. The air felt heavy around them, trapping them in an uncomfortable state of awareness. It had all been a stupid mistake. An unfortunate, accidental moment that had changed everything. And it was a painful realization.

So Xander and Deryn just continued to sit there, avoiding each other's eyes for a good, long while and focusing on the laughter coming from two floors below.

It was a strange feeling, being thrown together with your enemy, especially when they suddenly decided to save your life. Deryn didn't know how she was supposed to feel about Xander. She was trying to be grateful, but that hatred she had felt towards him still boiled strongly in the pit of her stomach. It would be easier if she could somehow get inside of his head. To be able to understand him just a little bit better.

"Why are you still here?"

Xander cocked an eyebrow.

"I mean here, as a Guardian for Saevus? It certainly doesn't seem like you want to be. If you did then you wouldn't be helping me."

Xander knocked some ash off his cigarette. "Same reason you didn't off yourself five years ago."

Deryn was taken aback. Her stomach lurched as she lifted her head to get a better view of him. "What does that mean?" she asked out of morbid curiosity.

"It means you did what you had to in order to survive. You might hate yourself for it, but at least you're alive."

Deryn gulped.

"Tell me something, Leon. Did you ever consider death as an option when they were tossing you from Guardian to Guardian?"

Monster to monster, she thought, watching closely as Xander began to breathe more rapidly. His breath was hot and visible against the cold air, his stormy eyes finally sparking to life as he spoke to her, trying to justify his own dark thoughts by finding a similar feeling in a soul more tattered than his.

"Did it ever cross your mind that just ending it would be the better solution?" he continued. "That maybe it would be your only salvation? You'd be free, which is all you ever wanted, anyway." Xander sucked in his raw, steamy breath and closed his eyes. "So did you?"

He slowly opened them again, turning his golden irises towards her and waiting for an answer. In the light of the moon, she could see that even with this spark, his eyes were still dead behind the haze of tears. Much like how hers looked when she saw them in the mirror.

Deryn choked as she drew back her own tears. She didn't want to appear weak in front of him, especially after all of the breakdowns she'd had already. But she knew she wasn't done yet.

"Of course I did," she answered honestly. "Nearly every day I thought about it. But the memory of what life once was - what it could be again - that's what kept me going. I could never have killed myself because it was too easy, and the best things in life aren't obtained by giving in. They're hard, but they're worth it."

Xander clicked his tongue. "I don't have memories like that. Even before all of this, I don't remember a time when I was ever really happy."

"Not even in your childhood?"

"No." After taking one final drag, he put his cigarette out on the balcony and tossed it over the side.

"So what is it that keeps you going then? When you have these thoughts?" she asked.

"Did I say I was talking about me?"

"You didn't have to."

"I wasn't. We were talking about you, remember?"

"You don't have to lie -"

"I'm not lying!" he snapped, turning sharply towards her. "I would never off myself. Too much depends on me staying alive."

"What does that mean?"

Xander paused. He stared at her, unblinking for a moment. "Nothing." He took out another cigarette.

Deryn stared at it with a growing curiosity. Cigarettes were a thing of their ancestors, almost forgotten until the Outsiders recreated them a few decades back. Saevus had banned them the moment he learned of their existence, hating all things made by Outsiders. Besides, tobacco was already forbidden. This was the one thing she actually agreed with him on, but for a different reason. "That's a very Outsider habit you've picked up there."

"Yes," he said unfazed. "You can blame the idiots downstairs. They got me into it and have to pick them up for me."

"Why?"

"They're in a part of the Black Market where even easily bribed Guardians aren't welcome." Xander held out the pack and offered her one.

Deryn recoiled. "Absolutely not. It's a horrid habit that I do not support."

"Of course you don't," he said with an amused grin. "Five years, countless hours of torture and you're still as predictable as ever."

"If you think you're going to pressure me into taking one -"

"Why would I waste my breath?"

Deryn watched Xander closely as he continued to smoke his cigarette. But, eventually, she became dazed and her mind quickly drifted back to her family and Dakota. She was the closest she had been to finding them in years but, instead of beginning her journey to them, she was spending her evening sitting on a balcony with Xander Ruby. Surely there were better things she could be doing with her time.

Still, she stayed. As much as she hated to admit it, over the years she had been starved of basic human interaction. Talking to someone about actual things, things that mattered to her - even if that someone was Xander - talking out loud made

Deryn feel almost human again.

"May I ask you something?"

Xander shrugged. "I suppose it doesn't matter. We both know you're going to ask whether I say yes or not."

Deryn frowned. She really was predictable.

"It's ... it's about my dad and brother," she said timidly. "What do you know of them?"

"Know of them?" he repeated. "I'm a Guardian, Leon. The two of them have probably spent a great deal of time making sure I know nothing."

"But surely you must know something."

"We almost caught that friend of yours, Trigger or whatever, a few months back."

Deryn's heart quickened at the mention of Dakota. She was so eager to hear more that she didn't even correct the name mistake, though it was most likely intentional. One day in training Dakota had been a bit too enthusiastic with his Element and from then on was known as trigger happy Triggs.

"During a raid on one of the Guardian's homes. He's made a few appearances over the years, and so has that annoying brother of yours, but your dad's stayed hidden."

"But they're together, right?"

"Probably," he said with a shrug of his shoulders. "They're all pretty active in the Resistance. They work together, but I'm not sure if they stay in the same place or not."

Deryn sighed in relief. They had found each other without her. She hoped with all of her heart that Dakota hadn't waited long for word from her, like she had promised. If she was lucky he had caught on pretty quickly and gone off to look for everyone else. But, even after all this time, she found it hard to convince herself this was true. Dakota had waited for her to return longer than necessary.

"I suppose, when you leave here, you'll look for them?"

Deryn awoke from her daze to find Xander staring at her. She nodded. "Part of me can't wait to see them again but another part ... maybe an even stronger part is dreading it."

"Why?"

Her eyes grew misty as she cradled her head back in her knees. "Because of everything that's happened to me. Because they would never understand."

"I thought you were close with them?"

"I am," she said with a sniffle. "But, after everything I've done, how can I face them?"

"What? What have you done?" asked Xander, cocking his head and trying to get a good look at her.

By now, Deryn was full on weeping. She didn't know why she was talking about this with him but, somehow, she knew she had to. She had to get it out. And, in this unusual haven she had stumbled into, Xander was the only one around to listen.

"I used to fight back in the beginning. I would fight and claw and hit and scream until my throat and limbs were raw or they beat me unconscious. But then I just ... stopped. I stopped fighting and I let them do whatever they wanted to me. It was easier. When I wasn't busy screaming, I had a better chance of closing my mind off and finding a happy moment. One that's buried somewhere deep inside of me that I could get swept into. The fight was killing me but it was still better than how I ended up. Instead, I just let myself die."

Xander said nothing as Deryn continued to cry into her knees. The two men downstairs had gone inside a short while earlier so, aside from the two of them, the world was still. An eerie silence engulfed them as her sobs resonated through the night. The unease between them grew thicker, enough so a knife could've cut through it. Just like the knife she had used to slit open Soren's throat ...

"Leon," called Xander, his voice quiet in her clouded ears. His untouched cigarette had burned to an ashy nub. "Why don't you ever say the word?"

"What word?"

"You know. The word of what happened to you. What they did. You've mentioned torture without a problem but you haven't said the other thing."

"Why does that matter?"

"I think you should say it," he declared.

"Why?" she asked, weakly lifting her head.

"It might make you feel better."

"It won't."

"You don't know that."

Unable to look into his eyes, Deryn watched the way his chest heaved as he inhaled the smoke of his newest cigarette. It stiffened as he let the smoke sink into his lungs. And then released as he blew it back out into the cold, night air. She needed to focus. She needed to stay focused on just one thing or else she was going to lose control, and Xander was the only thing in her line of sight that moved enough to keep her from sinking into her mind. Where the not-so-happy memories were kept much closer than the ones of her childhood living outside with the people she loved.

"Say it, Leon."

"No," she protested, still focusing on his chest.

"Say the word."

"No!"

"Say the word, Leon. Tell me what happened to you."

Her breaths grew short and frantic. "You *know* what happened to me," she snapped.

"Yes, because I know Guardians. But your dad, your brother, your fucking boyfriend, they know *nothing* about what goes on inside their heads. If you can't even accept what happened to you then how the hell do you expect them to?"

"They don't need to know everything."

"So you'll keep secrets from them?"

"N-no."

"If you don't tell them then that's exactly what you're doing. Keeping secrets."

"No, it's -"

"Tell me what happened to you, Leon," demanded Xander in a deep, drawling voice. "Tell me what Soren and the other Guardians did to you when they owned you. In their beds, in their hallways, in the filthy basements and pocket-sized closets they kept you in. What did they do to you there?"

"Stop it," she pleaded, her face growing hot as she pulled at her hair from the roots.

"Did they even bother to undress you? Or was it all just hurried and rough while they smacked you around and called you toxic trash? Did they let you shower after? Or were you left to soak in their sweat and your shame?"

Deryn's body was shaking. "Stop," she said through gritted teeth.

"Most of your owners hated you. They were repulsed by you and wanted to see you suffer. So they did it the only way they knew how. By breaking you."

"No."

"You're not the Deryn Leon I once knew. I can see that right now. The Leon I knew would have *never* let them defeat her."

"I haven't!" she protested, raising her voice.

"Yes you have!" said Xander, raising his voice to match hers. "That's why you can't say it. Because you're defeated. You're weak and you're defeated!"

"No!" Deryn jumped to her feet. "I am *not* defeated, Ruby! How dare you say that I am!"

"Then prove it to me," he demanded, also jumping to his feet. "Tell me what they did to you."

"Shut up!" Deryn lunged forward and beat her fists into his chest.

The glass door two floors below slid open. "Ruby, what's going on up there?"

"Nothing! Mind your own fucking business!" he shouted down at his nosy neighbors.

Xander wrapped his arms around the hysterical, thrashing Deryn and carried her inside. If she was going to have this outburst then it needed to be where she couldn't be heard.

"Tell me what Soren did to you at night when his wife wasn't home!"

"No!" she cried as he put her back down. Not for one second did she stop hitting him.

"Tell me, Deryn!"

At the sound of her given name, Deryn's whole body went

heavy. She sank to her knees, dragging Xander down with her. Her sobs were loud and frantic as she clutched the sleeves of his shirt, holding on so tight her nails ripped holes in the fabric.

"They ... they raped me, alright?" she finally admitted, her body instantly easing. "I was raped almost every day for ... for five years. Ruby ... why did this happen to me?" Deryn's head sank into his chest, tears soaking through his shirt and onto his skin.

"It shouldn't have happened to you," he said, stroking a comforting hand through her hair. "This world has become sick and cruel under the president's rule. But you're stronger than you think you are. And you're wrong."

"About what?" she asked through choked breaths.

"About you. Just because you stopped struggling doesn't mean you ever stopped fighting. I think we both just witnessed that there's still plenty of fire in you."

Deryn let out a painful laugh as she continued to cry into him. Her death grip on his shirt loosened as she finally let herself relax in Xander's arms. She never thought she would see the day where the two of them were willingly hugging, if that was what you could call this.

"I'm going to do what I can to help you find your family, Leon. As soon as it's safe for you to leave here, I'll find a lead to their whereabouts. I'm not without my connections in the Resistance."

"Thank you," she said with a sniffle.

"And when you go back to them, you can go knowing that you were a victim of this ongoing war. You've done nothing wrong."

"A victim," she repeated. "Like you."

Xander shook his head against hers. "No. You and I are not the same."

"How so?" she asked.

"I've done things, Leon. You've had them done to you. It's different."

Deryn wished she could argue, but it was hard to do that when she really didn't know what he'd done. He had mentioned to Veli on the tram that he was his superior now. She couldn't imagine he outranked someone several years older than him and so horribly devoted to the president without doing a few things that would tear his soul apart.

The clock that hung above the fireplace chimed. They both looked up to see it was six-thirty. It felt much later.

"Time to take your medicine," said Xander, standing up and pulling her with him.

Deryn still had the blanket somewhat tangled around her. She fixed it before following him to the kitchen. After swallowing a spoonful of the green liquid, Xander gave Deryn a sleeveless shirt and a pair of boxer shorts to put on so he could help her rub the ointment on her bruises.

"Who was the Guardian who owned you before Soren?" asked Xander as he got his first good look at the ankle that had been bothering her. It wasn't just sprained, it was full on broken. He would need to find something stronger to heal it tomorrow. There was no way he could leave it untouched.

"What good will knowing do?" she asked.

"I can find out on my own, but it'll be easier if you just give me a name."

Deryn sighed. "Aila Parrish. She was angry because her brother Lester was recently killed -"

"During that raid Trigger was part of -"

Deryn's jaw dropped slightly.

"- I know."

"Yes, well, she took her anger out on me. She came up with so many new ways to torture me that I'm surprised I haven't lost my sanity. Or maybe I have. That would certainly explain how I ended up here, if this was all just a figment of my disturbed imagination."

"Hmm," said Xander, pursing his lips as his mind began to wander. "You need to stay off your ankle for a while," he said, snapping back to focus. "No more walking around the apartment. You need bed rest."

Before Deryn had the chance to protest, Xander scooped her into his arms and carried her to the guestroom. He placed her carefully on the bed and helped her back into the sweater he had given her. Then he took a seat on the bed's edge.

"You look exhausted."

"I could say the same about you," she said, pulling the covers over her.

"I'm serious."

"So am I."

"You need time to heal. So lie down and get some sleep."

"What's with your incessant need to order me around?"

"What's with your incessant need to challenge everything I say? It's for your greater good, Leon, so, for once in your life, you should just listen."

"Fine," she conceded, scooting down on the bed and laying her head on the pillow. "You should really do the same."

"Is that an invitation?" he asked with a small smirk.

Deryn grabbed the spare pillow and smacked him with it. "Did you not just say we were being serious? Get some sleep, Ruby."

"Wish I could," he said, standing up and walking to the door, "but I'm actually heading out."

"But what about the -"

"Curfew?" he finished. "I'll be back long before then. And I'll have some company with me, so you need to stay in this room."

Deryn let out a frustrated sigh. "Fine. All these damn rules," she mumbled as she nuzzled into her pillow with her back to him.

"I also have duties in the morning, so I'll be leaving here fairly early and won't be back until evening."

Deryn turned in her bed so she was facing him. "Guardian duties?"

"Yes. Despite our current situation, I still am one and I have to keep up appearances."

"Yes, I suppose you do." Deryn's eyes fluttered. "Goodnight, Ruby. And, uhh ... thanks for tonight. Not my greatest birthday but at least I had one. And being able to smack you around a bit was definitely one of my better gifts."

She smiled softly before closing her eyes completely.

"Don't mention it."

Xander turned out the lights and shut the door behind him. Once he was out of there, he went to his room and cleaned himself up a bit. While all of that talk may have been beneficial for her psyche, it was horribly damaging to his. He did things. She had them done to her. He was guilty. She was innocent. There were no shades of gray here, only black and white.

Xander let out a deep and painful sigh before grabbing his coat and heading out the door. Deryn got her release that night. And now it was time for Xander to get his.

~

Deryn awoke several hours later to the sound of muffled voices coming from Xander's room. At first they seemed fairly normal and she thought nothing of them, but then they became more frantic and she started to worry that something was wrong. She was about to get up and check on him when she remembered he had specifically told her to stay in the room. He had mentioned company, but what sort of company would be making those horrible sounds?

"Ah! Mmm ... oooh ... yes!"

Deryn's eyes widened as it finally dawned on her what was going on in there. She was caught somewhere between horror and disgust, and she was quick to bring her hands up to her ears. Unfortunately, that did absolutely nothing, especially when the loud slapping sounds began.

Oh god, he was spanking her!

Deryn nearly vomited as an image of Xander and a faceless woman going at it in the style most appropriate for his slaps entered her mind. She grabbed her pillow and threw it over her head, trying desperately to drown out the noise. She didn't know what she'd expected when he mentioned company, but *this* certainly wasn't it.

Damn these thin walls.

"Yes! Yes! Keep going, uh ... whatever the fuck your name is! I don't care!" shouted the woman.

Deryn took a moment to roll her eyes in her tight, dark

space. Real class act, Ruby.

"Yes! Right there! Right there! Fuck! Fuck! Oh fuck!"

A few moments later, the noises stopped and Deryn thanked the heavens with more enthusiasm than ever before. Still, she remained hidden under her pillow as an extra precaution. Somehow, she got the feeling Xander was not against second rounds.

"That was amazing!" said the woman between heavy breaths.

"Yeah, sure," said Xander unconvincingly. Deryn heard his bed creak and then several footsteps. "You should probably get a move on. Curfew starts in an hour."

"What? But can't I stay here tonight?"

"No."

"Why not?"

"Well, I don't think my wife would like it very much when she gets home in about ten minutes."

Deryn chuckled. And then felt incredibly guilty about it.

"Your wife!" shouted the woman.

"That's right."

She could almost see the smirk spread across Xander's lips.

"You asshole!"

The bed creaked again, followed by many angry stomps as the woman shuffled around the room, probably looking for her clothes.

"I should've known better than to come home with a Guardian! The whole lot of you think you live above the rules!"

"We do."

"Fuck you!"

Xander's bedroom door opened and slammed, followed shortly by the front door. Deryn listened as Xander walked out of his room and across the apartment. There were several clicks as he locked the door. His footsteps returned to his room, and then he went silent.

Deryn lay in bed for a while after, trying to process everything she'd just heard. Earlier that evening she'd started to think that maybe Xander had changed. She wasn't sure if it was for the better or not, considering the life he presently lived, but he definitely didn't seem like the boy she once knew.

But now he felt familiar.

A smile spread across Deryn's face.

Nope. Xander Ruby definitely hadn't changed. Not entirely, anyway. Now, why did she find comfort in that?

CHAPTER EIGHT

Deryn ran through the dark halls of Eagle Center, her voice hoarse as she cried out for her father. Her heart was racing, and then she heard him call out, "Set our children free!"

Bodies littered the halls, causing the putrid smell of death to spoil the air. But there was no time to stop and look. No time to dwell on who had been lost in this horrible battle. Only one thing mattered. Finding her way back to her father. Together they could end this. Together nothing could stop them.

Finally reaching the room everyone was fighting in, Deryn stopped and stared at Godfrey, who was facing President Saevus, their weapons firing at each other. At first, it seemed like her father was going to win, but then, just when she thought he had him, a bright light grew around Saevus, shielding him and shooting an explosion back at her father. His body went stiff as he flew back against the wall, falling lifeless to the floor.

"Dad!" she cried, trying so hard to run for him but her feet wouldn't budge, her entire body feeling as heavy as lead.

"Deryn!"

Dakota was running towards her, his right arm outstretched as he reached for her. She lifted hers and did the same, wanting desperately to know what it felt like to touch those fingers again. Even if it was just once more.

He was so close. So close she could smell him, that intoxicating aroma of pine trees and rain and something else she had never quite been able to place. But, before he could reach her, she was knocked off her feet and being pulled away from him. Dragged farther and farther until his figure became nothing more than a speck in the distance.

"No! Dax!" she cried.

"Shut up, you toxic trash!"

Someone grabbed Deryn by the waist and flipped her so she was facing him. She screamed as he stared down at her. The cold and angry eyes of Atticus Ruby. Eyes she could never forget. Saevus and Elvira watched her from over his shoulder, amused grins distorting their already hideous faces. The smell of death had never been so strong.

"You belong to us now," said Elvira, cackling wildly as she stepped forward. "You will never see your precious Trigger again."

No.

"And your father's head will be mine," said Saevus. "It's over, Outsider. We have won."

No.

"Stop crying!" shouted Atticus, smacking her hard across the face.

"No!"

Those eyes ... Those piercing, cruel brown eyes.

"No!"

"Leon!"

"NO!"

"Leon, wake up! It's me!"

Atticus's eyes continued to stare down at her. Deryn thrashed around violently as he tried to hold her still.

"No! You can't have me! You will *never* have me!"

"Leon, it's me! Xander! You're having a nightmare! Wake up!"

Deryn's body eased slightly as the hold on her suddenly seemed gentle. She looked back into Atticus's eyes only to see them melt away and become Xander's. The differences were slight but they were there. A shade lighter with a gold ring around the pupil, slightly softer on the edges, and kind. These eyes were kind. Especially when waking her from a nightmare.

"Again?" said Deryn, sounding frustrated as she breathed heavily in his arms.

"I know," said Xander. "Third time since you got here."

Once Deryn's breathing evened out, she looked at him and frowned. "I woke you."

He shook his head. "I couldn't sleep."

"Why?"

"I rarely do," he said with a halfhearted smile.

"Too much on your mind?"

"No. Just a light sleeper."

Deryn's frown deepened. She knew he was lying.

"Any little noise'll wake me up and, once I do, I can never get back to sleep."

"So no solution then?"

"Of course there is. It's called whiskey," he said matter-of-factly. "Helps me during night's when sleep is necessary."

She smiled softly. "How about tea?"

"Whiskey is better but I guess I'll humor you."

Xander got up from the bed and walked out to the kitchen. Deryn took a moment to compose herself. Her nightmares were always the same. A combination of her most horrible memories and her greatest fears. And it always felt so real. So painfully and hideously real.

After wiping a single tear from her cheek, Deryn sucked back her nerves and followed him. She grabbed her favorite blanket off the back of the couch and leaned on the counter while he made tea.

"So did you get your lady friend out before midnight this time?" she asked.

Xander's shoulders bobbed as he chuckled. "You bet your sweet ass I did. I fucking took my eyes off the clock for two seconds the other night. Never again."

Deryn rolled her eyes. "You didn't have to be such a jerk to her about it."

"I thought I was a perfect gentleman."

"You made her sleep on the floor."

"I gave her a blanket."

"And a pillow?"

"Oh, right! I forgot about that." He glanced over his shoulder at her and smirked. "Whoops."

Deryn huffed. "You're an ass."

"Spare me your judgments, Leon, because I really don't give a shit."

Once the tea was finished, he handed her a red mug - which she had already decided was her favorite days ago - and the two of them took seats on opposite ends of the couch, as they were accustomed.

"Mind if I make one more judgment?" she asked as she settled into her seat.

"You mean you haven't already?"

Deryn narrowed her eyes.

Xander rolled his, a habit he quickly realized he was picking up from her. Only eleven days here and she was already getting under his skin. "On with it, Leon."

"I'm just a little surprised that you know how to make tea and -" She took a sip. "- it's not bad."

"Why?"

"I don't know. I suppose it's because, back in training, you hardly seemed self-sufficient. Didn't your family always have someone serving you? I know I saw someone doing your laundry once while you ordered them around."

"Of course we did. But I don't exactly have a wave here now, do I?"

Deryn had heard the term 'wave' over the years, but it still always sounded funny to her, probably because she had seen actual waves in the ocean before. It was what Guardians called their worker slaves. The ones whose heads they shaved and were forced to work all day. The less desirable who no one was searching for.

"Not that I've seen," she said.

"The Ruby family's wave spends all of its time at my father's house."

Deryn's head snapped up. "It?"

"Yes, the wave. We have just the one now. My family was downgraded after my mom's execution."

"Waves and slaves aren't *its*, Ruby. They're hes and shes."

"Says who?" he asked, clearly egging her on. "Besides, I don't know what *it* is. All waves have their heads shaved, and the one my father owns' sex isn't exactly discernible."

Deryn's jaw dropped.

Xander smirked. "Are you going to yell at me now?"

"You're damn right I am! What right do you have to say something so degrading about a poor, defenseless person?"

"Every right. I own *it*."

"*He*!" she yelled.

Xander froze. "What?"

"*He*! Not *it*! *He*!"

"How do you know my family's wave is a he? It was a woman who did my laundry." His eyes drifted slightly towards the photo on his bookshelf. The one where – he had noticed previously – she had covered the image of his father.

Deryn lost all color in her face. "Or she," she said quickly. "'He' is just a natural default."

"Like my 'it'?"

"No, Ruby" said Deryn slowly and clearly. "It's not the same."

"What a fucking double standard!"

Deryn had stopped listening. Xander watched closely as she sucked on her bottom lip, very visibly falling into the depths of her mind again. She did that a lot.

"Leon," he called.

It was a few seconds before she looked up and noticed him.

"I'm not serious. I understand all slaves are people, but I have to say 'it' when around other Guardians or the president. It's what's expected of me."

Deryn nodded. "I know," she said, taking another sip of her tea. "I think I'm going to take this to bed. I really need to work on getting past these nightmares."

She started to stand, but Xander reached across the couch and grabbed her arm before she got very far. "I've heard that, sometimes, it helps to talk about your nightmares."

Deryn blinked. "Talk about it?"

"Yes."

She blinked again. "With you?"

"That is what I was getting at. I can see now why everyone always thought you were so intelligent."

"And it's those sorts of comments that make me not want to

tell you anything."

Xander smirked. "Come on, Leon. I humored you with the tea. Even made a cup for myself instead of hitting the bottle. Now it's your turn to humor me."

Deryn pursed her lips and studied him. Since the day she got there, Xander had been putting on this persona that never felt quite right to her. Something was off, and she had a hard time believing he cared at all about her nightmares. If she had to make a guess, she would say that he didn't want to be alone. If he really did never sleep, like he said, then she imagined his nights were pretty lonely, especially when he was so unwilling to let anyone stay over. And it wasn't like she had to be anywhere in the morning. She might as well 'humor' him.

With a light sigh, Deryn sunk back in her seat. Xander removed his hand from her arm and returned to his side of the couch. They both sat with their feet up, hers crossed beneath her while his were out in front of him, one bent and one straight.

Deryn took another sip of her tea before starting. "I don't know what you're expecting. My nightmares aren't exactly cryptic. I just dream about that day at Eagle."

"Am I in it?" he asked while circling the rim of his mug with his finger.

"No," she said honestly. In all her years reliving the same nightmare, not once had Xander made an appearance. It was always President Saevus, Elvira and Atticus, with her other former owners occasionally sprinkled in. A shiver ran through her. "Why do you ask?"

Xander shrugged. "I don't know. I suppose it's the way you look at me every time I wake you. Like you're ready to kill."

The smallest of smiles crept onto Deryn's lips. "Sorry."

"It's probably my fault for even attempting to wake you. I wouldn't bother at all if your damn screams weren't loud enough to alert the whole fucking neighborhood."

Deryn frowned. "Well, maybe if you put a soundproof shield around my room, like I ask every day after you bring one of your women over, we wouldn't have that problem."

"You *know* I can't do that. It connects to my wristband and the president has all technology used by his guards and Guardians checked every morning, and he knows I live in an area that's basically deserted. It's his way of keeping us under his iron thumb. Then he has us check everyone else's homes so they're under *our* iron thumb."

"But you put one up every time I'm out on the balcony."

"Yes, because I can use it once and say I have loud or nosy neighbors downstairs." Which he did. "It's either a soundproof shield at night or your balcony privileges. I'll let you make the call."

Deryn's frown deepened. She looked down at her tea and quietly said, "Balcony."

"What was that?" he said, leaning his left ear towards her. "I couldn't quite hear your mumbling. Speak up."

"Balcony," she said slightly louder as she looked up and scowled at him.

Xander smirked. "I knew it. I knew you secretly enjoyed hearing me fuck."

Deryn's cheeks flushed. "N-no -"

"Don't deny it. I can see it written all over your face."

"Stop it."

"Come on, Leon. I might actually believe you if you weren't blushing."

Now her whole face was red. "I said, stop it."

"Not until you -"

"I *need* to go out on the balcony so I don't suffocate in here!"

Xander's eyebrows rose high into his hairline as he gave her a look of surprise. His face stayed frozen like that for a few seconds, unblinking. Until, eventually, that signature smirk of his returned. "If you'd like, I can give you a few pointers."

Deryn gazed at him, heavy breaths coming out steadily through her nose. Then she rolled her eyes. "You repulse me."

Xander's smirk widened. "Ah, now there's the Leon I remember. We'll have you cursing at me in no time."

The corner of her mouth twitched upwards. "Ass."

CHAPTER NINE

"**S**hit!"

Deryn popped awake at the suddenness of Xander's shouts.

"I'm fucking late!"

A bit disoriented, she looked around to see that she was still in the living room. A flash of blond hair ran by.

"I work for a sadistic psychopath and I'm late. Fuck!"

His door slammed and, a few seconds later, she heard the water running in his personal shower.

Deryn waited a few more seconds for the shower door to open and then close. Once she heard the click, she got up from the couch and tiptoed over to his bedroom door. She opened it just enough to slip in and went over to his bed, thoroughly searching the pillows for any stray hairs belonging to whomever he'd brought home the previous night.

This was Deryn's only chance to do this, since Xander always tossed his sheets in the washer downstairs on his way out, to rid them of last night's conquest. She was, of course, absolutely repulsed by this task, constantly fearing that she would accidently come across a different kind of hair, but it was necessary. She had been there eleven days now and her body was finally starting to feel normal again. It was time to prepare.

Her time spent in guard training was not all about Element usage and fighting. Upon entry, everyone was tested and the most intelligent of applicants were also used to help develop the ever-growing technology of Utopia. She had actually been chosen to start working in the Government Lab the day she turned eighteen, but that obviously never happened.

One of these technological advances was the wristbands everyday citizens wore on their right arm. They were connected to the wearer's DNA and were able to store all of their information. Hence the hair, and a project she had every intention of starting.

Deryn finally located one, long and honey-blonde this time. That made two blondes, one brunette and one raven haired girl since she'd been there, only missing one from the woman that first night. Hair in hand, she slipped out of his room and went to hers. She took out a plastic bag she'd found and put this hair in with the rest.

Once that was done, Deryn caught sight of the list she had written yesterday and slid it into her pocket. She then went back to the living room and waited for Xander so she could give it to him.

The water turned off and there was more shuffling around his room. Xander was rarely ever late in the mornings and was always really good about eating breakfast. Looking at the clock, she realized there would be no time for that.

On instinct, Deryn went to the kitchen and turned on the toaster oven. She took out a loaf of bread from the small pantry and cut two slices. While they were toasting, she grabbed some jam from the refrigerator and a knife from the drawer.

Xander burst out of his room, sheets in hand, just as she was finishing spreading the jam on the pieces of toast. His eyes scanned the apartment until they located her. She walked over and handed him a slice.

"Here," she said. "You should eat something before you go."

Staring suspiciously at the toast in her outstretched hand, Xander lifted his eyebrows.

"Just take it," she said, shoving it into his hand. He took it. While he still stood there baffled, she took a bite of her slice. "I have compiled a list of everything I need at the Black Market. Are you still going to be able to go for me today?"

"Yeah, I should have time," said Xander, aggressively chomping his toast.

Deryn took the list out of her pocket and handed it to him. He unfolded the paper as best he could with his full hands and carefully scanned it. After reading only a few items, he turned to her and cocked an eyebrow. "Are you making wristbands?" he asked.

"Yes," she said. "I would like to experiment with them to see if I'm able to create a false identification for myself."

"There really is no need. For the right price, I'm sure I can find someone -"

"No, I want to do it," she said sternly. "It's been years since I've worked on anything like this and I want to give it a try."

"You were second best when it came to these types of experiments in training. I doubt -"

"I was *the* best, Ruby. Don't delude yourself into thinking otherwise."

He sneered at her while taking another aggressive bite of toast.

"Be that as it may, I'm out of practice, and it's something to keep me busy so I don't go crazy locked in here alone all day."

Xander grunted. "Yeah, fine," he said, slipping her list into his pocket. "I want to get you trained with that knife of yours, too. You need some sort of protection and I refuse to get you a better weapon until you're fully healed. Even if you get a wristband with a false identity working properly you can't just go running out of here. You need a plan, and I suspect it'll take several weeks, if not months. Have you finally accepted that you're going to be stuck here for that long?"

"I suppose I have," she said, taking another bite. "You're late, remember?"

Xander's eyes widened as he released a loud, "Shit!" and ran to the door. "Don't forget! No balcony when I'm not here!"

She waved at him nonchalantly and shrugged a, more-or-less, affirmative yes.

"I mean it, Leon! You're in hiding. Never forget that."

"I know," she said firmly.

Xander narrowed his eyes and took a forceful bite before opening and slamming the door.

"You dropped a pillowcase!"

He stormed back in, grabbed the fallen item, sneering once more as he hurried off.

Finding herself alone again, Deryn made a cup of coffee before curling up in her favorite blanket on the couch. She really should have tried to go back to sleep, and in the proper location this time, but she knew it was pointless. By now, she had accepted that she would never get a decent night's sleep again. There were just too many things plaguing her dreams.

Deryn sat there in silence for a while, her finger absently tracing the rim of her mug as she stared over at the desk and the untouched portable computer Xander used for reading. Untouched by her, anyway. Xander had said she could use it to read anything she wanted and gave her the password days ago, thinking that maybe his lack of permission was why she hadn't already, but, for some reason, she just couldn't bring herself to pick it up. Even though her body was healing nicely, her mind still didn't feel quite right, and she was afraid to find out how much damage had been done. Not to mention the improper feel of a hologram of words in front of her eyes.

They were nothing compared to the paper volumes she read in her youth, most dating back to before the war that destroyed their world. While many books had become mush over the years, there were plenty that could still be read. Every time her father went out to explore a new region, he would always return with them for her. Books, records, music boxes, snow globes. Any knickknacks he came across that were still in good shape. Usually finding them in a rusted safe or bomb shelter. Once he had found an entire library that had been preserved by sheer, dumb luck. He had promised to take her there one day, but had never gotten the chance.

With a heavy sigh, Deryn stood from the couch and carried her blanket and untouched coffee out to the balcony.

~

"You're holding the knife wrong again, Leon."

"How many ways can there possibly be to hold a knife?" asked Deryn.

"Two. The right way and the wrong way," answered Xander. "Now correct your form."

With a grunt, she placed her hand the way she knew he wanted. For being the right way, it certainly felt wrong.

Xander stepped forward and readjusted her elbow, making her stance feel even more wrong. "From what I recall, you were a good soldier. Why are you so bad at this?"

"This sort of combat wasn't exactly touched upon."

"Yeah, because why would you want to fight with a knife when you have a gun that can turn someone to dust?"

Deryn gave him a look. "Which is exactly why I need something more powerful than this stupid thing. Get me a gun."

Xander laughed. "The Black Market is full of rebels and Resistance members. While they may want my money, not one of them would dare sell me a gun."

"You're a Guardian! Get me something from *your* side."

"Since you've been out of the loop for the past five years, I'll excuse your naivety and tell you a little story," said Xander with a grimace. "Once upon a time, a large group of Outsiders broke into our training center, took our weapons and used them against us. The president was not pleased, so when the battle was over he had every last Element collected and destroyed, ordering his team of top engineers to come up with a new design. One that could only be used by its owner."

He pulled back his coat and grabbed his Element out of its holster. While showing it to her, he placed his finger on a small gold square on the side. It beeped, a blue light scanning his finger before pricking it. The moment it had a blood sample, both his wristband and the Element started glowing.

"New weapons are only ever made anymore when we have a new recruit. And if you lose yours you're executed. No questions asked."

Deryn stared into his golden eyes and frowned. "Well, that blows."

"Yes, it does," he said, using his fingerprint again to turn the Element off before putting it away. "Now, proper form."

She did as she was told.

"When taking someone down, I can imagine going for their heart is the initial gut reaction. Or, in your case, slitting their throat."

Deryn gave Xander a look. He just smiled and moved so he was in front of her.

"I got him, didn't I?" she said with a sneer.

"Yes, but only because the bastard was an unsuspecting victim. Now imagine, if you will, someone coming at you. What do you do?"

Deryn looked at her raised knife, and then at Xander as he took a step forward. "You're right. I think heart." She tapped his with the tip of her blade.

"Exactly. But, from my experience, the heart is too unpredictable when acting quickly. You could miss or hit the ribcage, or even stab the heart successfully, but that doesn't mean your victim will die right away. They could still get one good whack at you."

"Stop calling them that. I can assure you, anyone I stab is *not* a victim. They will deserve it."

"Oh, I have no doubt," said Xander. "But when your *prey* comes for you, might I suggest that you raise your knife -" He grabbed her hand and lifted the knife higher. "- and get them right here." The tip of the blade touched his neck. "Sever the jugular vein." He positioned the knife correctly.

Deryn stared at the spot on his neck for a moment before meeting his eyes. "Slitting the throat worked just fine for me." She ran the knife gently across his neck.

Xander stared back at her and asked, "Then why did you stab him first?"

"I only had a moment to react and I hit him where I could."

He grinned. "That's all fine and dandy, but if you have more than a moment, do yourself a favor and go for the jugular vein." Xander stepped away from the knife touching his throat and began looking around. "Now, where is that holster I got you? I want to show you how to attach it and pull the knife out with ease on your unsuspecting vict - I mean prey."

She lowered the knife and helped him look.

"I must've left it in my room," he said, heading that way.

Continuing to look around the living room, Deryn finally found the holster between the couch cushions. "Got it, Ruby!" she called as she picked it up.

"Fine! Gonna take a piss if that's alright with you!" he called back.

Deryn rolled her eyes. She did that a lot when he was around.

While she waited for him to return, she took a good look at the holster. It was basically just a thin band for her arm with a little pocket attached. She put it on her right arm, slipping the knife into the pocket. It fit like a glove.

Deryn bent her wrist down but was unable to grab the handle. She lowered the holster and tried again, successfully grabbing the knife, but pulling it out a little too aggressively. The knife went flying, knocking something on the bookshelf that fell off the edge with a crash.

Deryn gasped.

She ran over and kneeled beside the broken object. She couldn't quite tell what it was anymore, but it appeared to be some sort of blue bottle. She thought apothecary, but considering Xander had spent his entire life living in the city she highly doubted he owned an Outsiders trinket.

"What are you doing?"

Deryn whipped around. Xander was standing in the doorway of his bedroom, his eyes drifting to the pile of blue glass on the floor. His face sank.

"Sorry, I ..." Deryn gulped. "It was an accident."

"How the fuck was it an accident?" he spat as he marched over and crouched down beside the broken glass. He lifted a couple of pieces and tried to match them together like a puzzle, but the thing was completely shattered. "What were you even doing over here?"

"I ..." Deryn lifted her arm and showed him the holster. "I

pulled the knife out too hard."

Xander stared blankly at her arm for a moment. Then his face fell into a hideous scowl. "I was gone for two fucking minutes! You couldn't wait that long for me to teach you properly?" he spat, dropping the pieces and rising back to his feet. "Fuck!"

"I-I'm sorry," she stuttered. "I didn't mean to upset -"

"Do I look *upset?*"

"Well ... yes, I would say -"

"No one asked you!"

"But you just -"

"Stupid, fucking toxic trash! Stay the fuck away from my things!"

Deryn's eyes grew wet as Xander turned on his heel and marched into his bedroom, dramatically slamming the door behind him. She was too stunned to move. He had called her toxic. Something he hadn't done since before. Maybe he truly did believe the lies he was told about the outside world. And suddenly he seemed a lot more like the boy she once knew in training, who thought less of her because she was from a world he had been taught to hate. A place he had never gone to without a gasmask for protection.

Xander's old self had never felt so close to her, so real. Every day she would justify her staying with a Guardian by convincing herself that he was different than the rest, but how different could he really be if he still saw her that way? Just a piece of toxic trash.

One outburst was all it took for Deryn to lose that ease she had been feeling for the first time in years. Now she was as scared as ever.

Without another thought, she grabbed her knife and put it in the holster on her arm. She stood up and ran for her room, knowing she couldn't stay here another minute. Not with *him.*

Deryn snatched her coat out of the closet and threw it on, then grabbed her map and chocolate bar off of the dresser and tossed them in her pocket. Once she had everything, she ran back to the living room, found her ragged old boots in the closet by the front door and put them on. Then, with a deep breath, she pulled on her hood, opened the door and left the apartment for the first time in almost two weeks.

Without looking back, she ran down the stairs two at a time and left that building as fast as she possibly could, barely noticing Bronson sitting in the hall outside of his apartment, eyeing her curiously as she sped by.

Xander was in his bathroom, splashing cold water on his face when he heard the door. He whipped his head around and tried to listen closer to see if his ears had deceived him, but there was no other sound.

He hurried to the living room, calling the name, "Leon," as he went into her bedroom. She wasn't there. So he checked her bathroom. Nothing. And then the balcony. She was nowhere. "Leon!" he called louder. No one answered. "Fuck!"

Xander went to the front closet and grabbed his coat. He noticed her shoes were missing when he put on his.

"Fuck, fuck, fuck!" he shouted before running out the door and down the stairs.

"Hey, Ruby, what's going on?"

Xander ignored Bronson as he ran by his door. He had no time for him right now. Every moment Deryn was outside was a moment too long. The search for her was still going strong and it was only a couple of hours until curfew. There was no way she could find a successful way out of Middle City, let alone a safe place in Outer City by then. Even he didn't know how to get out and he was a Guardian. He had to find her. *Now.*

CHAPTER TEN

Deryn didn't know how long she'd been running. She just wanted to get as far away from Xander's apartment as possible, but it was time for her to stop and think about where she was going.

Ducking into the first alley she saw, she took out her map and looked it over. She had already pinpointed where Xander lived days ago and she was pretty sure she had run east. One look at what she assumed was north - where President Saevus's lavish house resided, large and high for everyone to see - confirmed it.

An entrance to the underground, the remains of the tunnels their ancestors had barricaded themselves in for years, was not far. She had once asked Xander if the people hiding down there would be affected by the curfew and he'd said no. But it was still very dangerous, with S.U.R.G.E.'s patrolling and searching for life constantly, and he didn't envy whoever chose it as their place of refuge.

S.U.R.G.E.'s were also sent to attack people out past curfew, since they were able to detect body heat outside of registered residences and find all offenders within minutes. Some nights they took prisoners, others they killed. It all depended on what sort of mood President Saevus was in. For some reason, this technology did not work underground.

Despite all of that, Deryn knew she was out of options. If she didn't want to go back to Xander's then she needed to get underground before the curfew began.

Putting the map away, she poked her head out of the alley and searched for people. There were none. She walked back out and headed in the direction she was sure was right.

Deryn had barely turned onto the next block when someone did the same farther down the street. A tall figure hidden beneath a dark trench coat. They walked towards each other and she tried to remain calm, so as not to bring any attention to herself.

The person slowed as she passed, trying to get a good look at her, but she made sure he or she didn't.

"'Ey! Curfew's comin' soon. You got somewhere to go?" asked a male voice she vaguely recognized.

Deryn pretended she didn't hear him and kept walking.

"'Ey! I'm talkin' to you!"

She paused, turned slightly and said, "I'm just trying to get home." Then she kept going.

Deryn didn't even hear the footsteps, but they must have been there since someone was suddenly grabbing her arm and pulling her into the closest alley. He slammed her against the wall.

"Lemme see your wristband," he said, pulling up his sleeve so she could see Saevus's crest on his left wrist. A Guardian.

Deryn's breath hitched. She looked up and was immediately met with the shifty blue eyes of Dougal Fender, a Guardian who had owned her once.

He stared back at her, his eyes hazy. Obviously drunk. It was a long moment before there was a light of recognition. "Oh, shit! You're fucking Leon!" And then he smiled, giving her an up-close and personal view of his jagged teeth. "I can't believe it! I fucking caught Soren's favorite slave! The president's gonna reward me immisley for this!"

"I believe you mean *immensely*." She couldn't resist.

Dougal's smile quickly turned to a scowl. "Watch your fucking tongue. Guess I'll make this easy and just call 'im. His car can get 'ere pretty fast." He pulled up his right sleeve to uncover his citizen wristband, then got ready to press the button Deryn knew was used to call someone. All it needed was a name.

Deryn could not breath as she stared at the band, her palms sweating and her heart beating so hard she felt it in her throat. She needed her knife. She needed to get to her fucking knife but he had her pinned!

Dougal hesitated and looked closely at her. His smile returned. "Or we can have some fun at my place before you're executed. You know. One last hoorah."

Deryn grimaced at the thought. Dougal leaned into her. She tried to push him off, but he seized her wrists.

"This'll be fun."

"No!"

He took a small device out of his pocket, then pressed a button so it became shackles.

"Get off me!" Deryn kicked him away and bent her wrist into her sleeve, finally pulling out her knife. Even while bound, she still landed a successful slash across his chest. His jugular vein wasn't even an option right now. The cut wasn't deep, but it was enough to make him take a couple of steps back.

"You fucking -"

Both of their heads turned when they heard someone's feet skid and stop at the entrance to the alley. Deryn had never felt more relief than when she saw Xander standing there. He was panting heavily and had obviously been running for a while.

"Xander, what you doin' here?" asked Dougal, clearly unhappy about having to share his find.

"Leon?" asked Xander, looking at her unsurely for a moment.

Deryn pulled her hood slightly back and nodded.

"Yeah, Leon," said Dougal. "I found 'er. Was just goin' to call the president." He pulled up his sleeve again and put his finger on the call button.

Xander took a step forward and grabbed his Element out of its holster. He aimed it at Dougal. "Hands up."

Dougal looked at Xander, pursing his brow when he noticed the Element was pointed at him. "What the -"

Xander pressed a button on his Element that released a large

gust of wind, sending Dougal hurling backwards. He walked up
to Deryn and held out his hand. "Give it here, Leon."

Deryn hesitated only for a second before handing him her
knife. He used it to cut through her binds, which worked,
despite them being electrical. She took note of that.

"Next time, try using it before you're tied up."

"You helpin' her, Xander?" asked Dougal from where he sat
unmoving on the ground.

"Looks like it," said Xander, taking several steps forward
with his Element still aimed at Dougal, making sure he didn't
give the man a chance to reach for his own weapon.

"But why? You fuckin' 'er or somethin'?"

Xander said nothing. He would not even dignify a question
like that with a response.

"'Cause, I gotta tell you, I owned 'er before and it ain't
nothin' spe -"

Xander aimed his Element more forcefully.

"Alright, alright! I take it back!"

"Leon, did he really own you before?" asked Xander,
glancing sideways at her.

Deryn gulped and looked at Dougal. She nodded slowly.

"And did he treat you well?"

She took another moment to stare into Dougal's shifty eyes
before moving to Xander's fiery ones, which were currently
twinkling gold in the moonlight. She shook her head.

Xander looked back at his fellow Guardian and scowled.
"You were in the wrong place at the wrong time tonight,
Dougal. And now it ends."

"Ends?" repeated Dougal with wide eyes. "Wait, Ruby -"

Xander raised the knife he was still holding and threw it at
Dougal, hitting him on the left side of his neck. There was a
moment of fear and several choked breaths before his body fell
to the ground. He began to bleed out and quickly lost
consciousness.

Deryn gasped and turned away. "Why did you do that? You
didn't have to kill him."

"Yes, I did."

"But you could've just stopped his heart or -"

"No, I couldn't have," insisted Xander. "I told you, the president has our Element use checked every morning. I'm going to have to come up with an excuse just for that damn wind."

"But -"

"No buts. This is a fucking war, Leon. Aim to kill."

Deryn turned back and watched Xander as he stared at Dougal's lifeless body, the sound of his words instantly bringing her back to their encounter during the battle in Eagle Center. But, even with those same words, Xander had never seemed further from his old self than he did right then.

Xander remained placid as he stepped forward. He took some gloves out of his pocket and put them on before taking the knife out of Dougal's throat. Then he kneeled down, grabbed Dougal's left wrist and began cutting it off. Deryn turned away. But only for a moment.

"When I took off Soren's wristband I only had to cut it, not him."

"I know. That's why the president had them remodeled."

When she turned back, Dougal's hand was detached and the veins in his arms were quickly turning black. Xander removed the wristband and jammed the knife into it, destroying the tracker he knew would be activated when Dougal did not show up for his duties in the morning. He easily slipped off his citizen wristband and did the same. It was only a matter of time before citizens were upgraded to wristbands that burrowed into their skin, like the ones the guards wore, but for now the president was playing it safe, letting everyone adjust to the idea of wearing them first before taking it a step further.

Once that was done, Xander glanced farther down the alley at the closest dumpster. "Help me with this, will you?" he said, looking over his shoulder at her. "I don't want to get his blood all over me."

Deryn hesitated before walking over. Xander instructed her to take Dougal's arms while he grabbed his legs. She flinched as she held him below the bloody nub that was once his hand.

They moved quickly, tossing him in with a 'heave-ho'. He was immediately followed by his hand and broken wristbands.

The little bit of trash in the dumpster looked like it had been there for a long time, but Xander still rearranged it as best he could so it was at least covering Fender's exposed body parts. Then, after one last wipe of the knife on the dead man's coat, he turned to Deryn.

"What the hell were you thinking?" he shouted. "Do you have a death wish or something?"

"I ..."

"Saevus would already be planning your fucking execution if I hadn't been close enough to hear you scream! Dammit, Leon! Why did you leave?" Xander's face turned bright red as he shouted at her.

"You ... you called me toxic trash," said Deryn softly.

"What?"

"You called me toxic trash, Ruby," she repeated. "You try to act like you've changed but if that's how you view me -"

"That's not how I fucking view you, Leon! I was pissed! I didn't mean it!"

Deryn's throat tightened. "You didn't?"

"Of course not! If I saw you that way then why the fuck would I be helping you?"

"I ... I don't know -"

"I wouldn't!" Xander continued to stare at her with flaming eyes. They eventually softened. "Look, Leon, I'm not going to lie to you and say that all my beliefs have changed, because they haven't. The outside world is toxic, and anyone who lives out there will have a shortened life."

Deryn rolled her eyes.

"Don't fucking do that," he said harshly. "Let me finish before you go and judge me."

She waited.

"Yes, I believe what you consider to be nonsense, but I don't believe Outsiders should be treated as they are." Xander let out a deep sigh. He grabbed Deryn's arm and pulled back her sleeve, carefully returning the knife to its holster. Then he held out his hand to her. "Come on."

Deryn looked at it skeptically.

"I'm sorry I called you toxic -"

Deryn's eyes snapped back to his. He had never said that word to her before. *Sorry.*

"- but you can't stay out here. I don't know where you were going, but I can promise you it's not safe. Now, let's go."

Deryn looked back at his hand and watched closely as she placed hers inside of it, a weird feeling tingling in her stomach as he gave it a squeeze.

Without another word between them, Xander pulled her to the edge of the alley. He looked out to the street and made sure it was clear before leading her towards his apartment.

Deryn didn't take her eyes off of their clasped hands as they walked, her head still ringing with that word. *Sorry.* Xander was sorry for something he had done to her.

About halfway back, they heard several voices coming from around one of the corners. Xander grabbed Deryn and pulled her into another alley. He pressed her against the wall and held his body against hers, keeping them shielded from view until the people passed.

Deryn looked at his profile as he stared out towards the street, listening closely to make sure the people were gone. Xander had killed someone for her, and she wasn't sure how she felt about that. Dougal Fender was a bad person. He was vile and cruel, and countless lives had probably been saved with his death.

The line between right and wrong was so thin in this war, and Deryn could not decide where Xander stood. At one time, Dougal had been his friend. She didn't know the extent of that friendship, but he was around their age and the two of them were often together at Eagle. That had to have meant something. But tonight he had disposed of him so easily. For her.

Without even realizing it, Deryn lifted her hands and gripped Xander's coat. He turned and looked at her right as the tears fell. Her face pressed against his chest and his arms instinctually wrapped around her.

"Leon, what's wrong?"

"I don't know," she said, shaking her head. "I just ... I feel like such an idiot."

"What?"

"My mind has been so muddled lately. I don't know what I was thinking, leaving like that."

"People make mistakes -"

"Not me," she said, crying harder. "My mind ... It's not the same anymore, Ruby. It's not what it once was. They destroyed it. They ..."

Deryn's legs gave out and she collapsed. Xander tightened his hold and scooped her into his arms. "Come on, Leon. Let's get you home."

Home. Is that what this haven she had stumbled into was becoming? Her home?

Deryn gripped Xander's coat tighter and nuzzled into his shoulder. She hated that she felt so safe here, like nothing could harm her while she was wrapped in his arms. This dependence she was getting on him was not healthy. He was a Guardian and Guardians were her enemy. She could never forget that.

When they got back to his building, Xander headed up the stairs very carefully. Right around the third floor, Deryn noticed someone blocking their path out of the corner of her eye. She turned her head slightly and met the curious gaze of Bronson.

"What the hell is going on, Ruby? Who is -"

"I've never cashed in on that favor you owe me, Bronson, and, now, I need to do just that. Mention this to no one. Not even Quigley. Understand?"

Bronson looked back at Deryn, his face twisting with the slightest flicker of recognition, but it seemed like he couldn't quite place her. He nodded and moved aside, watching closely as Xander ascended the stairs with the mysterious woman in his arms.

Once they got inside the apartment, Xander kicked off his shoes and went straight to Deryn's room. He put her down carefully on the bed.

"What were you talking about down there?" she asked in a weak voice as he helped her remove her shoes, coat and holster. "Why does he owe you a favor?"

Xander's face remained unchanged as he emptied the pockets of her coat. "Bronson and Quigley are both Outsiders."

Something jolted in Deryn's stomach as all of the air was literally knocked out of her.

"I altered the information in their wristbands years ago. They were both born in Utopia, but left with Quigley's family when they were around twelve, I think." Xander put her knife and map on the dresser, but paused when he came across the chocolate bar. "Why do you have this?"

"You gave it to me."

"I know, but why haven't you eaten it?"

Deryn shrugged. "I don't own very much. If I eat it then that's one less thing that's mine."

Xander sighed and put down the chocolate bar. As he hung her coat in the closet, he asked, "What were you saying before? About your mind?"

Deryn shrugged again.

He went over and sat on the edge of her bed. "Is that why you haven't been reading? You think it's damaged?"

"Is that so farfetched?" she asked, wiping several tears from her eyes. "People have gone insane while enduring a lot less than I have. Sometimes, I wonder if I'm even really here. Like maybe this is all in my imagination or something. That would at least explain why you keep helping me." Deryn sighed. "I was considered one of the most intelligent in our training program, and now look at me. What a joke."

Xander took in the sad woman in front of him. "You're not crazy, Leon," he said. "The truth is I don't know why I'm helping you. It's not like we were ever friends. I mean, we were rarely even civil."

"We were never civil, Ruby," she said with a slight smile.

He smiled back. "I know. But I just ... I *have* to help you."

"Because of the guilt?" she asked, recalling their previous

conversation.

"No," he answered. "It's more than that. I want Saevus's reign to end and your father and brother are leading the rebellion against him. But they're always too careful, and most people believe it's because they fear for your life."

"So you think getting me to them will make them act?"

"It will definitely change things."

"Is that why you killed your friend for me tonight?"

Xander cocked an eyebrow.

"Dougal Fender," she said, as if it wasn't obvious.

"Dougal wasn't my friend. He was a fucking bastard and he deserved what he got."

"But you were always around each other during training."

"So?" said Xander. "That was years ago. Things were different back then."

Deryn's hands fidgeted with the edges of the comforter. "So is it always that easy for you? Killing people, I mean."

"It depends on who I'm killing," said Xander honestly. "I held Dougal with as much regard as you probably held Soren. My only concern now is what new restrictions will come with his disappearance. And I need to go back to clean up the blood."

Deryn sighed. "I'm sorry I broke your bottle earlier. I really didn't mean to." She glanced up and met his golden eyes with her sea-green ones. "Was it special?"

Xander nodded. "It was my mom's. An old perfume bottle. I kept it around because it still sort of smelled like her. Strange, I know. A grown man longing for the scent of his mommy."

"It's not strange," she said with a soft smile. "I still remember what my dad smells like, and I would give anything to experience that again."

The two of them stared at each other for a long moment.

"You should try to get some sleep," said Xander with a small gulp.

Deryn nodded and lay down in her bed, pulling the covers all the way up to her neck. Xander had just stood up to leave when she called his name. He looked back and, when their eyes locked, hers shifted slightly to the side.

"Will you stay for a little while? I'm not ready to sleep yet."

He looked hesitant. "You want me to stay?"

Her eyes locked back on his and she gave a shallow nod. "Just for a little while."

Everything in Xander's mind started screaming at him, telling him to say no. There was no reason for him to stay with her. But, in the end, he still heard himself say, "Yes."

He took off his coat and holster, climbed on the bed and lay down beside her.

Deryn turned to face him and slowly closed her eyes.

"For what it's worth, I don't think your mind is as damaged as you believe," he said.

"You don't?" she asked, her eyes opening slightly. "Why?"

"Well, leaving tonight was pretty fucking stupid and I hope the old you would've known better, but you keep recalling things like it all just happened yesterday. Even I barely remember that I used to hang around Dougal."

"Really?" Her eyes widened to their full size.

"Yes."

There was another moment of silence. Xander turned his head and the two of them gazed at each other. Before long, both of their eyes began to close.

As Deryn slowly drifted off to sleep she found herself asking, "Ruby ... are you sure I'm not crazy?"

"Positive," she heard him answer before falling into her first peaceful sleep in years.

CHAPTER ELEVEN

The next morning, Xander awoke to someone knocking on his front door. It started out soft enough, but quickly became more urgent. His eyes opened slowly and it took him a moment to recognize his surroundings. He was not in his bedroom, as he expected, but in the guestroom instead. Feeling something in his hand, he turned his head and found a delicate female one placed inside of it, and, beyond that, the serene face of Deryn, her eyelashes fluttering as the knocking grew louder.

Xander grunted and yanked his hand out of hers, wiping it on his sweater. Which one of them had made *that* terrible mistake? He could not for the life of him remember, so it must have been her.

Xander groaned as he climbed out of the bed and left the room. He shut the door behind him, went to the front door and shouted, "Who the fuck is it?"

"It's Bronson! Let me in!"

Xander groaned again and opened the door a crack. "What the hell do you -"

Bronson pushed the door all the way open and let himself inside. His face was glowing as he held a piece of paper in his hands. "I knew it! I fucking knew it, Ruby!"

"Knew what?" asked Xander, rubbing his groggy eyes.

"I *knew* I recognized your little houseguest when she came here the other week and I thought it was weird when I never heard her leave. But, hey, I know how this works. Don't ask questions, right? But then, last night, I just knew! I fucking knew she wasn't just *any* girl. She was someone. And now I have proof!"

Bronson held up the piece of paper, revealing an old wanted poster for Godfrey and Talon Leon with a photo of them in its center, an old family portrait confiscated from their home. And there, between her father and brother, was a young Deryn, no older than twelve but seemingly unchanged.

Xander went white.

"Don't you dare tell me it's not her because I know! I *know*, Ruby! You're hiding Godfrey Leon's daughter in your apartment! I mean ... *damn*. That's intense."

"Why do you still have that old thing?" asked Xander.

Bronson grinned. "Is that a yes then?"

"I didn't say that. Now answer." He took the poster from Bronson.

"Quigley keeps a scrapbook of every wanted poster he comes across."

"You told Quigley about this?" Xander turned red in the face. "I thought I told you not to!"

"Relax, Ruby. Quigley isn't even home. Stayed at some new broad's place last night. I haven't seen him."

"Get out of here, Bronson." Xander slammed the wanted poster against Bronson's chest and turned away.

"No!" Bronson said firmly. "Some weird shit has been going on here for a while now and I want to know what it is! You know you can trust me. I've never once given you a reason not to."

"Until now. Don't stick your nose where it doesn't belong, 'less you want to get yourself killed."

"Yeah, well, I risk my life every day by living here, don't I? Just tell me."

"No."

"Come on!"

"No! Get the fuck out -"

"Dammit, Ruby! I want to know what -"

The door to the guestroom opened and Deryn walked out. She went right over to Bronson, whose jaw had hit the floor, took the wanted poster out of his hands and looked closely at the photo. She sighed.

"Bronson, is it?" she said, looking up to meet his eyes.

"Y-yes." He paused. "Holy fuck. I was right?"

"Leon, what the hell are you doing out here?" asked Xander, looking livid.

"He already saw me, Ruby."

"Well, he obviously didn't get a clear view of you, or else he wouldn't be here questioning it."

"Clear enough that he recognized me in a photo taken over a decade ago."

Xander took several deep breaths, through his nose and out his mouth, to calm himself. "I was taking care of it," he said through gritted teeth.

"Yes, because your 'get the fuck out' approach was working really well." She rolled her eyes.

"Stop fucking doing that!"

"Doing what?"

"That fucking eye roll thing! You do it all the time and it's annoying!"

Deryn crossed her arms in front of her chest. "Well, maybe if you stopped giving me reasons to roll my eyes then it wouldn't bother you so much!"

"Stop. Fucking. Doing. It."

"I'll stop rolling my eyes just as soon as you stop using so many obscenities."

Bronson chuckled, which caused Xander to glare at him. He quickly shut his mouth.

"Why are you being so snippy?" asked Deryn.

Because you were holding my hand, thought Xander.

"Did you wake up on the wrong side of the bed or something?"

No, I woke up in your *bed.* "No. I'm just ... fucking annoyed that you came out here."

Deryn let out a deep, frustrated breath. She opened her mouth to say something, but before she could -

"Do you mind if I put this little tiff of yours on hold for a moment and ask a really important question?" asked Bronson, stepping between the man and woman who had begun to edge towards one another.

"What?" they both asked, snapping their heads to look at him.

"Perhaps this isn't the time for this, but I just have to know."

They waited.

"Are you the cupcake girl?"

Both Xander and Deryn's brows furrowed, their lips sneering as they stared at Bronson like he was the biggest idiot in the world.

"Is that a yes?"

Deryn could not help but roll her eyes again. She gave Xander a sharp look before he could say anything.

"Look, Bronson, let me level with you," she said, now focusing her sole attention on him and trying to ignore the annoying prick also in the room. "I really didn't want to go down this road, but your incessant need to meddle in our business has given me no choice."

Xander cocked an eyebrow.

"Ruby told me about what he did for you."

All color drained from Bronson. "He did -"

"So I need you to know that if you ever blab about my being here, he's kept virtual copies of your real identification information -"

Bronson's jaw dropped dramatically.

"- and he will not hesitate to turn you in if you ever decide to betray our trust. Do you understand?"

Mouth still agape, Bronson nodded slowly.

Unable to resist the urge, Deryn finally looked at Xander. He was smiling with pride shining in his eyes. Of course it wasn't true. Keeping evidence like that lying around would be idiotic and dangerous for everyone involved, but Bronson didn't need to know that.

"Alright then. I'm glad we're all on the same page." Deryn looked back at the wanted poster she was holding and frowned.

"It was a pleasure meeting you." She headed to her room -

"Umm ... I sort of need -"

- and shut the door.

"- that back."

"When you get the chance, I'm also going to need the wanted poster of Dakota Triggs!" she called through the door.

Xander laughed. "I don't believe you'll be getting it back, mate." He took Bronson's shoulder and guided the flabbergasted man towards the front door. "She's a piece of work, I know. And really hard to get used to."

"How ... here?" Bronson pointed at the floor.

"You walked here just now. Do you not recall?"

Bronson glared at him. "You know what -"

"The fewer questions you ask the better." Xander opened the door and used Bronson's shoulder to push him out. "And remember, tell no one." He slammed it.

"So is she the cupcake girl?" Bronson called from the other side.

Xander didn't answer. He went to the guestroom door and opened it without knocking.

Deryn's head shot up as he entered. She was sitting with her legs crossed on the bed, the wanted poster held in her lap. "What if I'd been changing?"

"Into what? Different pajamas?"

"Funny," she said, frowning as she looked down at the poster.

"You alright?" he asked, taking a step into the room.

"Fine." Her frown deepened. "I just miss my dad and Talon. It's been so long I'd almost forgotten what they looked like. I wonder how different they look now, especially Talon. Have you seen him at all?" She looked at him hopefully.

"No," he said honestly. "He stays hidden a lot."

"That doesn't sound like him," she said, looking at the poster again. "And Dakota?"

"I've seen Trigger several times. He looks the same." Xander thought about this. "Angrier."

"Hmm." Deryn stared at the poster for a moment longer

before standing and propping it against a lamp on the dresser. "Do you have Guardian duties today?"

Xander cringed at the way she said that. So casually. "Yes."

Her eyes moved to the small clock he had given her. "You're running late again. Should I make breakfast while you shower?"

"If that's what you want."

"I suppose I'll take that as a yes," she said, eyeing him curiously. "You're acting strange."

Xander was taken aback. "No, I'm -"

"Is this because I asked you to stay last night?" Deryn blushed as she avoided his eyes.

He blinked. "Uhh ..."

"I'm sorry if that was weird or inappropriate in any way. I just ..." She sighed. "I needed someone last night and ... well, you were here. That's all."

Xander's lips tightened. That hurt more than expected. "It's fine, Leon. No need to get your panty's in a twist."

Deryn lifted her eyes.

"I know what a fucking vulnerable girl looks like. How do you think I get so many back here?"

She raised her eyebrows.

"I'm just saying, I know the signs and I wasn't going to leave you alone if you didn't want to be. No need to read so much into it. I'm not acting weird."

"But you kind of are."

"Am not!"

Deryn blinked several times before smiling softly. "Fine, Ruby. You're acting completely normal." She looked at the clock again. "If you get in the shower now you'll still have time to sit and eat. I'll make pancakes." She walked forward and pushed past him, heading for the kitchen. "Shower, Ruby!" she called when she noticed he hadn't moved.

Xander grunted and went into the living room. He took a moment and watched her moving around in the kitchen while humming to herself. Less than two weeks there and she already knew where everything was, like she belonged.

The thought filled him with dread, and he slipped into his

room before she was wise to his watchful eye.

CHAPTER TWELVE

When Xander got home that evening, he was not surprised to find Deryn sitting on the couch, twiddling her thumbs. How she wasn't going insane was beyond him. He walked right up to her and tossed a book he held onto her lap. An actual book, not one of those electronic items that merely projected a hologram. He knew she liked to actually hold her reading material. She had certainly voiced it enough.

Deryn lifted it and read the title. *Complex Conundrums*. "What's this?" she asked, looking up at him.

"It's a book of riddles and brainteasers meant to challenge your mind. I thought it might help you sharpen yours a bit. To get you back to where you were."

Deryn tilted her head. "You bought this for me?"

"Obviously," said Xander, taking out his pack of cigarettes and readying one between his lips. "My mind's still solid."

Deryn smiled and looked back down at the book, running her fingers across the spine and cover. It was one more thing that was hers. "Do you think the next time you buy me something, you can pick me up some new underwear? I'm really sick of wearing whatever it is those women you bring home leave behind."

"I refuse to let you wear granny pants, Leon. The underwear stays." Xander winked and headed for the balcony. He used his wristband to activate a soundproof shield around the space outside, knowing very well that she would be joining him.

Deryn frowned as she wrapped her blanket around her shoulders and followed him out. Sitting down in her usual corner, she opened the book to the first page. This chapter was titled, *Bogglers for Beginners.*

"Let's hear it," said Xander, lighting his cigarette.

Deryn cleared her throat and read the first one aloud, "I am lighter than a feather, yet no man can hold me for very long. What am I?"

"Breath," they both answered. That was easy enough.

"Feed me and I live, give me something to drink and I'll die. What am I?"

"Fire," they both said again.

"Skip a few chapters, Leon. Your mind's not that fucking damaged."

She flipped through the pages until she came across chapter five, *Medial Mysteries.* That sounded all right. For the most part, Deryn didn't have a problem with the riddles. Occasionally, it would take her a minute and Xander would get frustrated waiting for her to come up with the answer, but he always waited. And then Deryn came across one she didn't like.

"Until I am measured I am not known, yet how you miss me when I have flown." She slammed the book shut.

"What? Don't know the answer?" asked Xander, taking a drag of his cigarette.

"No, I know the answer is time," she said. "I just ... don't like it. It's a bit of a harsh reality."

"That time is missed when it's gone?" He cocked an eyebrow. "How is that harsh?"

"I was thinking more along the lines of how quickly it can be gone. Like, five years." Deryn fidgeted with one of the corners of the book.

"Time hasn't flown yet, Leon. You still have plenty of it." Xander leaned back in his chair and took another drag. "So, listen."

She lifted her head.

"I have to head to my father's tomorrow."

She tried hard not to react to the mention of Atticus. If

Xander noticed, he didn't let on.

"To pick something up after my Guardian duties are complete. Unfortunately, one of the new restrictions the president has put into place prohibits me from using my hover-bike after dark, or transporting it between cities and there's no way I could make it back in time for curfew."

"Meaning, I'll be on my own for the night," she said.

"I was actually going to have Bronson stay over."

Deryn furrowed her brow. "To babysit me?"

Xander smirked. "If you hadn't pulled a runner last night -"

"I'm not going to do that again! I'm fine on my own, Ruby. I don't need -"

"I would feel more comfortable leaving if I knew someone was here. Who can protect you, you know? In case of emergencies."

"I'll be fine on my -"

"I already asked him on my way up here," said Xander. "He's ecstatic. Can't wait to spend time with the famous Deryn Leon."

Deryn frowned and hugged the book to her chest. "I loathe you."

"I'm starting to consider that a compliment."

CHAPTER THIRTEEN

Deryn sat on the couch with her arms crossed while Bronson sat on the other end, all smiles as he watched her. He had so many questions and it was starting to give her a headache.

"So where have you been since you disappeared? How'd you end up here with Ruby? Are you the reason there are all of these restrictions lately? What's your favorite color? Do you like pasta? Do you like cupcakes? Are you the cupcake girl? If so, why didn't you like Ruby's cupcake? What's your dad like?"

She answered none but the last, stating, "The less you know, the better." But that did not stop her from talking about how good and kind her father was, making her miss him even more, if at all possible.

"Oh, I almost forgot!" Bronson grabbed his overnight bag from beside the couch and unzipped it. "Quigley will kill me if he ever finds out any of his stuff is missing but, I assume, this is the wanted poster you were talking about?"

He handed her a piece of paper. Deryn's heart skipped a beat when she came face-to-face with Dakota, a photo that must have been taken during some altercation with the Guardians. His father Piz and brother Laramie could even be seen in the background. A tear slid down her cheek. She was quick to wipe it away before it could drip onto the paper and smudge the ink.

"Yes, it is," she said with a smile.

Bronson watched her curiously as she continued to stare

down at the photo. "How long has it been since you've seen him?"

"Five years and thirteen days," she said. Counting the days had become a regular thing for her.

Bronson raised the eyebrows. "Since the battle at Eagle Center?"

Deryn nodded.

"I'd heard you went missing shortly after, but I hadn't realized you'd never been found. Were you being held prisoner, or something? Did Ruby help you escape?"

"Not exactly," she said, stroking Dakota's face. "I'm not going to tell you anything, Bronson, so you can stop asking." She paused. "Is that your real name?"

"It's my real surname."

"What's your first name?"

Bronson grunted. "Something I detest."

"So does that mean you won't tell me?" asked Deryn, looking up and giving him sad, puppy-dog eyes.

He grunted again. "You won't start calling me it, will you?"

"Not if you don't want me to."

A third grunt, followed by a gulp. "It's Baldric."

Deryn let a chuckle slip out but quickly threw her hand over her mouth. "I'm sorry. That's ... well, it's very lovely." She chuckled again.

"There! You see? *That's* why I never tell anyone!"

"No, no! Ignore me. Baldric is a very nice name." Another chuckle. "And I do enjoy the irony since you have such an abundant head of hair."

"Thank you," said Bronson, running a hand through his thick, chestnut locks.

Even though romance was the furthest thing from Deryn's mind, she was also not blind. Bronson was nice to look at. He had that hair, obviously. It looked so soft and she was tempted to reach out and touch it, and it was accompanied by olive skin and striking deep-blue eyes. Not to mention that smile. It could make any heart melt. But she had a sinking feeling that she was not his type.

"So what's his story?" asked Bronson, looking at the photo in Deryn's hands and pointing at Laramie in the background. "He play for my team?"

That confirmed it. Definitely not his type. "Not that I know of," she said honestly. "I've never known Laramie to have a girlfriend but I always saw him as more androgynous than anything."

Bronson cocked an eyebrow. "Come again?"

Deryn smiled. "It just means that he's more interested in exploring than relationships. With a girl *or* boy."

"Not once I'm through with him." He laughed.

Deryn looked coyly at her fidgety hands. Bronson couldn't help but notice.

"Don't tell me you spend all your time with Ruby and you're shy when it comes to sex? How the hell does that work?"

She blushed. "Not well."

"That man really has no shame. Most nights we can hear him and his latest conquest all the way down in our apartment."

Deryn crinkled her nose. "You can?"

"Why the hell do you think we always keep the music so loud? Two floors and all windows closed means nothing when that guy's going at it." Bronson snorted. "Tell me he at least puts one of those noise shield things up between your rooms when he brings someone over?"

Deryn narrowed her eyes and shook her head. "He says that the bastard president checks his wristband activity every morning, so he can't do anything that looks suspicious."

"Oh, what a load of crap!"

Her eyes shot up. "You mean, he doesn't check?"

"No. Of course he does," said Bronson defensively. "But Ruby's his favorite. Any lie he feeds him, he'll eat right up."

"Did Ruby tell you he's his favorite?"

"No. He'd never brag about something like that. But he's in charge."

"In charge," she repeated.

"Of the other Guardians," said Bronson. "Ruby's the one who barks out orders. And, every time President Save-none-of-us has a gathering the whole city is required to attend, Ruby is always standing just behind him. Him and that bitch daughter of his. *Elvira.* I can't tell you how many times Ruby's sent her on what are supposed to be suicide missions, only to have her come back unscathed. I wouldn't be surprised if she's sold her fucking soul to the devil for eternal life or something, considering all of the crap she's survived without a scratch."

Deryn stared at him, unblinking.

"He's really never told you any of this?"

She shook her head.

"You and Ruby don't know each other very well, do you?"

"We don't know each other at all."

"So what have the two of you been doing here for the past two weeks? Staring at each other without a word passing between you or something?"

Deryn pursed her lips in thought. Huh. What *did* they talk about? Their conversations were certainly never about him. Every time she tried to get something out of him, he would turn it back on her.

"Can we change the subject?" she asked, putting the wanted poster down on the coffee table. "So were you just teasing me with your pasta talk earlier, or do you really know how to make it?"

"Spaghetti, Fettuccini Alfredo, Pesto, you name it, I can make it," said Bronson with a smile.

Deryn smiled back. "Pesto sounds perfect."

~

Xander sat on a white, stone bench in the middle of his father's backyard, staring blankly at an unmarked grave in front of him. The cold air stung his wet cheeks, only adding to the horrible ambiance that haunted this place. After the battle at Eagle Center, he couldn't move out of this house fast enough, and had only been back a handful of times since. And only to see her. His mother. Buried without a tombstone out of fear that the president would decimate her remains for disobeying his orders. Telling her son not to fight, but to leave out of fear for his life. He had been a terrible guard back then.

Xander had actually been chosen to work in the Government Lab after turning eighteen, but his father wanted him to be a soldier so that's what he became.

He had dug the grave for his mother with his bare hands, after his father had ordered him to come back here with her body. Before he dragged Deryn away, dooming her to the horrible life of slavery that almost destroyed her. But she was strong. Xander knew she was. That was why she was doing so much better than others who had suffered the same fate. Sure, she had her moments of insanity, but those were to be expected. You could not endure years of torture and come out untouched.

Eyes still on the disturbed dirt that covered his mother's shallow grave, Xander mindlessly took a cigarette out of his pocket and lit it.

"Xander," a voice called from behind him.

Without turning around, Xander blew the smoke out through his lips and slowly said, "Hello, Father."

"What are you doing here? The wave did not alert me of your arrival."

"Probably because he hasn't seen me. Your wave is a *he*?"

"What? Why in Saevus's name does that matter?"

"Just answer the question," said Xander, taking another drag of his cigarette.

"Yes, *he* is," said Atticus, stepping closer. He took a good look at his son. "Take that dreadful thing out of your mouth! What if the president found out you were smoking?"

"How would he find out?" asked Xander. He gave a small smile as he took another drag. "Are you going to tell on me?"

"Of course not!" shouted Atticus, turning red in the face. "Do not think that just because you're his current favorite you are exempt from the rules. It won't last forever, Xander. You cannot afford to make any mistakes."

"You mean like you?" said Xander, finally turning to his father with narrowed eyes. "I'm not stupid. I know better than to repeat *your* mistakes."

Atticus's face softened as he stared back at his son. "Xander,

I -"

"Leave me, Father. I only came here to visit Mom and I would like some time alone with her, if you don't mind."

Atticus gave him a shallow nod and moved to leave. "Will you be staying?"

"With the damn curfew it seems like I don't have much of a choice."

"So does that mean they haven't found Deryn Le -" Atticus stopped and sighed. "That toxic slave yet?"

"You remember her name?" asked Xander curiously.

Atticus said nothing.

"No, they haven't." But *he* had. "I don't know why we're wasting our time. She's probably halfway back to her father by now, if not there already."

"It would be impossible for her to travel like that. Someone must be helping her."

"Someone with a death wish." Xander had to laugh.

"If I had to venture a guess, I'd say she hasn't gotten any farther than Middle City. You should have your Guardians search every home."

"Who fucking cares?" He took another drag of his cigarette. "The whole point of keeping her was to lure her father out and, in five years, he's never come looking for her. Not once."

"He's sent others."

"Failures. Every last one of them. If we want to lure him out she's not the answer. We're wasting our time."

"Xander, I surely hope you haven't spoken like this to the pres -"

"Of course I haven't!" shouted Xander. "But it's the truth! Now, leave me."

Atticus left without another word.

Xander sat there mindlessly, staring at his mother's grave for a long while, only standing when the first drops of rain landed on his forehead.

He dropped his cigarette that had burned out and walked over to her, putting his hands in his pockets as he tried hard to remember her face.

"Mom, I've done something foolish. Something that will probably cost me my life. I don't ..." Xander gulped. "I don't want your death to have been in vain. You lost your life to save mine and, now, I'm doing the same for someone else. Please, don't hate me for it. I'm just so sick of this life. A life I know you never wanted for me."

He wiped his wet eyes, a mixture of cold rain and hot tears.

"You once told me a secret. I was very small and you told me that you dreamed of going outside, feeling a real breeze, maybe even seeing the ocean, and I wanted to see it, too. But you never got the chance to make that dream a reality because of the fear that's been instilled in us since birth. And father ... he's not like you and me. He believes every lie the president tells him. And, who knows, maybe sea air truly is the most toxic of all, but I still want to feel it. Someday."

He took a deep breath.

"I won't be like him, living in fear. That's why I must do this. Even if I die. I'm tired of being afraid."

Xander took a step closer and kneeled down, lifting a rock he had placed where her heart would be. He gulped back tears and dug his fingers into the dirt, moving them around until he felt metal, gripping his find and pulling it free.

It was an Element. A very old one, but an Element, nonetheless. He had found it on his mother's body after her passing and hidden it here for no reason really, other than he had no use for it at the time. But he always knew he wanted to hold onto it. In case one day he might need it. He had completely forgotten about it until he'd told Deryn how Elements now worked the other day, and after seeing her helpless against Dougal he knew she needed something more powerful than a knife.

In these current times it was next to impossible to find an Element that didn't have to be registered, let alone activated without a prick of its owners' blood. This very well might have been the last one out there.

"Thanks for keeping this safe for me, Mom. The person I'm giving it to will put it to good use. I'm sorry I haven't fought harder for the world you always wanted. I would change a lot of things if I could."

The light drizzle steadily sped up to a heavy downpour. Xander looked up and watched as a streak of lightning lit up the artificial sky, accompanied by a loud roar of false thunder.

"I don't know when I'll be able to visit again, but I love you. I look forward to the day I can take you to the ocean."

Xander kissed his hand and touched it to the earth.

"Soon. I will avenge you soon."

He stood up, put the Element away in his hidden inside coat pocket and slowly walked towards the backdoor of his childhood home. His father's wave met him there with some dry clothes in hand.

"I have already made up your old room for you, Young Master," said the wave, putting the clothes down and using a towel to help Xander dry off.

"Thank you," said Xander, definitely aware that the wave was, in fact, a 'he'. "Tell me something. Has a young woman ever stayed here? Perhaps in the basement, or a closet of some sort?"

"No woman has stayed here in many years, Young Master."

"How many years?"

"Ezra, my son is quite capable of drying himself. Please, continue with your other duties," said Atticus, walking into the room.

"Yes, Master." The wave hurried off.

As soon as he was gone, Atticus looked at his son and asked, "What were you asking him?"

"Nothing," answered Xander, walking towards the living room. "I'm pulling out the good brandy."

After a few drinks, Xander excused himself to his room, only to sneak off to the basement on his way there. He had a horrible feeling he simply couldn't shake. Deryn acted strangely at the mere mention of his father. Of course, she had every right to hate him. It was his final decision that forced her into slavery. But it seemed like it was more than that. The way she looked at Xander when he woke her from her nightmares, fear and hatred pouring out of her as she stared into the eyes that could have very well belonged to someone else. While Xander looked more like his mother, he had his father's eyes.

Xander descended the stairs and turned on the light. He began walking around the dreary space.

He didn't know what he was looking for. Just some small sign that she had been here, but there was nothing. If there was ever any part of Deryn in this basement it was long gone. He had kept pretty good track of her over the years, but not always. There were times, especially in the beginning, when he had absolutely no idea where she was. But, from what he understood, his father had never owned a sex slave. Just like him. Because the Rubys never just took women. They made them theirs. As it should be.

With a heavy sigh, Xander headed back to the stairs and turned off the light. He opened the door and left the basement behind, just missing the scratches low on the wall beside the doorframe. A young girl's desperate attempt to keep track of her days imprisoned there. Back when time still mattered to her. And when she still had hope that one day she would be saved.

CHAPTER FOURTEEN

Xander left the next morning at the first signs of light and began his journey home. He didn't even bother to say goodbye to his father.

The S.U.R.G.E.'s and patrolling guards let him back into Middle City without so much as a second glance. One of the few benefits of being the president's right-hand man. Anyone else would have been checked and then punished for trying to sneak in an unregistered weapon.

Xander had his hover-bike locked up near the gate and used it to ride home.

He reached his building and used the clicker on his bike's handle to open the garage. He took over two spots, since his hover-bike was the only vehicle ever in there. The building only had two other residents and neither of them made enough money to afford such luxuries.

After stepping off of his bike, he walked back out to the street and took a moment outside by himself. He rarely got those anymore. Not since before Deryn entered his life. Even when he tried to escape for a moment of peace on the balcony she always followed him. He understood she was lonely, but it was starting to get frustrating.

After a few breaths, the rain began to pour down again. Xander ran inside and up the stairs to the fifth floor. As he approached his front door, he could hear some strange sounds coming from inside. A flash of panic ran through his head. He hurried to unlock the door and burst into his apartment.

Both Deryn's and Bronson's heads shot up to look at him. They were in the kitchen and he appeared to be teaching her how to make an omelet. She had a spatula in hand and both were smiling, the faint remnants of a laugh still vibrating on her lips. It was the first genuine laugh he had seen since she got here. And Bronson was the one to make it happen. Now, why did that irk him?

"Hey, Ruby! You're home early," said Bronson.

"Uhuh." Xander eyed the two of them suspiciously. "It was not a leisurely visit."

"Should we make you an omelet then? Deryn's getting pretty good. Course, she burnt the first three."

Xander was not blind to the way Deryn smiled at the sound of her name.

"No, that won't be necessary," he said, kicking off his shoes and putting his coat in the closet. "I'm tired and want my own fucking bed."

Xander walked to his room. Noticing Deryn's bedroom door was open, he peeked inside and saw that her bed was untouched. She did make it every morning, but never first thing. He grunted, opened his own door and slammed it behind him.

"He's always so bright and cheery in the morning," said Bronson, completely unfazed by Xander's rude demeanor.

"Leon, get in here!" called Xander's unpleasant voice from his room.

"The prince is beckoning you. Better hurry." Bronson laughed as Deryn handed him the spatula.

She groaned before walking over to Xander's door and opening it cautiously. "You called?" she said, only poking in her head.

"All the way in, Leon. And shut the door behind you."

Deryn did as he instructed, but still hung near her only exit as a precaution. "Is everything alright?" She crossed her arms and waited.

"What the fuck was that?"

"What was what?" she asked, holding his fiery gaze with her

own.

"That! *That*!" Xander pointed at the door. "Whatever *that* was I just walked in on!"

Deryn crinkled her brow and said, "What? You mean my omelet?"

"Don't play fucking dumb! You know what I'm talking about!"

She crinkled her brow further. "Bronson?"

"Obviously!"

"I don't know what you mean," she said. "He was just teaching me how to make an omelet. Is that so terrible?"

Xander's nostrils flared. He closed his eyes and took several deep breaths to calm himself. "Look, I know you've made this decision for the two of us to trust him, but that doesn't mean you should let your guard down."

"I haven't." Deryn uncrossed her arms and pulled the sleeves of her sweater over her hands. It was always so cold in his room. "You're the one who asked him to stay here, remember?"

"Yes, but I don't recall telling you to get so chummy with him."

Deryn raised her eyebrows. "I'm sorry, but what did you expect? You threw me into an apartment with a man I hardly know for an entire night. God knows I get enough awkward silences with you, and Bronson is pretty impossible to hate. Besides, you trust him. Why shouldn't I?"

"Who says I trust him?"

"You wouldn't have asked him to stay here if you didn't. And he certainly knows more about you than I do."

Xander went red. "What the hell does that mean?"

"Nothing," said Deryn, turning her head and staring at a spot on the wall.

"Leon, don't you fucking go spacing out on me in the middle of our conversation."

Deryn's head snapped back.

"What did Bronson tell you about me?"

"Nothing," she said again.

"So you like him then?"

"Yes, he's very nice."

"Don't be fucking stupid, Leon! You're in hiding! This is no time for you to be going googly-eyed!"

Her brow crinkled again. "What?"

"You want him!"

Now her brow shot high up on her forehead as her eyes widened. "*What?*"

"That's what you just said!"

"No it's not! How on earth did your deluded ears hear that?"

"Because you said it! You said you like him!"

"As a person, Ruby! Not like that!"

"So you're saying you're not attracted to him?"

"No, that's not ... he's decent looking. I'm not going to say he isn't. But I'm hardly his type."

"What does that mean?"

Deryn instantly thought of Laramie Triggs. "He likes smaller breasts."

Xander crinkled his forehead. Clearly, he didn't get the joke.

"He's gay, Ruby. You know. Likes men ..." Her voice trailed off as she stared awkwardly off to the side.

A pause.

"He is?" asked Xander, looking absolutely baffled.

"Oh, yeah." She smiled. "You really didn't know?"

Xander's face calmed a little as he slowly shook his head. "So then ... he and Quigley -"

"No, Ruby. Quigley likes women. It is possible for a gay man to have a male roommate who isn't his lover."

Xander cringed. "Don't say that."

"What? *Lover?*"

He cringed again. "Stop it."

Deryn laughed.

Xander looked over at her and felt a strange sense of satisfaction. She had laughed, and because of something *he* had done. Not Bronson.

"So did you really just call me in here to act all fatherly, or was there a point to all of this?"

He smiled and said, "Well, someone fucking has to. Can't have you go jumping into the sheets with the first man to cross your path since escaping your former life."

"Technically, that would be you." Hearing what she'd just said, Deryn blushed and cleared her throat. "There's really no need. I already have a dad, and he raised me to be cautious."

"Hopefully you have a dad," he said flatly.

Deryn's face dropped. "What?"

One look at her and Xander immediately regretted what he had said. He really needed to learn to hold his tongue. "No, Leon, I didn't mean ... He just hasn't been seen in a long -"

"What did you want, Ruby?" she asked, looking at the floor and clenching her fists so tight they turned white, obviously trying not to cry.

"I brought you something," he said, reaching into his inside coat pocket and pulling out the old Element. Deryn did not look up, so he walked over to her and touched her fist, easing her fingers a bit before slipping the handle into them.

Deryn looked down at it and gasped. "What's this?"

"It's an old Element, created before either of us were old enough to train. Meaning, it doesn't have to be registered to work. My mom had it on her when she was killed."

"You kept it?"

"I hid it," said Xander. "I always knew I might need it one day. And, now, it's yours."

"Mine," she said slowly, carefully tracing the weapon with her free hand.

Deryn smiled and then, very unexpectedly, reached out and hugged Xander. He was a bit stunned for a moment, but eventually let his arms wrap around her.

"Is this weird?" she asked, but without making any attempt to let him go.

"Yes," he answered honestly. "But it all is, isn't it?"

He could feel her soft hair brushing against his cheek as her head bobbed. She pulled away and gave a coy smile. "Get some sleep, Ruby. You're no fun when you're grumpy."

"I'm always grumpy."

"Yes, I know." Deryn opened the door and slipped back out.

"Took you long enough," said Bronson without looking up from the plates he was garnishing on the set table. "I was afraid he might have murdered you or something."

The use of that word immediately wiped the smile off her face. *Murder*. "He would never," she said defensively.

"I was only joking," said Bronson. "So what did he want?"

"Just to give me something." Deryn took a seat at the table and put the Element down beside her.

"That's yours?" he asked, pointing at it.

Deryn smiled and nodded.

Bronson laughed. "Figures. Only Ruby could get an unregistered Element in the middle of this dark world. You definitely found the right Guardian to hide out with."

For the first time in two weeks, Deryn was starting to suspect that this was true.

After breakfast Bronson left, but not before promising to come back and visit her soon. When he was gone, Deryn made herself comfortable in her blanket on the couch, the book Xander had given her set comfortably in her lap. Every few minutes or so she would catch herself looking up and staring at Xander's door. It was several hours before he finally came out of it, a cigarette dangling from his lips, just waiting to be lit. He went to the balcony and motioned with his head for her to follow. She did just that.

CHAPTER FIFTEEN

Pretty much every day for the next week, Xander came home to find Bronson there with Deryn. Gay or not, he didn't like the amount of attention he was giving her.

Surely Quigley was starting to wonder why his roommate was never around anymore. But when he asked Bronson about it, all he said was, "Nah. He's been seeing this new broad for a couple of weeks now and spends most of his nights at her place. Curfew, you know?" And then he looked at Deryn and winked.

On this particular day, Xander walked in to find them both sitting on the couch, leaning in towards something that seemed to be talking on the coffee table.

"Evening, friend," said Bronson brightly.

"Ruby, look what Bronson got me at the Black Market." Deryn held up what he could now see was a small and very old radio. "Did you know the Outsiders use these to communicate? My dad used to broadcast messages to me and my brother when he was away exploring new territory."

"Careful, Deryn," said Bronson. "You don't want to go blabbing all of the Outsiders' secrets to the big, scary Guardian."

"I'm already fully aware of the Outsiders' use of radio broadcasts, but they never use them to say anything of importance. They know better," said Xander, taking off his shoes. "Did you steal my money to purchase that, too?" The Black Market was perhaps the only place that accepted real currency. Knowing the wristbands were coming, Xander had been storing it for years, and now it was quickly dwindling.

Deryn and Bronson looked at each other and laughed. "A woman needs her own underwear, mate. She shouldn't be forced to wear ones that belonged to your random bed buddies."

"*Thank you!*" said Deryn. "And if you're going to be angry at anyone for that, it should be me. I'm the one who gave him your money to get them for me."

"Yes, and I would still like to know how you knew where I kept it."

"Well, you didn't exactly make it difficult. Sock drawer, Ruby? Really? If you don't want me to take it then find a better hiding place."

Xander narrowed his eyes at her. "You're both getting too fucking comfortable here."

Deryn and Bronson looked at each other and laughed again.

"Don't worry. I bought it with my own money," said Bronson. "I *do* have some, you know?"

"Whatever." Xander groaned and headed for his room.

Deryn stood and followed him. "Ruby, I wanted to ask you something," she said, shutting the door behind her.

"Make it quick," he said, taking off his coat. "I'm supposed to meet Luka for a drink tonight."

"Well, I haven't had much of a chance to use my Element since you gave it to me, and I was hoping to get some practice with it."

"So practice." Xander dug through his drawers for some clean clothes.

"I mean *really* practice, Ruby. Like, for a war."

He stopped what he was doing and slowly looked over at her.

"You told me before that the only people who live in this building are you, Bronson and Quigley. So I had Bronson go and check to see if it has a basement. It does, and he says it's pretty well-sized. He cleared the space and says it will be perfect for -"

"No."

Deryn huffed. "Why not?"

"It's not safe for you to leave the apartment."

"But it's not like I'll be leaving the building. I'm not going to be staying here forever, Ruby. I need to prepare!"

"Just practice here."

"There's not enough space! I can't fire a gun in your damn living room! Ruby, please. Will you just look at it?"

Xander straightened up and crossed his arms. "Have you?"

"Have I what?"

"Have you looked at it?"

"No, of course not," she said. "I was waiting for you."

Xander knew instantly that she was telling the truth. It was impossible to miss lies in eyes like hers.

"Fine. I'll look."

Those same eyes immediately lit up. "Really?"

"I just said it, didn't I?"

"Yes. I just figured you would put up more of a fight."

"I can if you'd like."

"No, no! This is fine!" Deryn reopened the door. "Now?"

Xander followed her to the front of the apartment.

"He says he'll see it, Bronson!"

"Excellent," said Bronson, standing up and heading towards the door.

Xander went and put his shoes back on, then looked over at Deryn, who was watching him closely. "Is Quigley home?" he asked Bronson.

"No. He's out with that broad."

"Good." His eyes were still focused on Deryn. "You coming then?"

She stared blankly for a few seconds, then nodded. She went to the closet, pulled out her tattered boots and slipped them on. Bronson stared down at them in disapproval.

Xander opened the door and Bronson went out first. He then looked back at Deryn, who was staring hesitantly into the hallway.

"Do you want me to hold your fucking hand or something?"

Deryn bit her bottom lip. "I know you're being sarcastic but ..."

Xander held out his hand. She stared at it for a moment before slipping hers into it, suddenly feeling the urge to interlace their fingers for the first time.

Xander did not even flinch as she did this, squeezing her hand tightly and pulling her out the door. Bronson led the way to the basement and proudly showed them around the large space. It was dark and smelled a bit musty, but nothing that couldn't be fixed with a few air fresheners.

Bronson watched carefully as the two of them walked around the basement, noticing how close Deryn always stood to Xander and that their hands never once became unclasped.

"So what do you think?" asked Deryn once Xander had taken a good look around.

"I can understand why this might be a better place to practice, but I really don't feel comfortable with you coming down here without me."

"She'll be fine," said Bronson. "I'll look after her. And I'll make sure we only come down here when Quigley's not around."

Xander eyed him curiously. "I don't get you. Why are you willing to sacrifice so much of your free time for someone you don't even know?"

"Why are you?" retorted Bronson.

Xander said nothing, but he did finally let go of Deryn's hand.

"Look, Ruby, I want Saevus's rule to end just as much as you do. You know that. You're not the only one who hates him. You're just the only one who hates him while fucking working for him, not to mention housing refugees. Me wanting to help Deryn makes a hell of a lot more sense than you wanting to help her."

Xander narrowed his eyes and said, "Fine. If this is what you want, Leon, then I can't stop you now, can I? We are both fully aware that if I say no you'll just go behind my fucking back and do it anyway."

Deryn frowned. The thought had crossed her mind.

"Just don't be stupid about it."

"I won't."

"You better not," he said sternly. "Now, let's get the fuck out of here. I still have to change before I go out."

Xander reached for her. Deryn took his hand again, letting him lead her out of the basement and back up the stairs. Bronson followed closely behind them, still staring at their interlaced hands with a captivated skepticism.

Back in the apartment, Xander changed quickly and headed out the door without so much as a goodbye to Deryn. Bronson left at the same time, since he still had a late shift to get to. A side job he had cooking food at a bar.

"Hey, Ruby."

"What?" asked Xander, pulling out a cigarette and smoking it on his way down the stairs.

"Why haven't you gotten Deryn any clothes?"

"What?" he repeated, only with more irritation.

"Well, all she seems to have is pajamas and sweaters of yours. And don't even get me started on those remnants of what I assume were once shoes."

Xander grunted. "I don't really have time for this. Just tell me what you're getting at."

"It's not fucking physics."

"What isn't fucking phys -"

"Buy-her-some-clothes! And shoes while you're at it!" Bronson reached his front door and opened it. "Make her feel like a person again!" He stepped inside and slammed the door.

Xander stared at it, dumbfounded for a moment before continuing down the stairs. Somewhere between the second and first floor, he found himself getting angry and ended up hitting the wall. Why the hell did he never think of these things? It was so fucking obvious, but not once had it even crossed his mind to get her clothes.

"Fuck!" Xander shook out his hand. He would be feeling that in the morning.

When Xander got home later, he had his typical random

female guest with him. After a quick go on his floor - since they couldn't even make it to the bed before she was plunging onto him - he used his usual tricks to get her out the door.

Once that was done, he took a quick shower, grabbed his cigarettes and headed for Deryn's room. He walked right in.

"Balcony, Leon," he said, the same way he always did.

Only, this time he was not met with her usual rustling of sheets, but a whimper instead.

"Leon?"

Xander turned on the lights and stepped farther into the room. She was lying in the fetal position with the covers tangled around her. The small radio Bronson had given her was currently switched on and set on the nightstand.

"Leon, what's wrong?"

"Nothing," she said, shaking her head.

Xander went over and sat on the bed beside her. "Obviously you're lying."

"No, really, I'm fine. It's just ..." She looked at the radio and whimpered again. "The song."

"What?"

"I turned on the frequency my dad always used to broadcast messages to me and my brother, and there were voices. It was Talon and Dakota, and they spoke to me. They said my name and then they dedicated a song to me. Can you believe it?"

Actually, he could. Xander had, of course, listened to the various radio stations before. Orders from the president to see if the Resistance would ever reveal Godfrey Leon's location by accident. They never did. But there was one station that was always active. On a loop every hour, with the voices of Talon and Dakota speaking to the girl they loved and dedicating a song to her. Always the same one.

"It's an old song from our ancestors called *Blackbird*, and my favorite." She chuckled softly. "I've never appreciated its meaning so much before." With a heavy sigh, she looked at him and said, "I used to play it every night, and now it seems like they play it every hour. I know the message has to be old, but it was still so great to hear their voices."

Unsure of what to say, Xander reached down and stroked his fingers through her hair. More tears poured down Deryn's cheeks as she moved her hand so it was on top of his.

"Will you stay and listen with me? Just until their voices come on again."

Xander nodded. He moved so he was lying down beside her, pulled her body tightly against his, and hugged her from behind while static emitted from the radio.

And then the voices were there again, speaking to the girl they'd lost so many years ago.

"*Deryn, I love you,*" said the voice of Dakota, making her tremble in Xander's arms. "*I'll be waiting for you for as long as it takes, at our place.*"

Then the song began.

Then ended.

Then static.

But Xander didn't move. He knew the moment he lay down that he was not going to leave. He wanted to stay. And just knowing that was killing him inside.

CHAPTER SIXTEEN

"AHHH!"

The old woman screamed in agony as Finley Scout whipped her with the a blue streak of light coming from her Element, her body writhing in unnatural shapes while everyone watched, cold and detached.

"Where ..." Finley gulped. "Where was Deryn Leon going?"

"I know nothing!" shouted the old woman. "I admitted to giving her the knife, but that's all I did!"

Finley lowered her hand.

"And even if I did know, I would never tell you!" she hissed. "That poor girl deserved her freedom!"

"Hit her again, Ms. Scout," said a dark, male voice behind her.

"But I don't think she's lying -"

"I'm sorry, were you under the impression that someone asked you to think?" spat Elvira, stepping forward. "Do as your president says. Hit her again."

Finley glanced sideways at Xander, who was propped on a windowsill while Luka leaned against the wall beside him. He gave her a shallow nod.

Finley turned back to the woman, releasing a quiet sigh before whipping her again.

While the old woman thrashed and screamed on the floor, Elvira went up to her and slashed her with her knife. The same one she had taken from Kara Triggs all those years ago. "How do you like it, bitch? Can you imagine the pain my husband must have felt?"

"Is this all really necessary?" asked Luka in an almost bored voice. "She makes the best cottage pie. That's why my father and I always take her in. A world without it just seems so ... blah."

Xander glanced at him and successfully fought off an eye roll. Luka had a natural coldness about him that rivaled even Atticus's, and it was only getting worse with age. He hated to admit it, seeing as Luka was his oldest friend and all, but he really was a true Guardian. Not like him or Finley. She hated it, only ever becoming one to please her father.

"She's done evil," said President Saevus, turning his back on the old woman and walking towards the center of the room. "I show no compassion for criminals. You know this." He stopped. "Finish this, Elvie. We won't waste our time here a moment longer."

Elvira looked down at their next victim and smiled. "Xander, get over here."

Xander stood up from the windowsill and obeyed.

"Finish her," she demanded.

He began to take his Element out of its holster, but Elvira held out a hand to stop him.

"Not with that. With this." She slipped her knife into his hand. "Let her know what it feels like to have a knife rip her apart. And just a reminder," she said, falling to her knees and pulling the woman up to a seated position by her gray hair, "we will be doing this exact same thing to my precious cousin the moment we find her."

The old woman spat at her. Elvira flinched and smacked her hard across the face.

"Toxic bitch! You will regret trying to contaminate me!"

The woman sneered. "I regret nothing."

Xander's hand shook slightly as he tried hard not to let his mind wander to visions of Deryn being captured. He needed to make sure Elvira never got close enough to lay a hand on her.

The old woman's eyes moved to his trembling hand. He steadied it quickly.

Elvira stepped back and joined her father in the center of the room. Xander crouched beside the woman.

"Your soul ... it's different," she whispered, reaching out to grab his coat.

"What?" asked Xander, not moving quick enough to avoid her grasp.

Even in her weak state, she still lifted her head and met his gaze. Her hand came forward and gripped his chin.

"I read souls and yours is good." Her eyes stared through him, like she was entering the depths of his mind.

Xander pushed her off of him and fell back on his heels. When his eyes focused again, she was still sitting there. Only now she was smiling.

"It's alright," she said softly. "Do what you must. I'm not afraid."

Xander gulped. If only so many people weren't watching him, he could give her a tonic or something to take away the pain. But there was no way. The best he could do was make it as quick as possible.

Xander clenched his eyes shut and discreetly mouthed, "I'm sorry," before plunging the knife into her neck. The jugular vein. It only seemed appropriate.

"What the hell are you doing? Slice her fucking throat open!" shouted Elvira from behind him. But it was too late. The woman was gone, her death made quicker by her own will to leave this world.

"Well, I suppose it would be rude of me not to offer you all a piece of her very last cottage pie," said Luka with a frown. "Fucking waste."

"I'll pass," said Xander, walking over to Elvira and handing her back the knife.

"Me too," said Finley.

"Mmm ..." Elvira moaned, letting a tiny bit of blood drip on her finger and licking it off. "Don't you just relish in it, Xander?" She smiled wickedly as she smeared one side of the blood-covered knife on his cheek, and then flipped it and smeared the remaining side on the other.

"You're fucking twisted," said Xander, wiping his face. He turned to leave.

"I don't know what you see in him, Father. The boy is weak."

Xander stopped and tightened his fists. "Don't test me, Elvira."

"Xander, please, call me Elvie." Another infuriating smile. "I don't know why you keep him so close, Father. He's not -"

. In one swift movement, Xander had his Element out and aimed at her. He pricked his finger, turned on the wind, and sent her flying backwards with such force she smashed through a window and continued into the garden.

"Now, Xander, was that really necessary?" asked President Saevus, looking quite pleased.

"It always is," said Xander, putting his Element away. "I'm not weak and I will punish anyone who says otherwise. Never let her put a doubt in your mind about me. My loyalty is here."

"I know where your loyalty lies," said the president, displaying a faint smile that had always greatly disturbed Xander. "Now, young Voclain, about that cottage pie."

"It's this way," said Luka, taking one last glance at the old woman's still figure before leading the president out of the room.

Xander headed for the front door with Finley following closely at his heels. He had barely walked a block when he realized she was still behind him. "Did you want something, Finley?" he asked, turning around.

"I was just wondering what you're doing tonight."

"Going home to wipe this shit off me," he said, looking down at the blood that had already dried in his fingernails.

"And after?"

"I don't fucking know. Why?"

"I wanted to know if maybe you'd like come over. You know, spend the night? It's been a while since -"

"No."

Finley looked at him sadly. "Why not?"

"It's not a good idea."

"But I don't understand. Luka says you're with random girls all the time. Why will you go home with them but not me?"

"It's not personal."

And that was exactly how Xander liked it. Random meant it was never personal. It meant detachment, and detachment meant never caring.

Xander could care less about himself, and he could never get truly hurt as long as he felt that same way towards everyone else. He and Finley had history. They had dated off and on when they were teenagers. She was his first everything.

And then his mother died and it was all put in perspective. He had ended it with her for good shortly after. Sure, they had shared a few lonely nights since, but the deeper Xander fell into President Saevus's inner circle, the more he realized it was a bad idea.

"Goodnight, Finley," he said, and continued on his way home.

~

Deryn was lying in her bed with the radio on her stomach. Over the past week she had become accustomed to listening to it, flipping through the stations for any sign of life between the time *Blackbird* ended and Talon and Dakota's voices began. Just in case something important was to happen.

Upon hearing the front door slam, she put the radio on the nightstand, got up and walked out of her room. Xander's bedroom door slammed next. She went over and knocked.

"Ruby, are you alright?"

There was no answer.

Deryn slowly opened the door and poked her head into his bedroom. "Ruby?"

Nothing.

She stepped inside and saw a light coming from his bathroom. There was a weird mumbling just beyond it.

Against Deryn's better judgment, she walked on, stopping as she reached the doorway and gasping at what she saw.

Xander was inside at the sink, scrubbing vigorously at his hands. The water swirling around the bottom of the basin was blood-red. "Won't fucking come off ... Won't ... fucking ... come ... OFF!"

Deryn ran over. "Ruby, what happened? Are you alright?"

"No," he said, moving away from her. "Not fucking alright."

"Are you hurt?" she asked, grabbing his hand and turning it all around, looking for some sort of gash.

"Not mine."

"What?" Deryn's eyes shot up and met his. More blood was smeared on his cheeks.

"It's not fucking mine!" he said, pulling his hand away. "Get out of here, Leon!"

"Ruby, what -" She tried to grab his arm but he pushed her off again.

"Don't! I just want to get it off!" He rubbed his hands violently against a bar of soap. "But it won't ... Fucking. Come. Off!"

"Let me help you!" Deryn tried to grab the soap but he pulled it away from her.

"No! Get out! I don't want you to fucking see!"

"But I've already seen! Ruby, please -"

"No ... no ... no!" He pushed her away again, this time a little bit harder.

Deryn's eyes went wide as she stumbled backwards. "Don't push me!" she shouted, pushing him back.

Unprepared, Xander went flying into the wall and used it to slide to the floor. He brought his raw hands up to his eyes and cried into them.

With a sigh Deryn grabbed a washcloth, wet it under the running tap and lathered some soap into it. She turned off the water and took a seat beside him.

He glanced at her and she took this moment to grab his face and hold it still, using the washcloth to wipe it clean of blood.

"Why are you doing this?" he asked, keeping his eyes steadily fixed on her.

"I don't know. But you've helped me during my weak moments, haven't you?"

"I'm not weak -"

"It's alright to admit it. We all are sometimes."

Xander's eyes clenched shut. "Fine, I'm weak. I'm a fucking coward," he said, his voice cracking in agony. "Is that what you want to hear?"

"No," she said honestly. "I'd rather hear that this is Saevus's blood and the war against the Outsiders is over."

"It's not."

"I figured. Hands."

Xander held out his hands and let her use the washcloth to scrub them. "You'd hate me if you knew whose blood this is."

"Is it my dad's?"

"No."

"My brother's?"

"No."

"Dakota's? Or anyone else I was close to?"

"No."

"Then I don't hate you," she said, taking the time to really scrub underneath his fingernails. "You've done too much for me to dismiss you like that." She stopped scrubbing and looked at him. "So whose is it?"

Xander gulped and looked down at the hands she was still holding. He couldn't look at her as he said it. "That woman's. The one who gave you the knife."

"Oh," said Deryn softly. "You found her." She closed her eyes. Damn.

"Elvira put the pieces together. She tortured her, and then she made me do the dirty work. She always does. She's determined to break me."

"But she hasn't." Deryn began scrubbing again.

"Not yet," he said. "That woman ... she told me my soul was different. That she could read it and it was good." Xander felt Deryn's hands tremble in his. "She told me it was alright, and to do what I must."

Deryn stopped and put the washcloth down. Now she was looking at him with nothing to distract her. Just her and him. Xander tensed as he realized this.

"She looked me directly in the eye and told me it was alright to kill her, Leon. I don't know what I'm fucking supposed to do with that." He brought one of his hands back up to his eyes and wiped the tears that were still falling. "I just don't fucking know. What the fuck am I supposed to do with that? Does it make it okay?"

"No," she said in a dry voice.

"I know! I fucking know! But it's all I have! It's all I fucking have and I don't know what to do!"

"There's nothing you can do. She's already gone."

"She said she wasn't afraid," he went on. "She knew she was going to die and she wasn't afraid. But me ... every day I wake up fearing that it's my last. I could never not be afraid."

Xander wasn't looking, but he suddenly felt Deryn's hand slip into his. He stopped rubbing his eyes and turned to her. She looked at him without fear and smiled softly.

"I'm afraid, too."

They gazed at each other for a long time, neither flinching as they realized this was the closest they had ever gotten to really understanding one another. Deryn had been eager to get into Xander's head for a long time, and now she felt like she might actually be there.

He was afraid. Just like her. But, being born into a family of Guardians, he was forced down one path while she, being born an Outsider, was forced down another. Neither was easy, and both left their souls in tattered messes, even if they were good. Knowing that if you didn't murder someone you would lose your life ... there was no winning for a Guardian with a sense of right and wrong.

Deryn gave Xander's hand a squeeze.

Mesmerized by the faint upturn of her lips, Xander reached forward and touched her cheek. He cupped it in his palm and stroked it with his thumb, tracing the faint scars that still lingered there. Their eyes were still locked, neither of them breathing as their hearts started beating unbelievably fast. It had been years since either of their minds had felt so incredibly at ease.

Without another thought, Xander leaned forward and

delicately brushed his lips against hers. He kept his eyes open, staring deeply into her green irises as she slowly began to respond.

And then he was on her, holding her face between his hands as he kissed her zealously, slipping his tongue into her mouth only to be met with a matched enthusiasm.

Her hands clutched the sides of his sweater. Xander could tell she didn't know what she was doing, so he helped her by pulling it over his head. Then he took her hands and pressed them to his bare chest. He wanted to feel her. He wanted her to feel him.

Deryn gazed dazedly at his chest for a moment, stroking her hands across the perfect, porcelain skin that was untouched by sun, not stopping until her right hand was directly above his heart. Her fingers trembled as she felt the beating of it. It was so real. More real than anything she had ever felt before.

She looked at him and gulped.

Xander wrapped his arms around her waist and pulled her towards him, kissing her passionately as he lowered them to the floor.

"Ruby ..." he heard her moan as he moved his lips over to her ear, nibbling down her neck and towards her collarbone. His hands were tangled somewhere in her sweater, touching every inch of skin he could find. It felt so natural. So pure. So ...

"Fucking beautiful."

Xander didn't know how long he had wanted this, but these feelings of his weren't new. They had been there.

His lips moved back to hers and their tongues tangled once more. He brought up his left hand and stroked it through her hair.

"Ruby ..." she moaned again as he kissed down her jaw. She turned her head to the side to give him better access, opening her eyes for just a moment, but a moment was all she needed to come face-to-face with Saevus's crest imprinted on his left wristband. "Ruby!" she shouted suddenly. "Ruby, stop! Stop!"

Deryn pushed his chest. Xander pulled back, looking

confused. It was a moment before his eyes finally moved to his wrist, still resting beside her head.

Deryn was crying, her eyes closed tightly as she lay there trembling, her head turned in the opposite direction.

"Leon ..."

"Please, just stop," she said with a whimper.

Xander's eyes hardened. "I'm not fucking raping you."

Deryn's eyes shot back open. She turned and stared at his cold face. "I ... I know."

"Do you?" he said, stumbling to his feet. "Because it doesn't fucking look that way. I mean ... *Fuck*!"

Xander went into his bedroom and rummaged through his drawers for some clothes. After putting on a clean shirt, he noticed Deryn watching him from the doorway.

"Where are you going?" she asked as he pushed past her to get back in the bathroom.

"Finley invited me to stay over tonight," he said before turning on the sink and splashing his face several times. "And I'm taking her up on her offer."

Deryn's heart stopped at the sound of *her* name. "Ruby, I'm sorry, I just -"

"I really don't fucking care, Leon." Xander grabbed a towel and used it to dry his hands and face. "What happened just now ... that was a mistake. A mistake we will never make again. Do you understand?"

Deryn's bottom lip quivered as she slowly nodded yes.

"Good. Glad we're on the same page."

"But do you have to leave right now?"

"Yes."

"Why?"

"I don't feel like being alone right now, alright?" he snapped. "Simple as that."

He wasn't alone.

"But ... you want to be with *her*?" spat Deryn.

"Your enemies and mine are not the same, Leon. Never forget that."

Not wanting him to see her cry again, Deryn ran out of

there and to her own room, making sure to slam the door behind her.

Deryn stood against her door, listening as Xander left his room and then the apartment. There was a strange pang in her heart as she heard the front door shut that she didn't quite understand.

And then she realized. Maybe the problem was that she didn't want to be alone either. For five years she had been nothing but alone. But then, just now, lying on Xander's bathroom floor ... kissing him ... touching him ... holding him for those few moments ... that was the closest she had been to an actual connection with someone in a long time. And even though the ending was hardly ideal, she found herself craving more. More of *him*.

Lying on her bed, Deryn was suddenly aware that she wanted Xander to come back. Right now and without some random girl. Or, worse, Finley. Someone who she could not even think about without feeling the pain burning in the scars Finley had left behind. Back when her father had owned Deryn.

She sobbed into her pillow as her poor heart ached. Finley didn't deserve to be in Xander's arms. But she did. After the hell she had lived through, she certainly deserved some form of happiness. Even if it was just for a moment.

More than anything, Deryn wanted to hold him again. To touch him. To feel his lips pressed against hers. If only for the night, she didn't care.

What was happening to her? What was this horrible pain she was feeling?

"Not him," she whispered into her pillow. "Please, anyone but him. He has his eyes."

But they were not his eyes. They were a shade lighter with a gold ring around the pupil. And those eyes ... Xander's eyes had gazed at her tonight in a way that no man's ever had before.

"Not him," she repeated into the still of the night. Only, this time, she meant it differently. He was not him. Xander Ruby was not his father.

But that night when Deryn cried out from her horrible

nightmares, heavy with memories of Atticus's eyes, for the first time in a long time Xander's lighter ones were not there to wake her. And she hated that.

CHAPTER SEVENTEEN

Deryn let out a frustrated growl as she aimed her Element at Bronson, swiftly pressing a button for wind that sent him flying backwards at an incredible speed.

After a hard land on his ass, he jumped back to his feet. "The hell, Deryn? Calm down -"

She moved her fingers and pressed a button just below the wind, causing the earth to shake underneath the closest object, which was Bronson. He fell back on his ass.

"Okay, okay! You're the clear victor!"

Another button. Two strings of blue light shot out and wound tightly around his arms and legs.

"Deryn!" he screamed as he tried to stand again, which proved to be quite difficult with his ankles tied together. "Uncle! Uncle! Please, just take a breather and set me free!"

Deryn stared at him with hard, flaming eyes for a moment, weapon still pointed fervently. Then, in a quick flash, her eyes softened and her mouth fell. "Oh, god. Bronson, I'm sorry. I must've forgotten where I was for a moment."

"You don't say?"

Deryn didn't move.

"Uhh ... you gonna undo this now?" He lifted his tied hands.

"Oh! Right!" She aimed her Element and pressed the reverse button. The blue light disappeared. Bronson was just happy she had gotten so good at using that thing. One wrong button and he could be blown to oblivion.

"You sure you're alright?" he asked once he was free.

"Yes, fine."

"You've seemed off all week. The first few times we did this you never lost control."

"I know. I just ... I was trying to use that earth shaking button on the first move and when I missed I got frustrated."

"Is the problem with the Element?" he asked.

"No. It works alright," she said. "The problem is me. I forgot which one it was and hesitated. I'm having some trouble memorizing." She sighed. "My mind just isn't what it used to be."

"Why not?"

Deryn took a deep breath and shook her head. "No reason."

Bronson took several steps towards her. "Come on, Deryn. We've known each other for over three weeks now and I haven't told a soul about you. You trust me. I know you do. So don't you think it's time you told me where you've been all this time?"

Deryn cast her eyes to the floor. "I was in a horrible place, Bronson. Many horrible places. And the people who kept me there tortured me religiously. That's all you need to know."

Bronson stared at her straight-faced, trying hard not to show the pity he knew she hated. But it was impossible to hide it completely after a confession like that.

"Just answer one more thing for me," he said.

Deryn looked up and waited patiently.

"Ruby wasn't ... he was never involved in -"

"No, of course not," she said, cutting him off. "My mind's not that deluded. If he was then I definitely wouldn't be here."

"But I'm assuming his ... 'coworkers' ..." For lack of a better term.

"Ruby's not like them."

Bronson shrugged before looking down at the new brown boots she wore. "He gave you those, did he?"

Deryn followed his eyes and frowned. "I don't fucking know."

Bronson raised his eyebrows. He had never heard that sort

of language come out of her mouth before.

She held up one foot and took a good look at the boot. "When I went to the closet earlier my old ones were gone and these were in their place. I guess that means he gave them to me," she scoffed.

Bronson's face twisted in curiosity. "Are you two in a fight or something?"

"No." Deryn crinkled her nose. "I mean, when aren't we in a fight?"

"So you are then?"

"I don't know!" she shouted, throwing her arms up in frustration. "I haven't seen him in days. He comes home, goes straight to his room and then leaves! And he doesn't come back until the curfew's over, and then he just showers and leaves again! He doesn't even eat breakfast. I mean, he stopped fucking smoking, for god's sake!"

Deryn paused and took several deep breaths.

"It just seems odd, doesn't it? That three weeks ago he didn't even want to leave me alone for a night and now he's never here."

Ah. The reasons behind her recent animosity were slowly being revealed.

"Just because I have a way of defending myself now doesn't mean I'm any safer," she said, lifting the Element and giving it a shake. "Especially since I can barely fucking use it!"

"So he's avoiding you?" asked Bronson, fairly positive that he had figured out the real problem.

"I. Don't. Know!"

Bronson crossed his arms and eyed her curiously. "Deryn, you don't have feelings for Ruby, do you?"

"No! What do you think I am, a masochist?"

"I suppose not. Because that is what you would be, you know? No good could ever come from -"

"I *know*, Bronson. My mind may be damaged but I'm not an idiot. You have nothing to worry about," she said. "I have too much history with his family to ever look past it all." She sighed and gazed down at her Element. "Would you mind if I practiced a little more on you? I promise I won't lose control this time."

"Yes, of course. Just let me brace myself first," he said, spreading his legs apart and planting both feet firmly on the floor. "Okay, go."

Deryn raised her Element and pressed a button she had been tinkering with, for no other reason than to see if she remembered enough of her training to advance her weapon. She was quite pleased when Bronson fell back, laughing, feeling nothing more than some tickling. It may have been simple, but at least it was something.

~

Xander stood outside of a small store in the center of the Shopping District in Middle City. He stared dazedly at a robe on a mannequin in the display window. It was blue and fuzzy and completely practical in every way. Definitely not something he would encourage any woman to ever wear. But Deryn would love it. No matter how much he heated the apartment, she was still so damn cold all the time, and this seemed like the perfect solution.

He had just begun to take a step in the direction of the store's entrance when someone called his name. He stopped and turned, his face immediately dropping when he saw Finley running towards him.

"What are you doing here? Buying me a present?" she asked, leaning up to give him a kiss.

Xander made sure there was no response on his end. He knew going over to her place that one night was going to be a mistake, but he had done it anyway. Why he had done it he still didn't understand. He remembered spurting out some crap to Deryn about not wanting to be alone but, if that were true, he could have just stayed where he was. With her. She wouldn't have left him alone no matter how much of an ass he'd been.

In Xander's weak moment, he'd actually had the audacity to fondle a rape victim on his bathroom floor. One who had not touched another pair of lips willingly in over five years. Needless to say, he was more than a little embarrassed by the whole ordeal and had, perhaps, been avoiding her.

The avoidance was not all intentional, though. Finley had also been very persistent about wanting to come over to his apartment, probably in some attempt to reclaim possession over him, much like kissing him in public. So he had been going over to her place for the past few nights instead. *His* attempt to stop this from happening. The last thing he needed was for her to come knocking on his front door when he had a wanted criminal living in his guestroom.

"When have you ever known me to buy anyone gifts?"

"You bought me that bracelet for my birthday a while back."

"I was thirteen and trying to get my first tongue kiss. Worked well, from what I recall."

Finley smiled and leaned towards him again. Before she had a chance to make contact, Xander turned on his heel and walked in the opposite direction, glancing sideways at the robe that would just have to wait.

He heard Finley's hurried footsteps behind him and then she was grabbing onto his arm, clinging to him like an annoying barnacle as he walked through the streets of the Shopping District.

There was no particular reason why Xander was here today, other than to keep his eye open for something he might want to potentially buy Deryn. Bronson had been right before. He hadn't made an effort to consider her needs or make her feel like a person again. One book just wasn't going to do it after everything she'd been through. He knew this, especially since she still held on to that chocolate bar he'd given her because she didn't want to have even less than she already did.

He had gotten her boots the day before when he had run across a pair that seemed potentially her, but he hadn't even had the chance to give them to her properly before having to go running off to Finley's. Seeing her face when receiving them would have been nice.

Xander frowned.

"What's wrong?" asked Finley.

"Nothing," he said, quickly pulling his face back to his

signature scowl.

They were just passing the only bookstore that had actual physical books with pages when Xander caught sight of something familiar in the window. He stopped and looked at the copy of *Yesteryear* - a book on the history of the planet - sitting there, feeling more than a little surprised that it was out. The book had not been banned, like many others, but he was certain the president would not encourage anyone to read such material. He was very much devoted to the 'right now' in the planet's history, and certainly not the yesteryear. Still, Xander was not sure why it had made him stop.

"Yuck. That book always reminds me of Leon."

Xander turned to see Finley making a face as she stared at the same book. "Why?" he asked.

"Because she was in the same room as me at Eagle and read it almost every night, *and* during lunch. Soren took it away from her one day, saying if the president ever saw her reading it he would have her executed on the spot. Don't you remember?"

"No," he said honestly. Though something must have wedged in his mind. Why else would he have stopped?

"I guess the owner of this store didn't get the same warning." Finley paused. "Do you think if we put it on a giant mousetrap we could catch her?" She laughed.

"I don't fucking care," said Xander, walking away. He really wished Finley would leave him alone so he could go in there and buy that book.

The two of them had barely taken two steps when Xander noticed someone waving at him. He groaned as his father's friend Arron Von changed directions so he was heading straight for him, his daughter Lona smiling pleasantly on his arm. As always, she was picturesque in a fitted dress, her hair waving flawlessly as she tossed it over her shoulder. Her eyes glided ever-so-slightly to Finley's hold on Xander's arm - which only became tighter.

"Xander, my boy. It's been so long since I last saw you in the real world. How are you?"

"I am excellent, sir. And how are you and your lovely

daughter on this pleasant afternoon?"

Xander looked at Lona and winked. She beamed at him. He felt Finley's nails dig into his skin and tried hard not to react.

"Oh, fine. We were just picking up a few things. Lona will be moving to Middle City soon."

"Will you?" asked Xander.

He tried to look intrigued, but it was really hard to obtain when he had that horrible feeling in the pit of his stomach. There was only one reason a higher Guardian's child would ever leave Inner City. To offer their services to the president. Lona was a nice girl, barely eighteen. He very much doubted her soul would be able to take it. Even Finley had a hard time, and she was not pleasant at all.

"Yes, but I will not be officially moving here until the beginning of December. We've found my new apartment but my father wants to keep me at home for just a little bit longer." Lona looked at Arron and smiled dotingly.

"Well, you are my last little girl living at home."

There was a flash of sadness in Lona's eyes as she, undoubtedly, thought of her sister Odette. From what Xander understood, she had moved out shortly after turning eighteen and had rarely been heard from since. The rumor was that she was living somewhere in Outer City without a gasmask. He was pretty sure Finley kept in touch with her, since the two of them had been close, but, if she did, she didn't mention it now. Her focus still seemed to be on squeezing the life out of his arm.

"Perhaps when she's here, Xander, you will be kind enough to keep an eye on her for me. Maybe take her around, show her the ropes."

"I would be glad to." He really wouldn't. Xander was already taking care of one woman, and she was hard enough to handle.

"That would be wonderful," said Lona. "I'll make sure and contact you as soon as I'm settled." She glanced at Finley and smiled. "It looks like we are interrupting something. We won't burden you with our presence any longer. Father, perhaps it's time we head home. It looks like rain and I didn't bring a coat."

"Yes, dear," said Arron. "Xander, I was really hoping I

might trouble you with some questions before our Guardian meeting next week. Veli has been to see me recently, and he is greatly bothered by your lack of progress in the current investigation on the Leon girl."

Xander could not avoid an eye roll. Damn Deryn and her horribly addictive habits. "I'm sure he is. And, I suppose, he has some suggestions he would like you to pass on to me."

Arron smiled. "He simply does not understand why you haven't had your guards search every home for her. Clearly, the curfew has had no effect."

"I haven't done it because I don't believe she's here. But, if it will ease his troubled mind, I suppose I can waste everyone's time by doing just that. I'll have the president bring it up in our meeting. Anything to shut Veli up already."

Lona and Finley both laughed.

"Excellent. I will see you then. Come along, Lona."

"Goodbye, Xander," she said, completely ignoring Finley as her father pulled her away.

"Did you notice the way she looks at you?" asked Finley as soon as they were a fair enough distance away.

Of course he had. "No."

A clock chimed on a tower close by and Finley looked at it. "Crap. I was supposed to meet my dad ten minutes ago." She looked back at Xander. "Can I come over tonight? Maybe make you dinner."

"No."

She frowned. "Why not?"

"Why do you feel this incessant need to come over? What's wrong with your place?"

"Because I want to go to yours. *Please*. Just this once."

"No."

"I won't even ask to stay over. I know you hate that. Just let me come over for a little while."

Xander groaned.

"I swear, it's like you're hiding something in there. Have all your lies about having a wife manifested a real one, or something?"

Sort of, he thought. "Fine." Anything to shut her up. "But you better be long gone before the curfew."

She smiled as he caved. "I will."

"I mean it, Finley. You're not staying over."

Her smile vanished. "I know. You're such an ass, you know that?" Finally releasing his arm, she turned to leave. Calling over her shoulder, she said, "I'll see you at seven!"

With her gone, Xander turned back towards the bookstore and stared at the one he wanted in the window. He had just started to take a step towards the door when someone called, "Hey, Xander!"

"Fuck," he mumbled to himself. He turned to see Luka and Wyatt Firman walking towards him. So much for doing something nice today. Oh well. Deryn probably would have seen it as creepy, anyway.

CHAPTER EIGHTEEN

Xander did not make it back to his apartment until six-thirty. When he got there, Deryn was sitting on his couch with a cup of tea in her hand and *Complex Conundrums* on her lap. Her face was creased in thought as she read one of the more complicated riddles.

"Want to read it aloud?" he asked while hanging up his coat.

"No," she said coldly, without even so much as a glance at him.

Xander frowned as he walked over to her and handed her a paper bag. She took her eyes off the book and looked at it.

"What's that?"

"Dinner," he said. "Unfortunately, I'm going to need you to stay in your room tonight. Someone's coming over in thirty minutes and you can't be seen."

"Why on earth would you invite someone here?" she asked, finally looking at him. An hour here and there with one of his randoms she understood, but someone coming over during proper socializing hours? Unwise. Well ... really it was all unwise.

"I didn't. They invited themselves and I couldn't get out of it."

Deryn raised her eyebrows. "*You* couldn't get out of something? With that mouth of yours?"

Xander knew she was talking about his wit, but his mind couldn't help but drift to their moment together on the bathroom floor. He avoided her eyes and said, "I know.

Shocking."

Deryn stared at the bag in his hand for a moment longer. She frowned before taking it. "Fine, Ruby. I'll go and isolate myself for the night. What else is new?"

Xander sighed as she stood up and walked towards her room with the book, tea and food, and he couldn't help but think how pleasant she would look in that robe right now.

"Leon."

She turned as she reached her doorway.

"I don't have anything going on tomorrow. Would it be alright if I went down to the basement with you and helped you with your Element?"

Deryn stared at him with her mouth agape. He wasn't sure why she looked so surprised. He hadn't been that bad this last week, had he?

After several long seconds, Deryn blinked and smiled softly. "Sure, Ruby. But you're not going to be very impressed. The most progress I've made is adjusting one of the buttons to tickle my opponent."

"That's why you need me. I'm positive I'm a better teacher than fucking Bronson."

"He's a test dummy, Ruby, not a teacher." She chuckled and started to turn - "Oh!" - but quickly turned back. "And thank you for the boots."

Deryn smiled one last time before stepping into her room and shutting the door.

For a long moment, Xander just stood there, staring at her door. He would much rather be spending his evening on the balcony with her, but Finley was a persistent pain in his ass and he just needed to play this out until she finally took a hint. Besides, she wasn't the worst sex in the world.

Finley arrived at seven o'clock sharp. She had actually brought food to make him dinner and he was starting to get the dreaded feeling that she thought this was a date. After she cooked, Xander sat at the table and she opted to sit on his lap instead of in her own chair. She then proceeded to annoyingly feed him bites of the rancid tasting chicken she had cooked.

Xander chugged a bottle of whiskey he had brought out, knowing very well that he was going to need it.

As soon as he ate enough to satisfy her, she pulled him over to the couch, sat on the arm and positioned him between her legs. "Can we do it here tonight?" she asked, stretching up so she could nibble on his ear.

"No," he said sternly.

Finley pulled back and pouted. "Why not? We've had sex on your couch before."

"On my old one."

"Oh." She turned and glanced at it. "It looks the same."

"It's not."

It was. But looking at the spot Deryn so often occupied he knew he couldn't have sex there. It would be wrong to taint Deryn's spot like that.

"Just get on my fucking bed already, will you?"

"Whatever you say." She squealed as she ran to his bedroom.

Deryn's head shot up from her book. Until that moment, she had been making a point to ignore Xander and whoever it was he had out there, but she couldn't help but recognize that irritating shriek.

Standing up, she went over to the door and put her ear to it, but no sound was coming from the living room anymore. Then she looked at the wall separating her room from Xander's and gulped. She walked over to it and listened carefully.

"Come on, Xander. Lighten up. Seriously, what's with you tonight?"

"Just take off your clothes."

"You're not going to help me?"

"No. Fuck, Finley, you know I like to get straight to the point. Now, take off your clothes."

Deryn jumped back from the wall and nearly tripped on her own feet. She caught herself before her stumble could make too much noise, then she began hyperventilating as she realized what Xander had done. He had brought *her* here. Finley Scout.

Deryn couldn't breathe. She fell to her knees and gasped for air, urgently seeking some way to drown out the noise. But Xander was the only one capable of putting up a soundproof shield between their rooms.

"No," she mumbled to herself while still trying to catch her breath. "Not her."

Deryn's left side began to ache and she reached under her sweater, stroking her scarred flesh. This was the spot restricting her breathing. She cried as their noisy sex commenced, not even caring that her sobs were loud and hysterical. The two of them would be too distracted to notice anyway.

Finally able to get to her feet, Deryn grabbed her comforter off the bed and wrapped it around her. She went over to the window and sunk down beside it, keeping her ears close to the glass in hopes that the gentle sound of rain might distract her. It didn't.

Xander was having a hard time focusing as Finley bounced on top of him. He tried groping and sucking on her breasts - the one part of her he had always been quite fond of - to keep himself in the mood, but his mind kept wandering back to that damn robe. And it didn't help when his eyes drifted to his bathroom door. It had been only one week since he had been on top of Deryn in there, and Finley was the first girl he'd had in his room since.

Finley moaned his name as she pulled his head in for a sloppy kiss, forcing his eyes to leave their current place of interest.

Eager to get her lips off of his, Xander grabbed Finley by the waist and tossed her onto her back. He climbed on top of her and began thrusting vigorously, his gaze now focused on the wall in front of him. The one Deryn was behind.

His head was suddenly flooded with visions of her. Her full lips, her creamy skin, the rosy blush of her lightly freckled cheeks. And the sweet, sweet sound of his name slipping from her mouth as he trailed his tongue down her neck.

And then Xander was imagining her in that robe. That fucking robe which could hardly be considered sexy. He could see it wrapped around her, snuggled warmly against her skin.

Then he was moving towards her, slipping it off one shoulder and then the other, letting it drop to the floor. Her beautiful yet scarred body was a vision as he reached out and touched it, grabbed it, caressed it, pressed it against his. It *was* his, just like she was.

His.

His hands moved into that mess of mahogany-brown hair and pulled her head towards his. Kissing her. Touching her. Slamming her against the wall and fucking her. It was all there and he could taste it. The sweet tang of her mouth as she writhed around him, clutching him, clawing him, moaning his name between parts of their lips, holding him in a way no one ever had before. Because she needed him. She needed him and he wanted her. Just once. Just to taste.

Just to -

Thrust!

- fucking -

Thrust!

- taste!

"Xander!" screamed the woman beneath him as she came undone.

In three more thrusts Xander was finished. He bit down hard on his bottom lip to keep from screaming Deryn's name, tasting metal.

His body eased as he began to catch his breath. He was confused for a moment when he looked down and noticed that Finley was the one staring back at him. It was not who he had expected.

Xander rolled off of her, his eyes widening as he realized what he had just done. He had come while imagining he was having sex with Deryn.

"Fuck," he whispered to himself, suddenly feeling like he was going to vomit.

Finley moved so her head was resting on his chest. "Xander, that was ... wow. You've never fucked me like that before."

He looked down at her curiously.

"I mean, it's always good. You know it is. But *that* ... I don't know what *that* was but I can't wait for more."

She brought her hand down and began to stroke him, but Xander was quick to snatch her wrist and push her off.

"It's time to go, Finley."

"What?" she asked, sitting up. "But it's barely nine. Curfew doesn't start for another three hours."

"I don't care. I'm tired and I want to go to sleep."

"And you're sure I can't stay?"

"I said no, didn't I?" he yelled, rolling off the bed and getting to his feet. He headed for the bathroom. "I'm taking a shower." He had never felt so dirty before. "Be gone by the time I'm out." He slammed the door.

After a very long and necessary soak, Xander was happy to find that Finley had listened and left. He changed into some sweats and grabbed his cigarettes off the dresser.

On his way to the balcony, he glanced at Deryn's door. Even after that humiliating experience, he still had this strange urge to see her. As she was. Not the dirty image he had created in his own twisted mind. So he went over and let himself in.

"Leon?" Xander poked his head inside and looked around. The bed was bare of the comforter, but he found it in a strange bundle beside the window. "Leon, what the fuck are you doing?"

Silence.

"Leon?" Xander took a cautious step into the room. "Are you alright?"

Nothing.

Noticing the comforter fidget a little, Xander walked across the room and crouched down beside it. He reached his hand out and touched what he hoped was her shoulder. "Leon, what _"

Her body snapped and a hand shoved him back. "Don't touch me!" she shouted as he landed hard on his ass.

"Leon, what the fuck?" he said, grabbing the comforter and pulling it off of her head.

"I said don't touch me!" Deryn's hands flew out of it and she shoved him again, only much harder this time. "Stay the fuck away from me, Ruby!"

Crinkling his brow, Xander asked, "What the fuck is wrong with you?"

"With me? What the fuck is wrong with *me*? What the fuck is wrong with *you*?"

"What do you -"

"How could you bring her here?" shouted Deryn, her face bright crimson and soaked from what might have been an hour's worth of tears.

Xander's mouth dropped slightly. "Finley?"

"Who else would I be talking about?" Deryn pulled the comforter back over her head. "Get out."

"Look, Leon, I know the two of you never got along at Eagle, but aren't you being a bit dramatic?"

Her head popped back out. "Are you an idiot?" she asked, her face twisting in disgust. "I've been a slave! And she's a fucking Guardian!"

"Finley never owned you," said Xander, getting to his feet.

"No, but her father did!" stated Deryn, standing up with him while still clutching the comforter. "You said you kept track of me, Ruby! I have a hard time believing you didn't know he owned me several times!"

"I knew," said Xander, trying to recall exactly when that was. Maybe three years ago was the last time he took Deryn in. Before Finley was promoted from guard to Guardian, so she would have still been living at home.

"Yes, well, your fucking girlfriend didn't like all of the attention her precious father gave me when her mother was right there! So you know what she did? When he wasn't home, she came into the closet he kept me locked in and she tortured me!"

Xander stood frozen. He had never heard this before.

"But no, not just a lash or a cut! That was too easy for her, and she just thought she was so much cleverer than that! So you know what she did?"

Xander's throat grew raw as Deryn spoke. He shook his head weakly and said, "No," almost afraid to hear the answer.

Deryn let the comforter drop and lifted her sweater so Xander could get a good look at a large scar covering most of her right side. A large, indented scar that was still glossy pink and fresh looking, even though it was years later. Xander instinctually reached out to touch it, but Deryn pulled her sweater back down before he could.

"It's my biggest one. And it still hurts. It still fucking hurts me, Ruby! Finley thought if she scarred me then her father wouldn't want me, so she began experimenting with weaponry and developed a way to burn me and scar me with a wound that will never heal. And I have several smaller ones all over me. She wanted to get me everywhere but it wasn't fully developed yet, and it failed."

Deryn paused for a moment when she was unable to stop a whimper. She wiped her cheeks before looking back at Xander, a horrible, raging fire visible in her eyes. He didn't like it.

"And these." Deryn held out her wrists so Xander could get a good look at the dozens of marks all over them. "These deep ones here are from when her father used to tie me up so tight I couldn't even struggle. Back when I still tried!"

Xander really wanted to grab her right now. To take her in his arms and hug her, apologize for being such an idiot and promise to seek revenge. But he didn't do that. Instead, all he said was, "I didn't know."

"Of course you didn't! Because you never fucking asked! You should've asked, Ruby! You should've asked me before you brought a fucking Guardian here! You should've known! You should've fucking known better!" Deryn lunged forward and shoved him towards the door. "Get out!"

"Leon, I'm sor -"

"Get out!" she screamed, shoving him again and again until he was in the doorway.

Xander grabbed the sides of it and tried to brace himself. "Leon, stop! Please, just let me explain -"

"There is nothing for you to explain! I understand this is your apartment, and that you were *kind* enough to let me stay here! But this ... *this* is crossing the fucking line! Don't talk to me! Don't ever talk to me unless it's to say the curfew is over and security is limited enough for me to get the hell out of here! Understand?"

"Leon, please -"

"Get out, you selfish bastard!"

"No! I -"

Deryn grabbed her Element off of the dresser and pointed it at him, pressing the button for wind.

Xander went flying backwards and landed hard against the arm of the couch. As soon as his eyes focused, he looked at her door just in time to see it slam. He ran over and pulled at the knob but she had locked it.

"Leon!" he shouted while slamming his fist into the door. "I'm sorry, alright? I'm sorry!"

Xander knew he didn't say it much, but that was because he so rarely actually was. But this time he truly regretted what he had done, and he hated himself for giving into Finley. He didn't even want to sleep with her. It was all just a mistake. A horrible mistake.

Giving up on ever getting in, Xander went to his room and began throwing things around.

"Fuck! Fuck! Fuck!" he shouted as he punched the wall.

Xander hated this. He hated that he was so affected by a scar on someone else's body. *Her* body. The same one he had been imagining beneath him not even thirty minutes earlier. The urge to vomit was back.

He hurried to the bathroom and pulled the toilet seat up just in time to heave into it. When the sickness passed, he crawled over to the same wall he had sat against with her just last week.

What the hell was wrong with him? The whole fucking thing was really taking a toll on him and he didn't like it. For the first time in his life, he felt like he wasn't in control. *She* was.

"Leon," he whispered as he lay down on the cold tile. "Fucking bitch." Only, she wasn't, and he hated himself for even thinking it.

And then Xander's mind drifted back to that robe. For some reason, he really wanted her to have it, but there was no way he could go into a store like that without raising suspicion. It was only Finley who had seen him that day but what if it had been someone who might actually question why he was about to walk into a women's store?

And then he remembered. This was exactly what the fucker downstairs was for!

Getting to his feet, Xander ran into his bedroom and dug through his sock drawer for his extra money.

Once he had the cash, he ran out of his apartment, not even bothering to put on shoes.

Xander didn't stop until he got to the third floor, where he immediately began banging on Bronson's door. It was several moments before Quigley answered.

"Ruby, what the hell are you -"

"I need Bronson," he demanded.

Quigley raised his eyebrows. "Why?"

"We're fucking lovers, asshole. Now, get him out here!"

"Such language." Quigley smiled. "Hey, Bronson!" he called over his shoulder. "Your lover's here to see you!"

"My what?" asked Bronson, coming to the door. "Ruby? It's, like, five minutes to curfew. What do you -"

"I'll be quick," said Xander, stepping back so Bronson could come out.

The other two men eyed each other skeptically. They each shrugged and Bronson stepped into the hallway, shutting the door behind him. "You okay, Ruby?" he asked, taking in his disheveled appearance.

"I'm fine," he lied, "but I need you to do something for me."

"Go on," said Bronson, crossing his arms.

Xander pushed the money into his hand. "In the Shopping District there's this store. I don't know the name, but it's on the corner where that clock tower is. It's this women's store and there's this blue and fuzzy and completely ridiculous robe in the window."

"Uh-huh ..."

"And Leon needs it."

Bronson crinkled his brow. "Why?"

"She just does, alright?"

"Okay. So why can't you get it?"

"I tried! I fucking tried but every-fucking-where I go someone I know is there! I can't fucking get away from them!" Xander was fidgeting and pacing, clutching the sides of his head and pulling at his hair. It didn't even cross his mind that he probably looked insane.

"Ruby ... you're kind of freaking me out."

"Just get it, will you?"

"Okay," said Bronson. "Anything else?"

Xander thought about this. "A book. A real paper book in the bookstore right near there. *Yesteryear.* It's her favorite."

"Done," said Bronson, pocketing the money. "You sure you're alright? When I saw Deryn earlier I got the feeling the two of you were in a fight or something."

"We're not in a fight! Did she say we were in a fight?"

"No, but she seemed to think you were avoiding her."

"Why the fuck would I be avoiding her?" shouted Xander, his mind immediately returning to the bathroom floor.

"I don't know. You tell me."

"I'm not!"

Bronson paused and eyed him curiously. "Ruby, promise me you're not going to do something stupid."

"Of course I'm not going to do something stupid!" Again.

"So you're not ... you don't ... I mean, you and Deryn ..."

A loud siren sounded outside the building, informing everyone in the city that curfew was about to begin. "Get it, Bronson. Tomorrow."

Xander turned to leave.

"Ruby, wait," called Bronson. "I just wanted to warn you that there's supposed to be a thunderstorm tomorrow night."

Xander looked back at him and cocked an eyebrow. "So?"

"Well, I mean, I just thought you should know so you can prepare. Since Deryn's afraid of them and all."

Xander blinked.

"You didn't know?"

He blinked again.

Bronson rolled his eyes. Apparently, they were all picking up the habit. "The night you had me stay up there with her there was a thunderstorm. She got so freaked out that she ended up sleeping in the bathtub."

Oh. Well, that explained why her bed had not been slept in. Xander shouldn't have felt relief about that but, for some reason, he did.

"I'll take care of it."

Without another word, Xander ran back to his apartment, shutting the door and locking it with only seconds left until curfew. The punishment for being caught by a S.U.R.G.E. past midnight was always different, and Xander had no desire to find out whether it was imprisonment, torture or death on the menu tonight.

After staring at Deryn's door for several minutes, Xander went over and tried the knob again. Still locked. He sighed and headed to his room.

He looked at his bed for a long while before tearing off the sheets and stuffing them into his trashcan, ridding it of any signs of Finley. Luckily, he had another set.

"Fucking bitch," he muttered as he made the bed. And, this time, he meant it.

Climbing into bed, Xander closed his eyes and tried to sleep, but he found himself having to get up and vomit every time his mind drifted to inappropriate thoughts of Deryn.

"What is wrong with me?" he whispered while crouched over the toilet for the third time, his eyes drifting back to the spot where they had been together. He hated that spot. Only, he really didn't.

CHAPTER NINETEEN

The next morning, Xander was awoken by the sound of someone going through his desk in the living room, obviously not caring about the noise they were making. He rubbed his tired eyes for a moment before the events of the previous night came flooding back to him.

In a quick movement that was meant to be swifter than it was, Xander stumbled off of his bed and ran to the door. He threw it open just in time to witness Deryn's foot disappear into her bedroom. Her door slammed but he went to it anyway, aggressively pulling at the knob. Locked. Damn, she was quick.

"Seriously, Leon? This is fucking ridiculous! Get back out here, *now*!"

A weird surge entered through his hand. He looked at his desk and saw his portable computer was missing, something that didn't require a fingerprint to work as long as his wristband was in range, and he had mistakenly given her the password to it two weeks earlier. Somehow she had just hacked into his private settings and put a soundproof shield around her room. He would need to figure out some lie to tell whoever checked his daily activity report about that one.

Xander smacked the door in frustration before returning to his room and collapsing on the bed. He kept his door open, just in case she decided to come out and go to the kitchen, or something. She was definitely going to need the bathroom at least once.

Xander waited all day but Deryn never came back out. At

one point, he drifted into a daze. It was a moment before he realized his mind had immediately filled with images of her again, and they were hardly innocent. His eyes shot open and, as soon as he returned to full consciousness, he realized he was touching himself. He pulled his hand away quickly, feeling absolutely repulsed.

While he tried to tell himself the reason behind his repulsion was because she was an Outsider, he knew it wasn't true. It was because of everything she had been through. It seemed wrong to do those things to her without her consent, even if they were just in his head.

Of course, he could never ask her permission for such a thing. Xander would rather never have sex again than admit to these thoughts.

Sometime in the middle of the day, Xander's mindless staring at his ceiling was interrupted by someone banging on his front door. He got up to check, hoping it was Bronson with the robe and book for Deryn, but it wasn't. One look out the peephole and he saw that it was Finley. The loud cursing dropping from her mouth every few seconds was another surefire sign. She was angry. He didn't know why, but he didn't care either. There was no way he was letting her in. Even after Deryn was gone and out of his life forever, he would never allow her near him again. They were finished.

It was a good hour before she left, and Xander killed the time by smoking on his balcony. And then he killed more time out there. The sun had already long set when he started to wonder what he was doing. Why was he waiting around for Deryn? She clearly wasn't coming out. Not tonight, anyway.

"Fuck this."

Xander marched back inside. There was no reason for Deryn's actions to be affecting him so much, and he wasn't going to waste his time any longer.

After changing his clothes, Xander went to her door and knocked once more.

"Leon, if you can hear me I'm going out! I won't be back until late so come out, eat, use the bathroom, and then go back to your fucking cave before I return! I don't care!"

That sounded convincing enough.

Xander put on his coat and shoes, and left the apartment. He went to Luka's and dragged him out to his favorite bar for dinner and drinks. Lots and lots of drinks.

"Any particular reason you're chugging down that bottle of whiskey like it's the elixir of life?"

Xander slammed the bottle on the table and took a deep breath. "You act like me drinking heavily is rare, or something."

"You're right. It's not," said Luka. "But it's the way you're drinking. You pissed about something?"

"No!" he spat.

"You sure? Because it seems like you're pissed."

"I'm not!" He was. Why the hell wouldn't she come out of her room and talk to him? She was living there, for fuck's sake! Was she honestly planning to avoid him from now until the day she left?

Xander gulped as his mind suddenly became plagued by the idea of Deryn leaving. Would she take the robe with her when she left? The books? The boots? The fucking chocolate bar she still wouldn't eat?

Without thinking, Xander picked up the bottle again and chugged even more.

"Easy there, Xander," said Luka, reaching out and taking it from him. "Prime pickings for the night aren't even here yet. You can't be wasted off your ass before you even find some."

"I don't care. I don't feel like fucking some whore tonight."

Luka's eyebrows raised in surprise. "Really?"

"Really," he said, suddenly thinking of Deryn in that robe again. He grabbed the bottle back from Luka and chugged. "Got enough of that the last few nights with Finley. Can't even believe I went back down that road."

"Is that why she's looking at you like she wants to rip your dick off right now?"

Xander froze mid-sip. He put the bottle on the table and gulped down the remaining liquid. "What?"

"Finley. She's sitting over there." Luka motioned with his

head. "And she doesn't look very happy. What'd you do to her?"

"Nothing," said Xander. Yet.

Out of the corner of his eye, Xander could see Finley watching him. She had seemed pretty angry when she was banging on his door earlier and it appeared she hadn't calmed any. *Had* he done something to her? Other than the obvious of kicking her out, but it was hardly the first time. In fact, he even recalled kicking her out shortly after they lost their virginity to each other when they were fifteen. That was worse.

But the way she was looking at him now ... there was definitely something more.

Suddenly, Finley was out of her chair and on her way over to him. It appeared he was about to find out.

"You bastard!" she shouted, slamming something on the table. Xander looked down to see it was a piece of paper. "We've been part of each other's lives since we were kids and *this* is how you treat me? Fuck you, Xander!"

Xander eyed the paper curiously. Funny. He didn't remember sending her anything. "What the fuck are you talking about, Scout?"

"Scout? *Scout?* What, you can't even call me by my name anymore?"

"I am your superior, *Scout.* Outside of the bedroom, all you are is another subordinate. Accept it."

"Fuck you!" she repeated, storming away with tears in her eyes.

As soon as she was gone, Luka picked up the paper she had left behind. A few seconds later he was bursting out laughing. "Oh, shit! You *are* a bastard!"

Curiosity getting the better of him, Xander ripped the paper out of Luka's hands. He was instantly met with a short email she must have printed. But, instead of being typed out, someone had written the message, a feature rarely used on computers but still available for people who didn't like keyboards.

Scout,

While our last few nights together may have you starting to believe that something is rekindling between us, I would like to make it clear that these feelings are one-sided. I think you are a filthy whore and have little purpose beyond the sheets. You are an ugly person both inside and out and I have no intention of ever bedding you again.

Bedding? Who the fuck says ... Oh, shit!

I understand that since we are both Guardians we will be required to see each other from time to time, but that is the extent of our relationship. Never speak to me, never touch me, and never, EVER come to my place again!

Sincerely,

Xander Ruby

P.S. Your moaning sounds like a dying cat.

That little fucking ...

"Did you really write that?"

Xander's head popped up and he looked blankly at Luka. "What?"

"It doesn't really sound like you. Don't get me wrong, it definitely has a certain edge, but the language just seems ... dare I say proper? Until the end. That last line is fantastic! I used to hear her when you'd kick us out of our room at Eagle to have sex. You really hit it spot on."

Xander blinked.

"So did you write it?"

Xander blinked again. "Looks like it."

"Who knew you had such good penmanship? And here I thought it was a dying art." Luka laughed. "Dying," he repeated. "Like a cat."

Xander looked back at the email, his eyes still on it as he grabbed the bottle of whiskey and took several large gulps. She may have had access to his computer, but he had always made sure his email was locked.

"Hey, Xander! Snap back to reality!" shouted Luka, taking the bottle from him once again. "Seriously, th'fuck is wrong with you?"

"Nothing," said Xander, suddenly feeling furious as he crushed the paper in his hand. "I need to go." He stood up and stuffed it in his pocket.

"What? Go where?"

"Home. I need to take care of some shit." *Someone* in particular.

Luka watched with curiosity as his friend threw on his coat and sped out of the bar.

Xander couldn't let her get away with this! How had she done it? *Why* had she done it? Deryn had risked both of their lives by sending that email. What if Finley had seen right through those words? They were lucky she was an idiot.

Xander got back to his apartment in record time. On his way up the stairs he passed Bronson, who was smoking in the hallway. He stopped and stared at him, his eyes narrowing. *Him.*

"Hey, Ruby! I let myself into your place to drop off that - The fuck?"

Xander grabbed Bronson by the collar and slammed him into the closest wall. "I know it was you who helped her!"

"What are you talking about?"

"You're the only one who knows she's here! How the hell else could she of done it?"

Clearly, all logic had left Xander somewhere between those many chugs of whiskey, because it didn't even cross his mind that he had been in his apartment all day, and not once had Bronson and Deryn made contact. Not to mention that Bronson had just as much access to his email as she did, which was none. But rationality was not his top priority right now, so he punched him.

"Ah! What the hell you do that for?" shouted Bronson, clutching at the eye Xander had hit as he fell to his knees.

"Stay away from her!"

"What?"

"Stay. Away!"

And with that, Xander darted up the stairs again, the effect of the alcohol finally hitting his stomach somewhere between the fourth and fifth floor.

Still, he made it into his apartment and dashed towards the

toilet, glancing at her closed bedroom door as he went by. After a few rounds of vomiting, Xander got back up with as much vigor as before and marched out to the living room, where he banged on Deryn's door.

"Leon! Open the fucking door!" He kicked it when she didn't come.

"It's not locked!" she shouted from the other side.

Xander tried the knob and, sure enough, the door opened. He stormed inside. Deryn was sitting on the bed with the book of riddles in her lap and the radio playing on her nightstand. It was currently just static. She looked up as he entered, that fire in her eyes from yesterday slightly diminished but still burning deep. His gaze immediately fell upon her lips, as pink and plump as ever. He could just picture himself sucking that bottom one between his teeth.

"What do you want, Ruby?" she asked when he didn't immediately start talking.

Coming out of his daze, Xander tore the email out of his pocket and slammed it on the book in front of her. "What is this?"

Deryn lifted the piece of paper and unwrinkled it. "It looks like an email you sent from your account," she said.

"Only, I didn't. I didn't fucking send that, Leon, and you know it!"

Deryn smiled smugly before closely her book and putting it aside. "I don't know what you're -"

"How did you do it?"

Her sea-green eyes gazed up at him.

"Tell me how you fucking got into my email!"

"I hacked it," she said casually.

"You *hacked* it?"

"Yes, Ruby. Just like your damn soundproof shields this morning. I learned how to hack years ago during training from one of the instructors who saw potential in me. Email is one of the easiest things to break into, especially when you have your regular account saved on your computer."

"Are you insane?"

Deryn's face dropped. Xander didn't catch it.

"Do you have any idea what could've happened if someone found out it wasn't me who sent this? It doesn't even fucking sound like me!"

"You're right. I didn't put enough obscenities," she said, glancing down at the paper still clutched in her hands, her mind instantly going back to that word. *Insane.*

"Damn right you didn't! And you even handwrote it. I mean ... fuck! Do you want to get caught? Because, if you do, I can call the president right now and he can start planning both of our executions!"

Deryn let out a sound that was somewhere between a hiccup and a sob.

Xander froze. "What are you doing?"

"I'm not -" *Hiccup*! "- insane." Tears flooded and then poured from her eyes.

"What?"

"I'm not insane!" she repeated, glaring at him with her glossy, green pools. "How did you get this email, Ruby? I checked it not even five minutes ago and there was no response, and you had no reason to look in your sent folder."

"What?" he repeated.

"How *the fuck* did you get this email?" she shouted while getting to her feet. "When I curse does that make you *fucking* understand me better?"

"How *the fuck* do you think I got it? Finley gave it to me."

"So you went over there?"

Xander turned white. "What?"

"You went over there! You went over to her place to fuck her again after everything I told you!"

"No, I -"

"Don't lie to me!" shouted Deryn, crumpling up the paper and tossing it at him. "You don't even care! You don't even care that she tortured me!"

"Leon, no -"

Xander reached for her, but she pushed him away. "Don't touch me!"

His eyes and nostrils flared. He was getting really sick of this. "Fuck you, Leon!"

She looked up and the two of them locked eyes. Xander stepped forward so Deryn stepped back, not stopping until she hit the wall. Grabbing her wrists, Xander pinned her there.

"I did *not* go there," he spat, his breath hitting her in foul, heavy waves. "She found me when I was out with Luka. You understand? I wouldn't do that to you. What more do I have to do for you to trust me?"

Deryn squirmed. "How about not breathing on me after you vomit?"

Xander let go of her wrists and took a small step back, but he still rested his hands on the wall on either side of her, using it to brace himself while he breathed her in. That intoxicating natural floral scent of hers he had been missing all day.

"How much have you had to drink tonight, Ruby?" she asked, trying to look at his eyes.

"I don't know," he answered, avoiding those sad, sea-green irises he had become so accustomed to. Xander leaned forward and nuzzled into her hair. So soft. So incredibly soft. "Don't be angry with me," he whispered.

Deryn gulped as her body eased beneath him. "Please, Ruby ... please just go."

Xander nodded. He touched her hand with his before pulling away and turning, not looking back until he got to the door. Deryn had not moved.

"For what it's worth, Leon," he said, "you didn't have to write to her. It was already finished. I was wrong before. Your enemies and my enemies ... they're the same."

"Thank you," said Deryn weakly.

Xander shut the door behind him. He felt repulsive. For fucking Finley. For calling Deryn insane. For putting those tears in her eyes.

As soon as he got back to his room, he brushed his teeth and mouthwashed thoroughly before jumping in the shower. Even through the haze of the steam on the glass, his eyes kept drifting to that spot on the floor. He could still see himself there, lying on top of her while he caressed her skin, planting sweet kisses down her jaw and onto her neck.

Something inside of him was still forcing him to deny that he wanted her, but deep down he knew he did. He wanted her even before that moment. Possibly this went all the way back to that first night he had fallen asleep in her bed, when he awoke and found her hand in his. He hadn't admitted it then but he liked that feeling. Having her there. Needing him. Relying on him. He hated that he had to share her with Bronson. And that damn Dakota. He may not have been around physically, but he was never far from her mind.

But Deryn ... After everything she had been through she still seemed so innocent. So pure.

Even with her scars he could not find one flaw on her. And while her mind might have been damaged, she was still one of the most intelligent people he knew.

And her warmth. The beautiful warmth of her body the few times she'd let him hold her. He was picturing his arms around her now, running his hands along her hips, into her shirt, not stopping until he was caressing those perfect ... fucking ... breasts.

"Fuck!" shouted Xander as he came in the shower. He hadn't even realized he'd been jacking off. And to images of her. Again. "Fuck," he said more softly this time.

Xander looked back at the spot on the bathroom floor. The only solace he could find in any of this was that during those few moments he had her there, the feelings had not been his alone. She had kissed back. She had moaned his name. Until she saw that crest on his wristband she was into it.

Xander knew that deep down she wanted him too. Only, the hindrances in her mind were even worse than his. Xander was a Guardian, and Guardians had tortured and raped her for five years. No relationship in her future would ever be quite right. How could he even touch her without arousing those painful memories?

With a heavy sigh, Xander cleaned himself off and stepped out of the shower. He changed and climbed into bed, for the first time realizing how cold it was without someone there beside him.

CHAPTER TWENTY

Sometime in the middle of the night, Xander was awoken by thunder echoing through his room. A streak of lightning lit up the sky.

"Shit," he said as he remembered what Bronson had told him.

Not even a second later, footsteps stamped through the living room, followed by a slam of the bathroom door.

Xander got out of bed and left his room. Another round of thunder rattled his apartment, followed by a high-pitched squeal.

He opened the bathroom door and quietly said, "Leon?"

"Y-yeah?"

The room was dark, but another flash of lightning let him see that she was hidden underneath her comforter in the bathtub. He pressed a button on his right wristband that emitted a faint light.

Xander then went over to the tub and crouched down. He lifted the comforter just enough to see her wide and frightened eyes.

"Hey, Leon" he said softly. "You alright?"

Deryn nodded yes, but another loud burst of thunder and a high yip said otherwise.

"Bronson told me you're afraid of thunder. He said you slept in here the night he stayed over."

"I did," she said, her wide eyes darting around frantically.

"Have you always been afraid?"

She shook her head.

"Do you want to tell me about it?"

She shook her head again.

"I - Eek!" Another round of thunder.

Xander smiled. Those tiny sounds she was making were kind of adorable. Then he noticed the way her eyes were always on guard. He sighed.

"Do you want to go back to your room? I can put up a shield that will drown out the noise a bit."

Deryn shook her head frantically. "I don't want to move."

Xander nodded. He stood.

"Where are you going?" she asked, reaching out and grabbing his hand.

He looked at her. She was staring up at him pleadingly, looking almost as desperate as she had in that hallway at Eagle Center, right before his father dragged her away. He hated that look. "I'm just going to shut the door," he said.

Deryn reluctantly released his hand, and Xander walked to the door. Luckily, he was not gone long. When he came back, she instinctually moved so that he could climb into the tub with her. He leaned against the back of it before positioning her so she was nestled between his legs. Deryn wrapped the comforter around both of them and let herself sink into him.

"Maybe next time there's a thunderstorm you should make a point to run into *my* bathroom. The tub is at least twice this one's size."

"I'll try to remember that." There was a long moment of silence before Deryn said, "I'm sorry I wrote that email, but I thought I had the feature on to convert my written message to text. Even so, I know it was stupid but for some reason I just keep doing these reckless things. It's like my mind has lost all rationality."

"It was probably just the heat of the moment," justified Xander. "But maybe as you're doing these 'things', you should stop and ask yourself, 'what would the old Deryn Leon do?'"

Deryn chuckled softly. "That would certainly get me thinking. The old Deryn Leon was all about rationality."

Xander smiled into Deryn's hair and moved his arms so they were wrapped around her waist. When she moved her hands to rest on top of his, he could feel that she had something in her lap.

"What's that?" he asked.

"Oh." She pulled it out from underneath the comforter so he could see. "It's that book you had Bronson get. He came by and banged on my door earlier but I didn't answer. He said he was just dropping off some stuff you asked him to pick up for me and he left them on the desk."

Xander waited, but Deryn didn't say anything about the robe. She held up *Yesteryear* and, even in the dark, Xander could see her fingers tracing the cover.

"What made you choose this book for me?"

Xander put his chin on her shoulder and said, "It's your favorite, isn't it?"

He could feel Deryn tense in his arms. "How do you know that?"

"Well, you always had your nose in it at Eagle, didn't you?" He purposely neglected to mention that Finley was the one who had told him this. But it didn't matter. He was the one who stopped to look at it, somehow reminded of the vague memory of it all.

Glancing sideways, he could see the faint outline of a smile on her lips.

"Do you want to read some before we go to sleep?" he asked.

Deryn's hair brushed against him as she nodded.

Xander lifted his arm with the light higher. He rested it between Deryn and the tub, holding it out so she could see the pages. As Deryn began flipping through, he said, "Read one of the chapters about life before technology, will you? Preferably with castles. I always liked castles."

Deryn knitted her brow as she turned to look at him, their faces incredibly close. "You've read *Yesteryear*?"

"Of course I have," said Xander. "I've always been curious about life before our ancestors were forced underground, and this is just about the only book the president hasn't banned."

"Only because it's broad," she said. "There are many books we've found preserved that go into so much detail. I read this one for my fix but there are better ones out there."

"Maybe one day you'll be able to show them to me," he said, to both of their surprise.

Xander and Deryn didn't read for long. They only got about halfway through one chapter before they both drifted off to sleep. It was actually sort of peaceful in the bathroom, despite the unpleasant feeling from the curve of the porcelain pressing into Xander's back.

Sometime in the middle of the night, Xander awoke to the sound of a faint moan. He opened his eyes and realized he had been caressing Deryn in his sleep. One hand was gliding across her stomach on the inside of her sweater while the other was stroking the delicate area of skin just below the hem of her pajamas. The moan had come from her.

Deryn's head fell back against Xander's shoulder. He leaned towards her so that he could breathe in the aroma of her skin. Then he brushed his lips against her neck, his hand trailing down further until it reached the top of her underwear. And then his fingers stopped, fidgeting uncomfortably with the lace he was happy to find before removing his hand completely, settling both around her waist. Call him old fashioned, but he preferred his women to be conscious when he groped them.

After a gentle kiss on her temple, Xander leaned his head against hers and tried to fall back asleep.

"Ruby?" she whispered a short while later.

"Yeah."

"Would it be alright if I call you Xander?"

Xander smiled. "That would be fine, Leon." He kissed her cheek before closing his eyes and drifting off one final time.

~

The next morning, Xander was surprised to find himself alone in the tub. His neck was aching and stiff, and the rest of his body wasn't much better.

There was a rustling in the kitchen and he got up to

investigate. He left the bathroom and was more than happy to find Deryn mixing pancake batter while wearing her new robe. She smiled when she saw him.

"Morning, Xander. Do you want chocolate chips in your pancakes?" she asked, holding up a bag of them.

"Sure," he said, walking over to make the coffee. To his pleasant surprise, Deryn had already done that. He poured a cup and sat on the counter, watching closely as she worked flawlessly in the kitchen. That robe was even more appealing than he imagined. She looked so cozy in it and he was overcome with the strangest urge to snuggle her. Which was weird, considering he'd never had any desire to snuggle anyone before.

Xander's eyes then drifted down to her feet, clad in his too-large slippers. That would be next on his list.

A burst of thunder roared outside. Deryn shrieked and dropped the plate she was carrying. Xander was off of the counter in a flash and holding her in his arms. As it turned out, he had been right. The robe was delightful.

"I'm sorry," she said, looking down at the plate as she hugged her arms around his waist.

"It's replaceable," he said, nuzzling his nose in the top of her head. How did she always smell so damn good?

What Xander didn't realize was that Deryn was doing the same to him. He was always so spicy and fresh, and she took this moment to really breathe him in.

Thunder sounded again but Deryn didn't react this time. She was too caught up in the feeling of Xander's arms to even notice.

He stroked his hand through her hair and she looked up to find him gazing down at her. His lips parted slightly and hers did the same, both of them frozen as their eyes remained locked. Xander moved his hand from her hair to her cheek and slowly moved inward -

But their reverie was quickly interrupted by a knock on the door. Xander stared at it before reluctantly letting Deryn go. He walked over quietly and glanced out the peephole, sighing in relief when he saw it was only Bronson. And then he noticed his black eye.

"Shit." Xander slowly opened the door. "Morning, friend!" he said brightly as Bronson stepped inside. "Quite a shiner you got there. I'm sure the bastard who gave it to you was incredibly intoxicated and -"

Bronson swung hard and knocked Xander over with one solid hit to the jaw.

"Xander!" screamed Deryn as she ran over to help him. Bronson shut the door so she couldn't be seen.

"You. Fucking. Ass," said Bronson as he shook out his hand. "The two of you need to stop taking your damn frustration with each other out on me. I don't think my body can handle much more of this."

Deryn was doting over Xander on the floor for a moment, but then she glanced up and took a good look at Bronson. "What happened to your eye?"

"One guess," he said, looking scornfully at Xander.

"Oh." Deryn let go of Xander and stood back up. "I'm sorry, I didn't realize the hit was justified. Do you want pancakes?" she asked, heading back to the kitchen. "They're chocolate chip."

"Mmm, lovely," said Bronson, following her and making sure to knock Xander with his foot as he passed.

Xander groaned and stood back up. He should have known Bronson wouldn't take what he'd said the night before seriously. He supposed he should be grateful, since Bronson really did do a lot for them. But what terrible timing.

CHAPTER TWENTY-ONE

For the next couple of weeks, living with Deryn became very pleasant for Xander. The thunderstorms had stopped but she continued to ask him to sleep in her bed at night, which really gave him time to breathe in her intoxicating aroma.

She then woke up early every morning to make him these elaborate breakfasts. Bronson taught her most of it, since he was a sous chef at a popular restaurant on nights he wasn't cooking at the bar.

Deryn claimed she had never been much of a cook before, and Xander loved the way her face lit up every time she made something he was particularly fond of, like her spinach omelet. But his favorite part about her new morning routine was the robe she always cooked in, which was now accompanied by matching slippers he had sent Bronson back for.

By the end of the week, Deryn had already read through the entire volume of *Yesteryear* twice, so Xander asked her if there were any other books she might want, since she refused to read anything from a screen of any sort. Since she had no clue what sort of books they had in Utopia, she filled up an entire sheet of paper with different topics and - for fiction purposes - genres she enjoyed. Front and back.

It was definitely safe to say that Deryn Leon was getting back to normal.

"You still have to help me practice in the basement," she said as she sat on the floor of the living room, using the different tools and gadgets he had picked up for her to try and adjust her Element.

"So ... what? You want me to teach you Guardian tricks or something?" asked Xander.

"Well, it couldn't hurt. That way I can at least know what they might try on me."

"I'm not letting you run out of here unless there's a one-hundred percent chance no guard or Guardian will go after you, Leon."

"I know," she said. "I was referring more to the future. You know, like, a battle."

Xander froze. Of course he knew there would be more battles between the guards and the Resistance in the future. In fact, he was pretty certain they were overdue for one. But the thought of Deryn being caught up in the middle of it had never really crossed his mind before. When she left Utopia they would become enemies. Maybe they would even run into each other on the battlefield. Would she strike at him then? He already knew he would never strike at her. He did his best not to strike at any Outsiders. Though, sometimes, it was unavoidable.

"Fine, I'll teach you," he said. "There is one trick in particular I think you'd like. I'll need to make an adjustment to it for you, though."

"That's fine."

"We'll need Bronson for it, too. Test dummy, you know."

He winked and Deryn smiled. The two of them were just waiting for the day Bronson had enough of their shenanigans and retaliated. He, undoubtedly, had a few tricks up his own sleeve.

~

"Do I have to do this?" whined Bronson as Xander aimed Deryn's Element at him.

"You want her to learn, don't you?" said Xander. "Would you rather we sent our little fugitive out unprepared?"

"No," mumbled Bronson under his breath. "But it always fucking hurts."

"You won't feel a thing with this one."

Bronson let out a frustrated sigh before readying himself.

"Alright, Leon. Are you ready?"

Deryn nodded, her eyes focusing closely on her Element in Xander's hand.

She jumped as what looked like a streak of lightning shot out of the weapon and hit Bronson straight in the heart, making his eyes go wide and still as his entire body stiffened. He collapsed.

Deryn watched in awe. "He looks dead."

"Yes, that's the point," said Xander. "I designed it to look exactly like the shock of electricity that comes out and stops a person's heart. So any observers think that's exactly what happened."

She sucked in her lips and nervously asked, "What do you use it for?"

"When I first came up with it, the point was to catch members of the Resistance," he said. "I would use it on someone, and their comrades would leave the body behind, thinking they were dead. When they awoke, we would interrogate them."

Deryn shuddered. Xander didn't like it.

"But, lately, I only ever use it to stop other guards or Guardians from killing Resistance members first," he said defensively.

"How long does it last?" she asked, nudging Bronson's petrified body with her foot.

"Twenty minutes or so. But I can bring him back whenever." He walked up to Bronson, pointed the Element at him and pressed a button. Another streak of light came out and zapped him, making his body convulse.

Bronson popped up from the floor, gasping for air. He looked at Xander with the same wide eyes as before, struggling to breathe as he said, "What ... the ... fuck?"

"If you awake them too suddenly, it can be a bit unsettling," said Xander with a crooked grin. He handed Deryn her Element.

Deryn bit her bottom lip as she looked down at the button he had added. Even on this older model, there was always room for more. "I want to try."

Bronson moved his wide eyes to her as he continued to catch his breath. "Wha -"

"Alright but, this time, we should probably let him rest it out after. I'll show you how best to defend yourself against an attacker while he does."

Deryn nodded, and she and Xander moved back to the same spot as before. She readied her Element, but Bronson was still on the floor, clutching his heart. He held up a finger, letting them know it would just be one second, then he stood up and braced himself.

"Okay," he said with one last gasp for air.

Xander stood behind Deryn, running his hand down her arm until his fingertips were resting on top of hers. He positioned her hand correctly, adjusting it slightly so it was aimed directly at Bronson's heart.

"You need to make sure you hit him straight on. If not, even the real heart stopper will barely give him a shock," he said into her ear, feeling Deryn tremble beneath his touch. He smirked as he rubbed his other hand soothingly along her hip. "Ready?"

Bronson cocked his head, staring curiously at the way Xander was touching Deryn, and even more curiously at the way she was leaning into it. He was still stuck like that when Deryn pressed the button.

Bronson fell back, his head still in its tilted position. He would definitely be feeling that in twenty minutes.

CHAPTER TWENTY-TWO

Xander sat around the large, steel table with the other Guardians and President Saevus. They were in the president's home and a number of waves in chains were serving them a plethora of food. But Xander didn't want any of it. Not just because of the horrible conditions and torture their servers had to endure. Even now, Elvira was tugging on the chain around a young woman's neck, pulling her close and burning her with a candle from the table while she tried to pour wine without spilling a drop.

No, that was only a small part of why he didn't want to touch this food. The bigger part - and the more selfish one - was more focused on how Deryn was cooking her first dinner that night. She was excited and nervous, and he would be damned if he came home full.

"President, all I want to know is what exactly has this little shit done to recapture the toxic trash?" asked Veli.

Xander smirked. He hadn't even realized the conversation had become about him.

"Please do not use such tasteless language at my table, Veli."

"I apologize, President, but surely -"

"Xander, would you care to enlighten us with your reasoning behind your decision not to send guards out to search our citizens' homes?" asked President Saevus calmly.

"It's a waste of our fucking time," said Xander, smiling at Veli when it became clear that the president would not be criticizing his tasteless language.

"How so?" asked Veli.

"Because we gain nothing from recapturing Leon. You might want retribution but we have no use for her anymore. It's been years since they've tried to bargain for her, and months since they've sent anyone to retrieve her. Face it, Veli. They've given up. Or they will soon. We. Gain. Nothing."

"Speak for yourself," said Eamon Graham from across the table. He and Luka's father, Barath, exchanged grins.

It took everything Xander had to stop himself from lunging forward and beating them to a bloody pulp.

The president asked, "Soren, how do you feel about all of this?"

Everyone followed his eyes to the man at the far end of the table, alive and well, but his throat terribly scarred from the cut Deryn had given him and black veins that looked like tattoos climbing up his arms. His servant had fed him medicine to fight the poison only seconds before it would have killed him. And as for the stab wounds ... Unfortunately, they lived in an advanced society and he was saved pretty quickly.

Xander tried to hide the fire he felt as he stared at Soren. He had only just returned to Guardian duty a few days ago and Xander hated having to see his hideous face every day, even with that bit of satisfaction he felt every time he looked at Deryn's handiwork.

Soren's fists were clenched on the table, his knuckles turning white as his nails dug deep into the skin of his palm, obviously not over the humiliation of being mutilated by the Outsider he had fallen in sickening lust with. He looked up with weary eyes and shrugged without a word.

"Speak up, darling!" Elvira called to him. Even when he had been demoted to the other end of the table she still remained in the chair just beside her father. "Your president would like to know your opinion! Should we continue looking for your filthy pet, or are you fine with her slashing your throat open and, with that, obtaining her freedom?"

It was clear what *her* opinion was. Anything to overrule Xander.

"Do you think she's fucking that Trigger boy right now?" she asked with a cackle.

Soren leaned back in his chair and crossed his arms, glaring down the table at his wife. The two of them remained in a staring contest for a long moment before Soren moved his eyes to Xander. He wore a thick, silver band around his neck, having to press a button on it every time he wished to speak since his vocal chords had been maimed. He did that now. "Find her and let me deal with her. I do not want her returning to Trigger. *Ever.*"

"You do plan on killing her, darling, don't you?" asked Elvira with a wicked smile.

"In time," said Soren. "But first she must suffer."

He removed his hand from the band, which really looked more like a collar and not too different from the ones slaves wore. Xander felt great pleasure with that.

He then noticed several Guardians exchange grins. He knew what they were thinking. That they would all make Deryn suffer, but he would kill every last one of them before he ever let that happen. It repulsed him how many people in this room had had their way with her without her consent. He wished he could kill them all now. It would certainly be gratifying. But this was neither the time nor the place. Deryn would get her vengeance. Just not today.

"You heard the man, Xander," said Elvira. "Send out the search party."

Xander rolled his eyes and leaned back in his chair. "Waste of fucking time, but fine. You win, Veli." He scowled at the other man, determined to wipe that satisfied smirk off of his face. "But, when we don't find her, I want something in return."

The smirk vanished. Mission accomplished.

"What did you have in mind?" asked President Saevus.

"This is not the first time Veli has taken away my precious time. I'm sure we all recall that mission to Willow last year. We lost three guards and a Guardian when the Resistance bombarded us, and all because he wasn't smart enough to recognize a false fucking lead."

Everyone nodded in remembrance. Actually, the lead wasn't false, and Xander was the one who used his resources to get a message to the Resistance about the guards' arrival, but no one here knew that. No one anywhere did.

"If he's wrong again, I want him out. Not an execution. Just out." Really, he wanted an execution, but he was trying to be realistic.

Veli's eyes widened. "You little fucking shit. How dare you - "

"Done," said the president. "I suggest you work closely with Xander on this, Veli. Your future depends on it."

Veli looked at President Saevus, gulped and nodded. Then he moved his angry eyes back to Xander, keeping them focused on him for the remainder of the meeting.

"Now, onto our next order of business," said Elvira, looking at the hologram list in front of her. "Has no one heard from Dougal Fender yet?"

Keeping Veli's gaze, Xander grinned. It was all too fucking easy.

~

"So how does it look?" Deryn asked nervously as Bronson inspected the stew she had made.

"Looks good," he said, giving it a few stirs. He took out a spoonful and blew before stuffing it in his mouth. "Not bad. Of course, mine is better."

"I suspect it is," she said with a smile. "So it's really alright? I had this fear the meat would come out raw or something."

Bronson laughed. "You know it's not raw, Deryn. Stop being so insecure. It tastes great."

"I can't help it. I've never done anything like this before and I strive for perfection. Anything less and I'm dumping it down the drain."

"In that case, it's perfect," he said.

Deryn went over to the pot and took a bite. It wasn't perfect, but it was still pretty good. Maybe she could forgo the drain. "Do you think Xander will like it?"

Bronson's smile faded. "I'm sure he will," he said coldly, going back to his stirring. "When did you start calling Ruby by his first name?"

"Maybe three weeks ago," she answered nonchalantly. "Why?"

"Nothing. It's just ... is there any particular reason you no longer call him by his surname?"

"Of course there is."

"I guess I'll be blunt. *Why*, Deryn?"

She shrugged and checked on the vegetables she was steaming. "I have some history with his family, and I wanted to separate him from them."

"Why?"

"You ask that a lot."

"I know, I just ..." Bronson sighed heavily into the pot. "I'm concerned for you. I know Ruby's helped you out a lot. He's helped me, too. But people like us ... we can never forget who *he* is."

"Are you saying he's bad?" she asked, focusing very intently on her vegetables.

"No, of course not. We both know he isn't. But he certainly isn't good."

Deryn stared dazedly for a moment. "I know."

"And I don't want you to confuse your feelings for him. I don't know the extent of what you've been through, but I know no one's been kind to you in years and you should make sure you don't mistake gratitude with something else."

Deryn finally looked over at him and frowned. "I really wish you'd stop beating around the bush and just say -"

"Don't sleep with Ruby."

Deryn's eyes popped. "What?"

"Don't pretend you don't know what I'm talking about. For the past few weeks, let's say three of them, he's been angry and jealous, and I'm pretty sure he felt you up right in front of me in the basement last week."

"He was not feeling me up, Bronson. He was helping me."

"Okay, sure. The hand you were aiming I can understand.

But the hip? He was caressing it."

"He wasn't -"

"Ruby wants you, Deryn. Plain and simple. And from the looks of it you want him too."

Deryn blushed and looked away. "I don't. I know it's been a long time but when Dax and I parted we were together. It's not that I expected him to wait for me or anything, but I sort of hope he did. I wouldn't compromise that when I'm so close to getting him back."

"I hope that's true," said Bronson, putting the lid back on the pot. "Because I know the bastard you live with has a few tricks up his sleeve. Ruby's used to getting what he wants. Who knows what lengths he'll go to -"

"Xander would never do anything without my consent."

"But he might push."

"And I am fully capable of saying no. You don't have to worry about me. I can take care of myself."

"I'm sure you're right," he said, turning towards her. "I have to go, but I know your dinner is going to be great."

Bronson grabbed the back of Deryn's neck, kissing the top of her head affectionately before heading for the front door.

"Just be careful about what you serve for dessert."

Deryn rolled her eyes.

Bronson reached the door and opened it. "Oh! I almost forgot!" He turned back to her one last time and tossed her something from his pocket.

She smiled as she caught what she could now see was a small piece of chocolate.

"Happy Halloween. Next year, let's go trick-or-treating. Ancestor-style. I always thought it sounded fun."

Her heart suddenly feeling heavy, Deryn managed to maintain her smile and nodded. "That would be nice."

But she knew the chances of that happening were very slim. The war would have to be over, President Saevus would have to be defeated, and the world would have to somehow be restored to what it once was centuries ago. Nothing, even defeating the president and freeing the citizens of Utopia from its iron walls, could change all of that in a year. It was just not possible.

Bronson left then, forcing Deryn to be alone with her thoughts. While she had tried really hard to deny it before, a part of her was starting to wonder if she really did want Xander. Every line was fuzzy when it came to him, and this was one of the fuzziest. She wanted to believe that any feelings she might have were real, but how could she be sure? Xander was all she knew, all she'd been around for almost two months now. Other than Bronson, who hardly counted.

But these feelings she was having ... How could she trust them? Every day she found herself thinking less about Dakota and more about Xander. He was slowly taking over her mind and she didn't like it.

The night the two of them had spent in the bathtub together, Deryn had awoken to Xander touching her. He'd stopped, of course, the moment he realized what he was doing, but Deryn was not completely sure she had wanted him to stop. For the first time in years it had felt good to have someone touch her. Much like that feeling she got while kissing him on his bathroom floor.

It was hers. All of it.

Him. The moment. The feeling. The choice.

Especially the choice.

She had chosen not to stop him. Both times. Until she saw Saevus's crest on his wristband, and was reminded who he was. A Guardian. Favorite of President Saevus. Son of Atticus. A Ruby. He was all of these things and she hated it. But she didn't hate him. Not in the slightest.

Deryn gulped and sucked in her lips as she tried to fight back tears. She was sick of crying.

Grabbing a bottle of whiskey from one of the cabinets, Deryn went over to the couch and slumped down. She opened the bottle and drank straight from it, her eyes constantly drifting over to that photo on the bookcase. The one where she had covered Atticus.

This was his fault. She could look past Xander's

involvement with President Saevus and everyone else, but not him. Not his father whose blood he shared.

But there were differences. Differences she found herself becoming more and more aware of every day. There were his eyes, of course, and skin slightly tanner, a build slightly smaller, a more rounded nose and the faint traces of freckles sprinkled across it, despite never once having touched the sun. And she could never forget about that smile, with crooked lips and something else, something mischievous that let her know he was plotting. Always plotting. Now she smiled.

Atticus didn't have a smile like that. She was not even sure if he had one at all. If he did, she had certainly never seen it. If she was being honest, Xander really looked more like his mother.

But they shared blood ...

"I hate you," she whispered, staring at the blank piece of paper that covered a small spot on the photo. "I hate you," she said again. And then her eyes drifted to Xander, small and happy as he leaned into his mother, that same crooked smile lighting up his entire face. "I wish I hated you."

It would have made things easier if she did.

~

Xander watched curiously as some slave helped Soren into his coat. He remembered her. She was the one who had turned in the old woman, claiming someone from the slave trade van informed her of what she'd done. Her only request for this piece of information was that she be given to Soren permanently. The president had complied, forcing Soren to take her in, even after he said he didn't want her.

Still, she doted on him, even as he pushed her away, smacking her hard across the face and storming off. She only took a second to rub the wound before scurrying after him. Xander was mildly surprised. He had never seen Soren physically abuse a slave before. He had always been more interested in doing other things to them, but never hitting. The bruises on this slave's arms and face were a good indication that he had done both.

"Pathetic, isn't it?"

Xander looked over to see Luka standing beside him.

"Brainwashing the unwilling into the willing by doing something simple like *not* torturing them. And now look at her, being treated the same by him as all the others but, still, she begs to stay. I will never understand slaves."

"They're not all like that," said Xander. "That one is weak. But he never got any of the others. He never got Leon."

A pause.

"You know, you're the only one who ever calls her that. Leon."

Xander glanced sideways at him, noticing the faint hint of a smile on Luka's lips.

"Everyone else just calls her toxic trash or Outsider bitch or, on a good day, Godfrey Leon's daughter."

"You don't call her any of those things. And neither does Finley."

"I don't call her anything," said Luka. "I guess it's probably because we trained with her, so we see her as mildly more than just something belonging to her father. Do you really not believe we're going to find her, or is it something else?"

"What else, Luka?" asked Xander, staying composed but feeling slightly nervous about what his oldest friend was getting at.

"I was wondering if you might have a soft spot for her. That's what my father believes, anyway. I told him I didn't think so, but his theory is not without its valid arguments. You're being soft. We can all see it."

Xander took a deep breath. "I couldn't care less about Leon," he said. "But you're right. Since I knew her it does feel more personal. I don't care for Soren and I wish she was successful in disposing of him."

Luka glanced sideways at Xander, his mouth agape.

"But, from what I've heard, her mind's become completely fucked," continued Xander. "The Leon we knew would never stab someone in cold blood. She hated learning how to fight and only ever wanted to spend time in the engineering lab. She was not lethal. Her brain was her most prized possession and it's been destroyed. She's no more use to the Resistance than she is to us now. Executing her would be easy, but if we don't find her she has to live with the repercussions of what we did to her for the rest of her life. Is that not punishment enough?"

Luka closed his slacken jaw and knit his brow. "I never heard anything about her mind being fucked."

"Then you should ask Aila Parrish about Leon's stay with her just before her escape. That might put a few things in perspective for you."

Xander moved to walk away, but Luka quickly called him back.

"Th'fuck you going? It's Halloween, remember?"

"So?"

"*So*," said Luka dramatically, "we always go to the bar together on Halloween. You know, get sloshed, pick up a few women dressed up in those skimpy costumes. It's tradition. Wyatt's already out getting us a personal driver for the night so we don't have to take the tram."

"I don't feel like going out," said Xander, his mind instantly drifting to Deryn and the dinner she was making.

"Or sex?"

Xander shrugged his shoulders.

"*Again?*" said Luka, sounding absolutely appalled. "Seriously, Xander, what the hell is wrong with you?"

He shrugged again.

"You have a girlfriend or something?"

"What?" said Xander, turning to him with a look of disdain. "Of course not! I'm just sick of my fucking routine. Is that so unbelievable?"

"For anyone else, no. But you?"

Xander looked over and noticed Veli still sitting at the table with Aila, Eamon, Wenton and Arron. They were all watching him closely, obviously trying to listen in on their conversation. At least they had started out speaking softly.

Xander kept himself poised on the outside, but he was frowning deeply on the inside. It was unfortunate, but he had been given a part and he had to play it.

"Fine, Luka. I'll go. But I'm not staying for long. I'm tired and I want to get home."

And he really, *really* wanted to get home. He hated that being a Guardian meant Deryn's dinner would have to wait, but he needed to keep her safe and acting like his usual self was beyond necessary. Xander could not give anyone a reason to doubt him. If he did and his status dropped, the benefits he was given for being the president's favorite might be taken away, and his home would no longer be the safe haven he had made for Deryn. And, what more, he really was not ready for her to go yet.

"Glad you came to your senses," said Luka, putting a hand on Xander's shoulder. "Now, let's get the fuck out of here."

CHAPTER TWENTY-THREE

It was hell. The whole fucking night was hell.

All Xander wanted to do was get home, but *they* made it impossible. Not Luka or Wyatt. They were fine. In fact, Luka disappeared with some girl early in the evening and did not return for over an hour. And Xander was still stuck there when he did. Because of *them*. Veli, Eamon and Wenton. All there and watching Xander closely, eager to see some screw up or change in his personality that might be used against him, to get the president to question his loyalty.

But he would not give them the satisfaction.

Xander found a woman, a fairly attractive woman dressed in a modified version of a guard's uniform that showed off her long legs. She was completely enthralled by his Guardia wristband and the dark-blue trench coat he still wore, and she wanted to know all about being one. It was actually this band with the stupid crest on it that got so many women to come home with him. For anyone who lived in Middle or Inner City, it represented a sense of security. If these women could bed a Guardian and then keep him coming back for more, perhaps they could get him to protect them if need be. Little did they know, their cleverly devised plan was wasted on Xander Ruby. He had no interest in any of these women beyond one night.

Watching closely as the girl stroked the crest with her fingers, Xander couldn't help but find it curious how the one thing that made so many women desire him, beg for him even, was the same thing that made Deryn push him away. The one woman he actually wanted to have in his bed that night.

Thinking of Deryn sitting alone in his apartment with whatever dinner she had prepared made Xander sick. He stood up and pushed the girl off of his lap, which she had been straddling.

"You outta here, Ruby?" asked Luka as a different girl than the one he had disappeared with earlier sucked on his neck.

"I did my time," said Xander, taking a large swig from the bottle of whiskey on their table and then heading for the door.

He was practically outside before he realized the girl who had been so intrigued by his wristband was following him.

"What are you doing?" he asked when they got to the curb.

"I'm coming with you," she said, grabbing his arm and stretching up to kiss him.

Xander turned so she hit his jaw. "I'm not interested."

"I bet I could change your mind." She moved her hand downwards and began rubbing at the cloth of his coat, just over his groin.

He pulled back. "I don't know what you think you're going to get out of this, but you should know that no one gets more than one turn in my bed."

The girl moved towards him again and cupped him in her hand. "I'm not looking for more than one turn," she whispered seductively in his ear.

"Get the fuck off -"

"Evening, Xander. Leaving so soon?"

Xander glanced over her head to see Veli standing there with his own girl clinging to his arm. He had seen her with him before. A girlfriend of sorts.

Xander's nostrils flared as he stared back at him and nodded. "I have other plans for my night." *With your brother's attempted murderer and object of lust,* he thought. For some reason he found great satisfaction in that.

"Yes, I can see," said Veli, his eyes drifting to the girl still clinging to Xander. "Would the two of you like a ride?"

Right on cue, a long hover-car turned onto the street and stopped in front of them.

"No, we're -"

"Oh, yes, please!" said the girl excitedly as she pulled an unprepared Xander into the back of the car with her. He tried to jump out, but Veli was behind him now, prodding him in.

Once inside, Xander could see that they were not alone. Soren was sitting in the far corner, his chin on his palm as he stared dazedly out the window. His slave was sitting next to him with her hand stroking his thigh.

While Xander stared, the girl he was with pulled him into a seat across from them.

"Thanks for this," she said as soon as Veli was in and sitting beside his brother's slave, pulling his lady friend onto his lap. Xander noticed her slip her hands beneath his coat and then heard the sound of pants being undone. His face recoiled in disgust.

Veli signaled the driver and the car drove off.

"Is there any particular reason for your generosity, Veli?" asked Xander. "I have a hard time believing, after our encounter earlier, that you have any interest in doing me a favor."

"You're right. I don't," said Veli, his eyes rolling back in his head as the girl on his lap so obviously stroked him. "You and I are long overdue for a talk, young Ruby."

"You will not speak down to me, Veli. I am your superior and you will call me Ruby alone or nothing at all. You understand?"

Veli smirked. "I don't want to fight with you, Xander."

"Ruby!"

"Fine. *Ruby*. I'm not sure when this animosity between us began but -"

"Three years ago. You filed a petition to have my father executed for his failure during a raid on the Outsider villages. I'm sure you recall."

"I would have an easier time believing that's where this all began if you actually liked your father."

"You're right, I hate the bastard. But he's still my father and, thanks to *his* wife -" He pointed at Soren, who finally looked at him. "- he's the only parent I have left."

"Yes, that would truly be a shame if you lost your *only* parent," said Veli.

Xander narrowed his eyes. "Are you threatening -"

"Of course I am! You've left me no choice."

"You've had plenty of choices -"

"Shut your mouth, you annoying fuck!"

Xander raised his eyebrows.

"I've worked too hard to get in the president's good graces to be pushed out by a child on a power trip!"

"Child? What are you, five years older than me?"

The car pulled to a halt and Xander looked out the window to see his building.

Veli stretched across the car while he wasn't looking and swiftly pulled his keys from his pocket. He dangled them in front of the girl who was still on Xander's arm.

"I'm sorry, my dear, but I must request a bit more of your male companion's time. Top floor, only apartment there. These keys will get you in and he'll stop any alarms from sounding. I'll make sure to send him up shortly."

The girl happily took the keys and jumped out of the car. Xander tried to follow her but Veli grabbed him and tossed him back in, causing him to hit his head hard against the side window.

His wristband vibrated, letting him know the girl had made it into the building. He shut off the alarm before it could sound.

"These threats don't go over well with me, Veli. All you're doing is making me angrier," he spat. "If you're not careful, I just might -"

Veli pushed his lady friend off of his lap and set her on her knees in front of him. He threw his long coat over her head while simultaneously pulling something out of his pocket.

"What's that?" asked Xander, eyeing what appeared to be a small computer chip, no larger than a thumbnail. The right size to be easily installed in a wristband.

"Several of us have been talking and we all agree that it's

time for your reign to end."

"Is that so?" Xander smirked.

"Yes, it is, and we've also agreed that sacrifices must be made to keep you under control."

"I don't understand what that has to do with -"

"I'm sure you recall when the president ordered his Weaponry Development Team to create a mind control software that could be implanted into his citizens' wristbands a few years back."

Xander went white as he stared at the small chip between Veli's fingers. He gave a shallow nod.

"Well, they succeeded, but there are still a few bugs to figure out so I've asked the head of the project not to inform the president until it's absolutely perfect." Veli looked into Xander's eyes and smirked. "But it *does* work, and several Guardians have samples, all of which are very unsatisfied with how you've been running things. Including Eamon, who just happens to live very close to your beloved father and could easily install it while he sleeps."

Xander furrowed his brow.

"Like I said, you've left me no choice but to threaten you," said Veli. "I've compiled a list of everyone dear to you and I plan to dispose of them all if necessary. One by one. A short call to Eamon and the first one's gone. That's your father, who just might tragically fall out of a third floor window or something. If we're feeling generous, at least. I personally would like to make that piece of shit's death much slower and much more painful." He grinned wickedly. "Second is Luka. His father's already agreed to take care of it. Anything for the greater good. Third. Wyatt's father's agreed to the same thing. Need I go on?"

"You're bluffing," snarled Xander.

"Am I? Well, what do you say, brother?" He turned to Soren. "Shall we test it out then?" Veli pressed a button on his wristband. "Call Eamon."

It rang. Xander's heart beat fast.

It rang again. Then there was a click. "Is it time -"

"Stop!" shouted Xander, holding out his hand.

Veli smiled triumphantly and said, "Never mind, Eamon." He pressed the same button and the call ended.

"You certainly went to a lot of trouble," said Xander. "Dare I ask what it is you want?"

Veli looked at his brother and motioned for him to continue. Soren pressed the button on his collar and said, "Find the Leon girl. She needs to be punished for the embarrassment she has caused our family."

"I believe that embarrassment is on you," quipped Xander. "You both know as well as I do that even if we go door to fucking door there's practically no chance we're going to find her."

"Then torture everyone until you find someone who knows where she's gone!" shouted Soren, his face turning crimson. "I don't care how you do it, just fucking find her!"

Soren released the button and rubbed his throat. He had strained it with the yelling. His slave gave it a kiss and, for once, he let her try to please him.

"You're both fucking pathetic," said Xander, moving for the exit and having to step over the girl under Veli's coat to get out the door. He slammed it behind him and watched as the hover-car rode off into the night. "Fucking bastards."

Right then his wristband buzzed, signaling the alarm being triggered in his apartment. He turned it off before it could sound and hurried inside.

~

Deryn was sitting in her room, still holding the rapidly decreasing bottle of whiskey as she flipped channels on the radio. Xander hadn't come home and she just knew something had happened to him. She began to hyperventilate as the static continued, crying as she took another sip out of the bottle. She didn't know what she was waiting for. Perhaps some notification that there had been a battle and Guardians had been killed. Of course, they would never say the names. No members of the Resistance cared about such things, but maybe it would give her some idea, some indication that he was not all right.

What if he was dead? What would she do? Leave? Hide underground or in Bronson's bedroom and act like none of this ever happened? She could not just forget about Xander like that. He deserved more.

Finally, Deryn heard the front door open. She jumped off of her bed and ran for it, but stopped when she realized the footsteps were lighter than usual.

Deryn brought her ear to the door and listened as someone walked leisurely through the apartment, pausing every few moments to - what she assumed - look at something. And then they started humming. A high-pitched, sweet sounding, female hum.

Deryn went red as something inside of her burned.

The woman walked through the apartment, and opened a door that Deryn immediately recognized as the bathroom. She shut it just as quickly before heading to the next one, which was Xander's room.

There was a loud, "Oh," followed by a fit of giggles. Deryn listened as the woman's footsteps headed inside.

She stepped back from her door, nostrils flaring as she realized what was going on. The reason Xander had not come home was because he was out picking up some ... some *hussy*! He had her worried sick for nothing! And, more importantly, he had missed her dinner! Something she had worked really hard on for him!

Deryn froze.

For *him*? When had her wanting to make dinner for the first time become about *him*?

The front door opened again, the familiar sounds of Xander kicking off his shoes and hanging his coat entering her ears.

Then the sound of him walking across the apartment to his bedroom set a fire off in Deryn that she had not felt in years. Oh, he was not going to get away with this! Bringing some hussy here tonight!

She ran over to a bag she'd been storing everything Bronson picked up for her in, and dug through it, completely ignoring the voices coming from the other side of the wall. It was time for her to put Xander *fucking* Ruby in his place!

~

Noticing his bedroom door was open, Xander went right to it after kicking off his shoes and hanging his coat. He was glad to see there was no bloodshed, and that Deryn had most likely been in her room when this pest who would not go away came up here.

"Ah!" Xander screamed as he found her lying half-naked on his bed.

"Is your business all finished?" she asked, not the least bit fazed by his reaction.

"What the fuck are you doing?" he asked, picking up her clothes from the floor and tossing them at her. "How many times do I have to say I'm not interested?"

"What? But you brought me here!" she said, throwing her clothes back down.

It was only then that Xander noticed her shoes by his dresser. He went and picked them up. "Did you wear these across my white fucking carpet?" he yelled, his eyes bulging out of his skull.

"They're just shoes," she said, climbing off the bed and taking them from him. She threw them beside her clothes. "Now, I believe you are wearing far too much clothing." She reached out and pulled at his shirt, but Xander pulled back.

The two of them were in the midst of this wrestling match, and Xander was just about to pick her up and carry her outside of his apartment in nothing but her underwear, when they heard the door to the guestroom click open. They both stopped.

"What the hell is this?" called a voice Xander knew far too well.

He turned to see someone who looked an awful lot like Deryn, only her hair was honey-blonde, for some reason, and her eyes were blue. His forehead crinkled.

"Who are you?" asked his guest, who had finally let go of his shirt.

"Who am I?" said Deryn. "I am his wife!"

Xander cocked his head. Funny. He didn't remember having a wife.

"Who the fuck are you?" his 'wife' demanded, looking heatedly at the other girl.

"Oh. I'm sorry," she said, holding her hands up defensively. "I didn't realize you were married."

"Well, he is! Now, get out!"

The girl paused, putting her hands on her hips as she stared Deryn up and down. "I don't suppose you two would be up for a three-way?"

Xander raised his eyebrows. Well, that sounded intriguing. He looked at his 'wife' just as she rolled her eyes.

"Get out!" she demanded again, pointing at the door.

"Okay, okay." The girl grabbed her clothes and shoes, and headed for the front door. She put everything on quickly and gave the weird couple one last scan before exiting.

"Leon?" said Xander as soon as she was gone.

Deryn crossed her arms in a fashion he had become quite accustomed to. "Obviously."

"What are you doing?" he shouted. "And where did you get that fucking hair?" He grabbed at the honey-blonde locks, easily pulling them off of her head. A wig.

"I asked Bronson to get it for me," she said, grabbing it back. "So I can change my appearance quickly, if necessary."

"And the eyes?"

"Drops that change the color. It lasts an hour."

"And why the fuck are you using this shit now?" he demanded. "Why'd you do that? Saying you were my wife!"

"Because you should not be rewarded for worrying me!"

"What?"

"You didn't come home, Xander! You didn't come home and I was worried! Not once in all of my time here have you not come home when you said you were going to be here! What was I supposed to think?"

"I worried you?" repeated Xander, in a bit of a daze as he searched the strange blue eyes for Deryn.

"Of course you did! I thought you were dead!"

"I ... I'm sor -"

"But then I come to find that you're perfectly fine, *and* you sent some hussy up here to prepare herself for you! What if I'd been in the living room?"

"I'm not the one who sent her -"

"I mean it's all so ridiculous!"

"Leon."

"You're nothing but a selfish, inconsiderate, spoiled, ass!" shouted Deryn, turning bright-red.

Xander could feel his heart begin to slow. Those were harsh words coming from her wholesome mouth, and he hated that they were directed at him.

Staring into her flaming, unfamiliar eyes, Xander took a deep breath. "Sounds to me like you're jealous." He immediately knew that this was the wrong thing to say.

Deryn's eyebrows rose to her hairline. "What?"

"You heard me," he said. The words were already out. He might as well stand by them. "If you were paying any fucking attention then you'd know that I was trying to get her out, but you were too distracted putting on that getup. If you were that worried about me then shouldn't you just be happy to find out I'm alive?"

"I ... I was," said Deryn, blushing.

"Then admit it."

"Admit what?"

"Admit that this non-Deryn, rash thing you did is because you're jealous. Just like the last thing."

"The last -"

"The fucking email, Leon! The email you sent Finley! We both know that was not just about your scars!"

"Well, what else could it possibly be about?" she said, standing up straight and holding his firm gaze.

"You *know*! You fucking know! Just admit it!"

"No."

"Admit it!" he repeated louder.

"No!" she repeated, matching his tone. "I'm not jealous,

Xander! I love Dax! And you and me ... this whole twisted arrangement is just a matter of convenience! It doesn't mean anything!"

"Really?" said Xander, crossing his arms. "So me sleeping in your bed every night, that means nothing?"

"Yes."

"And the night I held you during the thunderstorm. Also nothing?"

"That's right."

"And that kiss in my bathroom. It really meant nothing to you?"

Deryn finally tore her eyes away from his, letting them fall to the floor. "You said yourself that you feed off of vulnerable girls, Xander. And that night we were both vulnerable."

Xander took a step back as he felt like someone had punched a hole in his chest. Deryn had his heart in the palm of her hand and she was literally squeezing the life out of it. "You're saying I took advantage of you," he said in a strained voice.

"No," she said quickly. "I'm saying we took advantage of each other. We're both lonely and we're stuck here. Together." She gulped. "In these close quarters it's easy to misconstrue feelings. We just need to learn to recognize them for what they are."

"And what's that?"

Deryn finally found the courage to stare back at him, her borrowed eyes looking sad but firm. "Nothing. They're nothing, Xander."

Xander quickly turned away from her. His nails dug into his arms as he tried to fight off any visible signs of what he was feeling. The heart she had been squeezing was now crushed. Nothing but dust in the palm of her hand.

"Fine," he said through gritted teeth. "If that's how you feel then you won't mind if I go out and find someone who actually wants my company."

Keeping his eyes cast to the floor, Xander walked out of his room, making sure to knock her shoulder as he passed.

"You're going out now?" she asked, following him.

"Looks like it." He took his coat out of the closet.

"But it's only two hours until curfew."

"Then I better be quick about it," he said, giving her a swift wink.

"Xander, wait! I -"

"I'm sick of fucking waiting, Leon. I've been trying to do the whole respectful thing, but now that I know where we stand there's not much point anymore, is there?" Xander's coat now on, he reached down and slipped into his shoes.

"I ... I didn't mean -"

"Don't try to fucking change your answer on me now. It's done." Last shoe on, Xander opened the door. He turned back, smiled and said, "Happy fucking Halloween!" before slamming the door behind him.

There was a small bar a few blocks from his apartment and he headed straight there. Once inside, he was immediately met by an abundance of women in costumes, all eyeing him as he entered. He had put his Guardian trench coat back on for this very reason.

Xander didn't know what he was looking for in a companion that night, but he definitely knew what he wasn't looking for. A woman dressed in a black dress and pointed hat came over to him first. She was pretty and blonde, and he immediately dismissed her.

Then he moved onto a brunette in a costume he did not even really look at. He went up to her and, when he got the smile, started sucking on her ear, only to be thrown off by the strong scent of too much perfume. It was wrong. All wrong.

They all smelled wrong. Every last one of them. Where were the women with the natural, floral aromas?

And then he saw her. Sitting in a chair and chatting with a friend was a simple girl with auburn hair and hazel eyes. She was more made-up than he wanted, but weren't they all? So he grabbed her hand, pulled her against him and placed his head in her neck. Perfume was present, but it wasn't overpowering in any way. And it was floral and feminine and everything he needed to pretend.

It wasn't long before Xander was pressing her against the wall and grinding his pelvis into hers. She moaned into his hair while he kissed down her neck.

There was no protesting as Xander grabbed her wrist and pulled her out of the bar, practically dragging her back to his apartment. The moment they got inside, he kicked off his shoes and demanded she do the same. She obeyed and watched closely as he tore off his coat and tossed it aside.

He picked her up and she wrapped her legs around his waist, the two of them kissing fervently as he carried her towards his bedroom, making sure to slam the door loudly behind them, just in case Deryn wasn't already aware of their presence.

But, of course, she was. Deryn sat up in her bed the moment she heard the front door open, hoping since Xander had left only a short while ago that he had come back alone. It didn't take her long to realize he hadn't.

She moved to the edge of her bed and just sat there, unable to tear her ears away as he clearly began to touch his guest.

Deryn didn't even realize she was crying until she felt the drops fall onto her hands, which were tightly gripping her pajama pants. *His* pajama pants. She wiped her wet cheeks.

"Stop crying," she demanded. Nothing happened. "Stop crying," she repeated. She cried harder. "Please, please stop crying."

Without another thought, Deryn stood up and grabbed her bottle of whiskey. She took several gulps before leaving her bedroom and closing the door behind her.

She seized her favorite blanket from the couch and wrapped herself in it, but even its warmth could not bring back the comfort she had just lost.

Deryn wiped her eyes some more as she went out to the balcony, lying down on the cold cement and trying hard not to let her mind wander back to what was happening inside.

Still, the tears flowed, and she was starting to wonder if they would ever stop. She took another sip from her bottle.

"Stop crying," she repeated once again. "This is what you

wanted. You can't be attached to him. You have to leave one day. You have to find Dad and Talon and Dax. You love Dax. You can't ... you can't have feelings for Xander. You just ... you can't. You can't."

Back inside, Xander was having a hard time focusing, since the woman he was currently thrusting into kept staring at him. So he turned her around and took her from behind, tangling one hand in her hair before tearing it away. There was too much of some product in there. It wasn't natural. It wasn't soft. It was wrong. It was all fucking wrong.

"Leon ..." he said under his breath as he continued to fuck this complete stranger.

"What?" she asked over her shoulder between heavy breaths.

"Nothing. Turn back around!"

She moved her head so it was once again facing forward.

Xander didn't know what he had to imagine to finish that night, but it certainly had nothing to do with the person he was with. He remembered mumbling something to get her out of his apartment, but he could not for the life of him remember what it was. He supposed it was the wife lie again. That one always worked well.

As soon as she was gone, he sat on the edge of his bed and held his head in his hands, breathing shallowly as it finally hit him.

What the fuck had he just done?

With a frustrated growl, Xander grabbed his nightstand and tossed it across the room. Then he grabbed his chair, his comforter, his curtains. Anything he could get his hands on. He threw it, shattered it, stomped on it, tore it, and destroyed it.

"Fuck! You pathetic asshole! What the fuck is wrong with you?"

He grabbed his clock, the only object still in one piece, and threw it hard against the wall.

Once he was satisfied enough with the destruction of his room, Xander put on some clothes and grabbed his cigarettes. He headed for the balcony, pausing momentarily by Deryn's door. He desperately wanted to knock on it, to have everything be all right and have her follow him out there. But if he knocked now he knew very well that this was not what would happen, so he walked on, his throat raw as he let it sink in how massively he had fucked up.

Xander opened the door to the balcony but was met with some sort of barrier.

Looking down, he found a small body wrapped in nothing but a thin blanket. There was an empty bottle of whiskey in her hand and the faint remnants of tears on her cheeks.

"Leon!" Xander collapsed to his knees and rolled her so her head was in his lap. "Leon, what happened? Are you alright?"

There was some incoherent mumbling he somehow translated to mean that she came outside to hide from the noise.

With a heavy sigh, Xander scooped her into his arms and carried her frozen body inside.

"Mmm ... Xander," she whispered as she rubbed her cheek against his chest. "Smells like you."

Xander kissed the top of her head and breathed her in. He hadn't recognized it before, but this was the scent he had been craving. So sweet. So intoxicating.

Tightening his grip on her, Xander opened the door to her bedroom and headed inside. He lowered Deryn onto her bed and wrapped the comforter tightly around her.

"Xander ... No more hussies," whispered Deryn.

Xander smiled. He moved his hand to her cheek and stroked it soothingly. "Alright, Leon. You win. No more hussies."

She smiled pleasantly before bringing her hand up to touch his.

Xander leaned toward her ear and whispered, "Only you." He moved his lips to hers and kissed them softly.

Even in her half-asleep, drunken state, Deryn's lips still responded. Xander smiled again and pressed his forehead against hers.

"Stay," she breathed into his hovering mouth.

"I can't stay, Leon. Not tonight. I don't deserve you tonight."

"Stay," she said again, opening her eyes slightly and looking into his.

"Soon," said Xander giving her another soft kiss.

And then it took everything he had to tear himself away from her, but he knew he had to.

Sometimes Deryn acted so normal that Xander forgot about everything she had been through. When he actually stopped to think for a moment, he understood her hesitance about him. But he knew these feelings were not his alone. She felt it, too. And now, more than ever, he was determined to make her see. Deryn Leon was going to be his. He was sure of it.

And, no matter what it took, he was going to deserve her.

CHAPTER TWENTY-FOUR

The next morning Deryn had a hard time opening her eyes, which were throbbing along with the rest of her head. She groaned and rubbed them, accidentally rolling so she landed in the large puddle of drool on her pillow.

"Gross," she said, moving out of the wetness, which only made her head pound harder.

As she turned in the other direction, away from the drool, the memories of the night before came flooding back to her. Her face crinkled with curiosity as she realized she didn't remember returning to her room. Had she come back here on her own? Somehow, she doubted it.

A nauseating smell that made her stomach churn currently filled the air, and it was soon accompanied by some very cheerful humming. She got up to investigate, stumbling slightly on her wobbly legs.

Deryn put on her robe and slid into her slippers. She yawned heavily and walked out of the room while scratching an itch on the top of her head. Her fingers got caught in a mess of tangles that could only have been caused by a lot of tossing and turning.

"Morning, sunshine!"

She stopped and looked. Bronson was smiling cheerfully from the kitchen.

"Or should I say afternoon?" He laughed and went back to cooking something on the stove.

Deryn groaned. She went over and sank down on the couch.

Not even ten seconds later, Bronson was handing her a glass filled with a hideous, muggy-green liquid.

"For your head," he said. "My own recipe to cure hangovers."

"Does it taste as disgusting as it looks?" she asked, reluctantly taking the glass.

"Oh yes, but you'll be happier in the long run."

Deryn frowned at the drink before plugging her nose and gulping it down quickly. She pulled a face as she finished. Bronson laughed and took the empty glass.

"How did you know I was hung-over?" she asked, turning to watch him in the kitchen. He really was an artist in there.

"Ruby told me," he said while chopping onions.

Deryn threw her hand over her mouth when she accidentally got a good whiff. And then her eyes drifted over to Xander's bedroom door. It was open.

"Where is he?" she asked, hoping there would be time to duck back into her room before he made an appearance. Anything to avoid suffering the humiliation of last night. Clearly, he had found her drunk and passed out on the balcony, probably just after his latest hussy left.

Deryn's fists clenched as the pain she had felt the night before returned. But she wouldn't cry. Not in front of Bronson. There was no reason for it. She had already decided that any feelings she had for Xander were unreasonable, so she would just have to forget about them. That should be easy enough. She had successfully shut her feelings off for five years. Become an expert at it even. This was the same. He was a Guardian and all she had to do was emotionally detach herself. Done.

Just then, the front door opened and Xander walked in carrying his rucksack. He kicked off his shoes before noticing her sitting there, his eyes falling upon hers.

Deryn gulped. No. Not done.

She stood up and darted for the bathroom. "I need a shower," she mumbled to Bronson, slamming the door behind her.

Bronson stared after her peculiarly, then moved his eyes to Xander. "Fighting again?"

Xander shrugged. "I don't know. Probably."

When Deryn got out of the shower, Bronson was gone but whatever he'd been cooking was still brewing. The curtains covering the door to the balcony were currently blowing, letting her know Xander was out there. She hurried into her room and shut the door, pressing her back to it and sighing with her eyes closed.

"What's with the dramatics?"

Deryn jumped as her heart literally skipped a beat. Xander was standing over her dresser, pulling things out of his rucksack and putting them next to the bag Bronson had bought her.

"What are you doing?" she asked, suddenly realizing that she was very naked underneath her robe. She pulled it tighter around her body.

"I bought you some medicine for when you go. And a few other things that might come in handy."

"Kicking me out already?" she asked, crossing her arms.

Xander smirked. "You're the one who said you needed to be prepared."

Once all of the medicine and other knickknacks were out of his bag - Deryn noticing a compass and an old flashlight among them - he began pulling out something else. Books. Many books.

Deryn's eyes widened in awe as the pile of volumes grew larger. There was even one specifically on weapon making. How he ever found a paper copy of something like that was beyond her.

"I was able to get a few of the books from training you requested, as well as some additions I thought might come in handy. There are more I plan to get but the weight of my bag was at capacity."

Xander put his rucksack over his shoulder and walked to the door. Deryn was still standing against it, her eyes focused excitedly on the books.

Reaching past her for the knob, he brushed her hip in a way

that could only have been intentional. He leaned down and whispered, "Excuse me, Leon."

The purr of his voice sent a chill through Deryn. Her body stiffened as he grasped firmly onto her arm, carefully moving her out of the way. He flashed her that crooked grin of his before opening the door just enough to slip out and shutting it behind him.

Deryn stared at the closed door for a long time, unable to move her gaze anywhere else. She had absolutely no idea what was going on in Xander's head. He had, more-or-less, confessed his feelings for her the previous night and now he just seemed ... off. What game was he playing?

Well, whatever it was, Deryn refused to let him win. She quickly changed into some clothes, then grabbed the book on weaponry and the blanket she had found tangled in her sheets. She wrapped it around her and went out to the living room, where she sat down on the couch.

Deryn opened the book and began reading.

Xander came over a short while later and handed her a cup of tea. Then he went over to the fireplace.

"There's supposed to be another thunderstorm tonight," he said nonchalantly as he pressed something on his wristband that shot out a flame and ignited the artificial wood. "You might want to prepare early."

"Fine," she said without taking her eyes off of the book.

"How is your head doing while reading?"

Deryn thought. The truth was, reading and retaining the information had proven to be much more difficult than before she suffered countless amounts of torture. She often caught herself reading sentences two or three times before fully comprehending them, but she simply said, "All is well."

Xander walked away and returned a minute later with his small computer and a cup of tea. He sat down on the other end of the couch and put his feet up casually before turning it on, a screen appearing as a hologram before his eyes. He scrolled a bit with his finger, then began reading something.

Using her peripherals Deryn saw the cover of a book at the

top of the hologram, and that he was reading about mind control technology. She had to ask. "Why are you reading that?"

Without looking up, Xander said, "It's come to my attention recently that this form of technology isn't far from the president's grasp, and I want to know more about it. Surely you, of all people, understand how necessary it is to be a step ahead on these things."

Deryn nodded before returning to her book. A gust of wind shot in through the open balcony door and she shivered. Xander put his computer down, stood up and closed the door.

"Sorry. I was airing out that onion smell," he said, returning to his seat.

"What was he making?" she asked, looking back at the brewing pot.

"Just some dinner for us. A new recipe he wanted to try."

"Oh." She suddenly frowned. "What happened to my untouched dinner from last night?" She couldn't resist.

"I ate it," said Xander casually.

Deryn whipped her head towards him. "All of it?" she asked.

He nodded. "I was very hungry, since I didn't eat anything all of yesterday."

"Why not?"

"Because I was anticipating your dinner. I know how much it meant to you, being your first time cooking it on your own and all -"

Deryn blushed. So, apparently, they were being blunt. She made a mental note.

"- and I would've been here if I hadn't run into complications."

"Complications," she repeated. "Is that what we're calling your hussies now?" So much for being the bigger person.

"Believe what you want, that girl had nothing to do with why I was late."

"Then why -"

"I'm a Guardian, Leon, and sometimes I need to keep up appearances," he said as he scrolled further down on the hologram. "Luka and I have spent every Halloween together since we were five. When I tried to get out of it, suspicions arose. Neither you nor I can afford to have anyone doubt my intentions. So I went. And when I tried to leave some girl followed me. Veli forced me into his car with her, and then sent her up here while he proceeded to threaten the lives of my father and friends if I didn't find you, which everyone realizes I haven't tried very hard to do. So that's it, the truth, which I'm sure is nothing compared to whatever you created in that head of yours."

Deryn's book dropped from her hands. "Veli threatened you?"

"He did. He and several others who were once my superiors don't like me very much."

If at all possible, Deryn felt like an even bigger idiot than before. She should have known he wouldn't worry her for no reason. "Xander, I'm sorry. I didn't realize -"

"Obviously," said Xander, putting down his computer. "I'm going to have some of Bronson's soup. Do you want a bowl?"

Deryn looked down at her stomach just as it growled. She hadn't eaten anything yesterday either and she was already feeling much better after Bronson's hangover cure. Food actually sounded like a good idea. "Yes, but I can get it," she said, standing up with him.

She followed him to the kitchen, and took out bowls and spoons while he put a ladle in the pot.

"So I wanted to purchase you some clothes, but I wasn't sure of your sizes," said Xander, giving the contents of the pot a few stirs.

Deryn held out the bowls while he poured. "I'm actually not sure of my sizes anymore," she said. "I've lost weight since ... since before." She looked down at her bony body and frowned.

After putting the lid back on the pot, Xander lifted her sweater a little and poked her stomach. "Looks like you've gotten plenty of it back."

Deryn's face sunk. *That* was definitely on the list of top ten things never to say to a woman, even one who had been starved for five years. "Thanks. I think," she added under her breath.

Xander took one of the bowls from her. "I really have no idea when it comes to women's sizes so you're going to have to help me out a bit." He grabbed his computer, and took it with his food to the table. The hologram shut off as he walked, but came back up again the moment he sat.

Deryn did the same, except she only had to turn to the correct page instead of have a bunch of words appear floating in front of her. So it seemed that whatever game this was they were playing, part of it entailed simply acting like yesterday never happened. And being blunt. She could do that.

Taking a seat, Deryn told him what her sizes once were, but mentioned that he should probably get a size smaller in the pants.

"I'll get your old sizes," he said. "We should be optimistic about fattening you up. Bronson will be happy to assist."

Deryn crinkled her forehead. "Umm ... alright."

What was with him? So another part of this game was being ... rude? No, that wasn't it. Oblivious? It was closer, but still not right. She got the feeling he knew exactly what he was doing.

As soon as they were finished, Xander took their bowls and washed them. He then grabbed his computer and said, "I think I'll finish this in my room. Night, Leon."

"Okay." Deryn turned to look after him. "Night," she said as he shut his door.

All right. So he wasn't giving her the silent treatment, but he definitely wasn't acting like himself. It was like he was ... "Disconnected," she whispered. She had finally found the right word.

On the other side of the door, Xander smirked before plopping onto his bed. His room was all back in order now since he had fixed what he could and replaced what he couldn't with a very early trip to the Shopping District, but not before going back to her room and sneaking a few more kisses from her drunk but willing lips. Of course, he assumed she wouldn't remember. Those were more for him than her, anyway. But the rest of it ... The light touches, the calm manner, the dull and detached conversations ... those were for her.

Xander could only imagine the millions of conspiracy theories going on in her pretty head right now. But if this was what it took to get Deryn to realize she wanted him - the way he was - then he was glad to do it.

He gave it a week before she cracked, and that was being generous.

CHAPTER TWENTY-FIVE

"President Saevus, I simply do not understand why we are suffering the same treatment as everyone else in the city," complained Wenton as the Guardians sat around their usual table. "I think you underestimate how humiliating it is to be stuck riding the tram at night with commoners."

"And just what is it you'd like me to do so that you might not suffer this *humiliation?*" asked Saevus, calmly folding his hands in front of him.

"I don't know. A personal car service? Not all of us can afford to order one every night," said Wenton, glancing slyly at Veli and Soren.

"Why not hover-bikes? We all have them," suggested Luka, looking rather bored as he tapped his fingers on the table. One stern look from his father made him stop.

Xander couldn't help but wonder if Luka would be so eager to please if he knew his father had put him on a hit list.

"The S.U.R.G.E.'s wouldn't like that," said Elvira, leaning towards her father. "They have a hard time differentiating between us and regular citizens. That's why we don't break curfew."

"We would end up having to increase our own patrol for that to work," said Xander, tapping his own fingers on the table for no reason other than to irritate Barath Voclain. "And we only have a few cars in each city. We cannot deprive them from the citizens who actually have the means to pay."

"Who cares about them? We're the ones who need to get around," said Wenton.

Xander stopped tapping and leaned forward in his chair. "Let me put a few things in perspective for you, Wenton. If we force the drivers to be our fucking chauffeurs, then they won't have time to go out and make any money, which means they won't be able to obtain the resources they need to survive. Therefore, they go out of fucking business and we're right back where we started. It's called cause and effect."

The others all stared at him blankly.

Xander rolled his eyes. "They work to *live*," he drawled. His smile faded as he leaned back again. "Cars are out."

Everyone was silent for a long moment.

"So why are hover-bikes out again?" asked Luka, scratching his head.

"Because we don't want the whole city riding around at night, and for us to use them we would have to reprogram the S.U.R.G.E.'s," said Xander.

"But aren't there ways to arrange it so they leave certain bikes alone?"

Everyone's ears perked up.

"We can have chips made that emit a wave to repel the damn things, then register each one so normal people can't get their hands on them and install them in our bikes. It's complicated, but it's possible."

They all looked at Xander, who would, undoubtedly, find some sort of flaw in this plan. Only, this time, he had nothing. So they all turned their attention to President Saevus.

"You may head to the Government Lab in Middle City now and arrange it, young Voclain. Xander, go with him. And take Soren and his car along with you. Ms. Scout?"

Finley sat at attention. This was the first time the president had addressed her personally and she looked damn nervous.

"You will wait here and send out a S.U.R.G.E. to test its reaction on the first bike once this chip is installed. Everyone else is dismissed."

"Wait!" shouted Veli before anyone could even get out of

their seats. "I believe Ruby owes us an update on his progress in finding the slave."

Xander groaned. "We sent a message to every citizen, asking them to submit their work schedules. This way, we will know the best times to *invade* their homes. Scout -" He motioned towards Finley. "- has already agreed to go through the responses and make a schedule for us. I hope you're all prepared to work overtime."

Now everyone else groaned.

Once that was done, they all dispersed. Xander and Luka followed Soren to his car, leaving Veli to find his own way home.

Getting the chip created was easy enough. While Luka and Soren handled the details, Xander excused himself to the bathroom. Of course he took a side trip, stopping by the lab he knew was being used to study mind control. It was empty.

As a Guardian, he had access to every lab there was, but he would need to make sure Luka was the one to check his wristband activity in the morning. He would believe whatever lie he told him, or at least pretend he did.

So Xander scanned his wristband and stepped inside as the door slid open. Knowing he only had a couple of minutes, he went straight for the lab's closet. Once inside, he looked around until he noticed several chips in glass beakers, each one labeled with a date.

"May I help you?"

Xander snapped his head around and saw a woman in a white lab coat staring at him.

"Mr. Ruby," she said, even though he was positive they had never met before. "Is there something you needed?"

"It's come to my attention recently that samples of your mind control chip were given to a Guardian," he said, looking back at the beakers.

"Yes, Mr. Veli Tash," she said nonchalantly. "To report our progress to the president."

"He's done no such thing," said Xander, turning to face her. "And if you provide me with the most advanced chip you have,

I'll make sure you and your team aren't punished when I report this."

The woman went stiff. "O-of course, Mr. Ruby. I had no idea."

Xander believed her.

She hurried forward and scanned the glass beakers, grabbing one labeled with a date from just under a week ago. "This is our most successful model to date. Nearly flawless, aside from slight memory loss when removed."

"Thank you," he said, removing the chip from the beaker and putting it in his inside coat pocket. "You called me in here to see your progress. Understand?"

She nodded, agreeing to the lie.

"Have a good day."

Xander left the closet and then the lab, hurrying back to where Luka and Soren were now waiting for him.

"So should we go to your place and test it?" asked Luka, swinging his bag of computer chips.

"Fuck no," said Xander, his mind flooding with the many disasters that could happen in that situation.

"But neither of us -" Luka motioned to him and Soren. "-lives even remotely close to here. There's no way we're going all the way back to Inner City to test them on one of our bikes."

"We already have to set it up for everyone anyway. What's the difference?" asked Xander.

"Exactly. What's the difference?" countered Luka.

Xander clenched his fists. He needed to stay composed. He needed to stay in control.

"We're going to *your* place," said Luka. "Why are you so private all of a sudden?"

Xander didn't have to think very hard to realize it was probably around the time he took in a runaway slave who sliced a man's throat open. A man who was with them now, and who he had neglected to mention to Deryn was still alive. This could not end well.

~

Deryn sat on the balcony, wrapped in her blanket while she

mindlessly flipped the pages in the book she was not actually reading. She had tried listening to the radio in the living room, but even the familiar voices of Talon and Dakota were not enough to hold her attention.

She couldn't stop thinking about Xander. For days now he had been playing what she knew was a game. He was cold and distant, but still always right there. Speaking was not the issue, he would answer anything she asked. Bluntly. But there was no passion behind it, no drive, no personality.

Xander was trying to get her to crack. She knew he was. He wanted her to admit whatever it was going on between them was *not* nothing. And Deryn knew he was right, because what she felt was definitely something. But how could she admit that to him when she still hadn't figured out what that 'something' was yet?

She knew she cared for Xander, that was not the question, but how much did she care? After everything that had happened to her, she hardly trusted her feelings. He had done so much for her, it wouldn't be so farfetched that maybe her gratitude could be misconstrued for something else. Hadn't Bronson said something along those lines?

But gratitude did not explain the safe and warm feeling she got that night he held her during the thunderstorm, or how beautiful his heartbeat felt under her hand when they had kissed, a memory that was never far from her mind.

Deryn tried to distract herself with memories of Dakota instead, but it was hard when he had never ignited the same fire in her she was currently feeling. She had been so young back then. So innocent. The most she had ever thought about was kissing him when their instructors weren't looking, something that had seemed incredibly ill-behaved and dangerous at the time.

But Xander ... when she thought about him her mind wandered to more than just visions of them sneaking a kiss while no one was watching. She wanted all of him. To touch him, to feel him, for him to feel her. She wanted to possess every part of him, not just his lips.

Did that make her sick? She had just escaped the Guardians, and now she suddenly found herself desiring one. Xander knew the people who had taken advantage of her. He knew them well and saw them every day. But, still, she wanted him. To feel what it would be like to have him not just on her, but inside of her.

Deryn grumbled at the realization of her dirty thoughts. After everything that had happened to her, how could she want this? With *him*?

She wished he was here now. So she could smell him, touch him, hold him. Everything she craved and more. God, he smelled good. It was intoxicating. Every time she breathed him in, she could never get enough.

Deryn bit her bottom lip.

Damn.

He was winning. She knew he was playing a game and, still, she was letting him win.

Deryn slammed her book shut. There was no point in even pretending anymore. She needed to talk to him. She needed to explain these feelings. How long until he would be home?

And then, as if some higher entity was reading her mind, she heard his voice. Coming from the street below and clearly talking to someone.

Deryn looked through the small crack in the balcony but she couldn't see anyone. She moved around until something came into view. Three figures in Guardian trench coats had just stepped out of a car. Xander pulled his hood down as he stared up at the balcony, gulping as his eyes caught sight of the crack he seemed to know she was behind.

One of the cloaked figures said something to him but she couldn't make out the words from this far away. Then he looked up to see what Xander was staring at. Luka Voclain. He squinted but saw nothing.

Xander looked away from her and spoke to the other two Guardians. The three of them disappeared from sight and, soon after, she could hear the garage door opening. When they walked back into view, Xander was leading his hover-bike by the handles. Luka took something out of his pocket and they all began scanning every inch of the bike. The third Guardian got on his knees and pointed at something. He moved out of the way so Luka could investigate. An artificial breeze hit him as he stepped back, causing his hood to fall off of his head.

Deryn's heart stopped. She tried to control her breathing as she stared at the ghost in front of her. Only, it wasn't a ghost. Soren looked completely solid, a visible white scar poking out of a collar on his once unblemished neck. It was a mark so large she could even make it out from her spot on the balcony five floors up. Her whole body was shaking.

Then Soren's eyes traveled upward, stopping on the crack in the balcony. She moved away and pressed her back against the wall.

"Shit," she whispered to herself.

"What are you staring at?" asked Xander, following Soren's eyes to the balcony.

Soren simply shook his head and pointed up at the sky. "Rain," he said in the crackly, barely-there voice that came out whenever he didn't use his collar.

"I think I got it," said Luka, getting back on his feet. "It should be dark in a few minutes so you can take it out for a test run."

"Fine," said Xander, mounting the bike and putting on his helmet.

"In the meantime, I need to use your bathroom." Luka held out his hand.

Xander sneered. "No. Go piss on a wall."

"That's really classy," said Luka. "Come on, mate. Give me access."

"I said no."

"Why not? You hiding something up there?"

Luka laughed but Soren eyed Xander curiously.

"Stop being so damn weird and hand your primitive keys over." Luka held out his hand again.

Xander grunted. It took everything he had to not stare at his balcony in hopes of giving Deryn a silent warning. Soren was already looking at him strangely. If he didn't let Luka in his apartment now then Soren might come back later, if he truly believed he was hiding something.

Reluctantly, Xander touched his wristband to Luka's and gave him temporary access to his building, then he reached into his pocket and took out his keys, slamming them into Luka's hand. "You better be quick about it."

"Yeah, fine," said Luka. "Sun's down. Better call Finley and get riding."

Xander pulled down the visor on his helmet and turned on his bike. It began to hover and he took off just as Luka headed for his building. One glance over his shoulder and he noticed Soren catch the door before it closed. He stared in Xander's direction for a moment before following Luka inside.

"Shit!" shouted Xander as he turned a corner. "Call Finley."

His wristband called her automatically.

"Is it installed?" she asked upon answering.

"Yes, I'm near my place. Now send the S.U.R.G.E. out quickly, and be ready to shut it off if it attacks me."

There was a momentary pause. "It's done. It should be there in a few minutes."

A few minutes felt like forever in that moment.

"Xander."

"What?" he said harshly.

"I just ... I want to know why?"

Xander grunted. She wanted answers now? Really? "No reason, Finley. But, like I said before, it's nothing personal." Only, this time, it was.

He heard Finley whimper. "Is this because of what I heard Mr. Von speaking with the president about?"

Xander knit his brow. "What?"

"You know. About you and Lona. When she becomes a Guardian."

"What?"

"You know. The marriage they're trying to arrange."

Xander's eyes widened as his body drained of blood. "What?" he repeated for a third time. "Where the fuck did you hear that?"

"Just now," she said. "The president and Mr. Von were talking about it. You didn't know?"

"I'm not marrying anyone!" Xander had never had much interest in marriage, and the current dark world they lived in only exacerbated those feelings. And since when did the president care about the marriages of his subordinates?

"Oh. So if that's not the reason you're blowing me off, then I guess it's just me," she said sadly.

"Damn right it is!" Xander turned another corner, circling back around to his apartment. "Want to get back in my good graces, Finley? Find out more about this 'arrangement'."

"Alright."

Just then, a S.U.R.G.E. flew into his vicinity. It fluttered around him for a moment before buzzing in approval and zooming off.

"It worked," he said to Finley through the line. "Let the president know we'll be installing the rest of them shortly."

Xander didn't wait for her to answer before hanging up. The test was done and he was heading home. Hopefully, there wouldn't be a mess to clean up.

CHAPTER TWENTY-SIX

Deryn stared at the street in panic as Xander rode off on his hover-bike and Luka headed for the door to the building. "Shit," she whispered to herself.

And then Soren hurried forward. She moved her position to follow him, just making him out as he disappeared through the same door as Luka.

"Shit, shit, shit!" she said much louder this time.

Deryn crawled to the door and slid it open, hurrying inside and back to her feet. Once the balcony door was shut and locked, she tossed her blanket and book into her room, then ran to the bathroom, grabbing every girly product Xander had given her and stuffing them in the cabinet under the sink. Then she moved like a whirlwind through the front of the apartment, searching for anything that was hers.

The knob on the front door rattled. Deryn went white before running into her bedroom, shutting the door quietly behind her.

"Th'fuck you doing, Sorey? If Xander didn't even want me up here then he sure as hell doesn't want you," she heard Luka say as he entered the apartment.

"I have to use the bathroom, too."

That voice ... that crackly, barely there voice sent chills down Deryn's spine. It was so different, but just the same.

"Like hell you do," said Luka. "If this wasn't an emergency I'd drag you back down to the street right now. But you better believe I'll be quick."

So would Deryn. When she heard Luka's footsteps head towards the bathroom, she moved around her room as quietly as she could, grabbing her things and stuffing them under the bed but holding onto her Element. Just in case. She wanted to clear out the closet too, but there was no time. All she could do was shut it and climb under the bed with her things, because Soren was already across the apartment and opening Xander's bedroom door.

He was out of there quickly, walking in a circle around the living room before stopping by her door.

Deryn put her hand over her mouth to drown out the sound of her breathing as her door creaked open. There were footsteps moving around the bed. She could see the shadows of his feet through the crack between the floor and the comforter. And then he stopped. By the closet. She didn't have much but she had enough to let him know someone was living here.

She clenched her free fist as she was sure he reached for the handle of the closet door, readying himself to open -

"Th'fuck you doing in here?" spat Luka, his angry footsteps marching into the room and shoving Soren back so his legs hit the bed. "You need to take a piss? Then go do it because you have no business in here!"

Something clicked and Soren spoke, his voice still damaged but somehow clearer. "That shithead you call a friend didn't want us coming up here for a reason and you know it."

"I know no such thing. That shithead's always been private. Now go take a piss!"

Another click. "I don't have to take a fucking piss!" shouted Soren, storming out of the room. Luka followed, making sure to shut the door behind him.

The two continued to bicker in the front room. Deryn kept hoping they would leave but their voices never got any farther. Until she heard the balcony door slide open. Then they both must have stepped outside.

She stayed where she was, not moving, not even breathing out of fear that she might give away her position, even though they were no longer near her.

When Xander arrived back at his building, he drove his hover-bike directly into the garage and leapt off of it, tossing his helmet somewhere as he ran out and shut the door.

When he got outside, he looked up at his balcony, his body burning as he saw Luka and Soren leaning over the side, Luka waving cheerfully.

"Shit," he whispered as he ran for the door, scanning his wristband and typing in a code since Luka had the key. The moment the door was unlocked, he ran inside and darted up the stairs three at a time. By the time he got to his apartment he was winded, but he didn't care.

The first thing he noticed was that all doors were shut. Then he went for the balcony, his eyes bulging as he caught Luka and Soren smoking his cigarettes. "What the fuck are you doing?"

"Hey, Xan," said Luka, glancing over his shoulder at him. "Better not let the president know you have these."

Xander looked at Soren. "Can you even smoke that with your throat?"

Soren shrugged.

"What would your brother say if he saw you with that?"

Soren chuckled and pressed the button on his collar. "He'd probably be more interested to know that *you* were smoking them."

"You going to tell on me, then?" asked Xander, walking to the edge of the balcony and glancing over the side. Deryn wasn't dangling, so that was good.

"I don't see any reason to mention this. As long as you do what I've asked."

Luka glanced sideways at him, obviously curious about what they were talking about.

"I said we'd look for her and we are. What more do you expect from me?"

"I expect you to find her," said Soren, standing up and tossing his cigarette over the side.

Xander could not help but notice the way Luka grimaced at the mention of Deryn. When he caught Xander staring, he quickly pulled it back.

"So did it work?" asked Luka.

Xander nodded.

"Guess we better get a move on then," said Soren, heading inside.

Luka took one last drag of his cigarette before putting it out and following him. Xander was right behind them.

"You two are fully capable of doing this without me," he said, walking over to meet them at the door. "If there are any complications figure it out yourself, because I'm done for the night."

"Whatever," said Luka, tossing him his keys and heading out first. "Come along, Sorey! Time to leave the hermit to his cave."

Soren gave Xander a curious look before following Luka. The moment he was out the door, Xander shut and locked it. He stood there for a second, trying to catch the breath he had been holding since the moment they got there. When he turned around, Deryn was standing in the doorway of her bedroom.

"Were you on the balcony before?" he asked with a gulp.

She nodded and slowly walked towards him.

"Glad you got in alright. Thank our lucky stars for five floors and no elevator."

She reached him, her eyes both cold and blazing as she stared at him for a moment. And then, without warning, her hand lifted and she slapped him hard across the face. He stumbled but still managed to stay on his feet.

"How dare you! How dare you, Xander Ruby! How could you not tell me that he was alive?"

"I didn't want to worry you," he said while rubbing his aching face.

"But I'm already worried! Every single day I'm worried! And Soren ... *He's* the one who wants you to find me?"

"Both him and Veli," answered Xander honestly.

"What does he want with me?" she screamed, tears visible in her eyes.

"He wants to possess you."

Deryn whimpered, but quickly covered her mouth. "It will

be worse. He will be so much worse to me after what I did to him." She paced back and forth. "I can't go back to him! I won't! I'd rather die! I -"

"Calm down, Leon!" shouted Xander, grabbing her shoulders and holding her still. "I'm not going to let him get close enough to lay a hand on you! You understand?"

"But -"

"No buts. Soren will never have you again. I promise. I won't let him, even if it means killing him in a room full of Guardians. You will *never* be his."

Deryn sobbed but still nodded. She wiped her eyes, which was pretty much pointless since the tears kept falling. Xander pulled her close and held her tight. Deryn wrapped her arms around his waist and melted into him, that wonderful scent of his filling her nostrils.

But he let her go far too quickly, without even so much as a kiss on the top of her head, which she had become quite accustomed to.

"What do you want for dinner?" he asked, back to that cold, detached manner he had been exhibiting for days now.

"I'm not hungry," she said following after him. "Xander."

He turned and looked at her.

"Xander, please stop playing games with me."

He said nothing.

"I know what you're trying to do and I won't let you manipulate me."

He cocked an eyebrow before flashing that crooked grin of his. He'd called it. Less than a week.

"Fine!" she shouted, obviously not appreciating the silent treatment. "You win, alright? I cave. I don't like you like this. I want you to be like how you were before. I want *us* to be like how *we* were before."

Continuing with his deafening silence, Xander crossed his arms and waited for her to go on.

"I was wrong," she admitted. "We're not nothing. *This* -" She motioned between them. "- isn't nothing."

Xander's mouth twisted. They were on the right track but ...

"So what is it then?"

Deryn blushed and cast her eyes to the floor. "I don't know. A friendship, I suppose."

Xander raised his eyebrows. "Is that it?"

She sighed while looking up at him sadly. "I don't know what you want from me."

He bit his cheek and looked off to the side. It was a good, long while before he looked back at her and said, "I want more, Leon. *This* -" He motioned between them. "- whatever we've been doing for the past few weeks isn't enough."

With a heavy sigh, Xander went to the closet for his coat. One step forward, two steps back. Fucking Leon ... Why wouldn't she just admit it already?

"Xander." she called, following him. "Xander, please don't go."

"Why?" he asked.

She didn't have an answer.

Rolling his eyes, Xander said, "I need some air."

"Please stay," she pleaded. "I'm sorry I don't feel the same way but -"

He whipped towards her. "You see, that's the thing. You *do* feel the same way. I know you do but, for some reason, you keep denying it, even to yourself."

Deryn choked as she tried to hold in another whimper. She hated this. Why couldn't she just be honest with him? Tell him everything that was holding her back. Tell him about his father.

"I understand you've been through something traumatic. I know it doesn't always seem like it, but I do. But you're never going to get past all this shit if you keep lying to yourself. Don't let those bastards win by denying your feelings for someone who actually cares."

"Are ... are you saying you -"

"Care?" he finished, his face igniting for the first time in days. "Of course I care! We wouldn't even be having this conversation if I didn't care! I care so much that it fucking makes me sick at night! I'm not ..." He gulped. "I'm not used to this, Leon, any more than you are. I've trained myself not to care and, for years, it's worked just fine. Then you come into my life and, all of a sudden, I don't know what I'm doing! I'm not even concerned for my own fucking life anymore! Just yours."

Deryn found herself slowly moving towards him. She just wanted to touch him, to hold him, to breathe him in. But, before she could get there, he turned away.

"I'm going out. When I get back, don't talk to me unless you've figured yourself out. I don't associate with liars."

And with that, Xander opened the door and slammed it behind him, leaving Deryn alone

CHAPTER TWENTY-SEVEN

Several hours passed before Xander returned. Deryn was lying on her bed and jumped to her feet when she heard the front door open, but stopped when her hand reached her knob. What if he wasn't alone? She clutched her aching heart at the realization that Xander coming home with someone wasn't so farfetched.

And then there were voices. Faint so she could barely hear them, but definitely multiple.

Tears were caught in Deryn's eyes as her greatest fear suddenly became a reality. Someone was with him.

Without even thinking, she left her room and followed the voices to Xander's bedroom door. She put her ear to it and listened, but was unable to make out anything. A horrible pang shot through her heart. She brought her hand up and placed it flat on the cold, artificial wood, just trying to feel some part of him in there. She had let this happen. She had pushed him away and into some other woman's -

Deryn stumbled forward as the door burst open. She instinctually took up a battle stance, even though she had no idea what or who to expect.

"Evening, Leon."

Xander was directly in front of her, watching her with amusement. She released her stance and looked around. He was alone. But then what was ...

Her eyes landed on the small radio sitting on top of his dresser. *Her* radio. Aimed at the wall separating their rooms.

Glancing at his clock, she saw that it was a few minutes past the top of the hour. Right around the time *Blackbird* always played. So the voices she heard were Talon and Dax and ... Paul McCartney?

Xander turned the radio off and leaned against the dresser, grinning widely.

Deryn scowled. "You jerk! I said no more games, Xander! How dare you trick -"

She didn't get the chance to finish before Xander had her in his arms and slammed against the wall.

"I knew you were a liar," he said, his grin never faltering.

And then his lips were crashing into hers. Deryn remained completely still as Xander kissed her, unsure of how she was supposed to react in that moment. She was angry. Definitely angry. But ...

"Admit it," he whispered into her ear before running his tongue along it. "Admit that you want this just as much as I do."

"I ..."

"Admit it." Xander pulled back and looked at her hungrily. He held his hands against the wall on either side of her, pinning her there as he continued to watch her with lust-filled eyes.

"No, I -"

The moment she began to protest, his lips were back on hers. Massaging, licking, biting, sucking, doing everything he could to drive her absolutely mad. And it was working.

Deryn tried to resist, but a few more moments of this and she knew she couldn't. Her eyes closed as she wrapped her arms around his waist, pulling him into her. Who was she trying to fool? She couldn't fight this. It was too strong, too powerful, too ...

"Fucking beautiful," he said, finishing her thought as she finally began to respond. "Tell me, Leon. I need to hear the words."

"I ..." Deryn gasped as he pressed his firmness into her. "I want this!" she blurted out to her own surprise. "I've wanted this since the night you first stayed with me." And that was the truth, something she hadn't realized until that moment. She'd felt safe with him that night, and that security had changed everything.

Xander pulled back, grinning widely as he tucked a stray strand of hair behind her ear. Victory had never tasted so sweet. "Then that's all you had to say."

He went in for her lips again and Deryn took this moment to completely take him in. His scent, his touch, the way he felt beneath her fingertips. She needed more.

"I'm still mad at you," she said between parts of their lips.

"It wouldn't be right if you weren't."

She loved the way she could feel his smile pressed against her.

Wrapping his arms around her waist, Xander picked Deryn up and carried her over to his bed. He threw her in its center and climbed on top of her, determined to keep any loss of contact as minimal as possible, so she would never get a chance to be overcome with doubt.

Deryn's hands gripped the sides of his shirt and Xander instantly knew what she wanted. He pulled back for just a moment to pull it off. After tossing it aside, he took something out of the drawer in his nightstand. Deryn watched closely as he pulled a black piece of cloth over his guard wristband.

"What's that for?" she asked.

"So we don't have a repeat performance of last time."

Before Deryn had a chance to ask any more questions, Xander caught her face between his palms and leaned down, kissing her tenderly as she ran her hands along his bare chest, once again stopping just above his heart.

Xander trailed his fingers down her face, her neck, her arms, not stopping until he reached the bottom of her shirt. He began to lift it, but her hands were quick to yank it back down.

He pulled back and stared down at her wide, frightened eyes.

"I'm not afraid of your scars, Leon."

"I know. But I -"

Xander reached over and turned off the lamp on his

nightstand. "Better?" he asked.

Deryn nodded. Her hands gave and he was able to take off her shirt. Even in the dark, Xander could still see the beauty in the body he finally had the chance to caress. While he was presently appreciative that he had never thought to buy her a bra, it did dawn on him that he should probably do that. Mental note for later.

Running his hands up her stomach and towards her breasts, Xander paused before gripping them for the first time. She bit her lip as he touched her delicately. He leaned down and pressed his lips to hers, kissing her softly as he finally took it all in. He was finally getting what he wanted. He was finally getting her. And it was as beautiful as he imagined.

Xander ran his hands through Deryn's hair while her arms wrapped around his back. His bare chest rubbed against hers, and the sensation of skin against skin caused him to moan into her mouth.

He needed more.

Xander wanted all of her tonight but, as an aspiring realist, he was fully aware that this might not happen right away. Which was why he was so taken off guard when her hands moved between them and started to undo his pants.

He pulled away and stared at her. She sucked on her bottom lip and sheepishly looked away.

"Don't do that if you won't be able to follow through."

Deryn took a deep breath beneath him, causing her chest to press harder against his. By god, he wanted to taste those breasts. But not yet. Not without the -

"Okay," she said, her voice cracking as she looked at him nervously. "I'm going to follow through, Xander. I told you, I want this."

"But we don't have to so quickly -"

"I *want* this," she repeated sternly. She reached up and stroked his cheek. "I promise."

The little resolve Xander had melted under her touch. He nodded slowly. "Alright."

He went back in and kissed her more aggressively. She

trembled as she brought her hands back to his pants. He helped her get them off before doing the same to her, leaving them both completely naked.

Xander kissed his way down Deryn's neck, distracting her while his other hand moved between them, making sure she was as prepared for this as she claimed to be. If the wetness between her thighs was any indication then she was more than ready for him.

He massaged her a little longer, relishing in the soft moans escaping her lips as he slipped a finger inside of her, and then a second. When she gasped, he moved his mouth down to her breast, sucking on the perky pink nipple that tasted as sweet as the rest of her.

Deryn closed her eyes as Xander continued to touch her, her hands clinging awkwardly to his shoulders as she realized she had no idea what she was doing. This was the first time anyone had ever tried to make *her* feel good, instead of just using her body to bring their own release, normally quickly and without any sort of priming.

Her mind was suddenly flooded with memories of these men. Using her, pounding her, hurting her. Never once caring when they were so rough they made her bleed.

"Leon."

Deryn opened her eyes. Xander was watching her, looking worried. She hadn't even realized he'd stopped. And then she felt it. The dampness stinging her cheeks. He wiped them with his thumb.

"We don't have to -"

"No!" Deryn shook her head urgently. She grabbed his arms and said, "Xander, please! I want this. I do. It's just ..." She closed her eyes again, letting more tears fall. "I can't shake the memories."

A pause.

"Open your eyes."

Deryn did as he instructed. She gazed up at him while he continued to stroke her damp cheek.

"If we do this, I'm going to need you to keep your eyes open at all times."

She nodded.

"Never take them off of me, not even once. You understand?"

She nodded again.

"That way if you ever start to feel that fear then you'll know it's me here with you." Xander leaned down and kissed her chastely, not once taking his eyes off of hers. "You ready?"

"Can you hold my hand?" she asked with a slight blush on her cheeks.

Xander smiled. He grabbed her hand off of his shoulder and interlaced their fingers, resting them on the pillow just beside her head.

Deryn could feel as Xander moved his other hand downward, stroking himself a few times before settling between her legs. She continued to gaze at him with wide eyes, refusing to break contact as he slowly began to enter her.

Deryn winced as he pushed all the way in, her hand squeezing his as their eyes remained locked.

"I'm going to move now," he breathed into her ear.

Deryn nodded, holding his back with her free hand as he began to slowly thrust inside of her. She sucked in her lips, trying to hold back any signs of pleasure as he panted above her. Realizing what she was doing, Xander touched her lips with his free hand, forcing them to part and release a small moan.

After a few minutes of this slow movement, he told her he was going to move faster. His free hand clutched her hip as he steadily increased his rhythm.

"Leon ... tell me you're alright," he demanded as his thrusts grew more frantic.

"I'm ..." Her head fell back as he hit a particularly pleasant spot. She moaned and brought her eyes quickly back to his. "I'm alright."

Xander kissed her then, biting her bottom lip hard as he finally let himself sink into her. In all of his fantasies, sex with Deryn had always been good, but nothing he imagined could have prepared him for the reality. Every small sound that escaped her lips had him growing harder in what was already an incredibly tight and beautiful fit. He had never felt this unbelievable grasping on his cock before. It was perfect.

Even though they had barely begun something that would, undoubtedly, lead to many incredible nights together, Xander already couldn't get enough. He could do this until morning if she let him, but he knew he couldn't keep it going too long. Her eyes were still so wide and terrified, and he would need to ease her into all of this before he could have her in each and every way he wanted.

Before long, Deryn was moaning loudly and freely. Xander moved his hand so it was between them, massaging with expert fingers to bring her to her climax that much quicker. To end the fear by giving her something beautiful. She sucked in her lips again, so he kissed them to free her sounds of pleasure from their prison.

Deryn's body writhed beneath his, and it was becoming harder for her to stay focused on his eyes. But, still, she did, never breaking their gaze as she moved closer. So, so much closer.

"Xander ... say my name," she demanded between heavy breaths. "I need to hear it."

Gripping her hand even tighter, Xander hovered his lips above hers and slowly said, "Deryn."

This was the last piece she needed. After hearing her given name, Deryn came undone, her tight muscles clenching around him as her back arched and her body lost all control.

Xander took this moment to wrap his free arm underneath her, pulling her as close to him as possible without merging into one entity, wanting to feel every bit of her orgasm vibrate against his body as it took hold. The look in her eyes as she came undone around him was all Xander needed to find his own release. One, two, three more thrusts and he was done, finishing inside of her as she fell heavy in his arms. He screamed her name once more, not just for her, but for him, as well. Reminding him that he finally had what he wanted right there beneath him.

The two of them stayed there for a moment, catching their breath as they kissed every inch of skin they could find. Their hands remained clasped, and Xander looked at them before attempting to move off of her. But, before he could, she wrapped her arm tighter around his back and held him in place.

"No. Not yet. Let me feel you for a little bit longer."

Xander smirked. "Leave me inside of you much longer and I'm going to have to demand a repeat performance."

Deryn said nothing. Just continued to hold him.

"You alright?" he asked, unable to see her eyes from his head's current position in the crook of her neck. He felt her nod against him.

"I like to feel you breathing," she said.

"Dare I ask why?"

"I don't know. It makes me feel alive, I guess." She took a deep breath, inhaled the sweet aroma of his hair, and said, "Okay." She let him go.

Xander pulled out and rolled off to the side, their interlaced hands finally coming undone. He landed flat on his back and pulled her into his side.

Deryn nervously put her head on his chest while he held her close. She moved her hand down to his stomach, resting it there while the feeling of his breath steadily moving it up and down soothed her. Only the faint sound of her name was able to break her from her daze. She looked up at him.

"Everything alright?" he asked once again.

She fixed her eyes on his lips and gave a shallow nod.

"Care to tell me what's on your mind, then?"

Deryn stared vacantly at those lips for a long moment before glancing back at his eyes and sighing. "If I tell you something, will you promise not to react?"

Xander stiffened.

"I mean, no being weird, no being angry. Just ... just act like it's nothing."

Deryn's hand began to shake on his stomach. In hindsight, she should've known who she was talking to, but she wanted to get this out and Xander was the one she wanted to tell. So, when he clasped his hand with hers on his stomach and nodded, she took several deep breaths to prepare herself. She wasn't going to tell him everything, but she needed to tell him this one small piece.

"When I first became a slave, I ..." She gulped, looked away and sucked back tears. "I was a virgin."

Xander's hand tensed on her shoulder.

"This was my first time by choice."

He shouldn't have been surprised. While she and Trigger had been together five years ago, the Outsider recruits were watched much more closely than those like him. They were never left alone.

But actually hearing the words come out of her mouth was different. She had been a virgin that day when his father dragged her away, and he knew it couldn't have lasted much longer. His hand clenched on her shoulder as he tried to keep his promise about not reacting, but that was really hard to do when he was suddenly overcome with this incredible urge to kill someone.

"Who?" he choked out.

Deryn glanced at him. "What do you mean?"

"Who was the first to touch you?" he asked through gritted teeth, still trying to maintain his composure.

She looked back at their clasped hands and used her thumb to stroke the top of his. "It doesn't matter."

"It most certainly does -"

"There were so many that first time. I just ... I shut myself off from it, just enough so all of their faces became a blur. I didn't want to know."

Xander tightened his grip and pulled her up so her head was level with his. He turned slightly and brushed his fingers through her hair. Deryn brought her hand up and touched his heart again.

"Would ..." She took a deep breath, gulped, and started again. "Would it be alright if I pretended this was my first time?"

Xander nodded as he continued to gaze at her, leaning in and giving her a soft kiss in hopes of stopping the tears that were stinging behind his eyes from falling. He wanted names, but he knew he wasn't going to get them. Not tonight. And probably not from her. He would need to dig deeper for that.

"Is that why you needed this?" he asked. "To have your first time of your own freewill?"

"Yes, but I wanted it to be with you. Don't think for one second that I didn't."

Xander kissed her softly. Her body was still tense, but slowly began to ease as she let herself sink into him.

Butterflies fluttered in her stomach. His lips were so incredibly delicate in comparison to the rest of him, it seemed almost unnatural.

When Xander pulled away, he planted chaste kisses on her cheeks and forehead before looking at her again. She looked beautiful like this. Her hair spread out in thick waves across the pillow, her sea-green eyes dancing in the small crack of moonlight shining through the curtains, and her pink, plump lips, always ready for him. His cock twitched and he knew he had to have her again.

"Do I have to go back to my room now?" she asked as she played with a strand of his hair.

"No," he said. "Why would you think that?"

"Well, you don't normally let women stay in your bed. If I stay you're not going to make me sleep on the floor, are you?" The corners of her mouth twitched upwards.

"No, Leon. Only one-nighters have to sleep on the floor, and you're not a one-nighter."

Her smile deepened.

Wanting to taste that smile, Xander kissed her again, this time with much more oomph. He ran his hands down her sides, caressing her with well-trained fingers. She moaned as he hardened against her.

"Shall we give it another go?" he whispered, grinning triumphantly as she nodded. Her stay there just got a lot more interesting.

CHAPTER TWENTY-EIGHT

Deryn gazed at Xander as he panted above her, his heavily-lidded eyes filled with lust while the feeling of his thrusting made her burn from the inside out. He had one hand on the inside of her knee, holding her leg upward so she was more open to him, the other one keeping a death grip on her hip.

The two of them had been having sex every night and most mornings for over a week now, and Deryn finally felt like she was getting the hang of it.

"Oh, fuck! Deryn!" he shouted as she grazed her teeth across his neck. Her nails were digging sharply into his back, which he had learned meant she wanted him to thrust harder. So he did.

Most days when Xander was gone and Deryn was left alone to really contemplate what it was they were doing, she couldn't help but realize the insanity of it all. This was Xander Ruby. Someone who had been her enemy for years - more or less - and she had willingly given him something no one else ever had before. Her consent.

Deryn hated herself for letting this happen. She hated herself before they ever did anything. She hated herself after. But during ... well, that was something different entirely.

From the moment Xander would start sucking on her neck, letting her know exactly what it was he wanted, any hate she felt melted away and become pure, raw lust. Never in her life had she felt so incredibly alive than when he was inside of her, making her feel in ways she'd never thought possible. No, she definitely didn't hate that.

Xander grabbed her waist and flipped them so she was on top. He must have been close because he knew she always liked to finish like this. So she was the one in control. In the beginning, he had helped her move her hips but now she never let him, wanting to bring them both to the finish line on her own.

Deryn put her hands on his chest and began bouncing fervently. He reached up and tightly gripped her hair, pulling her head down for a passionate kiss. He loved to feel the sounds she made while coming against his lips.

The two of them had created such a perfect sync that they always finished within seconds of each other, mainly because Xander held back until she was ready. Deryn was first tonight, the vibrations from the moans she was finally learning to let loose pushing him over the edge.

And then it was over, Deryn's body going limp while he wrapped his arms around her, both breathing heavily as the hatred they had for themselves returned. No matter what, they both knew this could never end well. Someday soon, Deryn would leave and they would become enemies once more.

But, still, they kept at it. Because they had found something in each other that no one else could ever give them. Someone who understood. Even though they fought on opposite sides, they still knew what the other had been through, what they were going through now. And Deryn realized that this was something Dakota would never be able to comprehend.

The closer she grew to Xander, the more she dreaded going back to her old life. She was afraid to lose that comfort. What if she never found it again?

"Leon?"

Deryn looked down to see Xander watching her. He reached up and wiped her cheek. More tears. She hadn't even realized.

"Sorry," she said, her eyes suddenly moving to the black cloth he wore over his guard wristband. She stroked it while putting her head on his chest and listening to his heartbeat. To hold onto that feeling of being alive for just a little bit longer. She smiled as Xander kissed the top of her head.

"Want to come out to the balcony with me?"

Deryn nodded, taking one last moment to feel his breathing against her cheek before slowly climbing off of him. She located her clothes, put them on and slipped into her cozy robe. When she finished tying the belt around her waist, Xander wrapped his arms around her, giving her a soft kiss before taking her hand and leading her outside.

When they got to the balcony, Deryn took her usual spot on the ground while Xander sat in his chair. He took out a cigarette and lit it, not blind to the way Deryn crinkled her nose. She never said anything, but he knew she hated it when he smoked, especially now that they were involved physically. Afterwards, she would always refuse to kiss him until he very thoroughly washed his mouth.

Deryn chewed her bottom lip as she stared down at the street through the crack in the stone. There was no movement down there, so he could not imagine what she was watching so fixedly. Probably being sucked into her mind again, overanalyzing everything they were doing, as she so often did.

"Something on your mind, Leon?"

She blinked back to reality. "No."

Xander continued to watch her as he took another drag of his cigarette. "You already know I can tell when you're lying."

"It's nothing new. Just the same things I always think about after."

Xander frowned. "You do realize you've never told me what that is?"

"Yes."

"It just seems a bit backwards, doesn't it? That you'll let me stick my cock in you but you won't tell me what you're thinking," he said, leaning forward on his knees.

"Please don't say it like that," she said, clenching her eyes shut. "I just ... I don't like feeling dirty about it."

Xander smirked. "No reason to feel dirty. It's all just a beautiful, natural -"

"Not for me!" she interrupted, her cheeks becoming flushed.

He glanced sideways at her. "I wish you'd stop doing that."

"Doing what?" She stared back through the crack.

"Blaming yourself for something that was out of your control. I mean, if you truly see what you and I are doing in the same way -"

Deryn whipped her head back towards him and shouted, "No! That's not what I meant!"

"Then how do you see what we're doing, Leon?"

She looked shyly to the ground. "I don't know."

"Does it feel wrong?"

Deryn shook her head. "But not right either. I can't really explain it."

Xander watched her and sighed. He put out his cigarette and held out his arms. "Come here, Leon."

Deryn stood carefully, making sure her hair covered her face from anyone who just might be able to see them from down below. They may have been five floors up but she was still paranoid, as she should be. When she reached Xander, he wrapped his arms around her waist and pulled her onto his lap.

"This isn't easy for me either. Wanting you," he said while nuzzling her neck. "Knowing no good will ever come of this. But I can't stop myself."

"Why do you want me, Xander?" she asked while tracing swirly patterns along his hand.

"There's no logic behind it. I just do."

"But you can have anyone. As a Guardian, pretty much all you have to do is point at a girl and she's yours."

Xander lifted his hand and pointed at Deryn.

She blushed and hit it back down. "You *know* what I mean."

"I guess I'm just sick of my usual bevy of women," he said with a smile. "None of them have ever left me completely satisfied."

"And I do?"

"Completely? No," he answered honestly. "But it's pretty damn close."

"Oh." She bit her bottom lip.

Xander tightened his hold on her and smirked. "That wasn't an insult, but I've been keeping myself pretty tame for you. I look forward to the day you're ready for me to let loose."

Deryn raised her eyebrows. "Do I even want to know?"

"You'll see," he said, planting a gentle kiss on her neck.

Deryn leaned into his lips. She closed her eyes and sighed.

"You know we can stop whenever. All you have to do is say the word."

Her eyes popped back open. "Is that what you want? To make it easier?"

Silence. Deryn's heart felt heavy as she turned to look at him. When she did, Xander grabbed her chin, pulled her in and pressed his lips to hers, massaging them gently before slipping his tongue into her mouth. For once, she didn't even mind the taste of cigarettes.

Deryn had been wrong before. During those rare moments when he kissed her like this - soft and sweet, her heart racing and palms sweating, making her feel like she was someone important, someone who mattered - she didn't hate herself. Because a kiss like this made her feel something she hadn't felt in a long time. Safe. Beautiful. Cared for. Maybe even loved. Of course, she knew that was crazy. But wasn't it all?

"I want *you*, Leon," said Xander breathlessly into her mouth as he continued to kiss her. "In spite of it all, I want you. From now until the day we part. The rest is up to you."

The two of them continued to hold each other, kissing tenderly, not even noticing as the air grew colder around them. The night stretched on and, still, they stayed like that. There was nothing passionate, nothing lustful, nothing desperate about that kiss, just the sweet and delicate feeling of comfort while having someone there. Someone to hold while being held. Someone who wanted you. Someone who needed you. Someone who looked at you through eyes without judgment, and who knew your past but did not define you by it. Who understood that you'd been through something horrible but did not treat you like you were made of glass.

Xander and Deryn did all of these things for each other, and they wanted to hold onto those feelings for as long as possible.

"We should get to bed," said Xander as the chill in the air began to pick up, but his lips never left hers.

"Just a little bit longer," she said, moving her hand so it was resting above his heart. Still beating. Still real.

And so they stayed. Seconds turning into minutes, minutes turning into hours. Neither of them had realized how much they needed this. It was something far more powerful than sex. A true connection.

It wasn't until Xander noticed how cold Deryn felt in his arms that he finally broke their contact. Eyes on her, he wrapped his hands underneath her legs and lifted her up, carrying her inside with great care.

Xander placed her on his bed, and helped her remove her robe and slippers. He turned off the lights and climbed in next to her. The two recommenced their kissing, slowly slipping off their clothes until he was inside of her once more, thrusting softly until the faint light of day shined through the crack in the curtains. Not once did their lips part, their connection remaining delicate as they began to memorize each other with every touch.

"Deryn," Xander breathed into her mouth as her face radiated soft pleasure. "This ..." He trailed off as her muscles pulsated around him, bringing him his release.

Xander gazed down at her as they both caught their breath, giving her one last kiss before rolling off and pulling her into him, taking a moment to breathe in the sweet scent of her hair before finally closing his eyes.

Part of Xander wished she had held on for a little bit longer, so he could have finished what he was going to say.

This is closer.

That was what he'd wanted to tell her. Because it was. This was the closest he had ever been to feeling completely satisfied. He had never had sex with anyone like that before. Not even Finley back when he almost sort of cared for her. But Deryn ... he cared a lot. More than he should. And knowing that he was experiencing this intimate moment with someone who had somehow managed to seep into him ... That was better.

CHAPTER TWENTY- NINE

Xander and Bronson walked around the women's lingerie shop, both looking a bit overwhelmed with all of the options available to them. How did women ever make such decisions?

Noticing their wide, tentative eyes, a shop girl walked up to them with a bright smile and asked, "Can I help you find something?"

"Uh, yes," said Bronson. "We're looking for some bras and sleepwear for my girlfriend, and we're not exactly sure where to start. But nothing too sexy," he added. "Just casual."

"Well, maybe not *just* casual," said Xander. "It wouldn't hurt to get her at least one sexy thing." His eyes immediately drifted to a red negligee in the corner. Damn, that would look great on Deryn.

"Casual would really be just fine," said Bronson, trying hard not to notice that lustful look in Xander's eyes as he glanced around the shop.

"Okay then," said the shop girl. "What size cup is she?"

Bronson crinkled his forehead. He looked over to see Xander doing the same. Huh. They had forgotten to ask.

Then Xander lifted his hand and said, "Like, a little less than a handful." He clenched his fingers like he was squeezing a breast.

The shop girl stared down at his hand for a moment before moving her eyes back to Bronson. "*Your* girlfriend?" she asked, raising her eyebrows.

"Um ... yeah," he said, feeling even more uncomfortable. He was getting this horrible feeling that his fake girlfriend might be cheating on him.

"Well, judging by the size of your friend's hands, I'm going to guess she is either a B or a C cup. Is she petite?"

"Yes," they both answered.

"This way, please."

While slowly following her, Bronson grabbed Xander's arm and said, "Hey, Ruby. Stop answering questions about *my* girlfriend. It looks weird."

"Sorry," said Xander, his eyes now drifting to a lacy, black nightie. There was so much potential here. Such a waste that he couldn't shop in places like this by himself.

It was a good hour before Xander and Bronson got out of there with several bags in hand. While Bronson had been pretty insistent about sticking with the basics - beige, white, and black - Xander had convinced him to get one lacy pink and black bra to 'make her feel like a woman'. He also convinced him to get one red one, by the slight chance that they might buy her a red sweater later.

They also bought her several pajama sets, so she would not have to borrow Xander's any longer, and one short nightdress for the 'warmer nights', as Xander had put it. Bronson didn't even bother to argue that it was mid-November. Warmer nights were hardly a concern.

On their way out the door, the shop girl grabbed Bronson and touched her wristband to his, transferring her information. "If things don't work out with your girlfriend," she whispered before eyeing Xander skeptically.

"You see what happens when you drag me to places like this?" said Bronson, when they got outside. "This is why I like men. Women can be so damn conniving. I mean, I'm taken for god's sake!"

Xander smirked. "Calm down, Bronson. You don't actually have to contact her."

"You want it?" Bronson held his wristband out to him.

Xander shook his head and Bronson deleted her

information.

"So how exactly do you know Deryn's breasts are a little less than a handful?" he asked, glancing sideways at Xander.

"Because I've looked." And he wasn't ashamed of it either. Actually, he really didn't care what Bronson knew about him and Deryn. She was the one against it. Apparently, he had already mentioned his disapproval of the situation before anything ever happened between them, and she didn't want to ignite any fires.

"But never touched?"

Xander could not help but smirk. "Any particular reason you're asking me this?" he said, slipping into an alley and pulling out a cigarette. He offered one to Bronson and they leaned against the same wall, smoking just out of view of wandering eyes.

"I don't know. But Deryn's become like a little sister to me, and I haven't seen much of either of you over the past couple of weeks. Seems like you've wanted privacy or something."

"We do," said Xander honestly. He leaned his head back against the wall and blew a billow of smoke straight into the air. "I'm sure you've figured it out by now, Bronson, but Deryn was a slave. They had a trade every few months and the next one is coming up. It was the night of the last one that she escaped and she hasn't been taking it well."

It wasn't a lie. Every day she dreaded the anniversary of the infamous slave trade. It just wasn't why they wanted their privacy.

There was a long moment of silence before Xander turned his head to look at Bronson. He was staring at him, eyes wide and jaw slacken as his cigarette dangled out of his mouth.

"What?" asked Xander, creasing his brow.

"What did you call her?"

"Leon?" Xander tried replaying his words in his head. He was unsure of what else he might have called her. He always called her Leon. Except in the bedroom, knowing very well that she got off on hearing her given name. But he supposed he might have let her first name slip.

"No. That's not what you said."

"I'm positive it is," said Xander, throwing down his cigarette and putting it out with his foot. "Better get a move on. We've barely gotten started."

Bronson nodded and did the same. Still, he couldn't shake the idea that something was off. Xander seemed different. Almost happy. And it was really creeping him out. A few weeks ago Deryn had finally admitted that she was the cupcake girl. *This* must have been the feeling she was talking about. How the nice gesture just seemed so not Ruby.

"Fucking creepy," said Bronson under his breath as Xander led him towards a women's clothing shop. Sweaters, shirts, and pants were next on their list.

~

"So how does it fit?" Xander called into Deryn's bedroom while sitting on the arm of the couch.

"Not bad," she said, walking out in black pants and a white sweater. "I actually think these might be a bit small." She began playing with the pants' waistband. Not much give.

"I disagree," said Xander, beyond pleased she was finally wearing something that showed off her feminine figure. His oversized sweaters and pajama pants just weren't doing it for him.

Deryn's cheeks flushed as she bashfully looked back into her room. Currently, her bed was overrun with shopping bags. "The two of you went a bit overboard. I really don't need all of this."

"Everyone needs options," said Xander, reaching out and grabbing her waist. He pulled her until she was between his legs. "Figures that we would finally get you into some proper attire and all I can think about is getting you out of it."

Deryn giggled as he nibbled on her neck. She let him nestle there for a moment before pulling away, giving him a quick kiss and heading back into her room.

"Next one," she said, digging through the bags and coming out with a red sweater. She then went through the bag of bras, her eyes freezing for a moment before pulling out the pink and black one. "I assume this is your doing?" she asked, holding it up for Xander to see.

He smirked. "Naturally. But there's a red one in there for that particular sweater. You can model the pink for me later."

Deryn rolled her eyes. She looked back in the bag and started laughing. Then she pulled out the small nightdress. "Really, Xander? How'd you convince Bronson to let you buy me this one?"

"Warm nights," said Xander with a shrug of his shoulders.

"Warm nights? It's been a high of maybe forty degrees out."

"Has it?" He raised his eyebrows. "Well, then, you're certainly lucky I radiate such powerful body heat."

Deryn wanted to argue, but he was right. His body was like her own personal heater.

Finally locating the red bra, she moved to shut the door.

"I've seen you naked, Leon."

"Not with the lights on, you haven't." She slammed it.

Xander frowned. Unfortunately, that statement was very true. Deryn often put her clothes back on before going to sleep and, when she didn't, she always made a point to be the first one up and out of bed in the morning. Xander had caught a hazy glimpse of her through his fluttering eyelids once, but she had quickly moved out of view. He would have to eradicate this small problem immediately.

After Deryn was finished trying everything on, she put all of the new clothes in her dresser and closet, smiling widely as she did so. Once that was done, she slipped into her robe and got ready to take a shower. When she walked back to the living room, Xander seized her hand and pulled her towards the front door.

"One more thing," he said, grabbing a bag from behind the couch and handing it to her. "It wasn't a necessity but I thought you'd like to have it."

Deryn smiled as she put the bag down on the back of the couch and pulled out a long, black coat. It was of great quality and felt incredibly soft in her hands.

"I never wanted to ask, but I always figured the one you

have now was Elvira's."

"It was," she said, her smile only growing as she continued to run the material through her fingers.

"So I was right to assume you would want one of your own, then?" asked Xander, rubbing his hand comfortingly along her lower back.

Deryn nodded. "Thank you, Xander." She looked at him with tears in her eyes. "For all of it. I know I don't exactly have a current need for any of these things but -"

Xander silenced her with a kiss. Her stomach fluttered as he continued to rub the small of her back.

When he pulled away, he flashed her a crooked smile and said, "Think nothing of it. Besides, you're going to need all of this stuff eventually. You won't be trapped here forever."

Deryn's heart sank a little. "I've been trapped before, Xander, and *this* -" She put her hand on his chest. "- isn't it."

Standing on tiptoe, Deryn gave him a quick kiss before going back to her room and hanging her new coat in the closet. She grabbed the old one off of its hanger and went to the blazing fireplace, tossing it into the flames. Xander came over and grabbed her hand. They stood in silence for a moment and watched it burn until there was nothing left but ashes.

Deryn stared blankly at the fire, her eyes not focusing until she felt Xander tugging on her hand.

"Leon?"

She looked up to see Xander watching her. When their eyes met, he pulled her body into his and tucked her hair behind her ear.

"You alright?" he asked.

Deryn smiled and nodded. "I'm just glad to be rid of the thing. It's like a weight's been lifted." She rolled her shoulders. "Now I just need that shower to relax."

Deryn walked away but Xander was quick to catch up and turn her around. "Any chance I might join you?"

Her cheeks turned bright-red as she quickly stared anywhere but at him. "Um ... I don't ... I mean, I'm not ..."

"Don't you think it's time you let me see you with the lights on?" he said as he pulled her close and ran his tongue along her ear.

"I ..."

"Don't you want to see me?"

Deryn shuddered. Xander took this as a surefire sign that he was right, so he lifted her up and sat her on the edge of the kitchen counter.

"You can see me first if you want," he said, settling between her legs.

She tried to hide it by biting her lip, but there was no disguising the throaty moan that escaped her.

"All you have to do is undress me," whispered Xander, catching her lips in a fervent kiss.

Deryn continued to moan into his mouth as he grinded against her, her shaky hands slowly making their way into his shirt. She pulled at the edges awkwardly for a moment before finally lifting it and, with a bit of assistance, yanking it over his head. At first her eyes drifted to the black cloth on his arm that he had gotten into the habit of wearing, but that was not where she wanted to focus. So she moved her gaze back to his bare chest, staring at it for a moment - creamy, chiseled and perfect - before running her hands along his skin, pausing slightly when she found a small, white scar.

"Two years ago, during a battle with the Resistance in one of their villages," he said before she could ask. "One of them almost hit me with an arrow, and when I dodged I flew into the edge of a table."

"Are there more?" she asked, looking at him hopefully.

"Oh, yes." Xander took her hand and helped her trace his form. He brought it up his ribcage and stopped somewhere near the top. "Broke a few of these when our beloved president had me tortured before I was back in his good graces. I eventually taught myself not to squirm so much. It really is more beneficial in the long run." And then he brought her hand down to his left hip, letting her fingers pull down his pants a bit. "A member of the Resistance got me here with a rock when they lost their weapon."

"A rock did *that*?" she asked, rubbing the well-sized scar with her index finger.

"It was a sharp rock." Xander then let go of her hand and turned around. "The one just below my right shoulder blade is from when a flying target hit me during shooting training at Eagle. And the one here on my arm," he pointed, "was from when I fell off of a wall I was climbing when I was seven."

When Xander turned back around, he was happy to see that Deryn was smiling.

"I have more," he said, leaning back in and hovering his lips above hers, "but you'll have to find them on your own."

Deryn's head plunged forward and she engulfed his lips with hers, kissing him vigorously while running her hands along his smooth skin. Before long, they were both gasping for air, and she caught his eyes with a lustful look before moving her hands down to his pants.

She had just begun to undo them when the door to the apartment clicked, and then opened. Bronson stepped inside, quickly freezing when he caught sight of Xander practically on top of Deryn on the kitchen counter. They both turned and looked at him, their eyes wide and guilty as they realized they had just been caught red-handed. And, speaking of hands, Deryn was quick to pull hers off of Xander, but then she had no clue where to put them and they just hung awkwardly in the air. Xander pulled back and she was finally able to use them to fidget with her robe.

"Evening, Bronson," said Xander in an even tone. "Something we can help you with?"

Bronson stared at him openmouthed. He slowly lifted a box. "I, uh ... Quigley brought me dessert from the restaurant before he went out and I thought you two might like some."

There was an awkward silence as no one moved from their current positions. Deryn could not even look in Bronson's direction. She was too embarrassed and did not want him to see how red she was.

"I'm sorry," said Bronson once he got sick of listening to the clock tick. "Have I interrupted something?"

Xander said, "Yes," while Deryn said, "No."

"Because it looks like I interrupted something. Like maybe Ruby was making sure that your breasts really are slightly less than a handful."

"Hey, my hands were nowhere near her breasts," said Xander defensively. "They were on the insides of her thighs."

"Okay," said Deryn, jumping off the counter and standing in front of him, since Bronson was leaning forward, obviously preparing to strike. "Bronson, I can see where this is going and I cannot stress enough how important it is for you to stay calm."

"Stay calm?" said Bronson, taking a moment to slam the still-open door and lock it before walking forward. "Are you fucking kidding me? He's a Guardian, Deryn! And *you're* an Outsider! What the hell are you thinking? I thought you said you weren't a masochist!"

"I'm not," she said weakly. "I can't help -"

"You can't help what? Your feelings?"

Deryn blushed.

"This is insane, Deryn! *You're* insane!"

Tears filled her eyes and she quickly looked to the side so he wouldn't see them. There was that word again. *Insane.*

"Hey!" shouted Xander, putting a comforting hand on her waist before stepping in front of her. "Don't you dare! Don't you fucking dare talk to her like that!" With flaming eyes, Xander looked back at Deryn and said, "Leon, go take your shower. I'll take care of this."

"But -"

"It's fine," he said, squeezing her hand. "I won't do anything rash. I'm not you."

Deryn smiled faintly. "Like you're any better." She gave Bronson one last disappointed look before heading to the bathroom.

The moment the door was closed, Xander turned back to Bronson and said, "Outside." He grabbed his shirt off of the floor and put it back on.

"I'm not going -"

"I said, outside!" demanded Xander, walking towards the balcony.

After letting out a loud grunt, Bronson followed him and shut the door. Xander pressed his wristband and put up a soundproof shield. The two of them stood on opposite ends with their arms crossed.

"What the fuck, Ruby?" began Bronson, staring daggers at him as he tried to remain somewhat composed in the small space.

"What the fuck, what, Bronson? None of this is any of your business!"

"Well, I'm making it my business! Someone needs to be the voice of reason for you two! I mean ... *fuck*! What the hell are you thinking?"

Xander smirked. "Isn't it obvious?" Bronson lunged forward but Xander held out his hand. "Stop right there."

Bronson froze. "What you gonna do, Ruby? Use your Element on me? I'm curious, what reasoning would you give the president for doing it?" he asked venomously. "Perhaps you were putting someone in their place."

Xander said nothing.

"Oh, come on, Ruby. We both know you'd love to do it, so why don't you already?" he baited.

Xander glowered at him. "All of these years and you still think so little of me." He sighed, slowly lowering his hand. "No, Bronson, I'm not going to use my Element on you and I never would, even if I did have it on me. Punch you, sure. Or bind you so you don't come at me again; I'm not against that either."

Bronson's face softened.

"You can think whatever you want about me," continued Xander. "I don't care. But don't you dare, don't you fucking dare come up here again if you're going to insult Deryn! She's been through enough in her life! She doesn't need to hear such horrible insults from someone she trusts!"

Bronson cocked his head in curiosity. "What are you talking about? I didn't insult -"

"Yes you did!" shouted Xander. "In there just now! Didn't you see her? Didn't you see her fucking eyes as she tried to stop herself from crying? *You* did that! You fucking did that when you called her insane!"

Bronson glanced upwards as he tried to recall everything he had said inside. "If I said that I didn't mean it literally."

"It doesn't matter! Her mind has been fucked with and she's been working so hard to get it back! And then, in one second, you make her doubt herself! That's all it takes with her! That's all it fucking takes for her to lose it! To not want to try anymore!"

Bronson cocked his head again and stared dazedly at Xander, his mouth agape as he tried to process everything he was hearing. Between the lines, of course.

"What are you staring at?"

Bronson blinked.

"Seriously, what is your problem? Deryn and I are both adults and we know what we're doing!"

He blinked again. "Do you?"

"Of course!" shouted Xander. "We're aware the circumstances are not exactly ideal, but she *knows* we can stop whenever! I've told her! I've told her over and over again that all she has to do is say the word and we'll stop! Because I'm not stupid! I know this is a fucked up situation! It's sick and it's twisted and it's wrong, but I can't stop! I can't stop until I know it's what *she* wants!"

Bronson cocked his head further. "Why?"

"Because!" Because Xander wanted her. Needed her. Desired her. Because no one else had ever felt so perfect while tangled in his arms, against his lips, around his cock. And he would be damned if he gave up those feelings before he had to. But he gave Bronson no further explanation. 'Because' would just have to do.

Straightening his head, Bronson stared at Xander for a long while, stuck in a blank expression before his lips slowly began to curve into a smile. "Holy fuck."

"What?" asked Xander, more than a little disturbed by this

man's growing amusement.

"Nothing, I just ... I get it now."

"Get what?"

Bronson laughed and said, "The fact that you don't know only makes it better!"

"What are you -"

"Don't you see, Ruby?"

Now it was Xander's turn to blink.

"Holy crap, you really don't!" He laughed louder. "You *like* her!"

Xander's eyes widened.

"You like Deryn! Ah, shit, I'm sorry, mate! If I'd known, I wouldn't have reacted that way earlier. I seriously just thought you were looking for a convenient fuck, but this ... this is alright! I can definitely get onboard with this!"

Xander's jaw dropped slightly. He really had no idea what to say. "I wouldn't ... I mean, I would never ... to her ..."

"It's alright, mate. I know," said Bronson, stepping forward and putting his hand on Xander's shoulder. "I mean, I still think this is going to fuck with both of your heads in the long run but, hey, who am I to judge? You know how many straight men I've been involved with? Big mistake. Mistakes, really. One right after another. Hmm ..."

As Bronson pondered his own life, Xander fidgeted from foot to foot, looking around uncomfortably as the words finally started to sink in. Bronson thought he *liked* her. That he, Xander Ruby, actually liked Deryn Leon. The girl who had suffered horribly because of something he had done. Who was in the shower now ... soaking wet and lathered in the sweet smelling soap he had purchased for her. And alone. So, so alone. *Fuck*, he wanted to be in that shower with her. But not because he liked her. Because he liked fucking her. There had to be a difference.

"Well, I suppose I should probably get out of your hair. I obviously *was* interrupting something before. Here." Bronson handed him the box he was still holding. "The dessert's all yours. They say chocolate is an aphrodisiac." He winked and went back inside.

Xander followed.

"Have fun," said Bronson, heading out the front door.

Xander went to the kitchen and put the box on the counter. He opened it and took a good look at the piece of chocolate cake. Picking it up, he took a big bite before putting it back and closing the box.

His eyes drifted over to the bathroom door. The shower was still running strong. His efforts earlier didn't have to be wasted.

Without another thought, Xander entered the bathroom, not even bothering to knock. He stripped off his clothes until he was wearing nothing but the black cloth over his wristband.

"Xander?" called Deryn from behind the steamy shower door. "Is that you?"

"Yes," he answered, walking over and standing so his silhouette was just out of view. "I was hoping we could finish what we started earlier."

"Oh, umm ... that sure ended quickly. Bronson isn't dead, is he?"

Unfortunately, "No. He got over it pretty quickly. So can I come in?"

"Uh ... how did you convince him to -"

"Quit stalling, Leon. I have a large scar on my ass from when a Resistance member sent me skidding across the ground that I would just love to show you."

She giggled. "I suppose it would be alright. If you came in, that is."

Xander reached for the door.

"Just don't ask for stories on mine. Not yet."

"Deal," he said before slowly opening the door, a large gust of steam seeping out and obstructing his vision.

When it started to clear, he could just make out Deryn's silhouette in the back corner. He stepped closer. Her hands moved so they were covering her body, so he kept his eyes upward, catching hers as she gazed at him nervously while sucking in her lips.

Xander smirked and took another step forward. "Ease up,

Leon. The point of this is so I can see you. Remember?"

Deryn looked away.

"Alright then. I'm not looking yet." He kept his eyes focused on her face as he continued to step forward. When Xander reached her, he rubbed her arms, easing them to her sides before taking her hands in his. "But you should look now."

Deryn glanced up and kept her eyes on Xander's as he took a step back. She bit her bottom lip.

"Go on. I'm not embarrassed."

Her eyes slowly trailed downward, taking a moment to stare at each and every part of him. His neck. His shoulders. His chest. Abs. Hips. Her breath sucked in when she finally reached his cock, growing hard as she gazed at it. She instinctually let go of Xander's hand and reached out to touch it.

He let out a throaty moan. "You like that?" he asked.

Deryn said nothing, but when she looked up at him there was no mistaking the lust in her eyes. Xander pressed forward and crashed his lips into hers, using his free hand to push her wet hair out of her face. Then he moved it downwards, not stopping until he reached her wet core, massaging it gently.

"Lift your legs around me," he instructed.

Deryn nodded nervously and wrapped her arms around his shoulders, lifting her legs as he raised her up against the shower wall. She linked them around his waist, her body trembling as he continued to kiss her, his lips moving to her neck as he guided his cock inside of her.

"You alright?" he asked.

"Yes," she answered. "You can move."

Xander nodded, plunging his hungry lips back on her neck as he thrust inside of her. There would be no going slow tonight. There was too much buildup. Too much anticipation. Too much time wasted with Bronson. And Xander needed to prove something. He needed to prove that this was just sex. A matter of convenience with someone he just happened to desire. Someone he cared for. Nothing more. You could care for someone without liking them, you could have sex with them every morning and every night and fall asleep with them in your arms but still keep those feelings separate. It was not impossible.

Deryn's nails dug into his back as his thrusting became more vigorous. He tangled his hand in her hair and pulled her head back, staring into her sea-green eyes for a moment before heading in for those lips. Those divinely delicious lips he simply couldn't get enough of.

"You taste like chocolate," she said with a breathy giggle.

It was not long before her head fell back and she quickly began to fall apart. He moved even faster, his hips nothing but a blur as her eyes closed and her moans grew louder.

Xander buried his head in her neck as he continued to thrust through his release, not wanting this incredible feeling to end just yet. *Closer.* Every time was so much closer to that complete satisfaction he craved.

Finally beginning to slow, Xander's legs gave out and he collapsed to the shower floor, taking Deryn down with him. She hugged her arms tighter around him and attempted to catch her breath.

"Fucking beautiful," he whispered while she planted lazy kisses along his neck.

She laughed quietly.

"Can I see you now?" asked Xander.

Deryn nodded. She slackened her hold on his shoulders and let him slowly push her back, not stopping until she was, once again, pressed against the shower wall.

The warm water continued to pour down on them as Xander sucked in his breath, taking in Deryn for the first time. All of her.

Yes, there were scars, but he hardly noticed them. How could he when there was so much more here? So much beauty. Milky skin with a few spattered freckles, especially on the shoulders, something he understood came from living under the sun. Her breasts were perfect. Still perky and young with vibrant pink nipples, obviously a side effect of being in the shower. He couldn't help himself, so flicked one.

"Xander!" she shouted, trying to act offended as she

smacked his arm.

"Sorry," he said, stretching down to kiss it. "Better?"

"For you, I'm sure."

Xander flashed his crooked grin and pulled back again, his eyes continuing to trail downward. His fingers traced circles around her bellybutton before he finally landed on their crotches, his cock still soft inside of her. She shifted, signifying her discomfort and, incidentally, making it twitch.

"Probably best if I pull this out now," he said, slowly backing away from her. But then he kept going, instinctually leaning downward so his head was level with the lovely haven his cock had just vacated. He couldn't help himself. He wanted to see all of her tonight. So he reached forward and pulled her nether-lips apart. Deryn fidgeted but he held her still.

Xander breathed her in. The aroma was intoxicating. He wanted to taste it. So he did, running his tongue along her slit once before engulfing her in his mouth.

"Xander!" she shouted while fidgeting again.

"Relax, Deryn," he said, moving his hands up to rub her hips. "Let me do this for you. I promise you'll be thanking me later."

"B-but -"

"Shh," he said, continuing to rub her soothingly. "Relax."

Deryn bit her bottom lip, her head falling back against the wall as he continued to pleasure her with his tongue. As a slave, several men had done this to her in an attempt to loosen her up. She had always hated it. But it had definitely never felt like this before.

A soft moan escaped her lips as he circled the tip of his tongue around her clit, her hands softly threading his hair as her hips began to buck. He smirked before bringing one of his hands down and inserting two fingers inside of her, pumping them slowly as her body weakened beneath his touch. He had always been an expert at making women reach that second orgasm in record time, and it was not long before she was pulsating around him.

Xander stayed down there until her writhing body eased. He

gave her soaking lips one last kiss before sitting up and going for the other set.

Deryn barely let him make contact before she was pushing him off. "Okay, Xander. You got what you wanted. You've seen all of me. Now, don't you think it's time you let me see all of you?"

"What did you have in mind?" he asked, smiling as he leaned inward once more.

Xander was a bit surprised when Deryn grabbed his left arm and yanked at the wet cloth he wore.

"What are you doing?" he demanded, trying to pull his arm away.

"Unashamed, right?" she said, managing to successfully maneuver the cloth off and tossing it aside, revealing the wristband with the president's crest burrowed deep in his wrist.

Deryn barely got a chance to see it before Xander was pulling his arm away and hiding it against his chest.

"I cover this for *you*," he said.

Deryn frowned. "We both know that isn't entirely true. I promise I'm not going to freak out like I did that first time. I just ... I want to see. I've never really looked at it before."

"Didn't you take Soren's wristband when you first escaped?"

"Yes, but I never studied it. Not even in training. I just never really cared before."

Xander looked down at his arm.

Reaching out, Deryn rubbed it soothingly, moving her head forward so that she could catch Xander's dark, clouded eyes. "Please, Xander. This wristband is your equivalent of my scars. You wear it against your will."

"Not entirely," he said truthfully, ashamedly.

Under her touch, Xander's arm eased. He let it slacken and Deryn took it in her hands, staring carefully at the crest as she traced it with her fingertips, the only sound being that of the water beating down on them as he watched her in fascination.

Her fingers continued downward, feeling the smooth transition from metal to skin. There were no physical signs to indicate how deeply the wristband ran.

Eventually, she looked up at him, her sea-green eyes sparkling as she crinkled her nose and said, "It's not very attractive, is it? I mean, why a dragon? They're folklore. Wouldn't a creature that actually existed be better?"

Xander couldn't help but laugh. "I never really thought about it. I think his great-grandfather came up with it. He was the first of the Saevus family to enter politics."

Deryn smiled and held up his arm. "Well, then maybe you should have a discussion with him about redesigning his logo to something more modern."

Xander laughed harder. He could not stop himself from reaching out and pulling her in for a soft kiss. He clonked his forehead against hers and the two of them gazed at each other, her hand trailing down his arm until it was interlaced with his.

Xander had never felt like this before. Accepted by someone whose opinion greatly mattered to him.

Other women made Xander sick, wanting him for his Guardian status, for his left wristband with the stupid dragon crest, for the part of himself that he hated most. But not Deryn. She wanted him in spite of all that, somehow looking past this small piece of him, a piece that so many thought defined him. But it didn't. Collin Saevus did not define him. He was something long before that man took over his life and now, thanks to Deryn, he was starting to think that maybe he could be something after.

"Thanks, Leon," he said, never breaking their eye contact.

"You know, I wouldn't be totally against you calling me Deryn. Outside of the bedroom. Or shower." She smirked.

Once their actual shower was finished, Xander and Deryn headed to bed. They kept the lights on while she lay wrapped in his arms, telling him the story behind each and every one of her scars, both of them feeling relief every time he found one from her life before slavery.

As they slowly drifted off to sleep, Xander started to wonder if perhaps Bronson was right. Maybe he did like Deryn. He definitely enjoyed her company more than any other woman's, but he had just assumed this was because she was always there.

Not to mention his current desire for her.

But Xander had had her now, many times, and it still wasn't enough. He found himself constantly craving more of her, and this need was not just fueled by sex. Because he didn't just want her physically. He wanted all of her. Body and soul. Was that what liking someone felt like? Or was it something else? Entirely.

CHAPTER THIRTY

"Three months!" announced Bronson as he popped open a bottle of champagne, ignoring Xander's scowl as he let it rain all over his white carpet.

"Thanks, Bronson, but there's really no need for this," said Deryn, leaning very stiffly against the kitchen counter while he poured the champagne into three crystal glasses. "It just doesn't seem right to celebrate my freedom when so many others are suffering through the slave trade as we speak."

"Come on, Deryn. Can't you just be selfish for once?" he asked, handing her a glass. "You're a free woman, more or less. You're having sex regularly." Bronson motioned towards Xander, who took a glass and nodded in agreement. "For the first time in years, you have clothes and a weapon -"

"And a chocolate bar," added Xander, flashing her a quick wink.

Deryn narrowed her eyes, but she couldn't hide her smile.

"Uh, right," said Bronson, clearly not getting the joke. "So shall we toast?"

"Fine," said Deryn, holding up her glass. "But if I'm still here in three months, we won't be doing this again."

Xander hardened at the realization that she probably wouldn't still be there when that time came. Instead, she would be with her family and Triggs. *With* Triggs. Maybe physically. He cringed at the thought. *Never.* He would never, ever let that

-

"Ruby, we doing this?"

Xander looked up to see Bronson and Deryn staring at him, both of their glasses slightly raised.

"Right," said Xander, lifting his. "So are we supposed to say something?"

"Oh, good idea!" exclaimed Bronson. "Go on, then."

Xander raised his eyebrows. "Me?"

Bronson smiled. "Uh huh. Tell us how you feel."

"How I feel?" repeated Xander, creasing his forehead as he glanced at Deryn, who was looking at him expectantly. "Well, I'm glad you're not a slave anymore. But I'm not glad that I haven't had a chance to kill anyone but Dougal for owning you yet. I do plan to."

Deryn smiled.

"Is this how Guardians woo women?" asked Bronson, darting his curious eyes between them.

"Pretty sure it's just me," said Xander.

"Well, I'm wooed." said Deryn proudly. "Shall we drink?"

"It has become clear that *I* am going to have to make the toast," said Bronson, lifting his glass a little higher. He cleared his throat. "Deryn Leon, I'm so grateful to have the honor, no, the privilege of knowing you in this bleak and desolate world. You have overcome obstacles and conquered fears, always coming out on top and -"

"Cheers!" interrupted Xander, clanking his glass against both of theirs and chugging his champagne.

Deryn clanked Bronson's and did the same, making a face as the bubbles tickled her nose.

Bronson huffed. "Are you not even going to let me finish my speech?"

"Nope," said Xander, taking the bottle off of the counter, and pouring Deryn and himself another glass. Bronson pouted before drinking his down, then held his glass out for a refill.

Just as Deryn was taking another sip, there was a knock on the front door. Her eyes went wide, and she swallowed her mouthful down quickly before dashing into her bedroom, glass in hand. She shut the door just as the front one began to rattle.

"Xander, you there?" called Luka's voice from the other

side. "Let me in."

Xander put down the bottle, went over and opened the door.

"Th'fuck you have so many locks on for? You live in a secure building."

"And, yet, here you are," said Xander.

Luka pushed his way inside, Xander shutting the door behind him. "Yeah, well, after you had to give me access last time, I went to the home bureau and registered my band with your building." He then noticed Bronson standing in the kitchen. Their eyes locked and Bronson's face brightened.

"How'd you manage that without any sort of lease?" asked Xander.

Luka shrugged. "I'm a Guardian. Everyone in this city gives me whatever th'fuck I want." His eyes drifted from Bronson to the bottle of champagne on the counter. "Am I interrupting something?"

"No," said Xander. "Bronson here -"

Bronson nodded.

"- works at a restaurant, and, on some nights, he likes to steal the good shit."

"True statement," said Bronson, taking a sip from his glass.

"Tonight he was kind enough to share," said Xander.

"How do you two know each other?" asked Luka, still standing near the front door.

Xander took a sip from his glass and swallowed hard. "He lives downstairs."

"Oh," said Luka, walking to the kitchen. "So he's the one who gets you those cigarettes at the Black Market?"

Bronson's face lit up. "Oh, Ruby, you've talked about me -"

"This is the good shit?" asked Luka, looking closely at the bottle's label. "What sort of cheap establishment do you work at?" He took a sip straight out of the bottle.

Glowering at him, Bronson said, "One that, luckily, isn't often populated by pretentious pricks with absolutely no manners or -"

"Did you want something, Luka?" asked Xander, walking

over and pulling the bottle away from him. "If you would like more then get a glass."

"Sorry," said Luka, wiping his mouth. "I just need a fucking drink. Can we get out of here and get a fucking drink?"

Xander frowned. "Everything alright?"

"No," said Luka, biting his cheek in an attempt to hold back tears. "Can we go already?"

Xander looked at Bronson, who shrugged. "Fine, you go ahead. I'll meet you downstairs."

"Why?" asked Luka.

"I need to use the bathroom. What's with all the questions?"

"I'll wait, just hurry up." Luka rubbed his eyes.

Xander flared his nostrils, glancing slyly at Deryn's door.

"Hey, buddy," said Bronson, putting a hand on Luka's shoulder. "You look like you could use a cigarette. Wanna come have one with me on the balcony while Ruby takes a piss?"

"Fine," said Luka, walking towards the sliding glass door.

Bronson crossed his arms and stared after him. "Straight, right?" he whispered.

"Yeah," said Xander. "Why?"

"No reason. I just often find myself attracted to straight assholes. Any chance he might forget his sexual preference if intoxicated enough?"

"Doubtful," said Xander, cringing as the horrible image of Bronson coming onto a drunk Luka entered his head. "Just get out there."

"Done," said Bronson, grinning widely. He took his cigarettes out of his pocket and headed for the open door, making sure to shut it behind him.

As soon as they were out of sight, Xander went to Deryn's door and slipped inside. She was presently sitting on her bed with a book in her lap. She glanced up as he entered.

"Deryn, I -"

"Yes, I heard," she said with a frown. "I suppose you have to go and be with your friend if you want to keep up appearances."

"I'd rather stay here," he said, sitting next to her and meeting her for a kiss. "You know, celebrate your freedom properly." He smirked and she did the same.

"There will be plenty of time for that later. Now, go on. Take any longer in the bathroom and he might get suspicious."

"I hope you know I plan to fuck you senseless when I get back."

"I figured as much," she said, giving him one last kiss before pushing him off of her bed. "Go, Xander."

He grunted and reluctantly slipped back out the door. Damn Luka and his problems. He had no idea how much of a cock block he was being.

Outside, Luka was leaning over the edge of the balcony, staring straight ahead in brooding silence while Bronson tried to make conversation. He turned when he heard the door open. "Ready?" he asked, putting out his cigarette.

"Yeah, sure," said Xander, stepping out of the way.

Luka took a step forward before looking at Bronson. "You coming?"

"Not yet," said Bronson, grinning as his mind filled with dirty thoughts. "But if that's an invitation -"

"He can't come, Luka," said Xander quickly. "Not if we ride our bikes somewhere. All bars in walking distance are absolute shit."

Luka reached into his pocket and pulled out one of the chips from the Government Lab. "I have an extra. Kept it in case I wanted to bring someone home on my bike. I link it to their wristband and then unlink it the next day." He smiled, obviously proud of his cleverness.

"Oh, sweet," said Bronson, taking the chip from him.

"But his name isn't registered."

"Who's going to check?" said Luka with a shrug. "It's fine. I've already done it maybe half a dozen times. No one has a clue."

"Half a dozen, huh?" said Bronson. "And all with different women, I assume?"

Luka's smirk was response enough.

"Looks like we have a mini Ruby on our hands. Well, let's get on with it," he said, following Luka inside and heading for the front door.

"I assume you want to go to the Pit," said Xander as they descended the stairs.

Luka nodded.

When they got outside, Luka headed straight for his hover-bike, which was parked sloppily on the curb. "Your boyfriend can ride with you," he said as he put on his helmet and mounted his bike. "See you assholes there."

Xander went into his garage and took out his bike. "We need to get him drunk and make sure he forgets all about getting this back tonight," he said, taking the chip from Bronson and installing it in his bike. "Got it?"

"You're the boss," said Bronson with a salute. He touched his wristband to the bike, waiting for it to click and register.

Once they both had their helmets on, they mounted the bike and followed Luka, Xander insisting that Bronson not hold onto his waist. He did it anyway. For fun.

By the time they got to the Pit, Luka already had a table and a bottle of wine. He was chugging from it hungrily and Xander had a pretty good feeling he didn't intend to share, so he ordered another bottle for him and Bronson.

As it turned out, the reason Luka was so upset was because his father had called him out about his and Xander's lack of progress on just about every mission against the Resistance right in front of the president. He was convincing enough that Saevus had Luka's mind swept- a very painful technique used to search someone's mind for secrets. It had never actually been proven effective, though the president seemed to believe in it. But that was not the real problem.

"You should've seen the look on my father's face when he found out I wasn't hiding anything. It was like he was disappointed! Like he wanted me to get executed or something! I mean, can you believe it?"

Actually, Xander could, but he kept quiet about it because he had to. He had to cooperate. For Deryn's sake.

"I'm his son and he doesn't even care if I'm dead!"

"Oh, I'm sure that's not true," said Bronson, trying to be supportive, but one glance at Xander and he knew that it most definitely was. "You Guardians sure have twisted families. Hey, waitress!" He lifted his hand and a young girl hurried over, making sure to flutter her eyelashes. "Let's see. How about ... one, two, three ... nine! Nine shots of your finest whiskey! Whiskey?" he asked, glancing around for reassurance.

"Gin!" shouted Luka. "I need fucking gin!"

"His comfort drink," Xander said to Bronson.

"Gin it is!" he said, smiling at the waitress. She blushed and scurried off.

"You have a pretty good way with the ladies for a pansy," Luka spurted out before taking another swig from his bottle. It was already half gone.

"How did you know he was gay?" asked Xander, cocking an eyebrow.

"It's obvious, isn't it? He's been eye-fucking me since I stepped through your door."

Bronson smiled sheepishly. "Guilty," he said. "Forgive Ruby. He's known me for years and only figured it out just recently. And not even on his own. He had to be told."

"Hmm ..." Luka brought his bottle back to his lips and chugged some more.

The waitress returned a moment later. She put the shots of gin on the table before slyly touching her wristband to Bronson's and slipping him her information. He was about to delete it when Luka stretched forward and touched his citizen wristband to Bronson's.

"Yoink!" he said, absorbing the waitress's information.

"Oh, Ruby, he's so adorable. I could just put him in my pocket."

"You seem a lot gayer tonight," said Xander, grabbing a shot.

"It's because I've found the new object of my affection," said Bronson, doing the same. "Shall we toast?"

"No," said Xander and Luka, both downing their shots.

Bronson took his slowly. He then slipped another one in front of Luka. "So tell me more about your father."

"He's a fucking ass," said Luka, quickly taking the new shot. "Always has been."

"I see," said Bronson, sliding another one over. "And what makes him so ass-like?"

"He just is. Been a strict follower of the president and his father before him since he was a teenager and he doesn't want anyone to outshine him. Not even his own son." Another shot down.

Xander watched closely as Bronson slipped yet another shot towards Luka. He smirked and took one more for himself.

It wasn't long before Luka's ramblings became incoherent. He closed his eyes and rested his cheek on his hand, beginning to drift off to a state of unconsciousness while Xander and Bronson finished their bottle of wine. But, about three-quarters of the way through, Xander realized he was drinking the bulk of it.

It was only then that he noticed he was a little drunk. "Why aren't you drinking more?" demanded Xander, angry since Deryn refused to have sex with him whenever he was intoxicated.

"Because I don't want to get drunk," answered Bronson. "All I need is a little buzz."

"Why?"

"No reason," he said, grinning widely as he watched Luka catch himself after falling off of his hand.

"Fuck. No," said Xander, his eyes flaming. "I don't think so, Bronson."

Bronson shrugged. "I would never do anything without permission first. I'm not a member of the guard."

"Th'fuck yeh talkin' bout?" mumbled Luka, before settling back on his hand and chewing something that clearly wasn't there.

"Nothing, sleepy," said Bronson, poking his cheek affectionately.

Xander shook his head in disapproval. "You're fucking

sick."

Bronson just smiled.

Once their bottle was finished, mainly thanks to Xander, they dragged an essentially unconscious Luka towards the door, but he wasn't moving very well.

Bronson eventually had to toss him over his shoulder and carry him outside while Xander went ahead of them to get Luka's bike's passenger car to initiate. It popped out like an inflatable balloon, but still felt like solid metal when touched.

Xander was starting to feel a bit woozy and had to brace himself against the wall while Bronson loaded Luka inside.

"Fuck ..." said Xander, falling to a crouching position. "I can't lead you right now."

"Why not?" asked Bronson. "Too eager to go back and have sex with Der -" He caught himself, stared at Luka moaning in the passenger car and gulped. "Your pseudo-girlfriend?"

"My what?" asked Xander, crinkling his nose.

"Who th'fuck yeh fuckin'?" asked Luka, popping up suddenly. "He fuckin' say Der?"

"No," said Xander, reaching in and pushing him back down. His head started to spin again, so he brought his hand up to brace it. "I feel sick. I can't even drive to my place."

"No worries. I got it!" said Bronson, gladly pushing Xander out of the way and mounting Luka's bike.

"Fuck. No."

"Why not?" he whined.

"Well, if we completely overlook the fact that I don't trust you -" Xander gulped. He needed to get out of here soon. "- it's also too dangerous. He lives in Inner City with his father and -"

"My father's not -" *Hiccup*! "- fuckin' 'round. He and Veli-fucker are doin' some shit out -" *Hiccup*! "- out -" *Hiccup*! "- side."

"What are they doing out there?" asked Xander, suddenly feeling a lot more sober. Then the next wave of nausea hit.

"Dun-fuckin-no. Who yeh talkin' bout before?"

"No one," said Xander firmly.

"It's settled then!" said Bronson, putting on Luka's helmet.

"Don't you worry about a thing, Ruby. Take a car home and I'll come back for your bike. Just give me money for my own car to get back here. Gotta make that curfew." He held out his arm.

Xander grunted but touched his wristband to Bronson's all the same, pressing a few things on the screen that appeared to transfer the money over. Then he switched over Bronson's chip to Luka's bike.

"Park it in the lot near the gate to Inner City. Once through walk left and his house is only two blocks away. Here's the address," said Xander, touching their wristbands once more, his thoughts giving him the address.

"Don't you worry, Ruby. I'll make sure to take great care of your friend." Bronson winked and rode off, Luka fast asleep and with his mouth hanging open in the passenger car beside him.

Xander had just enough time to run inside and make it to the bathroom before he was vomiting vigorously into the toilet. He waited a bit and got it all out before cleaning himself off. Then he ran to a nearby store and bought a toothbrush and toothpaste, getting rid of all traces of his vomit before flagging down a car and heading home. At least since they were so expensive, it was never hard to find one.

When he got there, he stumbled to his room and collapsed on the bed, more than a little disappointed to find it empty. It was another minute before Deryn's door opened and she appeared in his doorway, a blanket wrapped around her shoulders.

"You're drunk."

"No shit," said Xander, holding out his arms.

Deryn walked over to the bed and let Xander pull her into him. She nuzzled into the crook of his arm, letting his warm body consume her.

The two of them were silent for a long while and Deryn assumed Xander had fallen asleep. But then he turned his head and, when she looked up, he was staring right at her.

"Why are you never in my bed when I get home?"

"What?"

"On nights I go out, when I get home you're always in your bed, but you've been sleeping in mine for weeks now. Why aren't you just here?"

"Oh, I ... I don't know."

"Is it because you think I might come home with someone else?"

Deryn looked away and blushed. She hadn't realized it before, but something in her gut told her he was right. This was exactly what she thought.

"Because I wouldn't ..." He gulped. "I wouldn't do that to you. Not after everything you've been through."

Deryn frowned. "You've already brought one girl back here to spite me. What's to stop you from doing it again?"

Xander's throat ached as she looked at him once more. "That was a mistake. I don't ... I mean, I'm not ..." He sighed. "I'm not good at this, Deryn, but I like you, and I want you to be here." There. He admitted it.

Deryn's heart skipped a beat.

"There isn't going to be anyone else. Be here."

"I guess I can make a point to -"

"No," he said, shaking his head. "Not good enough. Move in here."

Her eyes widened. "What?"

"Get all of your shit from the guestroom and move it in here. The clothes, the books, the damn chocolate bar. All of it. I want it here. I want *you* here."

"Xander, that's crazy."

"So? It all is, isn't it?"

Deryn released a heavy sigh. "You're drunk."

"That has nothing to do with -"

"I'll tell you what. Ask me again in the morning when you're sober. If you remember to do that and you still feel the same way then I'll do it."

"You will?" he asked hopefully.

She gave him a faint smile and nodded. "If it's really what you want then yes."

Xander frowned. "No. It's not just about what I want. What

do you want, Deryn?"

She sighed again and brought her hand to his cheek, running her thumb along his soft skin. "I want you," she said simply, truthfully.

Xander leaned in and kissed her then. Softly. Sweetly. Gently massaging her lips with his, making her heart race and her palms sweat.

"Don't ever leave me," he breathed into her mouth before reclaiming it with his.

Deryn didn't answer, her chest feeling heavy as he continued to kiss her. She knew this was wrong, but she couldn't stop herself. Xander had become too special to her, too significant. She didn't want to leave him but, at the same time, she knew she couldn't stay here forever. It had already been three months. Three incredible months that she wouldn't trade for anything. But, someday soon, it would be time for her to go and she would have to leave Xander behind. All of him. It was the only way she was going to survive this.

When their kiss finally ended, Xander closed his eyes and pressed his forehead against hers. Deryn kept her eyes open, watching him closely as tears built behind them.

"I'm going to make some tea," she said. "Would you like some?"

He nodded.

Deryn gave him one last kiss before reluctantly climbing out of his arms. She went into the kitchen for a moment and just stood there, bringing her hand to her mouth and trying to hold in the sobs. She knew getting involved with Xander was a mistake, but she had done it anyway. Because she was selfish. Because she wanted something that was hers. Because she wanted *someone* that was hers.

Deryn's eyes drifted over to Atticus's covered figure in the photo on the bookshelf. She still hadn't told him about his father. But how could she now? Despite everything, she didn't want to lose him. And if he knew the truth nothing would ever be the same. Xander would never look at her the same.

Sucking back all of her feelings for yet another night, Deryn went to work on making that tea. Just as she was finishing, the lock on the front door clicked and she ducked behind the counter, mugs in hand.

The door opened and she heard someone humming. She smiled and stood back up.

"You're in bright spirits," she said, looking at Bronson. "Any particular reason?"

"Nope," he said with a wink.

"Don't tell me you and Luka -"

Bronson rolled his eyes. "Please. I was there for maybe ten minutes before I had to get back here for curfew. Did Ruby tell you I was going to molest him or something?"

"No." She smiled wider. "It was just an observation from earlier. Thin walls, you know?"

"Well, I can assure you I didn't. Anything that might've happened in those ten minutes was completely consensual."

"What does that -"

"This is for Ruby," said Bronson, handing her a small computer chip. "I figured he wouldn't want to keep it in his bike. Night, Deryn." He winked one last time before heading out the door.

Deryn put the chip in her pocket. She went back to Xander's room, tea in hand. When she got there, he was lying with his back to her. She walked over and saw that he was asleep.

After putting the mugs of tea on the nightstand, Deryn crouched beside the bed and gazed at him, unable to stop herself from reaching out and moving some stray hairs from his eyes. She kissed him softly and climbed in beside him, pulling the comforter over them and wrapping her arms around his back, surprisingly happy to be the big spoon for once.

The next morning, Deryn was awoken with a kiss. She barely had time to open her eyes before Xander was picking her up and carrying her to his shower. They joked around while he lathered her up with her floral soap, not once mentioning their conversation from the night before.

Even as he picked her up and had her against the shower wall, Deryn's mind was never far from his request, both anticipating and dreading that he would ask again.

While Xander got ready to leave, Deryn put on her robe and slippers, and made him breakfast. He pulled her onto his lap as he ate, giving her a kiss on her cheek, her nose, her lips between almost every bite.

And then it was time for him to leave. Deryn cleaned up while he headed for the door, stopping beside the couch.

"Deryn, come here," he said suddenly.

Deryn put down the dishes she was holding and walked over. Xander pulled her close and kissed her affectionately.

When he pulled away, he looked at her with his golden eyes. "I meant what I said last night. I want you and all of your things in my room today when I get back."

"O-okay." Her body quivered.

"You may have to do some rearranging in the dresser, but take whatever space you need. Just keep our underwear separate. I hate it when people share a drawer for underwear."

Deryn smiled and nodded.

Xander gave her one last kiss before leaving.

Deryn brought her thumb to her mouth and bit down on it, staring hypnotically at the door for a long while, a faint smile still visible on her lips.

This was a mistake. She knew it was. Everything inside of Deryn told her that she would regret this later, that no good could come from her moving into his bedroom. But then why could she not stop smiling?

CHAPTER THIRTY-ONE

It had been a week since Deryn moved into Xander's room and everything was going great. As far as either of them were concerned, anyway. Bronson hadn't been too thrilled about it when he went over there and Deryn was in the process of making the move, rearranging all of the drawers in the dresser and using the small ones at the top to separate their underwear.

No, Bronson was definitely not happy about it. And while he bit his tongue, it was impossible to hide the dissatisfaction on his expressive face, which was why Deryn hadn't invited him over in a few days. To avoid feeling that judgment.

But not today. Today she needed him, to be - if nothing else - a distraction. Because for the first time since she had been living with Xander he was sent on a mission to the outside world, to investigate what happened to two guards who went out for a routine check of the area and never returned.

She was worried. There was no doubt in her mind that Resistance members always had their eyes on the doors to the city, watching those who entered and exited.

Xander assured her that he had been out there many times before and he always came back safe, but that didn't make her feel any better about it. It only took once for someone to never come back.

So, on that day, Deryn had asked Bronson to join her in the basement to work on her Element. Over the weeks, she had turned it into a fairly good weapon,' but it was capable of so much more than that and she was determined to make its defensiveness as great as its offensiveness.

What she wanted was a shield that was large enough to protect more than just her. Two people, at least. Preferably three.

After some tinkering, she asked Bronson to stand behind her and gave it a try. Their upper bodies were protected, but if someone went for their legs there wasn't much they could do about it.

"That thing is coming along pretty nicely," said Bronson as she tinkered some more.

"I do what I can," she said.

"And with your Element working so well, don't you think it's time you came up with a plan to get out of here?"

Deryn didn't answer. Just kept tinkering.

"It's obvious the curfew won't be lifted anytime soon. Probably never. So shouldn't you consider trying to find some other way to escape the city? It's not impossible, especially since you're just one person."

She remained silent.

"Deryn ... you still *want* to leave, don't you?"

Nothing.

"Say something."

"I want to leave, Bronson," she finally said. "I want to see my dad and Talon and Dax and everyone else, but ..." She sighed. "But I don't want to leave Xander here. I already can't breathe when he gets home late. What's it going to be like if we're separated?"

"So ... what then? You're just going to stay here forever because you don't want to be worried about Ruby?"

"No, of course not. I just ..." She sighed again. "I don't want to leave him behind."

Bronson bit his cheek. "You want him to come with you."

Deryn blushed as she continued to stare at and tinker with her Element.

"You know he'll never go for that. Besides, you're planning to look for the headquarters of the Resistance. Sending him into their hive, even on the arm of their leader's daughter, is still suicide. Surely you realize -"

"Bronson, I know!" she shouted, her head whipping towards him. "I'm not an idiot! But he can't stay here! A bunch of Guardians already have it out for him!"

"But he can't leave. Staying is his best option."

"No, it's not!" Deryn put her Element down, stood and turned so she was facing the other direction. She brought her hand up to wipe her tears away before Bronson could see them.

"Deryn, I'm sorry, but you need to be realistic here," said Bronson with a frown. "Ruby will never be able to escape the president. Not until one of them is dead."

"I know that, too," she said after a small pause, her heart feeling heavy. "But I've already lost so much. I don't want to lose him, too."

"I know." He hugged her from behind. "But just because you have to separate doesn't mean you're going to lose him. There's still a chance you'll both survive this. If you can get your dad out of hiding and start a battle against that bastard we're forced to call president, then you can sure as hell bet Ruby won't be fighting on his side. Just tell your friends not to attack him."

Deryn smiled. "Yes, I'm sure that will go over really well with Talon and Dax."

Bronson's arms tensed around her. "Deryn, you're not ... I mean, you and ... and Dax. Are you still planning on going back to him?"

Deryn's smile faded. "I don't know."

"Have you thought about it?"

"Of course I have," she said. "Every day I think about it. But I haven't seen Dax in five years. How am I supposed to know if those feelings are still there?"

"Well, ask yourself this. On nights when you're feeling sad and missing home, who do you want there with you? Xander or Dax?"

That was simple. "I want Xander."

"Then shouldn't that be your answer?"

Deryn shrugged. "I don't know."

She knew it should be that simple. Xander was the one she wanted, the one she desired, the one she thought about constantly, but Dakota ... he was her past, her first love, one of her last ties to her old life, and she had always thought he would be her future. But now there was Xander. And a future without him just seemed so bleak.

~

Xander walked along the overgrown path, his gasmask on tight - molded perfectly so his face was still visible - and his hand on his Element, which dangled from his hip. Just in case. He had been sent out to investigate the disappearance of two rookie guards who had been on a routine sweep of the area. They were often conducted to make sure no Outsiders had taken up residence in their old villages on the border of Utopia. The villages had been cleared out shortly after the Resistance was formed and the president planned to keep them that way.

A light breeze rustled the bushes and trees, not to mention Xander's trench coat, and he found himself checking his mask again, making sure it was fastened properly. While he was fully aware the president was a liar in many aspects, he had never been able to shake the idea that perhaps the air outside really was toxic, and only some were immune. He feared he was not one of those some.

Deryn told him he was crazy. She was probably right.

Xander stood still and waited for the breeze to pass. He hated being out there. Especially alone. He supposed he could have brought Luka with him. He definitely would have come too, considering he had been persistently trying to speak to Xander over the last few days, but there was never any time for that with his beautiful fugitive at home waiting for him.

Luka had even tried to stop him before he came to the outside world that day, but Xander was eager to get his job done quickly, leaving enough time to report back to the president and still arrive home before curfew. Plus, he sort of feared the reason Luka wanted to talk was because something had happened between Bronson and him and he needed to tell somebody. Xander really didn't want to be that somebody.

When everything was still again, he released a breath of relief and looked up. Other than the wind, it was a beautiful, clear day. Unlike the overcast dome above the city, which supposedly mimicked the sky he was looking at now. Just one example of the many lies the president told.

After this realization, Xander wondered if maybe he really was being crazy and he could take off his mask. But the moment his hand started drifting upward it stopped. He sighed, let his hand fall, and continued on.

Knowing there was very little chance he would ever find those guards, Xander had decided to take a little side trip to the largest of the border villages. He stopped by the hand-painted sign and read the name.

Redwood.

All of the villages had been named after ancient trees. With no access to the rest of the world, it was impossible to know if they were extinct or not.

Xander walked through the village quickly, making sure to look straight ahead. Not to the right, where several houses had been burned, probably with entire families trapped inside, or to the left, where many graves had been dug by those who survived for their lost loved ones.

No, Xander did not dare look at either of those things. Even though he hadn't been there for the destruction of Redwood and all of the other villages in the vicinity, it certainly felt like he had.

And then he saw it. A wooden house near the back of the village slightly bigger than the rest. It was the house the leader of Redwood had shared with his two children before they were taken from him. The same person who also led the Resistance. Deryn's father, Godfrey Leon. Last seen that fateful night five years ago but still believed to be very much alive. President Saevus had no doubt in his mind that his cousin was still out there somewhere, refusing to show himself out of fear for his daughter's life. It was no secret that the president had every intention of executing her while her father watched, and not a day sooner, despite rumors to the contrary.

Xander shuddered at the thought. He closed his eyes and took a deep breath before walking up the steps and onto the porch. There was a swing to the right of the door that Deryn had spoken of once. On warm nights she would sit there sandwiched between her father and brother, leaning on her father's shoulder so she could read along to whatever book he had brought out that night. Even though he spoke aloud she always preferred to see the words. It made the stories more real for her.

Xander put his hand on the knob and turned, the door creaking as he pushed it open. The house was covered in dust and cobwebs with small, black spiders in the center of them. There were no spiders in Utopia but Xander still knew what they were. He had encountered quite a few large ones while wandering the forest in this area, and he was not fond of them at all.

Even though Xander had been to Redwood many times, he had never actually entered Deryn's house before. To the left there was a living room, and to the right a kitchen. He walked straight ahead, down a hallway, opening doors until he found a room that looked like it might belong to a young girl. It didn't look much different than the other rooms, aside from the lacey white curtains, but Xander knew it belonged to Deryn the moment he saw all of the books. Covering every flat surface, every corner, and every shelf nailed to the walls. They were even stacked up on a chair near the window. There was a good chance it had not once been sat in.

Xander knew Godfrey used to go exploring and always came back with books for Deryn, but this was a little ridiculous. He laughed as he entered the room, careful not to step on any books, especially ones left open. They were all very old and very delicate.

Aside from all of the books, the room was otherwise very neat. The bed was made, even though it hadn't been touched in years, the desk was well-organized and the closet was color coordinated. Not one object was out of place.

There was a box of records beside the dresser, and a square of dust on top of it, slightly less dusty than the space around it. At one point, there must have been a record player there, but it was long gone.

Xander found himself drawn to the desk, where a single framed photo stood. He picked it up and stared at the smiling faces of Deryn, Dakota, Talon, and several other children he didn't recognize. He didn't know why, but he was sort of surprised the Outsiders even had cameras.

It was taken at least ten years ago, by the looks of it. She was on Dakota's back and both were laughing.

He sighed and slipped it into his rucksack. She would want that.

After also putting a few of the open books and the two she had bookmarked on her nightstand in his rucksack, he went over to the bed and sat down, stroking the comforter as he tried to feel a part of Deryn here. This was her room, her house, her life before she was stolen from her home. This was where she came when she wanted to be alone. Her safe place. And she hadn't seen it in years.

He opened the small drawer in the nightstand, curious to see what she kept there. There were several bookmarks, a flashlight, a bag of gummy candy that must have come from Utopia and was probably horribly stale, a pen, and a journal. Xander picked up this last item and flipped through the pages. He knew he shouldn't invade Deryn's privacy like this, but maybe just one entry wouldn't hurt.

He opened to one of the last pages with writing, one paragraph popping out at him.

I'm not sure what to do about my growing feelings for Dax, especially now that Talon isn't around to constantly keep watch on us. The two of us have been best friends for so many years now, and I think we're both afraid to cross that line, but, somehow, I just know we have to. Dax and I are meant to be more than friends, I'm sure of it. Because the love I feel for him, it's different than the love I feel for everyone else. I hate to make a confession like this on paper, but I truly believe that I'm in love with -

Xander slammed the journal shut. That was enough of that.

He put it back in the drawer and erased it from his memory.

Standing up, he took one last look around the room. After grabbing an old snow globe with an ancient animal called a horse inside of it and adding it to his collection, he headed for the door. He wasn't ready to leave yet, but he knew he had to. He still had a job to do, as much as he wanted to stay and learn more about her life before.

Xander left the room and quietly shut the door behind him. He headed down the hallway but stopped when he heard the floorboards in the living room creak. Pressing himself against the wall, he opened his ears and listened closely. Footsteps.

The creaking stopped. Xander moved down the hallway slowly, making sure to stay hidden in the shadows. He stepped into the kitchen and stood so he could see through the archway leading to the living room. Someone was standing in there, their back to him while they stared at the photos on the wall. The figure reached out and touched one of Deryn in her teen years, probably just before she was taken from Redwood to join the guard. Then the person turned and glanced around the room. Even with a gasmask on, there was no mistaking those sinister eyes. Soren.

Xander's hand clutched his Element tightly as he glared at this man. There were few people he hated more. For owning Deryn. For raping her. But mostly for loving her, if you could even call it that. Soren's feelings for Deryn were sick, to say the least. He didn't just want to capture and execute her like the others. He wanted to possess her. And that, to Xander, was so much worse.

It suddenly dawned on him that if he wanted to get rid of Soren this was the place to do it. No one knew Xander was here, and he doubted anyone knew Soren was here. How hard would it be to make him disappear? Like Dougal.

Xander gripped his Element tighter and took a step forward. It was almost too easy. He lifted his arm, aimed, and -

The front door clicked open and Xander darted deeper into the kitchen, poking his head out just enough to see Veli walk into the house. *Shit.*

Veli headed straight for the living room. "I knew you'd be here."

Soren said nothing. Xander moved to get a better look. Soren was, once again, staring at the photo of Deryn.

"Oh, get over it already, will you? I don't have time for all of this pathetic nonsense."

Soren pressed the button on the collar around his neck and said, "Leave me be."

"Leave you be? I'm out here for *you*. Following my guys lead on that fucking brother of hers. Who cares what happens to him, as long as it gets her back for you?"

"I do," said Soren. "Her family is off limits."

"Well, it doesn't exactly matter now, does it? He's not here. It's over, not to mention a waste of time."

"Fuck you -"

"Oh, will you quit your whining already!" shouted Veli, stepping farther into the room. Xander was able to get a better look at him. His face was bright-red behind his gasmask as he glared daggers at his brother. "She's fucking toxic! A slave! She's worthless and so is her family! Just a filthy, revolting -"

"How dare you!" Soren took out his Element and aimed it at Veli.

"How dare I what? Speak the truth? She doesn't care about you, brother! She never did! That's why she slit your throat and left you for dead!" Veli took several deep breaths. "When we find her, she's going to loathe you even more than she already does," he said, his voice now calm. "What's to stop her from trying to kill you again? And maybe this time she'll succeed. Sometimes I think she'd be doing me a favor."

Soren lowered his Element but continued to stare coldly at his brother, angry tears fogging up his mask. He pressed a button on its side that cleared away the fog.

"When we find her I will let you have her once more. *Once more*, Soren. That's all you get before I take a knife to her throat, and I'll make damn sure there's no chance of survival for her. Maybe then you'll get back to your old self and stop being so pathetic over a toxic bitch," spat Veli. "Now, come along. I don't want to waste another minute in this filthy place."

Veli turned and walked out of the room. Xander noticed Soren slip a smaller frame into his pocket before following his brother out. While Xander desperately wanted to attack, he knew now was not the time. Two on one was too dangerous, and Xander couldn't risk any suicide missions. Not until Deryn was out of his apartment and somewhere safe.

Xander listened until their footsteps were out of range. With a faint growl from missed opportunity, he put away his Element and went over to the wall Soren had been staring at. The photos were all of Deryn and Talon at various stages of growing up, many also including their father and one with their mother when Deryn was just a baby. He grabbed that one and put it in his rucksack.

Looking around the rest of the house, Xander wished he knew what was sentimental and what wasn't. Part of him ached to know this piece of her life, but that same part of him understood that he probably never would. Even if Deryn made it out of Utopia, her life would never be the same. She had lost eight years, her confidence, and her innocence. All things she could never get back, at least not entirely. Chances were she wouldn't even want to return to the home she and her family had once shared. It held too many memories of the life that was stolen from her.

Xander sighed and took one last look at the photos on the wall before heading for the door. He still had a job to do and he needed to get back to Middle City before the curfew began.

Quickening his pace, Xander headed for the gated entrance to the forest near the back of the village. The missing guards had been sent to scope out an area just south of Redwood, following a rumor that Outsiders had built a new village there. If the rumor turned out to be true then they were to report back and the appropriate action would be taken. To the president that meant the termination of everyone in the village, aside from young children who had the potential to become his guards. Back in Deryn's day he only had them trained, but after the encounter with Godfrey and the Resistance he'd brought in master manipulators to make sure any Outsider children who joined the guard now rebelled against their families. And it looked like mind control wasn't too far off.

Xander activated the compass on his guard wristband. It hovered in a golden light above his wrist. He followed a path leading west until he found the southbound path the guards would've taken. He had to admit, he definitely preferred the green trees and yellow flowers out here than the gray stone and steel walls Utopia seemed to favor. Part of the reason he chose the building he lived in was because it was slightly more blue-tinted.

He hadn't walked far when he noticed there was a crack in the thick trees overhead, a streak of sunlight beaming down on the path in front of him. He stepped into it, looking up at the blue sky and getting a strong urge to feel the sun against his skin. His shaky hand lifted, then fell again, then lifted slowly, still shaking as it touched his mask, ready to press the release button and -

Crack.

Xander dropped his hand and turned towards the noise. It came from a very narrow pathway to his left that was overrun with brush and probably not very safe, but he had a job to do.

Taking out his Element, Xander very carefully headed down the pathway. He kicked at the bushes as he went, making sure he wasn't just following some animal hiding in them.

His eyes darted all around, searching for some sort of movement. But there was none. He realized then that it was too quiet. Someone was watching him. Two someone's. He could feel them on either side of him, closing in carefully.

Deryn's face entered his mind and he suddenly felt like he was suffocating. Drowning even. There was no way he could die that day when on a routine mission. He couldn't leave her behind. Not until he got her out.

Before Xander knew what was happening, he was running in a crouched position, two sets of footsteps closing in on him less carefully now. There was a whistling sound and he ducked. Something hit a tree behind him. He looked and saw a dart stuck in the trunk. The Resistance often used darts like this to sedate guards and Guardians. It made it easier to take them prisoner.

So these attackers didn't want to kill him. Well, that changed everything. Staying crouched, Xander stared through the bottom of the brush until he found some movement. The dart thrower. He shot up, aimed his Element and fired. He hit them dead on. There was a big thump as the person fell flat on the ground. Then another thump as his companion went into hiding.

Xander ran forward, not stopping until he was beside his attacker. He was not especially shocked when he saw the wide eyes of Talon Leon staring back at him. They were sea-green, like Deryn's, but nowhere near as striking. In his opinion, at least.

"He's only stunned but he'll be dead if you come at me again!" he shouted over his shoulder.

Not sure what to do next, Xander studied his surroundings. He had no intention of taking Talon prisoner but he wasn't sure how to get out of there without doing just that.

Then he saw something. On a path parallel to the one he'd been on before this little side trip. The wind blew and something waved, side to side. It was the steel-blue trench coat of a member of the guard.

Forgetting all about Talon, Xander walked forward until he was out of the brush. He froze as he stepped on the path, his eyes widening as he stared at what was in front of him. The two missing members of the guard were there, hanging from a tree. Their gasmasks were off and nowhere to be found, and their feet swayed in the wind.

Xander closed his eyes and took a deep breath. When he opened them again the men were still dangling. He glowered and turned towards the forest.

"For people who claim to be the good guys, you really do some fucked up things!" he shouted. "They were only kids! Barely eighteen! Believe me when I say there is nothing 'good' about what you've done!"

Crack.

Xander whipped around and aimed his Element down the path, just past the two dangling bodies. Veli stepped around a corner, holding up his hands when he saw Xander.

"Easy there, Ruby. It's just me."

"You act like that means something to me," said Xander. "What are you doing out here, Tash?"

"Following a lead on Leon's son. What are *you* doing out here?"

"Looking for these two." Xander motioned to the two dangling guards.

Veli looked above his head and whistled. "How tragic."

Xander grunted and went to the trunk of the tree they were dangling from. He took a knife out of his boot and cut the rope. Both bodies dropped to the ground.

"Who were you talking to before?"

Xander looked at Veli. "What?"

"I walked over here because I heard you shouting. Is someone else here?"

"No," said Xander. "I thought I was being followed for a minute, but if I was I'm sure they're gone now that there's two of us. What about you? Are you alone?"

"Of course," said Veli.

"Not even your brother to keep you company?" He arched an eyebrow.

Veli looked at him curiously. "You know he's not allowed out here since his demotion."

"Since when have rules stopped your family from doing anything?" asked Xander, walking to the bodies and cutting the ropes around their necks. It was only then that he noticed both bodies were badly burned. He backed away for a second, checking to make sure his mask was still tightly fastened before stepping forward again.

"Looks like they're allergic to the toxic air," said Veli with a laugh.

Xander grunted again and shook his head. He lifted one body and threw it over Veli's shoulder. Veli stumbled.

"Rigor mortis, Ruby. How the hell am I supposed to carry him?"

"Figure it out," said Xander, picking up the remaining body.

As he led Veli away, he looked back one last time at the place he had left Talon. Someone's eyes were staring back at him, but they weren't sea-green. They were dark-brown and accompanied by black hair and tan skin. Dakota.

Xander looked away and took a deep breath. He had just encountered two of the three most important people in Deryn's former life. If there was ever an opportunity to get her help on the outside, he had just missed it.

CHAPTER THIRTY-TWO

Whue down in the basement, Deryn and Bronson lost track of time. They didn't realize how late it was until they heard the door to the building open, signaling Quigley's return.

"Shit," said Bronson, walking over to the stairs leading out of the basement. "I really wish he and that broad never broke up. It was so convenient before."

"It's fine," said Deryn, walking up beside him. "Just head inside and tell him you went for a walk or something, and I'll slip upstairs."

Bronson nodded. "I'll make up some excuse and head up there in a bit. I'm pretty sure he thinks Ruby and I are screwing." He winked.

Deryn couldn't help but smile.

The two of them headed up the stairs slowly, Bronson taking the lead and listening closely for any signs of his roommate.

When they got to the second floor, Bronson held his hand out so Deryn would stop. "Someone else is here. But I didn't hear anyone else come in," he said, looking worried. "Go back to the basement, Der -"

"No," she said, stubbornly crossing her arms. "I'll wait right here until I know everything is alright."

Bronson wanted to argue, but Quigley's voice was becoming more urgent. He nodded and headed up the last flight of stairs to his apartment's door. It was currently wide open. Quigley was standing in the archway and yelling at someone on the inside.

Bronson walked over cautiously and put a hand on his roommate's shoulder.

Quigley jumped and turned, letting out a sigh of relief when he saw who it was. "Where the fuck you been? This ass says he's been waiting for you. *Inside!*"

Bronson looked past him, unsure if he should be happy or worried when he saw Luka stand up from the couch. The result of his mixed emotions was a strange, straight smile that was probably as unsettling to witness as it was to make.

"Luka. To what do I owe the pleasure?"

"Where th'fuck is Xander?" demanded Luka.

Bronson shrugged. "Hell if I know."

"Then where's that fucking chip I leant you?"

"I gave it to Ruby." Not a complete lie.

"And you really have no idea where he is?"

"Nope."

Luka huffed. "I don't believe you. He's avoiding me. Has been for days. Why th'fuck is he avoiding me?"

"Dunno," said Bronson, shrugging again. "Ruby and I hardly sit around chatting about our feelings."

"I thought that's what pansies like you were for," said Luka with a sneer.

Bronson smirked. "Ouch, Luka. And after everything I did for -"

Luka's eyes widened. "Just tell me where he is!"

"Why do you care?" asked Bronson, stepping further into his apartment. Quigley was still frozen in the doorway.

"Because I need to talk to him! *Now!*"

"Then go wait in *his* apartment, because he isn't going to come here first. I just gave him a new pack of cigarettes this morning."

"Tell me where he is."

"I. Don't. Know."

Luka's nostrils flared. "You think I don't know what's going on? Any help you give him is cause for immediate execution!"

Bronson raised his eyebrows. "You're going to have me executed, Luka?"

"Not if you cooperate. Now, let me check your wristbands. Both of you."

Quigley was taken aback. "Excuse me? What right do you have -"

"Every right!" shouted Luka, pulling back his sleeve so Quigley could see his left wristband with the president's crest engraved on it. "Now, let me see!"

"B-but Ruby is always the one to check our wristbands," said Quigley turning as white as a sheet.

"Not today he isn't." He held out his hand and wiggled his fingers impatiently.

Quigley grunted before walking over and holding out his arm, but Bronson hesitated. He had been helping Deryn in the basement all day, not going anywhere else. The tracker in his wristband would be stagnant, yet he had just walked upstairs, clearly coming from somewhere. There was no hiding that.

Luka checked Quigley's activity first, pressing a stick-like object against a small dot on his wristband, scanning through the material that appeared as a hologram in front of him. There was nothing abnormal, of course. He was not the one helping a fugitive develop a weapon in the basement.

"I'm waiting," said Luka, wiggling his hand at Bronson, who slowly held out his arm. "Do you want to tell me anything before I look at this?"

"Nope," said Bronson, grunting as he looked towards the door. He hoped Deryn hadn't returned to the basement, since that was bound to be Luka's next stop.

Luka checked the wristband. Bronson hadn't purchased anything so he pulled up a map of his activity. Other than going into Xander's apartment shortly after waking up, he had been in the basement all day. Luka played with the map, since it wasn't exactly clear where in the building Bronson had been at first.

"Th'fuck you been doing?"

Another shrug. Bronson stepped away from Luka and back towards the wall. With his peripherals, he could see Quigley staring oddly at him. "What have *you* been doing, Luka?" he asked. "I've been here all day and I didn't hear you come in."

"I was quiet about it," answered Luka.

"Why?"

Luka turned red. "I'm not the one being questioned here! What have you been doing downstairs in what I'm guessing is a basement all day? And you better answer me this time!"

"Or what?" he said, crossing his arms. "You obviously came here for a reason, so why don't you stop wasting all of our time and just tell me what you want."

"I want the truth!"

"The truth about what?"

"About what you and Xander are hiding! And maybe him!" He motioned towards Quigley. "I don't know! I honestly didn't know he existed until he walked through the door!"

"Ow," said Quigley with a frown.

"What do you think we're hiding?"

"Is this about you and Ruby being lovers?" asked Quigley before Luka could answer. "Because, I have to be honest, I've been suspecting it for quite some time now."

Luka rolled his eyes. "Fuck. No. This is about *you* and what you said." He was looking at Bronson. "I may have been drunk off my ass but I know what I heard!"

Bronson gulped. "And what was that?"

"I want *you* to tell me."

"I don't know what you're -"

"Liar!" Luka took his Element out of its holster and aimed it at Bronson, hitting him with glowing, blue light that bound his wrists. Not as painful as actual shackles but it still did its job. "Tell me now or I'll take you in!"

"Whoa!" said Quigley, holding up his hands and walking towards his friend. "I think we all just need to calm -"

"Fuck you!" shouted Luka, hitting him with the same blue light.

Quigley let out a high-pitched squeal.

"Luka, what are you doing?" asked Bronson, trying to walk forward, but Luka moved his Element back to him and he was quick to stop. "I don't know what you want!"

"The fucking truth!"

"About what?"

"Oh my god, oh my god, oh my god, oh my god!" repeated Quigley frantically.

"You *know*!"

"No, I don't! What is this about?"

"Just tell me!"

"Tell you what?"

"Tell me about -"

Deryn stepped through the door, her Element aimed at Luka. His eyes went wide.

"- Leon!"

She sent him shooting backwards into the wall, his Element flying out of his hand. Bronson ran and grabbed it, which proved difficult with his wrists still tied together.

When Luka tried to get to his feet, Deryn bound him with her Element. Bronson tossed Luka's weapon aside, moved forward and shoved him into a nearby chair. Then Deryn used a string of light from her Element him to it, first his chest, then his ankles. She was suddenly very glad she'd taken the time to add the additional button. All the while, Quigley was howling like a Yeti.

"Holy fuck! What's going on?" he shouted as Bronson slammed the front door shut.

"I knew it!" shouted Luka, struggling against his binds. "I fucking knew I heard you say her name!"

Deryn's jaw dropped. "You said my name, Bronson?"

His cheeks flushed. "Not all of it. Only the first half."

"Yes, and how many fucking Der's do you know?" spat Luka, still trying to break free.

"Unbelievable," said Deryn, rolling her eyes.

She took her knife out of her pocket and used it to cut Bronson and Quigley's binds.

"I can't believe you came in here," said Bronson.

"He was going to arrest you."

"He was bluffing."

"No, I wasn't!"

Bronson briefly glanced at Luka. Looking back at Deryn, he smirked and said, "Yes, he was."

"Holy fuck! Holy fuck, Bronson!" shouted Quigley, frantically pacing around the room. "What have you done? What are you doing? This ... *this* is Deryn Leon!"

"Yes, I know," said Bronson, following his roommate's chaotic movements before finally settling his eyes back on Luka, his hair askew, cheeks flushed, and clothes rumpled. Still pissed but obviously given up on getting out of his binds. They were solid. "So what are we gonna do with him?"

"I don't know," said Deryn. "Bonk him on the head and hope he forgets about this?"

"Don't you dare!" said Luka in a booming voice.

"I know the Guardians have ways to fumble memories a bit but I don't know how they work," she continued.

"With a mind like yours, I'm sure you can figure it out," said Bronson, patting the top of her head. They ignored Quigley as he continued to pace and panic around them.

"It's not something I could figure out right this moment. I think the bonking would be more affective." She took several steps towards Luka.

"Get away!" screamed Luka, trying his best to wiggle the chair away from her. "You're fucking mental if you think that's going to work."

"I'm not mental!" she shouted, kicking him in the shin. "What am I supposed to do, Bronson?"

"I don't know!"

Luka struggled harder as Quigley walked in circles, muttering to himself about what deep shit they were in. Deryn closed her eyes and tried to think, but there was just too much going on.

"Could you please keep quiet!" she shouted, lifting her Element and pointing it at Quigley. "Don't make me knock you out!"

Quigley shrieked. "Oh god, oh god, oh god!" He ran into his bedroom and proceeded to scream in there. Bronson followed him, but the noise wasn't any less.

Deryn's head ached as she closed her eyes and thought again. *Damn.* There was no easy way out of this. She brought her hand up and rubbed her temple.

Luka smirked. "Ruby said once that your mind was completely fucked. While he may have been exaggerating, it seems he wasn't so far off. There's really only one solution to making me forget about this, and you know it."

Deryn opened her eyes and narrowed them. "My mind is fine," she said. "It's all of this damn noise that's the problem!" She went to a nearby desk and searched through the drawers. She eventually found some strong tape and used it to tape Luka's mouth shut. Unfortunately, he wasn't the noisemaker driving her up the wall. "Wait here," she said with a frustrated huff before following Bronson and Quigley into the bedroom.

Luka started to ask where exactly it was he might go, but stopped when he realized his attempt would be wasted.

Outside the front door, Xander had just been running by to get to his apartment when he heard all of the yelling. He took out his Element and cautiously opened Bronson and Quigley's front door. He froze when he saw Luka sitting there, bound and silent, but his eyes did plenty of talking as they attempted to burn a hole right through him.

Xander stepped all the way inside and shut the door. He leaned casually against the wall and crossed his arms, all the while keeping his eyes fixed on Luka. Xander perked up his ears and listened to the voices in the other room. There were definitely three. One female. *Shit.*

The yelling finally died down and, a few seconds later, Deryn, Bronson and Quigley walked into the room. When they saw him, Bronson and Deryn froze but Quigley screamed all over again, frantically pulling at his hair.

"Holy shit, we're all going to die!"

Xander cocked an eyebrow. "Are you? At this point, I'm only targeting Bronson. But, looking at Luka, it's probably a pretty good assumption that he wouldn't hesitate to kill all of you."

"Ah!"

Bronson rolled his eyes. "Calm down, Quigley. Do you honestly think I could be harboring a fugitive in our building without the Guardian who lives upstairs knowing about it?"

Quigley froze and looked hopefully at Xander.

"Well, obviously," said Xander, stepping away from the wall. "I'm the one who brought her here."

Quigley let out a breath of relief and calmed slightly.

After locking the door, Xander turned to the group. "Now, how exactly did this happen?" he asked, darting his eyes between Deryn and Bronson.

Bronson sucked in his lips and Deryn cast her eyes shamefully to the floor.

"We lost track of time downstairs," answered Bronson after several seconds of silence. "And when we came up, Quigley was already home. He was talking to someone inside. I guess Luka had let himself in, all quiet and sneaky like, and -"

"He was trying to arrest them, Xander," interrupted Deryn.

Xander looked at her and raised his eyebrows. "So you decided to play hero?"

"Well, I wasn't just going to stand in the hallway and do nothing!" she defended. "I know you're probably angry but -"

"I'm not angry," he said in a calm, even tone.

Deryn looked at him curiously. "You're not?"

Xander shook his head, still keeping his eyes on Luka.

"Why not?"

"Would you rather I was?"

"Well, it would certainly be more normal."

Xander smirked. "I'm not angry because I'm not surprised. You're a Leon, and the whole lot of you have a damn hero complex I will never understand."

Luka breathed heavily as he stared at them with fiery eyes.

"Remove the tape, will you?"

Deryn went to Luka and ripped it off.

The first words out of his mouth, after a small yelp of pain, were, "You fucking bastard!"

"You Guardians really do have the worst potty mouths,"

said Bronson, slumping down on his couch. He tried to get Quigley to take a seat with him, but his friend was too busy fidgeting nervously to sit.

"Why were you trying to arrest Bronson?" Xander asked Luka.

"I wasn't going to actually fucking do it," he spat. "I was just trying to get him to talk!"

"Ah! You see, Deryn? I told you he was bluffing!" said Bronson proudly.

"Talk about what?" asked Xander.

"About *her!*" said Luka, motioning his head towards Deryn. "I heard you two fuckers talking about her the night we all went out and I've been trying to ask you about it, but you keep avoiding me!"

Xander crinkled his forehead. "I haven't been avoiding you."

"Then where have you been? I tried talking to you after the meeting the other day *and* today but -"

"I'm harboring a fugitive in my home. Forgive me for wanting to get back here in a timely manner. And today the president sent me on a mission outside. You knew that."

"Yeah, but what took you so long?" demanded Luka. "It should've been routine. Go to their destination and come back once you confirm they're not there. Simple."

"I never reached their destination. I found their bodies before I got there," said Xander.

"Then it really shouldn't've taken you so long. Where. Were. You?"

Xander grunted. He took off his rucksack and pulled out the photo of Deryn with her family. He handed it to her and put his rucksack down.

Deryn stared at the photo, her mouth falling open. "You went to my house?"

Xander nodded.

As Deryn looked at the photo, she brought her hand up to her mouth and tried to hold in a whimper. "And did it look alright? Still in one piece?"

Xander smiled. "Yes, Deryn. It was essentially untouched."

She reached out and touched her father's figure. Then her mother's. And, finally, Talon's. He was so young then, and she was just a baby, laughing in her mother's arms.

"I can't believe you, Xander! I can't believe you're risking your fucking life for Leon!" shouted Luka, bringing all eyes back to him. "You know they've been talking spy recently? I heard my father and the president talking about it in his study, and of course the fucking Tash brothers were there. Veli and them already have it out for you! No toxic trash is worth -"

Deryn's eyes shot up. Her hand curved into a fist and she lunged forward, punching Luka hard in the cheek. "How dare you! How dare you speak that way about me!" She punched him again.

Xander tried to grab her wrists, but she pulled away.

"You asshole! I bet you plan to tell them about me, don't you?"

"Deryn, calm down," said Xander, grabbing her again. "He won't -"

"No! No, I will not calm down!" she shouted, swinging to punch Luka again, but Xander hugged his arms around her before she could, causing her to drop the picture frame. He picked her up and carried her kicking and screaming to the kitchen. "Fuck you, Luka Voclain!"

Luka smirked. "Never thought I'd hear such language coming from the Outsider princess's mouth."

"Oh, she gets very passionate at times," said Bronson, picking up the frame and propping it on a table.

"Deryn, please calm down," said Xander just out of view in the kitchen.

"I'm sorry," said Deryn while sobbing. "I still have trouble controlling my anger."

"I know," he said. "At least you didn't think to take out your Element this time, like you did with me."

They both chuckled halfheartedly. And then they went very quiet.

"Th'fuck ..." muttered Luka while listening.

He whipped his head towards Bronson, who simply

shrugged before taking out a cigarette and lighting it in the middle of his living room. Quigley had finally calmed a little and was leaning against the back of the couch. He stole Bronson's cigarette and smoked it anxiously.

"Hey!" complained Bronson, rolling his eyes before taking out another.

Luka looked back at the kitchen. He couldn't see Xander and Deryn from where he was, so he leaned sideways in his chair, just making out Deryn's long hair. He leaned a little more. There were two hands cupping her face while she continued to cry silently. Then the hands were stroking her cheeks, calming her. And finally Luka saw Xander's face, leaning forward until his lips met hers.

Luka's eyes bulged as he leaned a little too far and fell over. "Whoa!"

Bronson laughed. He went over to Luka and put him and his chair upright, then glanced into the kitchen where Deryn and Xander were still going at it.

"Th'fuck?" said Luka.

"Yeah, I had a similar reaction when I found out," said Bronson. "So you remember me almost saying her name, but you don't remember what we were talking about?"

"I was drunk! I'm a little vague on the details! Wait." He paused and sat up straight. "Weren't you talking about sex? Holy fuck, are they fucking?"

"It's Ruby. What do you think?" asked Bronson, holding his cigarette down so Luka could take a drag.

Xander and Deryn walked out of the kitchen.

Luka blew out his puff of smoke and shouted, "You're fucking Leon?"

Xander went white and stared accusingly at Bronson, who held up his hands defensively.

"Don't look at me. He caught sight of your saliva exchange just now."

"If you wanted to fuck her then you should've just taken her as your slave like everybody else!"

The entire room went silent.

Deryn's face dropped.

Bronson burned himself while trying to catch his cigarette as it fell from his slackened jaw.

Quigley didn't fully understand what was going on, but he knew better than to open his mouth in that moment.

And Xander ... his entire body burned red while his face distorted. His fists clenched and he swung his arm, hitting Luka so hard his chair fell backwards.

"How dare you!" spat Xander. "How fucking dare you!" He grabbed Luka by his shirt collar and pulled him up, chair included, towards his raging face until their foreheads were practically touching. "Don't you ever, *ever* speak like that again!"

"Ruby, cool it," said Bronson, grabbing his shoulder, but Xander shook him off.

"Xander, stop!" shouted Deryn, grabbing his other shoulder.

"Did he ever touch you?" demanded Xander.

"No!" she said quickly. "No, I never even saw him! Just once my first time at his house, and then never again!"

"You wouldn't lie to -"

"Of course not! When Finley came over I told you exactly how I felt about her! And you go out with Luka all the time! Don't you think I would've said something if I had any negative feelings towards him?"

Xander huffed. "Fine." He put the chair back on its legs. "But if he says one more thing out of line -"

"So is she the one who wrote Finley that email then?" asked Luka, spitting some blood out of his mouth. "I knew it. I knew that didn't sound like you!"

Deryn frowned. "Yes, I admit, in my anger I failed to grasp Xander's proper essence."

"I want to talk to Leon," said Luka.

Xander huffed. "Go right ahea -"

"*Alone.*"

"Fuck no -"

"Xander, it's fine," said Deryn. "We have his weapon and those binds are strong. What could he possibly do?"

"Don't underestimate -"

"I won't," she said. "But we're not exactly resolving anything here. Why don't the three of you go wait on the balcony, and I'll get you when we're finished."

"Whoa, whoa, whoa! Hold on!" Quigley suddenly shouted. "Before I go anywhere, there is something very important I think we all need to discuss."

"And what's that?" asked Bronson.

They all waited.

Quigley looked at Deryn and asked, "Are you the cupcake girl?"

Bronson laughed.

Xander rolled his eyes. "Why are you both so obsessed with that fucking cupcake?"

"Is that a yes?"

No one answered and Bronson dragged Quigley outside. Xander looked hesitantly at Deryn before following. "Don't you try anything, Luka."

"Yeah, I'm tied to a chair!" he called after him. "Th'fuck you think I'm gonna do?"

As soon as they were all gone and the door to the balcony was closed, Deryn grabbed another chair from around the kitchen table and put it in front of Luka. She sat down and crossed her arms. "So what did you want to talk about?"

"Let's start with how you ended up here."

Deryn thought. "Well, it wasn't planned, if that's what you mean. I was out on the streets and Xander recognized me, so he brought me here."

"And you just willingly walked into a Guardian's apartment?"

"No. I didn't want his help, but there were guards and Guardians everywhere. I was out of options, so I took a chance." She smirked. "You almost caught me, you know. On the tram."

Luka's eyes widened. "You were the girl he told Veli not to wake?"

"That's right."

"Well, damn. But that was over three months ago. How long

have you two been fucking?"

Deryn's jaw clenched. "I'm not answering that."

"Why not?"

"Because it's personal and absolutely none of your business."

"And is it none of Xander's business that his father took your virginity?"

Deryn's heart stopped. Every part of her fell limp from her jaw to her arms, and she was unable to hold her body or spirit together as she looked sadly at Luka.

"He doesn't know, does he?"

Deryn cast her eyes downward and slowly shook her head.

"That's what I thought. Xander would never be with you if he knew."

"H-how ..."

"Do I know?" finished Luka.

She nodded.

"I was there, Leon. Forced to watch that disgusting display before the president upgraded me from guard to Guardian. I was just lucky I wasn't one yet, or else my father probably would've made me take my turn with you."

Tears dripped slowly from Deryn's eyes as she remembered that horrible night. The roaring thunder, the smile on Saevus's face, the shameful look in Atticus Ruby's eyes as his president pushed him forward, forcing him to steal her innocence only hours after losing his wife. And he did it. Even though he had no desire for her, he still did it.

"Leon!"

The sound of Deryn's name brought her back to reality. She looked at Luka and said in a cracked voice, "Please, don't tell him. I do plan to but ... there's no good way to tell someone that."

"You should've told him before."

"I know. And I meant to, but I didn't want him to look at me differently. For the most part, Xander is really good about holding back those pitiful looks I hate so much. But if he knows about -" She gulped. "- his father, then it won't be the same."

"Obviously," he scoffed.

Deryn sighed. "Please."

Luka gazed back at her for a moment, the desperation in her eyes making even him want to give her that pitiful look she apparently hated so much. To get her to stop, he nodded.

"Thank you."

"But for my silence we're going to have to come up with some sort of compromise," he said. "Even you have to admit you're an idiot if you really think clonking me on the head will make me forget about this."

Deryn shrugged. "Maybe. But I'm not letting you out of here without doing something. I have no reason to trust you."

"Other than agreeing to keep your disgusting secret?"

Deryn's jaw clenched.

Luka sighed. "I didn't mean that," he said. "For what it's worth, I'm sorry. About everything, but especially my father and his treatment of you. He can be a bit ... well, he's mental."

"Yes, I know," said Deryn. "Xander told me about what he had Saevus do to you."

Luka nodded solemnly. "I'm going to tell you something," he said after a moment. "To prove that you can trust me."

"How will I know what you're telling me is real?"

"You'll know," he said, his tone serious.

Deryn leaned back in her chair and waited.

It took Luka a moment, but then he began to tell her a story. A secret he had never shared with anyone before.

"My father has been taking in slaves from the slave trade for as long as I can remember, but it never affected me. Not really. It was just part of everyday life at my house. And then, five years ago, you came."

Luka stared deep into Deryn's eyes. As much as she wanted to, she didn't turn away, and she stared straight back at him. It was while looking into those dark eyes that she realized he was not challenging her. There was nothing but sincerity in those almost black eyes. Sincerity and regret.

"My father was the first to own you after Saevus decided the slave trade was the best place to hide you, and seeing you there - dragged in and already beaten - I suddenly realized that I *knew* you. You were a real person who I'd trained with, talked to, even laughed with once."

One corner of Deryn's mouth twitched upwards as she remembered the moment he spoke of. "When Elvira was teaching us the most efficient way to customize our Elements - according to her."

"And fell flat on her face while going over to criticize Wyatt on his heavy hands," finished Luka, chuckling softly. "She fell right between your table and mine, and we looked at each other and laughed our asses off."

"Even back then I couldn't fake sympathy for that terrible woman," said Deryn.

Luka's smile faded. "None of the slaves had ever felt real before you. They were nothing to me, just objects passing through the night. Faceless. But you ... you had a face, and it was defeated. That first night after my father was finished with you, I sat outside the basement listening to you cry. I wanted to get you out but I didn't know how, so I did the only thing I could. I brought you food and water, and slipped it through the door before you could see me."

Deryn blinked. Throughout the years, every time she had been Barath's slave there was always food and water for her. "You did that? I always thought it was a sympathetic servant."

"No, it was me," said Luka. "And after you left, suddenly they all had faces. Every last slave. So -"

He took a deep breath.

"- I helped them all. I gave them food and water, and on nights my father didn't come home I let them sleep in one of our spare bedrooms. I know it wasn't much, but I did my best to make it easier for them. For all of you."

Another deep breath.

"And then I met Anna." Suddenly, Luka was staring into her eyes again. The sincerity behind his was even stronger than before. "She wasn't your usual slave. Come to think of it, I don't even really know how she ended up in the slave trade. I guess the president wanted to keep someone from finding her. But Anna was older, and the only reason my father ever even took her in was because she was an amazing cook. He let her eat our leftovers and sleep on the floor in the pantry, even allowing her a blanket and a pillow, so she didn't need me the way the others did. But Anna ... she took me under her wing. Inviting me into the kitchen with her, teaching me things about cooking, just talking with me like no one had before.

"But as the years went on I became aware that Anna wasn't well. Maybe sleeping on a pantry floor with a blanket would be a step up for a younger person, but the slave trade was taking its toll on her. She needed out. So while she was staying with the Firmans I went there pretending I wanted to see Wyatt. After twenty minutes or so I said I had to use the bathroom, but instead I went to the closet where I knew they kept her and I ... I gave her a knife."

Deryn froze.

"I bought it at the Black Market so it couldn't be traced back to me. It was a silver knife with a spear point, and the handle was wooden with two lines spiraling around it that crossed each other. Ever seen anything like it?"

She had actually, and it was currently burning a hole in her pocket. "It might sound familiar."

"It sounds familiar because you used it. I know you did because Anna told me. She gave up her life so you could live. That's why you can trust me. Why you should let me help you. Because it's what Anna would've wanted -"

He gulped.

"- if she was still with us."

Deryn sighed and broke their eye contact to stare at a spot on the floor. She knew she shouldn't, but she actually believed him. The knife the old woman had given her was not an average kitchen knife, and Guardians weren't exactly known for keeping such trinkets. They preferred firepower.

"I never knew her name," admitted Deryn, fiddling with the knife in her pocket. "There isn't much conversation during the slave trade. The night I escaped was the first time she ever talked to me."

"It was Anna Bellamy," said Luka. "Her granddaughter is an Outsider who trained with us. Eva —"

"Evangeline," finished Deryn. "I remember her. We were from different villages, but taken around the same time so we were in isolation together." She paused. "What happened to her?"

"She escaped with the Resistance during the battle at Eagle. Her father's family still lived in the city and were taken into custody the moment it was discovered she was gone. Anna was the last of them."

Deryn frowned and continued to fiddle with the knife. She then stopped and took it out of her pocket. "I believe everything you've told me," she said, "but how do I know you're not out for revenge since my life was spared and Anna's wasn't?"

"Guess you'll just have to take a chance. That's what got you here with Xander, isn't it?" he said with a smile.

"Yes, but the difference is with him I was out of options, but with you I have at least three."

Luka cocked an eyebrow.

"I knock you in the head until your unconscious and hope you forget about this, I hold you prisoner, or I kill you. Of course, if we go into the ways I could kill you, the number of options drastically grows." She smirked.

He rolled his eyes. "We both know the only real option there is number two, and Xander will tell you that it's too risky."

At that moment, a voice outside grew louder than the others. Deryn turned her head and saw Bronson yelling about something. And then it clicked.

"I'll make you a deal, Luka. In a minute here I'm going to call Xander back in and he's going to decide what we're going to do with you. You're his friend and it's his decision, not mine." She paused and gave him a sly smile. "But he'll be much more likely to trust you if I say I do, which I will if you answer one question for me honestly."

"And what's that?" he asked, thinking there was no possible way the question could be that bad.

"What happened between you and Bronson the night he took you home?"

Luka blushed. As it turned out, it was 'that bad'.

"And there's no use lying about it because he already told me everything. I just want to hear it from you, to see if you're truly being honest with me."

He took a deep breath. "Umm ..."

"You have thirty seconds to tell me before I call Xander back in."

"Okay, okay!" he said hurriedly. "It's not that big a deal."

"You don't have to convince me," she said.

"I know." Luka stopped and took a deep breath. Then while staring at the floor he quickly blurted out, "Itoldhimtosuckmeoff!"

"I'm sorry?" said Deryn, leaning in. "I didn't quite catch that."

Luka grimaced but still cleared his throat. Then, very clearly, he said, "I told him to suck me off, and he did. Happy?"

His eyes shot up and met hers. He was a bit surprised to see the bewilderment behind them. And then came the laughter.

"Oh my god," she said, covering her mouth to stifle the chuckles. "He did? I thought maybe in your drunken state the two of you kissed or something, but -" Her laughter grew stronger.

Luka went white. "You said you knew!"

"I lied," she said, laughing away. "Bronson doesn't kiss and tell. At least he doesn't tell me."

Her laughter kept growing until she practically fell out of her chair, stumbling a little before catching herself. And then it tipped. She hit the floor hard, but her laughter didn't cease.

Hearing the commotion, Xander ran inside and knelt down beside her. "Deryn, what happened? Are you alright?"

She looked at him, and then past him to where Bronson was standing. The laughter continued as she practically rolled on the floor. And, she had to admit, the laughter felt good.

"It's not funny!" shouted Luka from his chair. "Why'd you do that?"

"Why'd you believe me?" she asked while sitting up. Seeing Luka sprouted a new round of giggles.

"What have you two been doing in here?" asked Xander, helping her back to her feet.

"Talking," answered Deryn. "Sharing secrets." She chuckled again. "He wanted to prove that we can trust him."

"There's no need for any of that," said Xander. "I can already tell you that we can't."

Luka glared at him. "Excuse me? We've been friends since we were fucking babies and you don't trust me?"

"It's not that I don't trust you," said Xander. "It's that I don't want to have to deal with another fucking person. Enough people already know about this. Besides, you enjoy being a Guardian."

"No I don't!"

"Could've fooled me."

"And *you* could've fooled *me*!" shouted Luka. "It's all a game, isn't it? We do what we have to to stay alive! That's it!"

"Why do you want in on this, anyway?" asked Xander. "If you want to stay alive so bad then helping Deryn isn't the way to go."

"You're right, it's a risk and I would rather not be any part of this!" Luka sighed and looked at Deryn again. "But Anna gave you that knife. She wanted you to live and I'll be damned before I let her death be in vain." He gulped. "I never had a grandmother or even a mother of my own, and Anna ... she was kind to me. I know she was a slave but I never saw her that way. I never saw any of them that way. Not after you."

"You gave me food," said Deryn with a frown. "It really was you?"

Luka blushed. He cast his eyes timidly to the floor. "I want to help you."

"Well, you can't," said Xander.

"Tell him about his father, Xander," said Deryn suddenly. "He should know what Veli and the others are doing."

Xander looked at her lividly.

"He should know."

Xander didn't like it, but every day he found it more and more difficult to say no to her. So he crossed his arms and turned to Luka. "Veli threatened me. He said he was sick of me and if I didn't find Deryn then he would have each and every person I cared about killed. You were second on the list, and your father has volunteered to do the dirty work."

Luka's mouth fell open as he continued to gaze at his oldest friend. He shook his head and said, "Why am I not surprised? That bastard's had it out for me ever since I took his seat."

Xander nodded. "So what exactly is your plan here, Deryn? I'm not just letting him walk out of here."

"I know," she said, "but I think he can be useful. And I would really feel better about you spending your days with other Guardians if I knew one of them was on your side."

Xander thought for a second. And then he remembered. He reached into the hidden inside pocket of his coat and pulled out a small chip. "This just might be your lucky day, Luka."

But Luka didn't look quite so sure. "What's that?"

"This is a prototype of a mind control chip. Something Veli informed me of by threatening me with it. Aside from minor memory loss when removed, it's said to be completely flawless. You're going to be my test dummy."

Luka's eyes widened. "Fuck. No."

"It really is our best option," said Deryn, taking a closer look at the chip. Xander had told her about its existence, but this was her first time actually seeing it.

"No!" shouted Luka. "No, I will not let you take away my freewill! I'd rather you bonk me over the head to try and erase my fucking memories than do that!"

"We won't take away your freewill," said Deryn. "We can order you to keep that. Can't we?" She looked at Xander expectantly.

"I believe we can."

"There you go!" she said enthusiastically. "We just need to make it so you can't talk about me being here outside of these walls."

"But what about him?" asked Luka, motioning towards Quigley. "Are you going to plant a fucking chip in him, too?"

Quigley's eyes widened in terror.

"No," said Xander. "I only have one."

"And we can trust him," said Bronson, leaning against the back of the couch. "Remember, Ruby, you have the same dirt on him that you have on me. So we're all good." He gave Xander a thumbs up.

Xander grunted. "Clearly, this was a fucking awful day for me to leave the city."

"Seems that way," said Bronson with a smirk. "Personally, I'm happy this is all out in the open. At least now I won't have to constantly convince Quigley that we're not actually lovers."

Xander ignored him and turned back to Luka. "So what will it be? The mind control chip, or are you mysteriously going to disappear for awhile?"

Luka narrowed his eyes and shook his head. "Mind control chip, you fucking ass."

"Oh, wonderful!" shouted Bronson, the only one who seemed pleased with this outcome.

"Fine," said Xander, walking behind Luka and crouching so he had access to his wrists. He had to rearrange the binds a bit, but he was able to get his citizen wristband positioned right to insert the chip. "I really am sorry about this, Luka, but it has to be done."

"Funny that I need to be kept under control when you're busy taking advantage of the former slave you claim to want to protect," said Luka under his breath, so only Xander could hear.

Xander said nothing, and Luka fixed his eyes on Deryn. She tried to give him a smile. Then Xander stepped between them, and Luka realized his binds had been released.

"Now, let's see what this thing can do. Luka, go fetch me a glass of water."

And before Luka had a chance to shout at Xander to get his own fucking water, his feet were pushing him up and carrying him towards the kitchen.

CHAPTER THIRTY-THREE

Deryn sat on the bed in the room she shared with Xander, fresh out of the shower and wearing nothing but her robe. Every few seconds, she glanced at the photos that were now propped on the nightstand. And then her eyes moved to the snow globe just beside them. She sighed and reached for it, giving the knob on the bottom a few twists so the song would play. She didn't know what it was, just some old song she had never been able to find on any of her records, but it was beautiful.

The front door opened. Bronson called his familiar, "Olly olly oxen free!" and she went out to meet him.

"Did you get it?" she asked.

"Get what?" asked Luka, who was lying on the couch and thumbing through *Complex Conundrums*. Ever since he found out about his father he didn't like to be home, but ever since Xander installed a mind control chip in his wristband he didn't like to be around him either so if they weren't working the same shift he made a point to leave before Xander got home.

"None of your business," Bronson said to Luka, "and you bet I did," he added to Deryn. "It's time to get this party started. And then I'll tell you all about the gorgeous hunk of man I met on the tram. We're going out later."

Bronson skipped over to her, his shoulder bag swinging from his hip as he eyed Luka with a sly smile. He grabbed a skeptical Deryn and pulled her towards the bathroom while Luka tried to hide his furrowed brow behind the book.

Once alone, Bronson sat her on the closed toilet seat and dug through his bag, first taking out mascara, then eyeliner, blush, lipstick, and some sort of beige-colored liquid.

"They didn't have any sponges so we're just going to have to make do with our hands."

"I have no idea what that means," she said.

"For the liquid foundation," he answered, holding up the small bottle of beige liquid. "Do you want to apply it or should I?"

"You do it." She closed her eyes tightly.

Bronson shrugged. "Okay, but I haven't exactly done this before either." He put a dollop in his hands and spread it over her face. He quickly realized he had used way too much. After a quick wash of his hands, he rubbed the excess off and focused on spreading it evenly.

Once he was satisfied, he moved on to the blush, applying just a small amount to the small brush it had come with and applying it to her cheeks. He didn't quite like the end result and ended up rubbing it in with his fingers.

"Bronson, could you stop please?" said Deryn, pulling away from him.

"Why?" he asked, crinkling his nose as he lowered his hand.

"I don't know, I just - I'm starting to have second thoughts about this."

"Why?" he asked again. "You said you wanted to do something to make Ruby happy and we both agreed that this is the best -"

"I know!" she shouted. "But I just don't think I'm ready!"

Deryn stood up. She pulled her robe tightly around her body and cast her eyes shamefully to the floor.

"You probably aren't," said Bronson with a frown. "But will you ever be?"

"I don't know," she said dryly, "but I want to be."

"Then I think you need to be more forceful about it. You've been through a lot, Deryn, and you're not going to get past all of it by sitting back and waiting to be healed. And if you're not going to just *tell* him how you feel ..."

Deryn chuckled halfheartedly. "I don't know if I'll ever be ready for that."

"Well, could you at least tell me how you feel?" asked Bronson with a wide, teeth-baring grin.

Looking at him very seriously, Deryn reached her hand out and took his. "Bronson, I like you very much. As a friend." She smirked.

Bronson rolled his eyes and said, "Not what I meant."

"I know," she said, letting go of his hand. "But, the truth is, I don't know how to describe my feelings for Xander. There are no words for it. Not the right ones, anyway." Deryn closed her eyes and took several deep breaths, images of Xander instantly flooding her mind. When she opened her eyes again, she retook her seat on the toilet. "Okay, let's try this again."

With a smile, Bronson finished fixing her blush. He then moved onto the eyeliner and mascara - relieved to discover that she wasn't much of a blinker and he had a fairly steady hand - but he refused to do the lipstick out of fear he would get it everywhere and ruin the beautiful job he had done with the foundation.

While working on her lips in the mirror, Deryn was too focused to notice Bronson leave the bathroom. He came back a minute later waving around her black and pink bra.

"Are you wearing this one?" he asked. "Because I remember Ruby being particularly fond of it when we got it for you."

Deryn turned bright-red before whipping around and grabbing it from him. "I don't know," she said. "I haven't really thought about it." That was a lie. Ever since Deryn had decided to do this, she had not stopped thinking about what she should wear. This particular bra had come up in her thoughts several times.

"Well, I think you should," he said, taking it back and holding it up to his chest. "With some lacy black underwear. I know we got you some."

Deryn blushed brighter.

"Aw, cupcake, after all of the time we've spent together you're still so shy around me." Bronson gave her cheek a pinch.

Deryn batted it away. "I don't see you telling me what you plan to wear the next time you try to seduce Luka."

Bronson smirked. "If I'm going to seduce someone then I won't be wearing anything." He paused. "And who says there will be a next time?"

Deryn rolled her eyes. "Oh, please. You've been messing with him ever since he made it clear that *he* wasn't interested in a next time."

"Have I?" he said innocently.

"Yes, you have."

"Maybe. But it's not like it matters."

Deryn looked at him curiously.

"Luka's not gay, Deryn. He's just lazy."

"What?"

"That night I *seduced* him," he said mockingly, "it wasn't even me who instigated it. It was him, and he did it for one reason and one reason only."

She waited.

"Because he was horny, and I was there and willing. He knew that and he used it to his advantage."

"His advantage?"

"Why do it yourself when you can have someone else do it for you?" Bronson winked. "The reason I've been messing with him, as you put it, is because I want to see how open he might be."

"And just what conclusion have you drawn from this little experiment of yours?" she asked.

"That he'd be open to a repeat performance. But I'm not sure he'd ever return the favor, and that's a problem."

Deryn looked to the floor so he could not see her blush again.

Bronson laughed. "Your innocence is so fucking adorable, I can't even stand it. Does this mean you've never returned the favor?"

She didn't answer.

"Well, if you do end up going through with this tonight then maybe you should start with that. I can already tell you that

Ruby is a fan."

Deryn's eyes shot up, going excessively wide as her jaw fell to the floor.

"No, no, not like that!" said Bronson quickly. "He's just told me things. About his past conquests, you know?"

Moving her eyes back to the floor, Deryn quietly said, "I wouldn't know what I was doing."

"And this is why you have me as a friend," he said with a bright smile. "Your little problem just happens to be my field of expertise."

~

Deryn stood alone in the bathroom, wearing nothing but her black and pink bra and lacy black underwear. She looked in the mirror at the face Bronson had painted on for her.

She tucked her hair behind her ear and walked into the bedroom. Xander would be home soon. She paced around, her hands fidgeting nervously as she waited. The clock was ticking much slower than usual.

Deryn sat on the bed and tried to calm herself. Her eyes drew to the large scar on her side. The one Finley had given her. She wished she could get rid of it somehow, even if it was just for the night. Bronson had tried to put some of that foundation on it but to no avail.

Tracing the scar with her fingers, Deryn sighed heavily. Even though Xander never stared at any of her scars for too long, never grimaced, she was still always so aware of them. She didn't want to be. She wanted Xander to view her as flawless, but that would never happen.

Deryn had been so caught up in her scars that she completely missed the sound of the front door opening. There were a few words exchanged between Xander and Luka before the latter was rushing out the door. A few moments later, the door to the bedroom clicked open and she jumped to her feet, standing nervously in the middle of the floor as Xander walked in. His eyes widened at the sight of her.

"Deryn, why are you -"

Deryn didn't let him finish. Sucking back her nerves, she

took several hurried steps forward, wrapped her arms around Xander's neck and pulled his head inward. She kissed him with more fervor than she ever had before, he normally being the instigator of their more intense kissing sessions.

Quickly forgetting about why Deryn might be doing this, Xander let her tear off his shirt while he undid his trousers. They fell to the floor and he barely stepped out of them before Deryn dropped to her knees, pulling down his underwear in one fell swoop.

"Deryn, why are you -" he started again, quickly shutting his mouth the moment he was engulfed in hers. "Holy shit."

His knees feeling weak, Xander fell back against the door, slamming it shut. Deryn shuffled right along with him, her mouth never stopping as it moved with a certain skillfulness he hadn't been expecting. He looked down and watched as her perfect, bright-pink lips stimulated him, his hand clenching tightly in her hair as he tried to hold in his release.

She suddenly moved off of him and looked up. "Don't hold it back," she said before plunging on him once more.

And so he didn't, letting her continue for several more minutes until he felt his release building up. He grabbed her hands off of his hips and pulled her to her feet, kissing her aggressively while she continued to pump his cock, not stopping until he was coming on her stomach.

Once he had a moment to catch his breath, Deryn kissed him softly. She went into the bathroom and cleaned herself off before joining him by the door again, kissing him with as much vigor as she had the moment he walked in.

Xander smiled as his arms wrapped around her waist. He picked her up, carried her over to the bed, and tossed her in its center. He climbed on after her, gently kissing up her thigh until he hit her black underwear.

"Your turn," he said while slowly pulling them off of her.

Xander discarded them to the side and fell into her, spreading her legs and lifting them over his shoulders before licking one delicate line up her slit. But that was the only gentleness she would be getting from here on out.

Engulfing his mouth on her clit, Xander sucked aggressively, nibbling on her most sensitive spot while she tried to wriggle above him. But he held her still and, when she finally began to relax, he plunged two fingers into her burning core. He loved that warmth, his cock growing hard again at the thought of entering her in a few short minutes.

It was not long before Deryn was on the edge, Xander biting down slightly harder on her clit to make her scream especially loud. He smiled triumphantly, knowing very well that she always liked that.

Deryn barely let her orgasm pass before she pulled Xander up so he was level with her and kissed him again.

Xander moaned into her mouth. Knowing where this was leading, he reluctantly pulled away, stopping her for just a moment. "Is there any particular reason you're like this tonight? Not that I'm complaining!" he added quickly as her face began to drop. "But you being the aggressive one isn't exactly usual."

Deryn stared deeply into his eyes and brought her hand up to stroke his hair. She gulped and said, "You once told me that you were holding back for me, and I don't want you to do that tonight."

Xander cocked an eyebrow. "Really?"

She nodded and, with all the confidence she could muster, said, "I'm ready."

He smiled and kissed her. "Should we have a safety word?"

Deryn laughed. "Safety word? Are you planning to start whipping me or something?"

"Well, if you're into that sort of thing."

She smiled coyly and shook her head.

Xander let out a dramatic sigh. "Alright, fine. No props tonight. Just you and me. But, seriously, a safety word wouldn't be such a terrible -"

"Xander, no," she said, tracing her fingers down his face. "I don't need a safety word. I trust you."

He smiled again. "Then let's start with something simple." Climbing off of her, Xander lifted Deryn and positioned her so her back was to him. With one quick flick of his wrist, her bra was off and discarded somewhere on the floor. "Put your hands on the headboard," he instructed.

Deryn did as she was told, suddenly feeling very nervous as Xander crawled up behind her. Until now he had always been somewhat gentle with her, letting her keep a certain amount of control even when he was on top. But tonight was going to be different. This was the first time they would ever be doing this in a position where she couldn't look into his eyes if she needed to. Maybe a safety word really wasn't such a terrible idea.

Then Xander moved her hair off of her neck, pressing his lips to it while caressing her hips. Deryn closed her eyes and sank into his touch. She knew the feeling of those lips, that tongue, those hands. They belonged to Xander and he would never do anything to harm her.

"Move back a little."

Deryn did just that, letting herself relax as he entered her.

Xander started out slow, running his hands along her thighs while thrusting inside of her, his lips never leaving her skin as she became putty in his hands.

It wasn't long before their movements became erratic, the two of them changing positions like it was a dance, and their hands and tongues everywhere they could touch.

There was a brief stint on the floor after they accidentally fell onto it, Deryn having her second orgasm of the night as she thrust her hips on top of him.

When it passed, Xander tossed her back on the bed and took his turn in control. Deryn writhed and moaned beneath him in ways she never had before, their wild sex causing the bed to bang hard against the wall and scrape the floor. Had the bed frame not been made of iron, it surely would have broken.

Deryn screamed his name, tossing her arms back and grabbing onto the headboard.

Xander put his arms behind her knees and lifted her legs over his shoulders. Placing his hands beside hers, he used the headboard to brace himself while he thrust mercilessly.

Xander was clenching his teeth so tightly together they may very well have cracked. If he lost any concentration then he was done, and he knew Deryn wasn't quite there yet. Just a little ... bit ... longer.

"Xander!" she screamed as her third orgasm washed over her, her body tensing and then falling weak as he gave two final thrusts.

Xander let out his own scream, along with a heavy breath he hadn't realized he was holding in. His body began to slow as Deryn ran her hands along his arms, rubbing them soothingly as he lowered her legs. He gave her body one last caress before pulling out of her.

Even though Xander and Deryn were both still out of breath, they managed to meet for a kiss as his body slackened on top of hers. Xander kissed her lips, her cheek, her forehead, jaw, neck, collarbone, anywhere he could touch, yet, somehow, it was never enough.

"So what did you think?" he asked once they had had a moment to catch their breath.

Deryn smiled. "Well, now I know why those girls you brought here always screamed so loudly," she said with a slight chuckle.

"I assure you, it's never been quite like that," he said, kissing her again. "That was -"

"Amazing," she finished.

Xander grinned and shook his head. "No. I've had amazing sex before, and that was beyond amazing, love. That was phenomenal."

Deryn blushed. Xander wasn't sure why until he replayed his words in his head. He had called her love. It was a complete accident, but one he hardly felt ashamed about.

Xander traced her lips with his thumb, tempted to say the word again. "Deryn, I -"

Knock. Knock. Knock.

Both of them shot up as they realized the knocking was on their bedroom door.

"Xander, if you're quite finished in there, I would like to have a word with you," called a familiar, deep voice.

Shit.

"Did I ever say your name?" asked Xander frantically while Deryn's fingers dug into his arms.

"N-no," she answered in a weak, terrified voice.

"Good." He reached down, pulled the comforter up from where it had fallen on the floor, and threw it on top of her. "Stay here. I'll get rid of him."

Xander kissed her forehead and hurried to get dressed. He looked back at her one last time before opening his door just enough to slip out.

In the living room, his guest had made himself comfortable on the couch and was flipping through the pages of one of Deryn's books.

"Father, what are you doing here?"

Without turning to look at him, Atticus said, "Is it not customary for a father to come and visit his son every now and then?"

"Not in our family."

He shut the book and put it down on the coffee table. "I'm worried about you, Xander. Everyone is."

Xander raised his eyebrows. "Are they?"

Atticus stood and turned to face his son. "Yes. They say you haven't been yourself lately. Do you have any idea as to why they might think that?" he asked, his eyes glancing slightly towards Xander's bedroom door.

"No," said Xander. "If I'm acting unusually, it's only because I'm being cautious. Several of our Guardian friends have made it very clear that they no longer want me in power, and I don't plan on letting them usurp me anytime soon."

"What? Xander, if someone's threatened you then I have a right to -"

"It's nothing I can't handle. Don't worry yourself too much or you might get wrinkles." Xander pointed at his forehead and made a face.

"This is no laughing matter," said Atticus, walking towards his son. "If those people have it out for you then it's only a matter of time until -"

"While they may have it out for me, it's not my life they're threatening."

Atticus stiffened.

"Don't concern yourself with this. Just make sure to watch your back when alone." Xander smirked. "Are we done?"

"Not even close," said Atticus. "I've been informed that Lona Von has reached out to you several times since moving to Middle City, but she has yet to receive a response."

"So?" He recalled seeing a few emails from her but never took the time to read them.

"Why haven't you contacted her?"

"I have no interest in Lona, though that doesn't seem to matter to you much, does it? Considering you're too busy making engagement deals behind my back."

Atticus was taken aback for a moment but quickly composed himself. "You know as well as I do that I have no say in such things. Any arrangements being made are done by President Saevus."

"But you knew about it, and you chose not to inform me."

"I was *ordered* not to inform you."

Xander shrugged it off. "Well, do me a favor and let those making the arrangements know that I will never agree. Marriage isn't in the cards for me."

"I'm afraid it's going to have to be."

"Nope."

Realizing he was standing a bit protectively in front of his bedroom door, Xander decided that it might be best to move away from it, so as not to arouse suspicion. Feeling his cigarettes in his pocket, he headed for the balcony. He kept the door open and leaned against the railing, keeping a sharp eye on his father as he took one out and lit it.

"It has also come to my attention recently that you cut Finley Scout out of your life in a very cruel fashion."

Xander took a drag of his cigarette. "Why should that matter?" And how had it come to his attention?

"Everyone says you've been going out less. And that, in recent days, you haven't been seen with your usual bevy of women."

"I don't see how my personal life has anything to do with -"

"Who is in your bedroom, Xander?"

Xander tensed. "What?"

"Is it someone important to you?"

"Of course not."

"Because if it is -"

"It's not!" shouted Xander, a bit too eagerly. He took another drag to calm himself. "I'm not going to lie, I have my usuals, and the girl in there is one of them, but that doesn't mean she's someone important."

"Good," said Atticus, walking towards the balcony door. "Because falling for someone right now would be very foolish of you."

Xander took a deep breath. "I know."

"I truly believe you should rethink your decision about Ms. Von. She would make a fine wife, and since you have no existing feelings for her -"

"Are you actually telling me to marry her because I *don't* have feelings for her?"

"Marrying for love only complicates things."

"You did," said Xander slowly.

"Yes, and look how that turned out," said Atticus, looking sadly at his son before heading for the door.

Xander put out his cigarette and followed him.

"Tend to your guest," said Atticus. "We will continue this discussion at a later date. I will see you soon."

Atticus opened the door and left quickly. Xander locked it behind him. He hadn't realized his father had access to his apartment. That would need to change immediately.

He stood by the door for a moment, staring at nothing while he thought about Atticus's words. His father had loved his mother, and when she died she took a part of him with her. He had never been the same since that day, which was perhaps why Xander loathed him so much. For letting her death break him. But now Xander was starting to understand what he must have felt. A world without Deryn didn't seem right, which was why he didn't plan to live in that world for very long.

Finally returning to the here and now, Xander went to his bedroom. When he opened the door, Deryn was running around in a panic, dressed messily in day clothes while she threw everything she could find into her bag.

"Deryn."

Her head shot up and she looked at him, her eyes filled with tears and her cheeks flushed.

"What are you doing?" he asked.

"I ... I need to leave. If he's here then -"

"He's not here. He left."

She shook her head frantically. "No. He'll be back. He can get in. He'll -"

"Deryn, calm down," said Xander, walking over and putting his hands on her shoulders.

She flinched.

Xander pulled away, his heart sinking as his old suspicions arose once more. "You're being irrational. I'll make sure he never comes back here. I promise." He reached out to stroke her cheek. "I -"

"Xander, no!" Deryn hurried away from him. "There have been too many close calls lately! I'm not safe here anymore!"

Xander took a step forward. She took one back. This repeated until she was against the wall. Tears poured down her cheeks while he looked sadly at her. She knew what was coming. She had brought it on herself. But how could she act normal when that monster had been so incredibly close to her?

"Deryn, I need you to be honest with me," said Xander, standing close but not touching her, even though he desperately wanted to. "I've been afraid to ask before now, but I need to know."

Deryn whimpered, scared to look into his eyes but unable to look away. A shade lighter with a gold ring around the pupil. Xander's eyes. She reached out and grabbed his hand.

Feeling her fingers interlace with his, Xander feared he already knew the answer. "Did my father ever ..." He gulped. "Did he rape you?" he asked in an almost whisper, his voice hoarse.

Deryn didn't answer, just continued to cry while squeezing the life out of his hand. He reached up and wiped her tears away.

"Deryn, please," he pleaded, his eyes becoming glossy as she kept staring back at him.

She nodded slowly.

Xander's tears spilled over. His eyes clenched shut as his fingers tensed on her cheek.

"No," he cried as his whole body began to shake. "Please, god, no!"

"Xander, I'm sorry," said Deryn as his forehead fell against hers. "I meant to tell you. I did. I just -"

"It's not your fault," said Xander, shaking his head while his hand moved into her hair, gripping it hard as he tried with everything he had to stay in control. "I should've known. I saw the signs. I even suspected it in the beginning. The way you always looked at me after your nightmares. But I didn't want it to be true."

"Neither did I," she said, leaning forward just enough to brush her lips against his.

He pulled away. "Please, don't. How can you look at me? How can you be with me after what my father did to you?"

"Because I don't see him when I look at you, Xander. Not anymore. You're not like him."

"Yes I am," he said, yanking his hand out of hers. "I'm exactly like him. I pushed you into this."

She shook her head wildly. "No. No, you didn't."

"Yes I did! You didn't want to so I tricked you and forced you into this!"

"No, that's not true!" she screamed. "I wanted to be with you! I -"

"I fucking forced you, Deryn! I forced you to be with me, just like him!"

"You would never -"

"But I did. You were vulnerable and I didn't care!" he shouted. "I fucking took what I wanted anyway. I *knew*. Deep down I knew that my father raped you and I fucked you anyway!"

Deryn went white. Her whole body felt heavy as he slowly stepped away from her. "Xander, please." She reached out for him but he only pulled away again.

"I'm selfish. I'm so fucking selfish that I chose not to see. But I can't be selfish when it comes to you, Deryn. Not anymore."

Xander stared deep into her eyes, the whites of them bloodshot while her sea-green irises were dim behind the tears. He hated seeing her like this.

"I'm getting you out," he said. "As soon as I can."

Deryn started to take a step forward, but stopped when Xander took a step back. "Xander, please. This is why I didn't want to tell you. You're already looking at me differently."

"How can I not?" His heart sank as she looked at him so desperately. "I need some air." He headed for the door but quickly stopped. "If I go, will you still be here when I get back?"

Deryn whimpered and nodded. "Should I move back to the guestroom?"

Xander tried to say yes, but he couldn't. "I don't want you to, but if that's what you -"

"I want to stay with you."

"Then stay. I'll be back shortly."

Without waiting for a response, Xander headed for the front door. He put on his coat and his shoes, stopping for a moment to punch the wall with all he had, not caring that he hit it so hard his knuckles started to bleed. He needed to hurt something and his father wasn't there.

Feeling himself losing control, Xander opened the door and ran out. As he leapt down the stairs two at a time, he started to think about where he should go. He didn't want to be alone right now, but he knew he couldn't stay there with Deryn since he was only moments away from breaking. As much as it pained him to admit it, there was only one other person he wanted to see.

CHAPTER THIRTY-FOUR

Once outside, Xander went into the garage, took out his hover-bike and rode off in the direction of Luka's house.

When he arrived at the Voclains front door, their wave let him in and he hurried towards Luka's bedroom. Luka's father Barath was sitting by the fireplace in the living room, drinking some brandy.

"Ah, young Ruby. To what do I owe the pleasure?"

"Obviously I'm not here for you, you sick fuck," said Xander as he passed on by.

When he got to Luka's room, Luka was lying on the bed, his head hanging over the edge with a half-finished bottle of gin in his hands. He looked at him upside-down.

" Long time no see. To what do I owe the pleasure?"

Xander grunted. "Like father, like fucking son," he said, shutting the door behind him. He walked over and tore the bottle from Luka's hands, taking several large gulps while his friend watched in amazement. By the time he came up for air, the bottle was pretty much empty. "Why are you drinking here? You should be out finding some girl or something."

Luka sat up and took the bottle back. He frowned at the small swish of liquid left. "Well, you see, the asshole I used to go drinking with recently fell for this girl, and I haven't really seen much of him since."

"I doubt I've been that bad."

Luka raised his eyebrows.

Xander grunted. "Fine. I've been an ass, but you don't have to worry about that anymore because it's over." He winced at the words, grabbed the bottle again and drank the last bit of gin to stop himself from breaking down.

"Really?"

Luka froze suddenly. He stared at his door for a moment, then jumped up and walked over to it. He threw it open with such a force that Barath nearly toppled over.

"Is there something you needed, Father?"

"Uh, no," said Barath as he stood up straight. "Xander seemed distressed when he came through just now so I thought I would see if everything's alright."

"Everything's fine," said Luka, slamming the door in his father's face and locking it. "So why is it over?" he asked, leading Xander into a small study connected to his room. This was the only entrance, so they would actually have some privacy. "You finally smuggle her out of Utopia or something?"

"No," said Xander, his eyes glossy as he took a seat on the chaise lounge in the corner. "She's still here."

"Then what -"

"It's my father." Just the mention of Atticus was enough to make Xander's tears spill over. He wiped them. "He ... he raped her. He fucking raped her, Luka."

Luka gaped at him. "She told you that?"

Xander nodded. "After I asked. My father came by my apartment. He didn't see her or anything, but after he left she began acting crazy. I suspected it before but I didn't really want to know."

"Why not?"

After taking several deep breaths, Xander looked at his friend sadly and said, "Because I'm in love with her." His words were sharp and painful.

Luka's eyes widened in surprise. He looked off to the side. This was awkward.

"I'm fucking in love with her, Luka. I've *been* in love with her but I don't know what to do now. This changes everything. I want to kill my father for what he did to her. I want him fucking dead! I want them all fucking dead for ever thinking they could touch her and get away with it! I want them all to suffer!"

Luka smiled at the floor. "It's good to know you're as cold as ever."

"You were right before," said Xander. "When you said I took advantage of her. I didn't think I did but -"

He gulped.

"- but what girl in her right mind would ever want to be with the son of a man who raped her unless pushed? I pushed her into this. When I first started feeling something for her, I knew she felt it too, but she kept denying it so I pushed. I pushed her to the point of pinning her against a fucking wall and holding her there until she admitted she wanted me."

"Sounds kinky."

"It's not kinky!" shouted Xander. "It's sick! I'm sick!"

Luka took a deep breath and sat beside Xander. They stayed there awkwardly for a moment before he lifted his arm and patted his friend on the back, nearly knocking him forward.

"What are you doing?"

"Being comforting," said Luka, continuing to pat.

"You're doing a lousy fucking job."

"Yeah, well, I've never done this before so you're going to have to deal." Luka stopped his patting. "For what it's worth, I was angry the other day. You were in the middle of installing a fucking mind control chip in my band. But I don't actually think you're taking advantage of her. Not from what I've seen, anyway."

"You don't?" asked Xander hopefully.

"Yeah," said Luka. "Don't get me wrong, what the two of you are doing is fucking twisted. But the whole world is fucking twisted right now, so it's kinda hard to place any proper judgment on you."

Xander laughed halfheartedly.

Luka smiled. "So you're really in love with her?"

With a shallow nod, Xander said, "Yes."

"Is it just, like, amazing sex or something?"

Xander smirked. "It's fucking mind-blowing, but it's not just that. It's everything. Just being around her makes me happier than I've ever been."

Luka crinkled his nose. "This is weird."

"I know."

"Xander Ruby with feelings. Never thought I'd see the day."

"You and me both."

"It's kind of unsettling, isn't it?" asked Luka with a smile.

Xander smiled back and nodded. "I hate it."

As the two of them were overcome with a bit of an awkward silence, Luka opened the small cabinet beside the chaise lounge and took out a new bottle of gin. He popped it open and took a swig before handing it to Xander.

"When did you start hoarding this shit in your room?" asked Xander as he took a large gulp.

"When I found out my father wants to kill me, and it started to get really uncomfortable drinking with him in the living room. It really puts a damper on things."

"Why don't you ask Saevus if you can move into your own place in Middle City? He offered a few years back, didn't he?"

"Yes, but I'm trying not to look suspicious, remember? You're the one who ordered me to act this way and I must obey," said Luka scornfully.

Xander frowned and handed back the bottle. "It's not that I don't trust you."

"Oh, I'm sorry. Are you not the one who said I couldn't be trusted that night your girlfriend *tied me to a fucking chair*?"

"I didn't want to install that chip. I didn't want you to be any fucking part of this, but, if you're going to be, it's safer this way."

"Safer my ass! You know I would never do anything to -"

"Safer for *you*," said Xander sternly. "You and I both know that Deryn's not getting out of here without some shit blowing up in our faces first. I don't expect to survive this, Luka, and when I don't they'll come for you. At least if you have this chip installed they won't think you were a spy or something. It's your safety net. Fucking embrace it."

Luka laughed. "So this is all for *my* benefit? Liar." He took a swig.

"It's a partial truth," said Xander. "I do trust you. And Deryn told me what you did for her when she was your father's slave. She told me what you've done for all of them. And the old woman with the knife ..."

Luka tensed beside him.

"I made it quick for her, Luka. She didn't feel much. I promise."

Luka gulped and gave a shallow nod, but he didn't say anything. Because, he knew if he did, he wouldn't be able to hold back the tears he was currently fighting.

A bright streak of lightning shot across the sky outside of Luka's window. Loud thunder followed, resonating through the room.

Xander winced. "Shit. I didn't know there was going to be a thunderstorm tonight."

"Why does that matter?"

"Deryn's afraid of thunder." Xander shot to his feet. "I shouldn't have left her alone in the first place. Just more proof that I'm a selfish bastard."

"You won't hear any arguments from me," said Luka, taking another swig. He swallowed hard. "But, for what it's worth, I don't think you should give up on this twisted romance of yours just yet. Your father's a bastard. You've known this your entire life. And I kind of like this lovelorn Xander. You've been pretty fucking miserable these past five years. At least now you're mildly happy, which is more than I can say for me."

With a faint smile, Xander said, "We'll get you out of this house, Luka. But, for now, just stay out of your father's way."

"Yeah, yeah." Luka waved him off as he fell back on the chaise lounge. "Night, Xan. Go protect your girlfriend from the big, bad thunder."

Xander flipped him off.

"I saw that."

"You were meant to."

Xander returned to the living room, where Barath was

sitting once more. He watched in curiosity as Xander more-or-less ignored him and ran out the front door.

It was not a long walk to the gate and then a ride home, but he still got soaked.

When he arrived at his apartment, thunder was echoing loudly throughout it. He tore off his coat and shoes, tossed them aside and hurried to his bedroom. His bed was bare of its comforter, and the gentle sound of weeping came from behind his bathroom door.

Xander opened the door, tiptoed inside, and climbed into his large, round bathtub. He slumped down next to the heap of blankets, rummaging through them until he found the warm body he was seeking.

"Hi, Deryn," he said, lifting the comforter so he could see her face.

She looked at him with tear-filled eyes and sniffled.

"Are you alright?"

She nodded.

"I'm sorry I left," he said, wrapping his arms around her. He found comfort in the feeling of the oversized, flannel pajamas she wore so often.

"I-it's okay," she said, whimpering as she buried her head in his shoulder. "I understand why you're mad at me."

"Is that what you think?" he asked, stroking her hair out of her face. "That I'm mad at you?"

"Aren't you? For not telling you -"

"You shouldn't have to tell me, Deryn. I should've known. But I just -"

Xander gulped.

"I don't understand when it happened. My father's never owned a slave. I would've known if he -"

"I was never his slave, Xander. His house is where they kept me in the beginning. Before Elvira recommended I join the slave trade."

"They kept you in his house? While I still lived there?"

Deryn nodded. "They kept me in the basement. I could hear your voice sometimes."

Tears filled Xander's eyes as he continued to gaze at her. "Deryn, if I'd known -"

"It doesn't matter," she said.

"And my father ... did he take advantage of you often?"

She shook her head. "Only once."

If there was ever a moment to tell Xander more, she knew this was it. But, for some reason, the words never came. She didn't have the courage to tell him that his father had been the first, because she could already feel him pulling away from her, and that was something her heart couldn't bear.

Xander closed his eyes and pressed their foreheads together, his tears dripping down his cheeks and onto hers. "I'm so sorry, Deryn. I wish I could have saved you sooner."

"I'm just grateful that you're here with me now," she said, digging her fingers into the sides of his sweater. "And I know it's not what you want to hear, but I'm not ready to leave you."

Xander cried harder as he pulled her even tighter against him. "It's not fair," he said. "It's not fucking fair."

Deryn didn't have to ask him what he meant, because she already knew. It all wasn't fair. The feelings they had, the short time they were given together, the horrible realties that would always try to tear them apart. Life wasn't fair. And the cruel world they currently lived in wasn't making it any easier.

CHAPTER THIRTY-FIVE

Xander sat at the president's table, unable to focus as his eyes constantly drifted to his father sitting about halfway down on the other side. He hadn't been on active duty in a few months, a benefit that came with age, but he was back now and couldn't have returned at a worse time.

Atticus kept catching his son staring at him, his eyebrows creasing in curiosity at the look of contempt he was receiving.

"How reliable would you say your source is?" asked Saevus, staring down the table at Veli.

"Very reliable, sir. They've never been wrong before."

The president tightened his lips. "And you realize this source is taking you to the same place you had that embarrassing display last year, don't you?"

Veli blushed. "I do, sir. But I trust -"

"Xander."

Xander removed his eyes from his father and looked at the president.

"You will take the lead on this."

Veli's mouth dropped.

Xander looked at him and smirked. "Of course, Mr. President."

"Choose your team."

"Well, I think it would only be fair to have Veli-belly come along with me."

His eyes narrowing, Veli said, "How dare you call me -"

"And who else?" interrupted Saevus. "Perhaps your father -"

"No, I think not," said Xander quickly, glancing at Atticus out of the corner of his eye. He was still unsure of what to do about his father and, since he was planning on setting up a deathtrap on this mission, it simply was not the place for him. "His skills are better suited here. "I will also take Luka -" For backup. "- Sorey," he winked at Soren, "Aila, Wenton, Orson and Gordon." A good mix of trash.

"You may have one more," said Saevus.

Xander thought. "I'll take Finley." He knew he had a soft spot for Finley because of their history together, but she had hurt Deryn, just like the others, and he could never forget that.

"I will also send two S.U.R.G.E.'s and a team of guards with you. You will leave in the morning. Everyone is dismissed."

Xander stood up first, as he always did, and motioned for Luka to follow him. He had barely stepped out of the room when someone grabbed his shoulder. He turned to see his father.

"Xander, I was hoping you and I could speak over dinner and -"

Xander pulled away from Atticus and took several steps back. "Don't touch me," he spat.

Atticus cocked an eyebrow. "Is there a problem?"

Xander wanted to shout at him, "*You raped the girl I love!*" but he knew how important it was to hold his tongue in front of his current crowd. So, instead, he said, "No, Father. None at all."

"Then why have you been looking at me like you want to rip me apart all evening?"

Because he did. "I don't believe I have."

Atticus studied his son. "Xander, what is -"

"Ready?" asked Luka, walking up to them and looking anxiously at Xander.

Glancing around, Xander noticed they had an audience. He always did. "One second." He looked back at his father. "I'm afraid I've already made other arrangements tonight. Another time. Let's walk," he said to Luka, heading for the front door.

"Where are we going?" asked Luka once they were outside.

"I need to get a message to someone. You're my lookout."

"Let me guess. I'm going to have to be extra cautious tomorrow."

"You should always be extra cautious."

"And *you* should be a little more discreet with those death stares you're giving your father."

"Well, I can't help that," said Xander. He perked up his ears. "So who's following us?"

"Our precious Veli-belly, as always," said Luka, who was an expert at spotting people by the distinct sounds they made while walking. "And Gordon."

Xander groaned. "Let's just get to Middle City. Bronson works a couple blocks from the gate. We can duck into his kitchen and slip out the back. He's let me do it before."

Luka crinkled his nose.

It was a straight shot from the president's house to the gate, since it was towering in Utopia's center. When they arrived at the Middle City gate, the guard and S.U.R.G.E. approved their entry immediately and opened the large, iron doors that ended about ten feet up where they hit an invisible and impenetrable force field. The doors didn't even have a chance to close before Veli and Gordon were walking through. Xander led them around a few twists and turns, eventually stopping in front of a busy restaurant.

"He works here?" asked Luka as Xander pushed through the waiting crowd and headed for the door.

"Yes," he answered. "Ever been?"

"Brought a few of my usuals here to keep them happy before." He paused. "So all this time I could've gotten a free fucking meal?"

"Guess so."

Xander opened the door and they headed inside, the hostess looking up from her chart and smiling as they walked towards her.

"Oh, hello. You're Bronson and Mason's friend, aren't you?"

"Mason?" asked Luka, cocking an eyebrow.

"Quigley," said Xander, right as Quigley walked by holding

several plates of food. He nodded at them. "We need to see Bronson. It's important."

"Absolutely," she said, her smile broadening. "Give me just one second and I'll -"

"I'll take them," said another hostess, popping up and giving them a smile to rival her coworkers.

"No, Jemma. *I'll* take them. You stay here."

Jemma glared at the other hostess as she left her station to lead Xander and Luka to the kitchen. She made sure wink at Luka as he passed.

"So ..." The hostess slowed her pace so she was walking side-by-side with Xander. "Has Bronson ever said anything about me?"

"No," scoffed Luka from behind them.

The hostess frowned.

Inside the kitchen, Xander immediately spotted Bronson throwing ingredients in a pot while a waiter standing incredibly close to him whispered something. Glancing sideways, Xander caught Luka scowling. When Luka noticed him looking, he pulled it back.

"Bronson!" the hostess called, not even noticing the obvious flirting happening right in front of her. "Your friends are here."

Bronson looked over and smiled. "Well, if it isn't my two favorite Guardians."

The kitchen went very quiet.

"Relax, everyone. They're not here to arrest you," he announced to the room. "To what do I owe the pleasure?"

"Nothing. We just need to slip out the back," said Xander.

"Being followed by those dick-holes again?"

"Always."

Bronson nodded. "Farrah, be a dear and make sure to keep any other Guardians that walk in here busy, will you?"

The hostess blushed and nodded. "Anything, Bronson." She hurried back to the front of the restaurant.

Looking at Bronson, Luka puckered his brow.

Bronson smiled. "I don't just go around announcing my sexuality, Luka. I shouldn't have to. If she ever asked I'd tell her." He winked at the waiter, making him blush even redder than the hostess and fumble with the plates he'd just picked up. The embarrassed waiter hurried out of the kitchen.

"I believe you know your way to the back door, Ruby," said Bronson, tossing them each a piece of bread that had barely come out of the oven.

Luka sniffed it before taking a bite. His eyes lit up. "Holy fuck."

"Focaccia," said Bronson with a smile. "I'll make it for you sometime." He winked and Luka blushed. He seemed to have that affect on a lot of people.

Xander and Luka slipped out the back door and the two of them headed for the Shopping District, this time without any followers.

"Anything you want to tell me, Luka?" asked Xander as they walked.

"Th'fuck you talking about?"

He supposed that was a no.

The Shopping District was not too far from where Bronson and Quigley worked, and the building Xander needed was right near the edge of it. Seemingly abandoned, the place was old and made of brick, in opposition with all of the newer metal buildings around it. The new Utopia was not about style, it was about safety and practicality.

Xander led Luka around the boarded up building to an alley just behind it. He asked him to keep watch while he did a very specific knock on the back door. Several seconds passed before something on the door shifted. A small section in its center pushed inward and was replaced with a pair of eyes.

"You're early," said a woman's voice.

"I'm not here to stay," said Xander. "There are rumors that Outsiders have once again taken up residence in the village called Willow. If there's any truth to these rumors, I suggest you inform your people to get the citizens out before tomorrow."

"*And* bombard the stupid Guardians," said a young man's voice from behind her. The eyes vanished and there was a loud cracking noise. "Ow!"

"I was actually going to suggest the same thing," said Xander.

"Will you be there?" asked the woman, her eyes returning.

"Of course. I'm the head on this mission."

She blinked and moved her eyes away from him. "I really wish you would let me tell them about you."

"No," he said quickly. "This is a war, and if someone from your side is captured, what's to stop them from supplying information about me to bargain for their lives?"

"But someone might hurt you by accident," she said, looking back out with worried eyes.

Xander sighed. "That's a risk I have to take." He glanced over his shoulder at Luka - who was watching him more than keeping watch - and beckoned him forward. "There's someone you should meet. In case something ever happens to me. He's my oldest friend and, even though I've installed that chip I told you about in his wristband, he's trustworthy without it."

"If he's trustworthy then he should meet more than my eyes," said the woman. Her eyes vanished and were replaced by darkness, then the darkness was replaced by the original chunk of the door.

There was some arguing going on inside, and Luka was sure he heard at least four voices. Maybe more. Despite all of that, the door still opened, but only one person stepped out of the shadows. A woman with dirty-blonde hair, faintly streaked with gray, and tired blue eyes. She was pretty, probably in her late forties, and very familiar looking.

"Hello," she said with a faint smile. "You're Luka Voclain, aren't you? Perhaps you don't remember me. I'm -"

"Adelaide Saevus," finished Luka, finally recognizing the president's wife and Elvira's mother who had vanished shortly after the war on the Outsiders had been declared.

"Formerly Saevus," she corrected. "It's Adelaide Norris, but you may call me Del."

She lifted her right hand, Luka only now noticing that it was made of metal. It squeaked like a S.U.R.G.E. that needed to be oiled. He shook it and let go as quickly as he could. The metal was surprisingly warm. Looking at Xander, he said, "Your double life just keeps fucking growing, doesn't it?"

"Language!" shouted a child's voice from deep within the building.

"We should go," said Xander. "I just wanted you two to meet. You know. In case."

Del smiled and said, "Nice to see you again, Luka. I will get your message out as soon as I can, Xander. And, please, be careful."

He nodded and she disappeared inside the dark building, shutting the door behind her.

"In case of what?" asked Luka as they walked towards the street.

"I think you already know," answered Xander.

"How is she living there with the curfew? It's not a residence."

"Back when it was a store, the owner lived on the top floor. When he died and no new buyers came forward, it just slipped through the cracks. It's still registered as both a business and a residence."

"Oh." Luka looked down at his feet and went quiet.

Neither of them said anything more as they walked towards the gate. When they got there, Luka returned to Inner City while Xander collected his hover-bike from the lot and rode off.

When Xander got home, Deryn was not in the front room like she normally was. He took off his shoes and coat, and headed for the bedroom, where he found her asleep with a book laying open on her stomach. He smiled and took it off of her, carefully marking the page before changing his clothes and climbing in beside her.

It had only been three days since Xander found out about his father, and he and Deryn had not so much as kissed since. Other than the occasional cheek peck. Even wrapping his arm around her now didn't seem right, but it had become a habit that he really didn't feel like breaking.

"You're late," she said quietly as he pulled her into him.

"I had to pass along a message to your people," said Xander. He had told her a while ago about Del and the others. But while he'd told Deryn about Del, he hadn't told Del about Deryn. There were too many risks involved if the Resistance found out she was free and in hiding, namely them coming for her in idiotic fashion. Talon and Dakota tended to lead missions in the Resistance, and neither of them were known for subtlety.

"Why?" she asked, turning and looking at him with fluttering eyelashes.

"We're following a lead on Outsiders said to be living in Willow tomorrow. I had to warn them."

Deryn blinked. "But ... the Resistance doesn't know you're a spy, do they?"

Xander sighed. "No."

"Then how will they know not to attack you?"

"They won't."

Deryn froze. Her lips quivered. "Xander, you can't go on that mission. It's a deathtrap."

"I'll be fine," he said. "I've done it a dozen times before."

"But -"

"There are no buts, Deryn. I have to go. Would you rather I didn't warn them and let the Guardians take them by surprise?"

Deryn sighed. "No. I would rather you weren't a Guardian."

"Too late to change that now," he said, giving her cheek a stroke. "You remember what to do if I don't return?"

Deryn gulped. "Go to Bronson the moment the curfew's lifted and have him take me to Del." If he wasn't around it was the only option.

"And you remember the knock?"

She nodded shallowly and did the knock on his chest.

"Good," said Xander, taking her hand in his. He brought it up to his lips and kissed it. If he couldn't have her lips then this was a close second.

"Promise me you'll be careful."

"Of course I will."

She nuzzled against his chest.

Now it was time for the big question. "If I see anyone you know and opportunity presents itself, should I tell them you're free?"

Deryn thought about this. "I suppose you should tell Talon or Dakota. But *only* if you can actually get them to sit down and listen. I don't want either of them finding out and then breaking into the city to get to me. Just tell them ..." She gulped. "Tell them I'll be with them shortly."

He nodded against the top of her head. "I should tell you now that this opportunity is highly unlikely."

Xander couldn't see from his current angle, but Deryn was smiling. She'd already told him she wasn't ready to leave him and she'd meant it. Not until she knew where the two of them stood and, after her confession about Atticus, it was even more unclear now than before.

It wasn't long before Deryn's breathing grew shallow against his chest. She'd had a nightmare the night before about Atticus, but tonight her dreams were all about Xander. About what their lives could have been if they lived in a different world. One where there were no obstacles threatening to tear them apart, other than their own stubbornness.

At least, if a world like that were at all possible to obtain someday, they would appreciate each other more than if an easy life had just been handed to them. The silver lining.

CHAPTER THIRTY-SIX

Xander walked through the forest outside of Willow, the S.U.R.G.E.'s following silently behind the Guardians and guards, and erasing their footprints as they went. He stopped at the edge of the trees and stared into the small village. Everything appeared peaceful, and several old buildings were even overgrown with vines and flowers.

"Looks very threatening here, Veli," said Xander, glancing over his shoulder at his fellow Guardian.

"I doubt they would clean up the outside to live here. They're in hiding," he spat.

Xander rolled his eyes. "Whatever you say. Everyone scatter around the village, enter from different pathways and search the homes and shops. Do *not* wreak havoc, even if you find someone. That's not why we're here. Understand?"

Everyone grunted and nodded before dispersing along the edges of the forest. Xander and Luka were the only ones to stay where they were, waiting a few moments before heading into Willow.

The two of them walked forward through the village square and towards the residential streets. Willow was much larger than Redwood, and was located in the center of the forest instead of on the outskirts. The entire place was sheltered by large trees that grew together in a dome-shape, only small cracks of sun poking through the leaves. The majority of Outsiders had lived here at one time, but it had been abandoned several years before President Saevus declared war on the Outsiders by citizens who wanted to protect their children from recruitment, which was really just the president's fancy word for kidnapping.

Xander and Luka noticed Veli and Soren staying rather close to them. Of course.

Stopping in front of an old house, one of the largest in the area, Xander turned to Luka and said, "Stay out here and keep watch. I'll call if I need anything."

Luka nodded and took his stance. He was having fun squishing footprints into the damp earth and watching the closest S.U.R.G.E. zoom forward to make them disappear. Xander had to roll his eyes a bit, slightly disturbed that this was the man he had chosen as his ally.

Xander stepped inside, frowning as he looked around at the clean floors and freshly built wooden furniture. This place was definitely lived in. He felt a chill, even through all of his protective layers, as a breeze slipped in through the broken window. Something that couldn't have been fixed in order to keep up appearances on the outside.

There was a faint creak on the second floor. Xander's head jerked upwards. He wasn't sure if it was the sound of an old house settling or something more but, either way, it was worth investigating. He had hoped the silence meant that Del was successful in delivering his message, but occasionally there just wasn't enough time to inform those involved.

Xander would have liked to think that the Outsiders wouldn't hide in the most obvious of places, but he supposed that was the brilliance of it. He slowly ascended the stairs, his Element at the ready as he tried not to touch anything. Call him sentimental, but it just seemed wrong to taint this home with Guardian hands. He reached the top of the stairs, unsure of where to go until he heard another creak coming from behind a door at the end of the hall.

Xander headed towards the sound, suddenly feeling very nervous at the thought of dying here and never seeing Deryn again. Never seeing her roll her eyes or scrunch up her face when deep in thought. Or the way her beautiful sea-green irises lit up whenever she did something she was particularly proud of, like cooking a meal he really enjoyed instead of just pretending for her benefit. She always knew when he pretended.

Reaching the end of the hall, Xander pushed the door, which was already open a crack. He took a slow step inside, and then another. Looking around, he saw that he had entered a baby's nursery. Stopping his movements, he now heard a very clear whimper.

With a sigh, Xander walked a few more steps and lifted the floorboards just beside the crib. Three children were crouched inside, one just a baby and the obvious inhabitant of this room. The oldest, a girl, took a protective stance in front of the other two, a dull blade held out in front of her.

It was cute, really, but Xander had to roll his eyes a little. He reached down and pulled a dagger Deryn insisted he bring with him out of his boot. Before the child even had a moment to get over her fear and react, Xander had the dull blade out of her hand and the sharp one in it.

She looked at it curiously, and then up at him.

"Head down to the broken window in the front room. Once you see the coast is clear climb out of it and run as fast as you can to the forest. Hide until we're gone. Do not get lost, do not get caught. If someone else sees you I cannot protect you. Do you understand?"

The girl gulped and gave him a small nod. Xander stepped out of the way. She climbed out first, taking the lead with the knife while her little brother carried the baby. He couldn't have been more than six and was struggling to hold her.

"Wait," said Xander, looking around the room until he found a blanket. He tied it around the boy in such a way that it became a sling for the baby. It wasn't great but it would have to do.

Without a word, the three children disappeared from sight. Xander went to the window and watched for a moment. It wasn't long before they came into view, their eyes sharp as they ran as fast as their little legs would carry them. And then they made it, hidden in the safety of the trees without ever looking back.

Xander smiled to himself, only going back on alert when he heard another creak. These wooden floors really were terrible. In a swift motion, he whipped around and aimed his Element sharply at the door, not incredibly surprised to see Dakota doing the same right back at him, only he held a primitive gun. It had just one use, and it was deadly.

"I had a feeling you'd be here, Trigger." A feeling of dread. "Never too far from the action. Some say you have a death wish."

"And I see you're as charming as ever," said Dakota scornfully.

Xander smirked. "Naturally."

"Why are you and your Guardians here, Ruby?"

Xander shrugged. "Nothing really. Just following what I'd hoped was a false lead on a few Outsiders trying to take their old home back."

"You all have no business -"

"Spare me your tirade, Trigger. I didn't come here to fight with you."

"Clearly," said Dakota. "You didn't come back for Talon the other day."

"Why would I do that when his boyfriend was there protecting him?"

"You lied about being attacked."

"You weren't my mission."

"You just let those kids run out of here."

"I'm not in the business of harming children," said Xander. "All of that shit was before my time. You remember."

Dakota scowled at him. "Why are you -"

"You and I need to have a chat. Sans weapons." Xander lowered his and carefully put it in its holster. "Now, I'm trusting you not to strike an unarmed man."

"Pick it back up!" spat Dakota.

"Put yours down," said Xander, crossing his arms. "We won't start our chat until your weapon is away, and you will want to hear what I have to say."

Dakota sneered and pointed his gun sharper.

"It's about Deryn."

Dakota's eyes widened, his hand slackening slightly as he asked, "What about her?"

"Not until you -"

"Just tell me if she's alive, Ruby!"

Xander grinded his teeth. He really hated this. "Of course she is. Now, lower your weapon."

Dakota stared unsurely at Xander for a moment, the inner debate in his head quite visible in his expression. Despite all of that, he slowly began to lower his hand, eventually putting his gun away.

"Go on," he said in a shaky voice.

Xander cleared his throat. "I'm sure you've already guessed this by all of the rumors circulating and increased security in the city, but Deryn is no longer in the president's possession."

"She escaped?"

"Yes, that is what I'm getting at."

Dakota took a deep breath, clenching his fists as he cast his eyes to the floor. "Why are you telling me this? I have a hard time believing you have no ulterior motives."

"Oh, big word!"

Dakota's eyes shot back up and glared at him.

Xander smirked. "Sorry. Old habits, you know? But I have no ulterior motive. I am simply telling you to ease your woes."

"That's it?" asked Dakota, teeth now baring.

"Sure," said Xander with a shrug. "And I might know where she is."

Dakota tensed. "Where -"

"I'm not telling you that. If I did then we both know you and that brother of hers are just going to end up doing something hasty and, undoubtedly, stupid. She'll be back with you soon enough."

"I don't believe you," hissed Dakota.

"You don't have to. I am simply relaying a message."

"You're a fucking liar! Saevus has ordered you to infiltrate us, hasn't he? That's why you're pretending to help us!"

"I *did* help you," corrected Xander. "You can't fake letting people go. I could have taken you down the other day once you had an unconscious comrade to protect. You know I could have, and that would have looked damn good for me, bringing in Godfrey's son and fucking trigger happy Triggs. But I didn't. Now, move along, you're boring me."

A floorboard creaked.

Both of their ears went on alert.

And then another creaked. And another. Someone was walking up the stairs. It was impossible to be subtle in a house like this.

"What do you think? One of yours or mine?" asked Xander, taking out his Element. "Probably mine, since the idiots all seem to lack the art of guile."

Ignoring him, Dakota moved out of the doorway and stepped more into the room, getting in a position that gave him access to shoot at both Xander and whoever was about to walk through that door.

Staying where he was, Xander quickly recognized someone in a Guardian trench coat heading down the hallway.

"Mine," he said quietly so only Dakota could hear.

"You in here alone, Ruby?" asked the familiar voice of Aila Parrish.

Xander grimaced. *Damn.* He had hoped for someone with less of a vendetta against Dakota. This would surely end in a mess.

"Do you see anyone else?" he said.

"I heard voices."

"Don't worry about it, Aila. Get lost."

"What makes you think you can order me around?" she said, taking a few steps closer.

"I'm sorry, did you not hear the president yesterday?" asked Xander mockingly. "I am the lead on this mission. Now. Get. Lost."

"No," said Aila, taking a few more steps forward.

Xander aimed his Element at her but she did not stop,

entering the room and immediately looking to the left at Dakota. The two locked eyes.

"*You!*" spat Aila.

She aimed her Element and fired. Dakota was able to duck in time, but it was clear by the huge hole blasted through the wall behind him that she was aiming to kill.

"You killed my brother, you bastard!"

Dakota barely steadied himself before she was trying again. It would have hit him too, if Xander hadn't grabbed him and yanked him out of the way.

"What are you doing?" shouted Dakota.

"Saving your ass, apparently."

"Well, don't!"

He pushed Xander off of him and darted for the window. When he got there, he fired his gun at Aila, forcing her to dodge. It gave him enough time to climb onto the roof. Xander stared out at him and watched as he jumped into some bushes on the ground.

Aila shoved Xander away from the window and followed Dakota, landing slightly less smoothly. Judging by her reaction, the bushes were pricklier than Dakota had let on.

Xander grunted and ran down the stairs, practically slamming into Luka as he rushed out the front door.

"Xander, what's going -"

"You let Aila get inside!" shouted Xander.

Luka froze. "I didn't ... I mean, she must have gone in the back or -"

"Doesn't matter. She's gone after Trigger. We need to move."

Xander ran in their direction with Luka just behind him.

Dakota and Aila had headed for the forest. When they found them, Dakota was in the middle of a small clearing, shooting at Aila while she darted behind trees. He ran out of bullets quickly, letting out a loud grunt and hurrying to reload. Aila took this moment to tackle him to the ground.

"You'll pay for what you did to my brother!" she shouted, trying to aim her Element at him while he grabbed her wrists and wrestled it away.

"Seriously, Aila?" said Xander, leaning casually against a tree. "Your family's inbreeding has become a real nuisance. You'll find another lover. Maybe a cousin."

"Shut your sick, twisted mouth, Ruby, and stay out of this! It doesn't concern you!"

"Actually, it does," he said, picking at his nails.

Luka cocked his head and stared curiously at the sight in front of them. His Element was out and ready, but he didn't seem especially eager to use it. Aila wasn't winning. She had gone for a tackle, for some reason, when she had a dangerous weapon in her hand.

"You interrupted a very important conversation between Trigger and me. And do you really think the president would appreciate you killing the Resistance's top fighter?"

"I'm not going to kill him!"

"Really? And I suppose those blasts you were just shooting at him a moment ago were simply to make him wet his pants?"

"I was surprised!" she shouted. "All I plan to do is torture him to the point where he'll be begging me to die! Just like what I did to his toxic bitch!"

All three men tensed. None more than Xander ,whose blood now boiled. His breaths became deep and heated.

"Do you want me to tell you all about what I did to her, Trigger? As payback for you taking my brother's life?"

In a quick moment, Dakota was tossing Aila off of him and jumping back to his feet. She did the same and they aimed their weapons at each other, ready to attack.

"How dare you touch her!" he shouted.

Aila smiled wickedly. "Oh, I'm not the one who touched her. I merely tortured her so horribly that she faded in and out of consciousness for days." She laughed wickedly. "You should've seen her tattered body once I was through with her, not even aware of all the men I brought in to have their way with her while she was in too much pain to even realize what was happening -"

A light shot out of Xander's Element in the form of a long

whip.

Dakota winced, positive that it was aimed for him. But then Aila was on the ground, screaming in agonizing pain as Dakota stared at her, dumbfounded.

The attack must have confused her, because she seemed to have no idea where it came from. Dakota was still in too much shock to move, so she leapt at him, tackling him into the mud and rocks once more before aiming her Element at his heart.

"You will suffer, you little -"

"Take me!" shouted Dakota suddenly.

Aila furrowed her brow. "What?"

"You need one of us, right? I'll come with you obediently if you let Deryn go!"

Xander felt sick as he noticed the desperate look in Dakota's eyes as he spoke. This was not just about saving his friend. After all this time, he was still very much in love with her. For some reason, Xander was overcome with a surprising amount of anger.

"That's stupid, Trigger," he said, moving off of his tree and taking several steps forward. "Surely, even you know better than to make a deal with a Guardian."

"I'll take the risk!"

Aila looked at Xander and smiled.

"I already told you. We don't have her anymore."

Aila's smile faded. "Why would you tell him that?"

"It doesn't concern you," said Xander, lifting his Element and pointing it at Aila. Another whip of light shot out of it and struck her.

She fell backwards, writhing and screaming in the mud.

While Aila was down, Dakota got back to his feet and aimed his gun at Xander. "What the hell are you doing?" he shouted. "Why do you keep helping me?"

"I thought I already made that clear," said Xander, watching Aila carefully. When her squirming died down, he hit her with the whip of light once more.

"Is that really necessary?" asked Luka, taking a few steps into the clearing.

"Of course it is," said Xander, striking her with the whip three more times. "I've wanted to do this for a long time."

"*DAKOTA!*" An earth-shattering scream echoed through the forest. All three men glanced around frantically.

"Neetles!" shouted Dakota, still keeping his gun aimed at Xander.

Xander knew the name. It was a nickname for a girl named Nita. She was another Outsider who had been 'recruited' to join the guard and had escaped the day of the attack on Eagle Center. He hadn't seen her much since, but he knew she was around and active in the Resistance.

Xander suddenly found himself wishing that Nita was the one he had run across instead of Dakota. She had been friends with Deryn too and, from what he remembered, she had always been pretty sensible. It was safe to say that his conversation with Dakota had been a waste of time and energy.

Dakota looked back at Xander and pointed his gun more fervently, but Xander didn't flinch, still keeping his Element aimed at the struggling Aila.

"What are you going to do? Kill me?" asked Xander with an amused grin. "You don't have it in you."

"I've killed before."

"Of course you have. We all have. But I've obviously put enough doubt in your mind that you're not going to take the risk. If I hadn't then I would already be dead. Or you would."

Dakota's nostrils flared. "I don't believe a word you've said to me, Ruby. You're a manipulative bastard who mentioned the one person you knew would make me cooperate. Even going as far as calling her by her first name."

Xander pursed his lips. Oh, right. Dakota was used to him calling her Leon. In training they were required to use surnames. If there weren't so many damn Guardians who were family members he would still do it now.

"But you saved me up there." Dakota motioned towards the house, which was barely visible through the trees, and slowly lowered his gun. "So we're even."

And, with that, Dakota turned on his foot and took off

running, heading the long way back to the village, probably so he could be discreet.

Xander sneered. "Go after him, Luka. Make sure he doesn't do anything stupid."

Luka nodded. He looked down at Aila, who had finally stopped struggling but was too beaten to do anything more than lie there and catch her breath. "You going to kill her?" he asked.

"Yes," answered Xander.

Luka nodded again. "Don't be gentle about it."

When Luka was gone, Xander took a few more steps so he was standing directly above Aila. He crouched down and placed the mouth of his Element on her heart.

"W-why?" she asked in a strained voice.

"So sorry, Aila." Not really. "But you sealed your fate the day you touched Deryn. I saw your handiwork and you must suffer for it."

"Y-you know w-where she is?"

"That's right." Xander reached into her inner coat pocket and searched until he found a small chip. One of the mind control chips. "I had a feeling you'd be carrying this." He took out his dagger and pressed his Element harder against her skin. "Goodbye, Aila."

He stabbed her first, so her death would look like the Resistance's handy work, then he pressed the button on his Element, hitting her with a shock that caused Aila to thrash around wildly before going stiff. It was the same shock that had killed his mother. While it may have been quick, it didn't feel that way to the victim. The pain was worse than being stabbed with a thousand daggers at once.

Aila's wide eyes were still staring at him as he slipped the chip inside his inner coat pocket. He would have liked to torture her more, but this was hardly the place. Someone could run by and catch him at any moment.

Xander left her body there and returned to the village. When he arrived, Resistance members and Outsiders were scattering towards the forest while several Guardians and guards chased after them.

"They're in the trees!" someone shouted.

Xander looked up and, sure enough, several ropes had pulled all of the Outsiders up in the trees, where they ran as fast as they could along bridges hidden in the leaves. His eyes widened. That was new.

The guards and Guardians all returned shortly, unable to get up there and follow them.

Glancing around, Xander saw that a guard and Orson Yam were lying dead on the ground. A S.U.R.G.E. had also been beaten down, something that, until now, he had believed to be impossible. Another one buzzed over to him. He ordered it to follow the Outsiders, but not to attack. It zoomed off.

"What the hell happened?" shouted Veli, stomping over to Xander.

"They obviously knew we were coming. It looks like your source steered us wrong. *Again.*"

"No they did not!" he spat, his entire body shaking. "There is no way they could -"

"Why not?" asked Xander. "The Resistance wouldn't have been able to take out three of us with absolutely no casualties on their side unless they knew we were coming! And how the hell did they take down a S.U.R.G.E.?"

"It was some weird weapon," answered a guard. "Looked like a satellite and knocked it right out of the sky."

Veli ignored the guard. "Three?" he asked Xander.

Xander nodded. "Aila is dead in the forest to the east. Go retrieve her," he ordered.

Veli took several deep and angry breaths before walking off with Gordon.

When Xander looked back at Orson's body, Finley was leaning over it. He didn't like how relieved he was to see she hadn't been hurt. She kneeled down and sighed before carefully closing his eyes. Xander walked over and knelt down beside her, searching Orson's pockets until he came out with another chip.

"What's that?" asked Finley.

"None of your concern." Xander slipped it beside the other one in his inner pocket. "But, if you happen to see your father with one of these, I suggest you grab it and give it to me."

Finley nodded. She stood and went to close the eyes of the guard.

Feeling a bit off, Xander walked away and leaned against the stone hedge that was designed to protect the village's produce, which was currently just overgrown weeds. And one green tomato.

While staring at the lonely tomato, a streak of light shining through the trees hit something that twinkled in his eye. He stepped inside the sad garden, walking towards the twinkling light until he noticed another bit of green beside the tomato. He cleared away the brush and eventually came up with a ring. It had a jade stone in its center and a gold band in the shape of a lion. While he recognized the animal, he couldn't for the life of him remember if they were real or folklore.

Suddenly, someone was grabbing the ring out of Xander's hand. He turned to see Soren standing there, gazing at it mesmerizingly.

He pressed the button on his collar and said, "It's the same color as her eyes."

With a painful grimace, he tossed the ring across the garden. Xander grunted.

"You're needed, *boss*," he said mockingly.

Soren turned and left in a hurry.

As soon as Xander was alone again, he ran to where the ring had landed and dug around until he found it again. He didn't know why he wanted it but, with Christmas coming up, it would be a nice present for Deryn. And Soren hadn't been wrong about the stone being the same color as her eyes, or at least similar. Her eyes had a hint of blue in them.

He put it in his inner pocket, opposite the chips. He didn't want something so cruel tainting his gift.

The ring now in his possession, Xander headed back to the others, hoping to get out of there quickly. He would, undoubtedly, be punished for his failure that day, and he wanted to get it over with before Deryn had a chance to worry too much.

CHAPTER THIRTY-SEVEN

Deryn sat alone in their room, just below the window with the radio playing beside her. *Blackbird* had just ended and she was currently listening to static. She had tried to read but was unable to concentrate.

The sky outside grew dark and Deryn was becoming more and more worried. She chewed on her thumb while listening closely for Xander's hover-bike zooming to a halt outside of their building. Everything was silent, other than the radio static.

Before long, Deryn was feeling sick. She hated this. She hated everything -

"Hello?" said a familiar voice on the radio. *"Deryn, are you out there?"*

Deryn sat up straight. It was Dakota, speaking to her in a new broadcast.

"I know this is a long shot, but if you are and you can hear me then please ... please, come home. I'll be waiting for you. Every day. At our place. And if you can't get there, I promise I will find you. Two Guardians were killed today -"

Deryn's head shot in the direction of the radio. "What?"

"- and two of those robots of theirs, too. They can be defeated, and I'll take down every last one of them if that's what it takes to get you home." Silence. *"I'm going to change the song, just for tonight. To the one you and my mom used to sing together. I miss you every day, and I ... I love you."*

Dakota's voice cut off, soon replaced by Ringo Starr singing *Good Night*.

Deryn sat there motionless, not even listening to the song as Dakota's words sunk in. Two Guardians were killed, and Xander still wasn't home.

She lifted her hand to her mouth. No. It couldn't -

The clock in the living room chimed, signaling the top of the hour. She looked at the smaller clock on the nightstand. Midnight.

"No!" shouted Deryn, shaking her head in disbelief. "No! No! Please, no!"

Deryn listened, but Xander's hover-bike was not in earshot, and no one was coming through the front door. First it was a minute after midnight. Then thirty minutes. Then two hours.

"No."

She brought her knees to her chest and sobbed into them.

"Please, tell me he didn't. Tell me Dax didn't -"

Deryn choked. She couldn't even say it. If Dakota had killed Xander, she could never forgive him.

"Xander, please ... please come back to me."

The night went on and, still, Deryn sat there. She knew she was supposed to be preparing to leave, but she refused. Xander was coming back. She was sure of it. And, when he did, she would be waiting for him. Because that's what you did when you loved someone. You waited.

CHAPTER THIRTY-EIGHT

Xander lay on the couch by the fireplace in the president's house, his body in a great deal of pain as he waited impatiently for the clock to strike four a.m. So he could get home and stop Deryn from leaving.

He hadn't expected Saevus to torture him for so long - a lashing, beatings, a poison that made him feel like he was being torn apart from the inside out, the whole works - and, after the hours of agony Veli had endured first, it was already well after midnight by the time it all ended.

Finley walked in the room, carrying a glass filled with some green medicine she had mixed up for him. Xander tried to sit up but she pushed him back down.

"Save your strength," she said, tilting his head back and carefully feeding it to him.

Atticus was watching from a nearby armchair, his eyes sad and heavy as he never took them off of his son. Luka was there too, also watching the clock with great anticipation. He had tried to leave to warn Deryn of Xander's late arrival, but the president had wanted to question everyone.

Unfortunately, they had to pin Aila's death on Dakota, claiming the lashes on her body were from Xander as he tried to get Dakota off of her. He had always been a target, but now there was an even bigger price on his head. Xander hated himself for losing control like that, but Aila needed to die. She deserved to after everything she had done to Deryn. Surely Dakota would understand.

"The president should not have treated you this way," said Atticus, his fists clenching on his knees. "This wasn't your failure. That damn Veli -"

"He got it worse than I did," interrupted Xander. "Besides, this was my mission. I was in charge. We all know the punishment for failing."

"But -"

"This is nothing I can't handle. If you remember, President Saevus did much worse to me after the battle at Eagle."

Atticus cringed at the memory. "Your mother would be so ashamed if she knew I let this happen."

"Probably," said Xander. "But it's too late to change any of that now. I'm a Guardian, and I made the decision to become one on my own."

The clock struck four. Xander stood up, his limbs still stiff and in pain, but much better with the medicine in his system.

"I'm going home." Looking at his father, he said, "Tell the president I won't be in today. I need my rest."

Xander headed for the door. Luka and Finley hurried after him, helping him walk outside. They summoned the president's private car and had the chauffeur take them to the gate.

His car was special.

While the cars and bikes belonging to citizens hovered no more than three feet off the ground, his car could rise above them, avoiding all traffic. Of course, Inner City was the only place there ever was traffic, since residents in Middle and Outer City couldn't afford cars or bikes. The majority of traffic was from trams.

When they arrived at the gate, Luka headed home, but for Xander and Finley it was only a quick scan through and walk to their hover-bikes.

"Do you need me to drive you?" asked Finley.

"No, I'm fine," he said, wincing as he sat on his bike. She put his helmet on for him, and he didn't even protest.

Without another word, Xander rode off, eager to get home and stop Deryn from leaving. He had tried to contact Bronson several times throughout the night but there was never any response.

When he arrived, he abandoned his bike on the curb, not even bothering with the garage. He tossed his helmet to the side as he entered the building and ran up the stairs, completely forgetting about the pain. He stopped by Bronson and Quigley's door and listened. Silence. He continued on.

When Xander got inside his apartment, everything was still. Looking at the coffee table, he saw the snow globe she loved so much. She would never have left without it. He wasn't sure whether to be relieved or angry that she hadn't followed his instructions.

Coat and shoes still on, Xander ran to his bedroom and threw open the door. "Deryn!"

Her small figure was hunched below the window, her knees to her chest with her face buried inside of them. She slowly lifted her head, her swollen eyes widening as they fell upon him.

Deryn burst into tears as she struggled to get to her feet. She ran to him and threw her arms around his waist, squeezing him tightly as she wept against his chest.

Xander winced, but her embrace was worth the pain. His eyes grew misty as he brought his arms around her shoulders. "Thank god you're still here."

"I knew you'd come back," she cried. "I knew you'd never leave me."

Deryn pulled back so she could look in his eyes. The two of them gazed at each other, Xander using his thumb to stroke her cheek as he realized how happy he was to be here with her. Without a second thought, he leaned down and kissed her.

It wasn't long until that need they both constantly felt took over. Before they could stop themselves, the two of them were naked on the bed.

The familiar sound of Deryn's moans gave Xander the comfort he'd been missing. He hated himself for doing this after what he'd found out about his father, but he was already too invested to just give her up. He loved her and he needed her, despite what he tried to tell himself.

It didn't take either of them long to finish but, for a while after, Xander stayed inside of her, savoring the familiar feeling as he kissed her, unable to get enough of those lips.

It was well into the day before Xander finally told Deryn everything that had happened, the two of them interlacing their fingers on his chest while she used them to stroke the bruises from the torture he had endured.

"I'm sorry I failed you."

Deryn shook her head. "You didn't, Xander. You tried to talk to Dax. We both knew it was a long shot. I'm more upset about Aila."

Xander looked down at her and cocked an eyebrow.

"You shouldn't take those risks for me. I care more about your safety than I do about vengeance. Please don't let what happened to me run your life. It's not worth it."

Putting his hand on top of hers, Xander stared deep into her eyes and said, "But you're worth it."

He leaned down and kissed her then, hearing no more objections as the two of them got lost in each other for the remainder of the day.

CHAPTER THIRTY-NINE

Dakota marched through the dark halls of the Resistance's base, everyone he passed avoiding eye contact but still whispering about him in not so secretive voices. But he didn't care. He had no one to impress.

When he reached Talon's door, he walked in without knocking. The young commander was currently leaning over a large map of the underground beneath Utopia, drawing in the latest routes his scouts had discovered. They had yet to find one that led inside. Nita was standing beside him, scanning the various notes of the scouts. Neither looked up as he entered.

"Well, if it isn't the lover boy," said Talon. "I see you switched the song back." He motioned to the radio in the corner, which was currently playing *Blackbird*.

"Maybe you should've kept it on the other one," said Nita. "If Deryn is listening, favorite or not, I'm positive she's as sick of it as I am."

"She'll never get sick of it," snapped Dakota.

Talon finally looked up from his work and sighed. "So I take it she wasn't at your special place?"

"If she was do you think I'd be here now?"

"I would hope so," said Talon with a tightened brow. "She is *my* sister."

"Really? Because you don't fucking act like it."

Talon's face burned. "What did you just say?"

"You heard me," spat Dakota. "You sit in here drawing your maps when she's out there somewhere!"

"Dax, that's not fair," said Nita, holding out an arm to keep Talon from lunging. "We haven't had word on her whereabouts in a long time. You know that."

"But she's out there!"

Nita looked from Dakota to Talon. She sighed. "That's something we don't know."

"I do," said Dakota with tears in his eyes. "Why else would they lock up Utopia? Why else would they enforce that curfew?"

"There could be a million reasons -"

"They're trying to keep someone inside! And then there's that damn Ruby -"

"Ruby?" said Talon, his stance calming. "You saw him again?"

"Yeah, in Willow," said Dakota. "He told me she's escaped and he knows where she is."

"Neetles told me you said he killed that other Guardian, too. Aila Parrish."

"I didn't see him kill her. I saw him attack her and then I saw them carrying her body away later," corrected Dakota.

Talon pursed his lips in thought.

"Talon, I know what you're thinking and you're wrong!" said Dakota, bringing Talon back to the here and now. "We cannot trust him."

"Those children from Willow did say they were saved by a Guardian who fit his description," said Nita, catching Talon's eye.

"No!" snapped Dakota. "He's trying to trick us, don't you see? Which is exactly why I want to bring him in! To find out why!"

"We already tried that, and it didn't go particularly well for me," said Talon.

"You tried to kidnap a Guardian?" asked Nita, her eyes widening. "When? Why?"

"We weren't trying to kidnap him," explained Talon. "We were trying to stop him from taking Reynard and that other guard's bodies."

"Yeah, and he seemed to think we were the ones who killed them," added Dakota.

"Yes, because Saevus wants *us* to look like the bad guys!" she shouted, bonking Talon on the head. "Idiots!"

"Yes, we're idiots," said Dakota. "When we don't have a plan. Give me permission to bring him in, Talon, and I promise I will come up with something brilliant."

"Talon, no," protested Nita. "Bringing Ruby here would be stupid and reckless."

"Then we won't bring him *here*," argued Dakota. "We'll find somewhere else."

Nita stamped her foot. "No! We don't take prisoners. If you go through with this it's a slippery slope until we're just as bad as they are."

"But nothing else has worked, Neetles," said Talon, his sea-green eyes as weary as ever. "It's been five years and the Resistance has barely made a mark. I want my sister back."

Nita sighed and shook her head. "Your father would never agree to -"

"Yeah, well, he's not exactly in a position to make that call right now, is he?" said Talon. "But I am. I'm in charge and I say if the plan is good then, Dax, you have my blessing. I'll find a way in. You find a way to get Ruby."

"Wise choice," said Dakota, smiling smugly at Nita. "You won't be disappointed."

"Make sure that I'm not," said Talon, returning to his map.

Dakota turned to leave.

"Do me a favor and turn off the radio, will you?"

He did just that, silencing the static that had taken over when the song had ended. Then he left Talon's room, and then the base, heading off to come up with a plan while waiting in his and Deryn's place. For as long as it took.